Sandpiper Island

DONNA KAUFFMAN

ZEBRA BOOKS
KENSINGTON PUBLISHING CORP.
http://www.kensingtonbooks.com

ZEBRA BOOKS are published by

Kensington Publishing Corp.
119 West 40th Street
New York, NY 10018

All Kensington titles, imprints, and distributed lines are available at special quantity discounts for bulk purchases for sales promotion, premiums, fund-raising, educational, or institutional use.

Special book excerpts or customized printings can also be created to fit specific needs. For details, write or phone the office of the Kensington Special Sales Manager: Attn.; Special Sales Department. Kensington Publishing Corp., 119 West 40th Street, New York, NY 10018. Phone: 1-800-221-2647.

Zebra and the Z logo Reg. U.S. Pat. & TM Off.

First Kensington Books Trade Paperback Printing: September 2014
First Zebra Books Mass-Market Paperback Printing:
February 2015
ISBN-13: 978-1-4201-3695-1
ISBN-10: 1-4201-3695-X

eISBN-13: 978-1-4201-3707-1
eISBN-10: 1-4201-3707-7

10 9 8 7 6 5 4 3 2 1

Printed in the United States of America

ACKNOWLEDGMENTS

Thank you to Pete Nelson, the tree house man, whose abundant enthusiasm and creativity when it comes to tree house living is as educational and en- lightening as it is charmingly contagious. Thanks to you, I've been eyeing that old oak tree in my backyard in a whole new way. Expect another call.

And a very special thank-you to everyone at Audubon, the Cornell Lab of Ornithology, and the various and sundry organizations and support net- works, many of them staffed by volunteers, who assist in seabird migratory monitoring and preservation ef- forts here in Maine, as well as in Newfoundland and Norway.

Though some fictional license was taken for story purposes, I've tried to stay as true as possible to the data and information you've so graciously shared with me. May your valiant and dedicated efforts continue to reap rewards that benefit us all.

Chapter 1

If you ever truly cared about her, you need to do something.

Ford Maddox stared at the message that had popped up on his laptop screen and scowled. When, exactly, had he lost command of his oh-so-carefully controlled world?

He looked away from the screen, back to the entire summer migratory season's worth of notes he was steadily working his way through, but it wasn't so easy to turn away from the request. That only served to deepen the scowl. There was no question whom the note was in reference to. Not because he was aware that Delia was in need of something, particularly something he might be able to provide, but because, with the lone exception of the person who'd sent the message, there simply wasn't anyone else it could be about.

He'd come to Blueberry Cove to get a grip on his life, and on himself. At the time, those two things had been synonymous. He'd arrived in Maine having narrowed his life down to one person who required his care, one person whose well-being he was responsible for: himself. At the time, he hadn't been at all certain he could even pull that off.

That had been thirteen years ago.

In the intervening years, he'd done everything in his power to keep that list from growing. He'd only been marginally successful where his work was concerned; any number of seafaring critters, both flippered and feathered, relied on him to preserve their continued existence. But where people were concerned . . . that population he'd maintained strict control over. *No one gets close, no one gets hurt. Or dead.* Simple math for the not-so-simple life he'd lived.

Granted, the only thing bombing him these days were bird droppings, but it had been the real deal for enough years that he knew he could no longer be the go-to guy when things got rough. Not personal things, anyway. He had no problem being the guy in charge on Sandpiper Island. Out on his patch of rocky, sea-locked real estate, perched at the outer edges of Pelican Bay, the only battle he fought these days was the one against the relentless forces of nature.

Other than the twelve weeks every summer when the annual crop of interns invaded his sanctuary to help study and record the various nesting populations, it was just him, the wind, the sea, and the tides. His troops these days consisted of a few thousand migratory seabirds, along with whatever harbor seals found their way to the tumble of boulders and rock that hugged his shores. That he could deal with. That was what he preferred to deal with. The animals he'd devoted his life to were simple creatures, relatively predictable and, most important, minded their own business. Human animals . . . well, that was an entirely different story.

Getting involved in the personal matters of that particular breed, especially in a small town like Blueberry Cove, and even more particularly in matters of any kind that involved one Delia O'Reilly? "Pass," he muttered under his breath, steadfastly ignoring the twinge in his chest. The Cove had saved his life, no argument there, but he was giving his life back to it, in the only way he knew how, the only way he could.

Of course, if he were being honest, Delia had played a pivotal role in that rescue as well. And one thing he was, to a fault, was honest. Most critically with himself. The truth in this case, however, was that he definitely wasn't the man for the job. Or any job that had Delia's name on it. And he was pretty damn sure she'd be the first one to agree.

He went back to the painstaking and often frustrating task of deciphering his notes on the recently completed nesting season, reluctantly looking up again when a *ping* indicated another incoming message.

I've only known her a few months, Ford, and I can already state with fair certainty that she's never going to come out and ask for help. Not from me, and most definitely not from you.

"My point exactly," he retorted, even though the note sender couldn't hear him. He and Delia had a past, a distant and some might say a complicated one. They weren't on bad terms. More like they weren't on terms of any kind. Hell, he hadn't seen or talked to her in . . . longer than he cared to figure out, much less admit. Because figuring it out would mean admitting he'd been intentionally avoiding her. Which meant there was something between them that needed avoiding. Only there was nothing between them. Good, bad, or otherwise. Other than her brother, and Tommy had been gone a very, very long time.

That didn't stop a mental scrapbook of photos from flipping through his mind's eye. It had been quite some time since he'd thought about Tommy, at least in any specific kind of way. Tommy O'Reilly would always be with him, in the ways that mattered, every day. Over the past several months, however, memories of the most specific kind had popped up. Tommy, fresh out of boot camp, being assigned to Ford's small platoon, and to Ford personally as his battle buddy. Tommy had been a few years older, but in all other ways, Ford had been the mature one, the one with more experience. In battle, and in life.

Coming from a small town in the northern coastal reaches of Maine and being about the most unworldly person Ford had ever met hadn't kept Private O'Reilly from being a cocky know-it-all around his fellow grunts. Around Ford, however, he'd been almost tongue-tied. Ford remembered how annoyed he'd been by that, especially since he'd done his damnedest to be more— how had his CO put it?—accessible. Less threatening. Ford had had enough self-awareness even then to know he was intense, focused, motivated. It was why he'd been groomed early on for the army's special forces unit, the rangers. But he'd never threatened anyone. Well, not anyone on his side of the trigger, anyway.

He forced his thoughts away from Tommy, away from the grinning kid who'd weaseled his way under Ford's skin with wisecracks and sheer force of will and, eventually, even into Ford's good graces. More shockingly, Tommy O'Reilly had managed to do the impossible. He'd found a way to be a friend. Ford hadn't had many of them. A choice he'd made very early in life. Life, he'd discovered at a very young age, was simpler when you didn't need people. Or even like them all that much. Especially in his line of work. Didn't mean he wouldn't have risked his life for O'Reilly, friend or not, battle buddy or not. He had. More than once. Tommy had saved his sorry ass, too, ultimately sacrificing his own while doing just that.

It was for all of those reasons, as well as the ones that Ford had been careful not to examine too closely, that he'd accompanied Tommy's body home to Blueberry Cove, intent on making sure his family knew he'd not only died a hero but a damn good soldier, and an even better human being. Those last two things didn't always go hand in hand. Ford knew that to be true every time he'd looked in the mirror.

Ford? I know you're reading this because the little green dot is next to your name. If you don't want me messaging you, then make yourself invisible.

Ford tossed his pen on the desk, leaned back in his chair, and scrubbed a hand over his face, wishing he could scrub away the message screen and the voice he heard behind it just as easily. He'd spent the past thirteen years being deliberately invisible. He wasn't used to anyone caring whether or not he was accessing the Internet, much less feeling compelled to communicate with him whenever the mood struck. The folks he needed to communicate with as part of his work knew that when information and data needed to be shared, he did so via e-mail or fax and responded in kind. Suited them, suited him, don't fix what's not broken.

Don't make me come out there.

"Dammit, Grace." Even as he barked the words, he felt the corners of his mouth briefly twitch upward. She was impossible to ignore when she wanted something and made a nuisance out of herself until she got her desired result. She'd been like that from the time she could stand upright and string more than two words together. She was a lot like him. In more ways than he wanted to admit, much less think about.

One thing was certain, that name flashing on the screen next to the message bubble was exactly the reason he'd lost control of his carefully contained world.

Grace Maddox. His baby sister. Not that there was anything baby about her these days. She might be thirteen years his junior, but she was thirty-two now, had a law degree, and was currently the proud new owner of an eighteenth-century boathouse she was converting into an inn. In Blueberry Cove. Where she'd moved, lock, stock, and stray dog, four months ago, specifically so she could be near her only family. Namely, him.

Grace had been another one of those things he'd carefully removed himself from. He'd told himself at the time he'd done it for her own good, which, he supposed even then was something he'd known would come back to bite him on the ass. It was one thing to join the army at age eighteen, certain he was doing what was right for him, telling himself his five-year-old only sibling would eventually understand, and even be better off without him. Their mother had finally passed away, so he no longer needed to play protector, shield his baby sister from the disaster that was their only known parent. Neither he nor Grace knew who their respective fathers had been—it was unlikely their mother had even known—and he damn sure knew they were better off for that, too.

The same friends who had been loyal to Sara Maddox the last few years of her life, for reasons that had never been clear to Ford other than some folks just needed to be needed, would see to Grace. That he knew, that he trusted. It had been the only thing he'd trusted back then. Not much had changed.

It had been quite another thing, however, to see just how wrong he might have been on his first return home again. Grace had been shuttled around to quite a few of those caretakers in that short time, and though their hearts had been in the right place, and they'd managed to keep her out of the government-controlled foster care system, the result wasn't all that different at the end of the day. It wasn't the life he'd have chosen for her, thought he had chosen for her. He'd already re-upped for another four, though, and was heading into the kind of training that precluded toting along family members, so there hadn't been a damn thing he could do to fix it.

By the time he and the army had parted ways . . . hell, he could barely fix himself. By then it had been too late for him to mount any kind of rescue, and even if he could have, Grace had hardly needed it, not from the likes of him, anyway. She'd gotten herself through primary education, four years of college, and on into law school. She'd made something quite good out of the crap deal life had handed her.

Staying away, letting her start her life on her terms, do things her way, had been the right thing to do at that point. He'd abandoned her, for God's sake. Why the hell would she want anything to do with him? He'd taken the only chance he had, gone down the only path he'd seen available, to make a life for himself. She'd deserved no less than the chance to do the same. So, he'd kept track, but he'd stayed away. For her own good.

You're so full of shit, too, he thought, *then and now.* He reached out to flip the screen off, but his hand paused mid-reach.

Both Maddox siblings had made their way in the world, chosen their own paths, but only Grace had had the balls to reach out for what she really wanted, for what really mattered: family.

He curled his fingers into his palm and let his hand

drop to the top of the desk, her words still staring him in the face. What he saw wasn't the words, but her face, those eyes, that stubborn chin, the way she lifted one eyebrow as if to say *"Seriously? You expect me to buy that?"*

Grace was his one weakness. When confronted personally, there was no way he could deny her anything she wanted. Even if what she wanted was to rebuild a relationship with him. But that didn't change the fact that he sucked at it, that he was supremely uncomfortable with it, that allowing even the tiniest chink in his damaged and beat-up armor to be revealed was the single most terrifying thing there was for him, because being vulnerable in any way, on any level, put his carefully constructed new self at risk. He'd survived a lot, more than most men could and still lay claim to their sanity, if not their souls. He wasn't sure he could survive letting her down. Again.

She'd given him no choice in the matter. She'd simply shown up, made it clear she wasn't going away again . . . and then she'd wrapped her arms around him, hugged the life out of him, and told him she loved him. Loved him. After all he'd done. After all he hadn't done. *How was that even possible?* He didn't even know what the hell love was anymore.

He only knew he couldn't tell her no.

And now she wanted to drag him into other people's lives. Namely Delia's. But while Ford owed a debt he could never adequately repay to his one and only sibling, he and Delia were square. Ford would figure out how to continue to manage his world and have his sister somehow be part of it, but he'd be damned if he'd open himself up to anything—or anyone—else. Delia knew better than anyone—*anyone*—even Grace, that that was, by far, the best for everyone concerned.

He shoved his chair back and stood, too restless

now to simply sit there and let the thoughts, the memories dive-bomb him like a sitting duck. He strode across the corner of the open loft space he used as an office and climbed down the ladder to the open space below that comprised kitchen, dining, and living area. He crouched down to check the pellet stove that squatted, fat and happily chugging out heat, in the center of the home he'd built himself, but it was going along just fine, which he'd known it would be since he'd just reloaded it that morning.

Swearing under his breath at his uncustomary restlessness, he straightened. Then, skirting the corner area that was both kitchen and dining room, he gave the rough bark of the heavy white pine tree that formed the far corner an absent rub with his palm before pushing open one of the triple-paned double doors. He stepped out onto the side deck. The dense, coniferous tree canopy provided year-round shade as well as much-needed protection against the elements. But the unseasonably brisk, late August sea breeze blowing inland through the treetops didn't bring him the peace of mind it usually did.

Back when he'd been working toward his degree, he'd spent almost every minute of his spare time researching alternate living spaces. Initially it had simply been a brain puzzle, a way to keep his thoughts occupied when he wasn't studying so they wouldn't veer into territory better left in the past. But that particular puzzle—off-grid living—was more than a distraction. In fact, it had captured his attention so completely that he'd eventually admitted it was the best possible solution for someone like him. Someone for whom the term "normal" didn't apply.

The first time he'd laid his eyes on a drawing of a sustainable, livable tree house, he'd known, instantly, that that was what he'd been searching for. After spending his school hours studying the habitats of the various endangered species he was learning about, he'd understood in that moment that he'd also been studying his own environmental habitat and that, being endangered himself, he'd needed to find the right home where he could, if not thrive, at least survive.

He'd already begun his work out on Sandpiper then, as an intern to Dr. Claude Pelletier, a man he'd greatly admired, and whose wisdom and formidable intellect he missed very much. It had been his first summer on the island when Ford had discovered the exact right spot, deep in the thick thatch of white pine forest that filled the center of the heart-shaped surge of boulders, soil, and rock that comprised Sandpiper Island.

The whole of Sandpiper was like a fortress, hugged entirely—barring the indent of the natural harbor— by a rocky, boulder-strewn shoreline, then surrounded by sea. There, deep in the tall, old forest—in the heart of the heart—he'd found his home.

By the time he'd graduated and taken over operations on the island full time after Pelletier had taken ill, Ford had long since figured out every last detail of how his tree house would be constructed. Multileveled at the core, then spread out to satellite structures he'd added over time, connected by a series of rope bridges, decks, and ladders, through a sturdy group of perfectly matched pine, naturally spaced, so as not to overly burden any one of them. It had taken him eighteen months to complete the main structure, and that had been with a relatively mild winter by Maine standards tossed in the middle of it. He'd hewn every log, cut every board, driven every nail, so he knew and understood its every strength and weakness. It was both his aerie and his bunker. It had given him the one thing he'd known he needed to survive, the freedom to feel completely safe for the first time in his life.

Only even his sanctuary couldn't save him now from the entirely different set of images that flashed through his mind. Images he'd kept tightly sealed away from all conscious and subconscious thought for a very long time. These images weren't filled with horror, weren't the seeds of the endless nightmares he'd once suffered both while asleep and wide awake.

No, he'd kept these particular memories under lock and key for entirely different reasons. Polar opposite reasons.

He'd learned to live with his past, with the things he'd done, to the degree any sane, rational human being could. He'd made a certain kind of peace with himself by making a deal of sorts, that he was giving back, balancing a score that could never be measured, much less rectified, but that he was nonetheless working toward anyway. That deal had been carefully constructed with the knowledge that his work was where he funneled whatever passion he had left in him, where he gave whatever might resemble his heart, if not his soul. He wasn't sure he'd escaped with even remnants of that left.

His work was the only place he could allow himself even a thread of the luxury of caring, of wanting, of being needed or necessary to something other than himself, greater than himself. The flip side of that deal was that he'd never allow those same parts of himself to be compromised by another person. He would never let someone in, allow them to rely on him, to need him or, God forbid, want him. And he'd most definitely made certain he'd never want those things for himself. He didn't deserve them, for one, and he sure as hell hadn't earned the right to even think he could be trusted with the care and well-being of someone else's heart.

Yet he was helpless to keep the images of that long-ago night from roaring in. As if it had happened only the night before, he could see the storm-lashed windows of the small rooms above the tiny restaurant on the other side of Half Moon Harbor, flickering like bold neon as lightning strikes illuminated the walls. The twisted linens on the foldout bed were wrapped around his bare legs, and Delia was astride him, gloriously naked, her red hair glowing in the storm's strobe lights, like some kind of flaming, otherworldly halo. She was completely unapologetic about taking her pleasure from him, wrenching his release in return. Mother Nature relentlessly pounded the shores of the harbor, unleashing her fury, while the two of them pounded their way just as relentlessly through each other, unleashing themselves, as if the delirious pleasures of the flesh could somehow simultaneously free them from the soul-ripping grief threatening to drown them both.

Delia sinking under because she'd lost her brother, her only sibling. And Ford feeling swallowed alive, because he'd known already, even then, that his grip on humanity, maybe on his very soul, had begun to slip away. Tommy was gone. Loyal, dedicated, good-will-always-beat-evil Tommy. Yet Ford had been left to live another day. So he could take more Tommys from the world. Cast more families into the devastating throes of grief he was witnessing, firsthand, on Delia's beautiful, heartbroken face.

She'd been gone when he'd woken up the next morning. When he'd made his way downstairs, she'd already been hustling in the restaurant kitchen. Her grandmother had been the one to push his breakfast plate across the bar in front of him, her expression neither open nor shut, but simply vacant. She'd lost a grandson . . . but there was work to be done. One foot in front of the other. Delia hadn't so much as looked his way, so he'd stayed out of hers. He'd eaten his breakfast, paid the bill, said his good-byes . . . and gone back to hell.

He heard the *ping* from the other side of the door he hadn't closed behind him and headed back inside and up to his loft office, drawn inexorably to the screen, already feeling fate wrapping its long, clever fingers around his neck . . . only the tightness he felt was in his chest.

He sat down, intending to find the words to explain to Grace that while he understood her concern, and appreciated her trying to help Delia, that he wasn't going to be of any help. Not because he wasn't willing, so much as he had no help to give. Only instead of typing, his fingers closed into fists as he read the words on the screen.

She reached out to help me before she even knew me. Because she cared enough about you to want you to have what you really needed. Family. We both should have listened to her then. We both need to help her have what she really needs now.

Another *ping* came, making him almost viscerally flinch. Memories, so long held at bay, roared in like thundering waves, breaching any and all walls, drowning his futile attempts to block them. Not just of that night, but of all the long mornings, afternoons, evenings he'd sat in her diner after returning to the Cove, drinking in the energy, the vitality, the *life* of her very presence. Her smile, her hearty, infectious laugh, listening as she alternately goaded a smile out of a gruff fisherman or a grudging apology from a short-tempered townie. He'd lost count of the number of times she'd lent an ear and a shoulder, offered a hug or a free meal, scolded, sympathized, lectured, loved, bussed cheeks, and even pinched the occasional ass. Hundreds of moments he hadn't even been aware of were there for a detailed, exact recalling.

Through the torrent, he read Grace's final message. This one was simply a cut-and-pasted a news story from the local Cove newspaper.

LOCAL DINER OWNER AND TOWN SCION IN BATTLE OVER LAND RIGHTS

He skimmed the article, and the tight clutch in his chest matched the ones he'd made with his fists. "Hasn't she lost enough in her life, you smug bastard?" It had been a while since he'd felt the need for physical violence. A very long while. But at that moment, he wanted to drive his fist through something. Or, more to the point, someone. "You have every other goddamn thing," he said aloud to the absent "town scion." "Why can't you just leave her the fuck alone?"

The scion was Brooks Winstock, descended from one of the oldest families in the Cove, who still owned a fair chunk of it, and was richer than Croesus. Now he wanted Delia's Diner. Or, more specifically, the piece of prime harbor-front property it sat on. For, of all things, a yacht club. What in the fresh hell would Blueberry Cove do with a damn yacht club? It was a tiny town with a three-hundred-year legacy of lobster fisherman, shipbuilders, and sailors. Hardly the yacht club type.

The diner, he knew, just as Brooks Winstock damn well knew, was all Delia had. And not just in terms of earning a living. It was the foundation and focus of the life she'd carved out for herself in Blueberry, as her family had before her, with their own blood, sweat, and tears. She loved her life and her livelihood, and had earned the right to enjoy it. And the town loved her right back. Delia's had become a Cove landmark . . . both the diner itself, and its colorful, saucy, outspoken owner.

He couldn't imagine her taking this lightly or well, much less going quietly. If he hadn't been so pissed off, the image of her taking on Winstock might have gotten what passed for a smile out of him.

Instead, he punched the screen dark, took the ladder down in a step and a jump, then stalked to the other side of the kitchen and grabbed his boat keys from the hook on the pot buoy attached to the wall by the single door there. He took the fast exit, shimmying down the knotted rope that extended through a hole in the deck to the forest floor below. He was halfway down the path that led to the only pier on the island before he realized what the hell he was doing. *Just what in the hell are you doing?*

"Dammit, Grace," he muttered again, under his breath this time, as he unknotted the ropes and jumped onboard the old lobster boat he'd bought off Blue years before and kept running with a combination of spit and sheer power of will.

So, he'd been wrong. There were apparently two people in the world he couldn't say no to. *Not that Delia asked you to stick your nose in her business.* In fact, he'd be lucky if she didn't bite it off and hand it back to him, wrapped neatly in a takeout box. Hell, he wasn't even sure what he thought he could do. But he'd stayed on the sidelines once before in his life, and he knew now, every time he looked into Grace's pretty hazel eyes, what his choice had cost her. He might not be able to do a damn thing to help Delia, but sitting on the sidelines wasn't going to be an option.

God help us all.

Chapter 2

She'd dreamed about him. Again. "And that is *so* not a good thing." Delia O'Reilly plunged her rubber-gloved hands back in the steamy, soapy water. "Understatement of the week." *Month. Year.*

Her livelihood—which was the same as saying her entire life—was being threatened with extinction, or at the very least a complete overhaul and relocation, which to her felt like the same thing, and what was she doing about it? Having hot sex dreams about a man she couldn't have kept as a twenty-one-year-old with a failed marriage already behind her, much less nine years later when he'd shockingly returned and she'd been old enough to know better. So, what was her excuse now? She hadn't made it to forty-three without learning a thing or ten about the opposite sex. She was old enough and wise enough to know that Ford Maddox wasn't a man who could be caught, much less kept, by any woman.

Not because he couldn't settle on just one, but because he'd long since opted not to settle on any. Ever.

Hadn't she opted for that very same thing? Yes, yes, indeed she had. "So where the hell did all this lusting come from?" *Lusting*. A tame word for the up-against-the-wall, take-no-prisoners dreams she'd been having about Ford Maddox. Lusting she could handle. Hell, lusting was a normal, healthy state of being, if you asked her. The kind of dreams she'd been having, however, left her feeling empty and emotionally wrung out, without the actual real-life sexual satiation to at least provide a little balance. "Talk about your lose-lose," she muttered.

For the first few years after Ford's return to the Cove, she'd entertained the idea—okay, fantasy—of proposing a no-strings relationship between them. By the age of thirty, she'd become an expert at no strings. Besides, no one in Blueberry knew him the way she did, and he was one of the rare few to have seen her at a most vulnerable moment. They shared a singular bond, the kind that made him someone she'd always care about, always watch out for, worry over. How could she not? He'd shown her courage, strength, and compassion at a time when he was suffering untold trauma of his own.

She had known, even at barely twenty-one, that the one night they'd shared had simply been an extension of the pain and grief they were both suffering through, part of it shared, over Tommy's death, and some of it intensely intimate, known only to each of them in their own hearts, minds, and souls. He couldn't know what else she'd been dealing with, devastated by her husband choosing a life somewhere else, without her, plagued with self-doubt after choosing family obligation over the vows she'd made to him, feeling betrayed that he hadn't stood up for her, either, and deeply confused by the mix of anguish, anger, and guilt.

Just as she couldn't know, couldn't even begin to fathom, what Ford had been dealing with after every-

thing he'd seen and done while in battle. Her brother
had died in his arms, mortally wounded after a second
land mine had exploded as he'd dragged Ford and
half his unit to safety from the burning wreckage of
the first one, all while taking direct fire. Delia couldn't
begin to fathom what any part of that did to a person's
psyche.

Still recovering from his own injuries, Ford had
accompanied Tommy's body home, making sure his
family knew he'd died a hero. He'd stayed for the funeral . . . remaining stoic, closed off, closed up throughout. Until he'd escorted Delia home afterward, and
she'd invited him in. And he'd accepted the offer.

It was for the best that he'd left after what she'd
come to think of as That Night. Even then, she hadn't
romanticized it. She'd known it for what it was, even as
she'd been doing it. It had been grief counseling mas-
querading as marathon sex. Afterward, when he'd
gone, she'd made herself focus on the good that had
come of that singular night. There had been a very
powerful sense of sanctuary created in the intimate
space they shared. She'd felt secure, safe, in a way she
never had before.

And, yes, though her battered ego hated to admit it
mattered so much, she had reveled in the fact that
he'd found her desirable. His strong, protective arms,
his body over hers, had been like a buffer, walling off
the outside world and, because of that, she'd finally
been able to let go, to truly grieve. The loss of her
brother, of her husband, and, maybe most important,
the naïve ideal that life came with a happily ever after.

She'd kept her focus on that singular truth, telling
herself she was lucky she'd learned it early on. She'd
wondered what, if anything, Ford had taken from that
night. Then he'd come back. To stay. Which she'd

taken as proof that he had indeed carried something from that night with him back into battle, back into hell. What else would bring him to Blueberry of all places nine years later? She was the only connection there could be.

Her hands paused on the lobster pot she was scrubbing as her thoughts took her back to that moment, the day he'd come striding back into her life. She'd just turned thirty and, when it came to relationships, she'd considered herself not merely battle-hardened, but bulletproof. Then he'd strolled into her diner. And her stupid, foolish heart, which she'd sworn she'd boxed up and stowed tightly away after Henry's abdication, shoving it even more firmly back to the darkest corners of the shelf after losing Tommy, then her grandmother . . . had fluttered. *Fluttered.* Like she was some kind of ridiculous, innocent schoolgirl, all hearts and flowers, being teased and taunted by the stirrings of her first crush.

Except one thing Delia O'Reilly had never been, at any age, was innocent.

Foolish, however, she was beginning to think was a life sentence.

That was the only explanation for allowing Ford Maddox to make her think about things she had no business thinking about. Knew better than to even consider thinking about. Over the ensuing years she'd eventually managed to tuck him neatly up on that same shelf with those other things better left in the past.

So why now? Why had he invaded her sleep, her dreams, tantalizing her with memories of a night that her head still knew was about grief, even if her body was perfectly happy believing otherwise?

It was an easy out to say that it was because his sister,

Grace, had come to Blueberry back in May, hoping to reunite with her estranged brother. Grace had gotten to know Delia, initially because she was aware of Delia's link to Ford and wanted to know more about her brother from the one person who knew him as he was now. Over the past three months, though, a true friendship had blossomed between them, to the point that Ford was only a small part of their ongoing conversations.

Delia scrubbed her forehead with the back of her forearm, shoving the damp red curls aside, and wishing she'd tied one of her handkerchiefs around her forehead when she'd finally kicked the night crew out and sent them home. Most nights she was thankful to have the help, but there were times when she just needed everyone to clear out so she could have peace and quiet, some time with her own thoughts, which was a rare and therefore precious thing in her world.

Her employees were family to her and, as such, teased her mercilessly about her kerchiefs, nicknaming her Lucy, after Lucy Ricardo, who also had red, curly hair, and whose kerchief-wearing updo was a well-known part of her iconic legacy. Old-fashioned though they might be, Delia had learned from her grandmother that short of shaving her head, nothing else did quite the same job of keeping curls and sweat out of her eyes when doing dish duty.

She smiled briefly, memories tripping through her mind of growing up, and all the late nights spent in her grandmother's restaurant, back in the kitchen, the mingled scents of fresh seafood, crispy bacon, and coffee always lingering, no matter the time of day or night. Delia had happily stood on the old, green, paint-chipped footstool next to her grandmother, both in matching kerchiefs, both with red curls, though she knew Gran's had come more from a bottle of Miss Clairol at that point than nature. She'd rinse after Gran had scrubbed, then carefully put the dishes in the rack, sorting the silver into the different drain buckets. Delia had just been happy to get to stay up late, after the locals and the crew had all gone for the night, finally having her Gran all to herself. Delia would have happily done any chore for more of those moments.

"Still would," she murmured, the smile and memory lingering. "What would you say now, Gran? Four generations of O'Reillys have taken on the care and feeding of the fine citizens of Blueberry Cove, and they all managed to do so through fire, flood, feast, and famine. Now I'm going to be the one to lose my place here—our place here—because I wasn't paying attention to business like I should have been." *Because I let myself get distracted by a man.*

Maybe even hard lessons had an expiration date, and she'd have to learn them all over again. *Well, this is one lesson I could do without repeating.* Determined to keep Ford Maddox completely blocked out of her mind, at least while she had the conscious ability to do so, she plunged her hands back in the soapy water and turned her thoughts to the man she should be thinking about.

"Brooks Winstock," she muttered, scrubbing as much wool off her steel pad as she was grease off the grill rack she tackled next, putting her elbow into it with perhaps a bit more force than necessary. "Arrogant bastard. Thinks money trumps tradition. Well, Mr. Winstock, not if I have anything to say about it."

"I'd put my money on you."

The sound of the deep male voice startled a high-pitched squeak out of Delia, who sent the steel pad one way and the suds-covered, half-clean grill rack clanging back into the soapy dishwater, spraying her face and front with a foamy splatter. Not because the intrusion itself had startled her—Blueberry Cove wasn't a lock-your-doors kind of place—so much as who had done the intruding. Surely it was thinking about those dreams making her hear things. Those oh-so-pulse-pounding, hip-thrusting, headboard-banging sex dreams. She'd just imagined that voice. But the shiver of knowledge—carnal knowledge—that shot straight down her spine and that very specific bit farther, even as she whirled to find him lounging in the open doorway, told her he was very real. And very . . . there.

"Ford," she breathed. "You about knocked five years off me. Not that I couldn't do with losing a few, but if it means not dying of a heart attack, I'll keep those five years, thanks."

He didn't smile. Ford wasn't much of one for anything so . . . affable as that. But even though it had been a good while since she'd laid eyes on him, she could still read every nuance of that face. The glimmer that passed through his gunmetal gray eyes was his equivalent of a slow, sexy grin. Or it was in her mind. Her poor, obviously overworked and undersexed mind. *That's all it is,* she told herself. *You just need to get laid.*

What little tourist season the Cove had was over, which reduced the no-strings list down to zero, and the only other man to show her any interest of late was overseas at the moment. Probably buying a small country. *At least he knows how to throw his money around.* Normally, the thought of Grace's famous architect friend, Langston deVry, who'd taken an interest in Delia over the summer while helping Grace convert her newly purchased boathouse into an inn, would make Delia's lips curve. Theirs had never become a physical relationship, mostly due to lack of time, but the very charismatic Langston knew how to make a woman feel like a million bucks with little more than a wink and a smile. She'd soaked that up like a dried-out sponge left forgotten on the drain rack. *Maybe if you'd made some time for more than a wink and a smile, you wouldn't be fixated on a decades-old one-night stand.*

At the moment, with six foot, two inches of pure alpha leaning in her doorway, somehow sucking every last molecule of steam-filled air from the room while he did so, she was hard-pressed to even picture the older man's face.

"Why are you—" She broke off, her expression changing to one of immediate concern. The hormonal fog finally lifted along with the steam from the sink, allowing rational thought to seep back into her steam- and sex-dream-addled brain. "Oh, no! Is—did something happen to Grace?" Something happening to his sister was the only reason Delia could fathom that would pull him off that damn island of his. "Why didn't you just call me? Where's Brodie? Is he with her? What hap—?"

"Grace is fine," he broke in calmly, his gaze steady on hers.

Of course, she was, Delia thought. Grace's brother would hardly be leaning against the doorjamb, all laconic and leonine in ancient jeans and casually tugged on layers of faded tee, even more faded sweatshirt, and an old lumberjack plaid jacket, if his one and only family member was in trouble.

How was it he looked even sexier in that ensemble than in a sharply tailored, exquisitely pressed military uniform? And she'd seen him in both. His hair was much longer these days, bordering on shaggy. It matched the two-day-old beard that shadowed his hard jaw. She hadn't thought his hair would be wavy when it grew out from the military buzz he'd sported when she'd first met him, though she couldn't have said why. Maybe because he was all hard angles, and even harder edged. Nothing about him would dare to be soft. But the dark mop, streaked heavily by the sun now as summer began closing up shop, tossed about by the sea wind from his boat ride in, hung in unruly clumps that she wouldn't go so far as to call curls, but begged a woman to run her fingers through and untangle just a bit.

She wasn't a woman given to vanity—she ran a diner, for God's sake—so function won out over form every time. But with Grace not in danger, and him still standing there looking about a hundred times better in the layers-of-clothes flesh than he had in her very unclothed dreams—and he'd been pretty damn amazing in those dreams—she was suddenly acutely aware that while he was all tree-house-dwelling-Crusoe sexy, she, on the other hand, quite probably resembled a stewed tomato. Damp hair plastered to her forehead and cheeks. Splattered with soapsuds.

"Why *are* you here then?" she asked, her brisk tone more directed at herself than him, but she couldn't deny a small part of her would be relieved if he simply turned and sauntered right back to his boat. She might not be vain, but she was still female. Besides, he wouldn't be the first man she'd sent packing. Eventually, they all sauntered off anyway. That was how she liked it. How she needed it to be.

"Heard you got yourself some trouble," he said. "The diner."

If he'd gotten down on one knee and proposed, she

wouldn't have been more stunned. He'd come all the way in from Sandpiper . . . because he was worried about her diner? She tried to conceal her shock. There had to be another reason. "The diner is fine," she lied. And it was. Or it would be. Just as soon as she came up with a plan to save it.

"That's not how I heard it."

She propped her fists on her hips, which was when she realized she was still sporting those oh-so-sexy bright yellow rubber gloves to go with the steamed hairdo and stewed-tomato face. *Fabulous.* "Exactly what did you hear? And from whom?" As soon as the words were out of her mouth, she knew the answer to that. "Grace. She got you to come, didn't she?" She waved a rubber-covered hand. "Rhetorical question. No one else could have done the impossible." He frowned at that last part, but she plowed onward, not wanting to discuss why he'd disappeared from her life or, more to the point, how she felt about him disappearing from her life. From the Cove in general, she understood. He needed sanctuary.

But she'd thought . . . well, she wasn't sure what she'd thought, but she guessed, at the very least, she'd thought that she was a part of that sanctuary, and not part of what he needed to get away from. How was it that she hadn't realized, until that very moment, just how deeply his departure had hurt her feelings? *Oh, yeah, you're bulletproof, all right.* Apparently, there wasn't armor strong enough for some bullets. "Listen, I don't know what Grace told you, but everything is—"

"—not fine," he finished. "Or Grace wouldn't have contacted me. So let's cut the crap."

Her eyebrows lifted a bit with that, but no one would ever accuse Ford of being a sweet talker. Or any kind of talker. "What crap are we cutting? Whatever is going on with the diner is my problem, not Grace's, though, of course, I appreciate her being worried about me. Truly. But she doesn't need to be. Her plate is full to overflowing as it is, what with her inn conversion project and Brodie building a damn full-size, seventeenth-century clipper ship in her backyard."

"Schooner."

Her eyebrows narrowed. And she could have sworn that glimmer in his eyes reached all the way down to the corners of his mouth. His hard mouth with those finely chiseled lips that had done amazing things to the softest parts of her—. "Whatever," she said, possibly a bit too shortly, but she was scrambling to get a foothold, a toehold, any kind of hold on her reaction to him. "And I know how thrilled Brodie is to have the contract. I know it will be a boon to Monaghan Shipbuilders, to Grace's new inn when it's finished, and to the Cove. But, the truth of it is, if it wasn't for Winstock commissioning that damn boat, none of this would be happening."

"And what, exactly, *is* happening?"

She folded her arms now, heedless of how soaked her apron was at this point. "I haven't seen you in . . . I don't even know how long it's been. Since you went full-tilt Crusoe, living out on a deserted island in that tree house, playing Dr. Dolittle, no one sees you. But suddenly you're here and you want to know what's going on?"

He stared at her for a beat, and then lifted a shoulder in a slight shrug. "Pretty much."

"Why?"

"Because you need help."

Four little words, said so matter-of-factly, shouldn't have made her knees go the least bit weak. She eased a hip against the edge of the industrial sink, because they had. A little bit. "I—I appreciate that," she said, humbled now by the offer, especially coming from him. "But, I can handle it."

"Story in the paper made it seem otherwise."

Delia swallowed a swearword. Grace had obviously sent him a link to it. "Don't believe everything you read."

He shifted a bit straighter, and shoved his hands in his pockets. "For someone who knows the business of everyone on this island, you sure get prickly when folks bring up yours."

She eyed him. "Some folks."

"You make it this hard for everyone?"

"Make what hard?"

She thought he might have sworn a little himself, under his breath, of course. He might have left the military behind a long time ago, but all those years of training were imprinted so deeply they were simply part of his DNA. He was polite, respectful, sometimes to a fault. Of course, she was probably the only one in the Cove who knew what he could be like when he wasn't feeling the need to be so . . . polite. And her knees might have wobbled a bit more at the thought of how, exactly, that was.

He gave the appearance of someone who couldn't care less about what was on anyone else's agenda because he was too busy keeping his focus on his own. Mostly because that was exactly who he was. And yet, he was here. In her kitchen. Offering, apparently, to help her. She knew it was because Grace had asked him to come, just as Delia knew that, recluse or not, Grace mattered to him. Deeply, in fact. So, of course he'd come. But that didn't mean he'd wanted to. Quite likely the opposite.

She let go of some of the rigidity that was holding

her up. It also wasn't his fault that she'd been having ridiculously indulgent sex dreams about him and, if she were being honest, those images were making her more prickly than the fact that he was forcing her to admit she needed help.

Under his continued silent scrutiny, she loosened her grip around her waist, and then finally let her hands drop to her sides. "Listen, I know you don't want to be here. And I appreciate—as will Grace, once I get done wringing her neck for telling you—that you came all the way in to the Cove to do . . . whatever it was she asked you to do." She let go the rest of the breath she was holding, and with it came a surprising dry smile. "You could have just called. Then I could have been a complete, unappreciative bitch over the phone and saved you the boat trip."

His lips did twitch then, just the tiniest of bits. "Problem is I'd have let you."

She sighed. "But Grace wouldn't have."

He shook his head. "And, tell you the truth, I'm more afraid of her than I am of you." He straightened fully, but kept his hands in his pockets. "So, here I am."

And, God help her, here was exactly where she'd like to have him. And on the counter. The floor. Up against the nearest wall, too.

She ducked his gaze, pushed at her hair, and the reminder of her stewed-tomato appearance was enough to snap her out of it and back to reality. Sometimes reality sucked. For more than a few reasons. "Well, you're officially off the hook. I'll talk to Grace. She'll understand."

His expression said *Good luck with that,* but he didn't look relieved. Or as if he was intending to leave anytime soon.

"It's something I need to figure out on my own."

When he still didn't budge, she said, "Listen, if there was something I thought you or Grace could do, I'd tell you. But I got myself into this situation by not following up on the whole lease thing. I mean, it's been twenty years, so . . ." She trailed off. Twenty years. That should have sounded like a long time. A very long time. And yet, it had seemed like just yesterday when the town council, and Eli Compton, who'd been the mayor back then, had come to her rescue after Gran's restaurant had burned down, taking everything from them except the house she'd grown up in.

"The article didn't explain much. How did Winstock wedge himself in between you and the land bureau? Or whoever oversees the lease deal you made with the town?"

"That's just it. No one has really been overseeing it. It wasn't much more than a handshake deal at the time, with a signed, typed-up sheet I've only ever used for tax purposes. I don't think anyone would have cared if I paid the dollar fee annually or not, that was just to make it legal. I did, of course, but—"

"Dollar fee? What does that mean?"

"It means the town more or less gave me the building that became my diner, and the land it sits on, but in a lease arrangement, to save me from paying back taxes, and a bunch of other financial red tape." She took in a breath and eyed him levelly. She had nothing to be ashamed of, and she wasn't. It had been an act of charity at the time, yes, one she'd been grateful for then and every day since, but what she'd done with her diner, and brought back to the Cove, had more than evened things up in the ensuing years. That still didn't make talking about it any easier. "The deal was a dollar a year for twenty years." When he merely nodded, she let go of some of the awkward tension. "It's been more or less the honor system ever since; no one has overseen it directly. I've offered to buy the property outright more than once, but I kept getting waved off. So once I'd paid off all the loans I took out to get the diner up and going, I took the money I'd been paying the bank, that I'd have put toward real rent, and set up a private thing with the local food bank. It was the best way I knew to give back, give a hand up to someone else, like they'd given to me. Anyway, no one knows about that and I'd appreciate it staying that way. I always figured I'd just do whatever was mutually agreeable to everyone once the lease finally expired."

"And when is that?"

"Was that," she corrected, disgusted with herself all over again.

"Twenty years," he said. He paused a moment, and then said, "That would have been right about the time O'Reilly's burned down."

Her defenses naturally wanted to kick up, but there was absolutely no pity on his face, merely curiosity and an expectation that she would explain.

"Yes. Boiler exploded. Mercifully, no one was hurt, because it happened in the middle of the night. Burned straight to the ground before anything could be done. We lost it all."

"Insurance didn't cover enough?"

"There was no insurance. I didn't—" She broke off. It had happened a long time ago, but that didn't make it any more pleasant a memory now. "Gran had let it lapse. I didn't know."

"I thought the place did well."

"It did. It wasn't the money. Gran was . . . well, she was getting forgetful, and I was in denial that she was having problems. I chalked it up to losing Tommy and just . . . a lot of things. But the fact was she was struggling a lot more than I knew, and a number of things had fallen through the cracks. Things I found out after the fire when all the bills and other attendant stuff came due. We managed to keep the house, but only because my grandfather had paid it off before he'd passed away. But we had nothing to rebuild with. I had to mortgage the house just to pay off the multitude of bills and levies involved after the fire. I couldn't keep the property the building sat on. The bank took it."

"Whatever became of it?"

"Nothing. It's a gravel lot now that folks use to pull in and look at the water on their way into the harbor. It's the first place you come to with a decent view."

"Why doesn't Winstock take that land then?"

"We had docks that ran out from the back of the restaurant, but they burned, too. You can still see the stumps sticking out of the water. We could only take small vessel tie-ups, though. It's not deep harbor, and it guts completely at low tide. That won't work for the kind of boats Winstock envisions. This place is right in the heart of the harbor, deepwater docks, and a better view. Perfect for what he has in mind."

"How did the lease come about? Can't whoever it was who did the deal or knew about it back then stick up for you? Step in, make a ruling, something?"

She shook her head. "Eli Compton made the deal. He was mayor back then. He grew up with Gran, passed away a few years after she did. His family had been eating at O'Reilly's since they were both kids, before Gran had become an O'Reilly. It was run back then by her future father-in-law and by his father before that."

"So a longtime Cove tradition, even before you," he said. His gaze caught with hers, and held.

She tried, and failed, not to react to the way he'd said that, as if she was somehow the be-all and end-all. She was wading deep into the harshest waters of her past, and yet her body was still happily clamoring for any little crumbs he might toss her way. Even crumbs that weren't really crumbs at all. He was just being polite. Doing as Grace had asked him to do. She wasn't the be-all and end-all. She was just going to be the end.

"Yes," she said. "Five generations of O'Reillys—four that have actually run the place. My father had other ideas, goals. . . ." She trailed off, then took yet another breath and waded deeper. "He and my mom died when Tommy and I were little, so even if he'd wanted to run the restaurant, it wouldn't have come to pass. Gran was still running it then, and did until it burned down. My grandfather died before I was born," she added, sensing that was the next question.

She forced a brighter tone and continued before he could say anything. She just wanted this conversation over. "Anyway, Eli came up with the deal once he realized the situation we were in. Gran's health took a major dive after the fire, so I stepped up."

"But you were only, what, twenty—"

"Twenty-three," she finished, nodding. "But I was all Gran had left, all I had left, for that matter. Working the family restaurant was all I'd ever done. All I wanted to do. I gave up my marriage to stick with our family legacy." She stopped abruptly, realizing what she'd let slip. Not that it wasn't common knowledge, but Ford Maddox was not a common man. And for all he'd been in Blueberry a long time now, he didn't spend much of it in the actual town, and he wasn't exactly the chatty, gossipy type. About as far from it as they got. She had no idea what he knew and didn't know. And hadn't she exposed enough already?

"I knew about that," he said, apparently sensing her apprehension. "I'm sorry."

"I was, too, at the time. I could take the cop-out route and say I was young and foolish—and Lord knows, we both were—but I also loved him, and I took vows. I just . . . I thought Henry would stay here, work for his family. But he wanted a bigger life, wanted to see the world. Or at least more of it than Blueberry Cove, Maine. His family ran a small fishing company here, and he got this big idea to move to the Northwest—*way* in the Northwest—and launch a new branch of the business there, a salmon fishing guide business. In Alaska. I . . . I didn't want that. And I didn't want to leave Gran. Tommy had enlisted and gone off and I knew he was never going to work at the restaurant anyway. Plus, I knew Gran wasn't doing that well physically. I mean, I didn't know the mental stuff she was really dealing with, but restaurant work is hard and it had taken a toll on her body. I just . . . I couldn't walk away from that. And truth be told, I didn't want to. I felt a lot of guilt about the breakup of my marriage, but I also didn't regret my choice once I'd made it, if that makes sense."

"I've never been put in that position," he said quietly. "I think you just have to do what is right for you. What you think is best. You can't make everybody happy, and that's not on you anyway. That's on them."

She stared at him for a long moment, wondering how he applied that wisdom to his own choices, how he'd felt about the ones he'd made. She knew he regretted—deeply—leaving his sister, but that was the last thing she wanted to talk about. Right after the current topic of conversation. "Well, that's what I did. And then Tommy was killed not long after Henry left and I didn't have time to question the what-ifs. I was too busy dealing with what was."

"That's all any of us can do." He looked around the interior of the kitchen. "Looks like you did what was right. By your grandmother. By yourself. By the town, too." He looked back to her. "Everyone benefitted from what the town did for you back then. The least they can do is step up for you now."

"I think the town and me are even on that score. Or at least, I'm not interested in keeping a score. I'd have caught up with and settled the lease situation when I closed my books at the end of the year, which is when I always paid my dollar, along with license renewals and whatnot. That's when all the bank loans had started up way back when, and so I always did all that at the same time. It wasn't like I had to worry about it. It was mine. I mean, it certainly felt like mine. The town thinks of it as mine. I've paid taxes on it for twenty years like it's mine. And I'm fully prepared to buy it and make it properly mine if they'll sell it to me now that the lease is up. It never once occurred to me, even after the stuff Brodie went through with Winstock earlier this year, that he'd come after my property. Or what I thought of as my property." She blew out a sigh, and let her hands drop to her sides. "The bottom line is, the twenty-year lease technically ended on the fifteenth of this month, which was last week. First thing the morning of the sixteenth, Brooks Winstock made the town a very, very generous offer on this land. An offer I couldn't meet in my wildest dreams, not without a substantial lottery win."

"And they're just going to sell it to him? Sell you out?"

"I don't know. I'm still here. No one has come to shut me down. Mayor Davis hasn't made a decision. He's getting ready to retire after the fall elections and frankly, I really don't think he wants to be the one responsible for this. The town is very divided about Winstock's plans. No matter how Davis decides, people are going to be angry with him, and I don't think that's how he wants to end his tenure."

"I can't imagine folks here are dying for a yacht club."

"It's not that so much as the money the yacht club might bring with it. Small businesses here do okay, but of course we struggle, as all small towns do. Most of us like things the way they are, struggles and all, because we like the way of life here. More money is never just more money. Along with it comes change, and I don't think people really understand just how far reaching those kinds of changes could be. Will be, if he builds that yacht club." She lifted a shoulder. "But with the tricentennial coming, the lighthouse being restored now, the schooner tours in the bay that will start when Brodie's ship is done, change is already coming."

"But those changes don't affect the fabric of the community," Ford said. "Brodie's ship tours—"

"Brodie's building the schooner, but Winstock owns it, so they're his tours."

"My point is when the tours start up, that will increase tourist revenue, but that won't otherwise change the nature of the town. Businesses will do better with the bump in income, and the town might see more small businesses pop up to take advantage of the increased summer tourist flow, but that's just an enhancement of what's here now and not a bad thing, all in all. A yacht club, on the other hand—"

"Changes the nature of the town," she finished.

"And the kinds of services the town offers. It attracts things like chain hotels and resort-minded developers. The kind of bigger money that then attracts other kinds of developers, for shopping centers and housing development, looking to expand the community in hopes of pulling in those deep pockets year-round. Which is exactly what Winstock wants, because who do you think they'll partner with? My point about the lighthouse, the ship tours, even Grace's inn, because Langston's name is associated with it, is that Winstock is using that 'we're already changing' tune right now, using it to his advantage, making people feel like it's already happening, already a forgone conclusion, and don't we want someone from the Cove deciding what kinds of things should be developed, and what direction we should take? Like he's our savior or something." She swallowed several choice swearwords. "And I'm stuck in the middle of it, though I didn't ask to be. Anyway, that's neither here nor there. I will deal with whatever happens, because that's what I do."

"But if you don't own this place, technically, then whatever equity you've built up—"

"Goes back to the city as well. Not that that matters, because Winstock is just going to bulldoze the place to the ground anyway. And no," she said, before he could go to the next logical step. She'd already taken that mental step and long since discarded it as a potential option. "I'm not interested in another charity handout from my town. It was one thing when I was twenty-three and in very dire need and had my grand-mother's well-being to consider. I don't need or want a handout now. If I have to, I can start over again. Ground up." The headache that had been building as the conversation continued began to throb in earnest now. The very idea of having to start over again . . .

"Is it just the mayor who makes the final decision? Or is it a council vote—" Ford broke off and his expression soured.

Delia nodded, knowing he'd put two and two together. "Mayor Davis decides, but the council has veto power, and he won't want a veto, so of course he's communicating with them, listening to their thoughts on the matter. And yes, Winstock's son-in-law is head of that council. And I know you've been out on the island, so you may not know that Ted Weathersby just tossed his hat in the ring for the mayor's race. He and Stanley Davis have always gotten along well. Stanley is an old golf buddy of Winstock's and has been touting Teddy for years as his most obvious replacement. I have been pushing Owen Hartley to run—"

"He owns the hardware store."

She nodded. "He'd be wonderful in the role, and though I've been championing the idea for the past few months, if he says yes, that would help me, because he's definitely on the side of the small business owner, being one himself. But I can't see the town or Winstock letting Davis drag this out until after the election."

"And yet Davis hasn't already accepted his golf buddy's big-money offer. So . . . what's holding him back?"

"His sense of fair play, I think. He's very close to Brooks Winstock and to Ted, but Stanley Davis has always been an honest man. He's run the town since Eli passed. He was town council leader back then and he's very well respected here, fourth generation, his family goes back."

"But he doesn't have the same connection to the O'Reillys that the previous mayor had."

"No, not directly. I mean, he may have eaten at

Gran's place back in the day, or his family might have. He'd have grown up with her, too—they're the same generation. But he comes from money, so he's always run more in Winstock's circles." She smiled briefly. "He's never eaten at my diner, I'll put it that way. The problem is I think he knows that everyone assumes he'll rule for his buddy, and he doesn't want to be seen as being bought, so to speak."

"That gives you some leverage. Have you talked to him?"

She shook her head. "Not yet. It hasn't even been a full week since all this happened. He hasn't spoken to me or Winstock; at least that's what his office is saying. He wants time to go over all the implications, talk to the council, do his own research or whatever. And who knows, maybe he is, but I can't help thinking he just wants to make it look like he did his due diligence before ruling in favor of his golf buddy. I don't know what Davis's plans are for his retirement, but I'm thinking he wouldn't say no to a lifetime yacht club membership, if you know what I mean."

Ford nodded, frowned, but didn't say anything as he took in everything she'd told him. She'd just opened her mouth to thank him again and more or less kick him out the door when he said, "I still think you have an opportunity. You have to know you have the support of a good percentage of this town."

"I don't necessarily know any such thing. I know they like my diner, and respect me, but money does strange things to people."

"All I'm saying is you don't have to stand there and stoically go down with the ship. There's nothing wrong with asking for help. Or taking it when it's offered."

Says the man who barricaded himself on an island, she thought. And yet, he was here. Offering. "I appreciate that you came all this way, Ford, I do. And listened to my lengthy tale of woe. It wasn't—you didn't need to do that, but it was very kind of you to do it anyway. And thank you, but . . . I need to do this on my own."

"You don't *need* to," he said, his tone a little sharper now, a thread of impatience showing through. "You're just too stubborn, or proud, or both to admit you might have to if you want to stay afloat."

"Well, if I am all those things, it's still up to me to stay afloat. If I drown, I drown."

"If that's all you're thinking about, yourself, then you deserve to lose this place." He turned to leave.

Her mouth dropped open at that, and then snapped shut again. "I'm not even sure what *can* be done," she shot back, her voice rising to match his. "But I'll be damned if I'm taking anyone else down with me. This isn't some kind of military mission where you get to just charge in and play hero—" She could tell herself later it was the snap in his tone that had made her lose her cool, but she knew it was fear. Fear he was right. Her throat closed over in horror at the words that had just pushed past her lips, mercifully stopping any more of them from coming out. But it was too late.

He'd paused, frozen maybe, for the briefest of moments, his back still to her, and then continued down the short hall that led from the kitchen to the rear door, saying nothing.

"Ford," she said, the word more of a croak. "I—that was unforgiveable. I don't know where that even came from." Then she hung her head, and felt her throat close over and her eyes burn, even though no tears formed. Shame, however, burned like fire in her gut.

He turned and walked straight toward her. For once

she couldn't read his face, couldn't guess his intent. She was rooted to the spot, held there by the sheer power of his presence, his focus, so very specifically on her. Whatever his intent, she would stand there and take it, because God only knew she deserved it.

He stopped a bare breath away, until she had to tip her head back to look up into his eyes. Eyes so dark gray they looked like a storm at midnight now. "You lost everyone you loved in the span of three years. If you don't want to let anyone get close, then don't."

She had had no idea what he was going to do or say, but compassion wasn't it. Wasn't even close to it. The burn in her gut burned a little brighter still. "I was a kid when that happened, barely an adult."

"You were human. Then, and now."

"You were a kid, too, barely an adult, and you—I lost people, but you . . . you saw unspeakable things."

"Did unspeakable things," he said, his gaze on hers, as if looking for the flinch, the wince. Or worse, the pity.

She hoped what he found was compassion. That's what she felt. And gratitude, for his undeserved understanding. "I must seem so weak, so . . . ridiculous," she said. "Letting people in, but only so far. Everyone loses people in their lives at some point, and they grieve, and then move on. Most days I think I have. Know I have. Just—you caught me off guard. I wasn't expecting . . ." *You.* She couldn't sustain the intensity of his gaze. She looked down. "I am sorry," she said, and then cleared the roughness from her throat. "And I do apologize." She looked up again. "Because you, out of everyone I have ever met, are the very last person I should be afraid of letting get too close. No one has ever been closer. I have nothing to hide from you.

You're the only one who knows that part of me. The only one who was there. Really there." And even as she said the words, she realized just how true they were.

She knew the events of that summer, and the eighteen months that had followed, had shaped her entire life, but until that second, she hadn't fully realized, fully appreciated that he was the only person left who could truly understand why.

He held her gaze for another long moment, and then whatever else might have been there for her to see receded. And the curtain slid back into place, so silently, so seamlessly, she couldn't so much see it as feel it.

"Your reaction was a defense mechanism, and they exist for a reason, Dee," he repeated, calling her by a name she hadn't heard in twenty years. The name her Gran had called her, that he had called her when he'd very first come to Maine with her brother's remains, unaware that everyone else always called her Delia, and were corrected if they didn't. She'd never corrected him. She didn't know why then, exactly, and she still didn't know now.

"Don't ever apologize for that," he said. "Life happens to you, and it keeps happening. It's relentless like that. So, you either find a way to stand up, or you let it flatten you. You stand up. You stand up just fine."

Her bottom lip quivered. *Quivered.* And, a little mortified, she felt tears start to gather at the corners of her eyes. But she was still rooted to the spot, unable to so much as lift a hand to blot them away before they fell.

"And because you do, this town stands up for you. And with you. You say this isn't a mission, but that's how I was trained to see things. You have a mission, to save your diner, your home. Your life. And you have an army, ready to go into battle with you, stand for you.

It's their diner, too. Their home. Their life. So now, of all times, is not the moment to sit down, to let Brooks Winstock, or anyone else, flatten you."

"I'm—"

"Don't. Apologize." He made each word its own statement for emphasis.

She stood there, stewed-tomato face, hair most assuredly frizzed out beyond all belief, inelegant tear tracks on her forty-three-year-old cheeks—redheads did not make pretty criers at any age—and, shocking them both, she smiled. "I wasn't going to say I was sorry." Even though she was. It was one thing to be strong and self-protective, quite another to be an insensitive jerk. "I'm scared. That's what I was going to say . . . I'm scared. Scared that standing won't be enough. That I won't be enough. That I won't just lose everything I am to myself, but everything I am—that Delia's is—to Blueberry Cove. I'll let everyone down. And that's so much worse than letting me down."

And the shield dropped, just like that. The glimmer slid back in. His eyes weren't so much impenetrable gunmetal as the rich depth of the black sky on a clear hot summer night. And she wondered for a brief moment what he would be like if the stars would just wink back on.

"So, don't," he said, and for the first time there was something in his voice. Something, rather than . . . nothing.

And memories from that long-ago night blitzed through her mind, in hyper-speed flashes, how he'd sounded when he'd finally let his guard down, when he'd finally given over to the moment, given himself over to her. There had been a lot of something there that night.

There must have been something of that . . . something, in her eyes, because his gaze, so certain, so focused, so specific . . . dropped, ever so briefly, for barely a whisper of a moment, to her lips. And she went from rooted to the spot to feeling like her legs, her entire insides, had suddenly turned to liquid . . . if hot, molten lava could be described as something as innocuous, harmless as liquid.

And then he was walking back to the door. And she was gripping the side of the doorframe, wondering how the yellow rubber gloves covering her forearms hadn't simply fused to her overheated skin. This time she didn't shoot him in the back, didn't let fear take the lead, where words built walls meant to keep her in, and others out, out, out.

There was a gust of cool, evening air rushing in, but like a whisper trying to put out a flame, it did nothing to soothe the fire.

She wasn't sure how long she stood there, but she finally turned back to the kitchen, returned to the sink and, by rote more than thought, picked up the grate, found the steel wool, and went back to work.

Because work was what she would have to do if she planned on being ready to feed Blue's lobstermen at the bare crack of dawn before they headed out for the day's catch, and Ceil from the town hall offices, who'd need her coffee if she had a chance in hell of dealing with her boss, Ted Weathersby—or Teddy the Letch as Delia had privately always called him. She guessed if he and his daddy-in-law managed to steal her place out from under her, she could add a few more names to that list.

She pushed her mind back to the morning regulars, and Old Lou, who sat on the second stool from the back, and liked his oatmeal with raisins and pecans, the way his late wife used to make it, and his coffee with more milk and sugar than actual coffee. Then the lunch crowd would start up, and Lou would still be there, in full storytelling mode, regaling sweet Jean Reister, who ran the jewelry store, with the tale of how he'd met Clara, his wife of forty-seven of the best years of his life, and Jean wouldn't have to pretend to be charmed, because she sincerely would be. Every time.

Being late August, what passed as the tourist season in a town this far up the coast was over, so dinnertime would just be the locals, her neighbors, who had put in a full day being useful to somebody, somewhere and weren't in the mood for the more rowdy goings-on over at Fergus McRae's pub, The Rusty Puffin, but not quite ready to go home to a house that was too quiet or, for some, not quiet enough.

So they came to Delia's. Not because the menu was trendy—she was a firm believer, as Gran had been when she'd run O'Reilly's, that folks don't come to the local restaurant because they want cutting-edge cuisine—they go local because they want the comfort of familiarity, both with the menu and with the people. Which worked out really well, because what Delia wanted was the comfort and familiarity of the people of Blueberry Cove.

"So, I suppose I'd better figure out how to make sure we all get to keep what we want."

Lord knew she'd have plenty of time to do that, seeing as the only way she'd ever keep Ford Maddox from invading her dreams now was quite simply to never go to sleep again.

Chapter 3

Ford rolled up his notebook and shoved it in the side pocket of his plaid flannel coat, but still paused before reaching for the Wonderland-themed croquet mallet door handles. He wasn't even certain why he was there.

It definitely wasn't because he needed an antique piece of furniture, no matter how interesting, eclectic, or compelling. And Eula March's Mossycup Antiques contained all of those things. Every piece she sold, whether charming, practical, or both, came with a story, and if local lore were true, had been lovingly restored not only by Eula's skilled eyes and hands, but possibly with a wee bit of magic thrown in for good measure. That particular legend was made easier to believe, and embellish upon, because the centuries-old building had a giant mossycup oak tree growing straight up through the middle of it. The unique little shop sat perched on High Street, looking out over Half Moon Harbor, just up the hill from Delia's, and had been run by Eula March for as long as anyone in the Cove could remember.

Ford had seen the shop when he'd come to town

the first time for Tommy's funeral—it was hard to miss—but he hadn't actually gone inside until years later, after he'd left the military and moved to the Cove full time. He'd begun his work with Pelletier out on Sandpiper, his interest in livable tree houses by then a personal mission, so he'd initially been drawn in by the oak tree, hoping to learn something about how the shop and tree had coexisted so harmoniously over such a long stretch of time. However, it had been the unexpected conversation he'd had with the shop's eccentric owner that had brought him back, periodically, over the ensuing years.

Depending on whom you talked to in Blueberry, Eula was either a crotchety old woman with an opinion she never minded sharing, a gifted seer with uncanny insight into the lives and souls of all of the Cove's denizens, or a clever witch who kept elves in her secret workshop.

Or all of the above, Ford thought, as he tugged the door open, wondering which one he'd encounter today. He paused, as he always did, to take a look at the tree. Hardy and huge, it squatted in the center of the store like the gatekeeper to some magical realm located far below the earth's surface, if only one could figure out how to find the hidden portal. The trunk of the tree was so thick it would take the arms of three adults to circle it. There was a large knot on the side facing the door that had sunken in at the center, creating a dark crevasse, which had become a constant source of dares by children—and more than one adult—to test the bravery, or lack thereof, of those willing to reach inside. Stories were told with delighted glee and much embellishment of the less-than-savory results that had befallen those who attempted to reach inside the grand oak.

Ford laid his hand on the rough gray bark and looked up to the heavy branches that reached skyward into the eaves and out through carefully constructed portals in the steeply pitched roof. Well, he could only assume the careful part, given the health of the tree, and the shop. Eula had never been exactly forthcoming on the whys and wherefores of the original construction, nor had she been keen on letting him climb the thing to see for himself.

"It's in a boy's nature, you know."

Ford hadn't heard her come out to the front of the shop, but he didn't startle easily. Or at all, actually. Ever. Some training stuck for life. "What nature would that be?" he asked idly, still looking up into the branches that reached in the eaves.

"To climb what is climbable, whether it wants to be climbed or not."

"I didn't ask." He hadn't for years now.

"Didn't have to."

Something that resembled a smile touched the corners of his mouth as he finally shifted his stance, moved back from the tree, and turned to look directly at the shop's owner. "Good morning, Ms. March, ma'am."

He could see the ingrained look of the long suffering that came with his continued stubborn refusal to stop ma'am-ing her. Couldn't be helped, he thought. It simply wouldn't be polite. He'd done a long list of very impolite things in his forty-five years, including the most impolite thing one could do—take another's life—but disrespecting women of any age was not one of them.

She folded her arms over the thin middle of her tall, wiry frame. She kept silver-white hair of indeterminate length tucked up in a neat bun, always wore a simply styled dress—made by her own hand, he'd heard—with a work apron tied over it, and the sort of sensible shoes worn by someone who'd spent most of her life standing in them. He couldn't have said what color any of her dresses had been, but he could tell you every apron she'd ever worn. At least the ones he'd been present to see. It was the sheer incongruity of them more than it was the detailed needlework that went into their design that made them so memorable.

Of course, Eula March was a study in contrasts. Her stiff New England posture, the patrician nose that she'd long since perfected looking down, the no-nonsense bun, and an attitude to match, seemed to be at complete odds with the whimsical nature of her shop, starting with the croquet mallet door handles, and continuing throughout the place with the various eclectic storybook collectibles tucked in nooks here and crannies there, not to mention the giant tree that sat in the center of it all.

That dichotomy was reflected on her person as well, with her buttoned-up, neatly collared, calf-length dresses and sensible shoes, always paired with shop aprons sporting deep front pockets that featured a veritable who's who parade of hand-embroidered characters from those same beloved childhood storybooks. He'd finally decided that if the morose gentleman farmer from those iconic, vintage cornflakes ads had ever had a love child with Mother Goose, the result would have been Eula March. If he wasn't mistaken, today her pockets featured the full cast of A. A. Milne's *Winnie-the-Pooh*.

"What's so amusing about insolence?" Eula wanted to know.

Ford realized he was smiling, but didn't smooth his

expression, despite her censure. "Nothing, ma'am," he said easily, thinking it had been too long since someone had gotten a true smile from him.

"Then you can wipe that smirk off your face. If you'd been paying attention, you'd have noticed I didn't remind you that I don't care to be ma'am'd to death."

"Didn't have to." There might have been a flash of teeth with that comment; then he ducked his chin and smoothed his expression before lifting his gaze to hers once again. "Ma'am."

She huffed and turned toward the back of the shop. "Some of us have work to do. Can I help you with something, or did you just come by to make googly-eyes at my oak tree again?"

Ford was already walking toward the back of the shop behind her, but almost stumbled over his own feet at that last part. *Googly-eyes?* He shot a quick glance at the tree, and fought another smile as he realized that maybe she had a point. How pathetic was it that just the night before he'd stood, stone-faced and stock-still, in front of the vibrancy of pure womanhood that was Delia O'Reilly, with her looking up at him like he was Thanksgiving dinner and Christmas morning all wrapped up in one . . . and instead of doing anything about it, he'd locked up like the tongue-tied, fumble-fingered kid he'd never been, even when he was a kid, and delivered a lecture instead.

This morning, however, he had no problem whatso-ever putting his hands on the trunk of an inexplicably thriving three-hundred-plus-year-old tree and trading banter with a woman old enough to be his grand-mother. He didn't need a shrink to spell that one out for him.

"Don't go prettying it up for me," she went on, still

moving to the back of the shop. "We both know it's not me you come to visit."

"You would be wrong about that, ma'am," he said, earning a baleful glare delivered over her bony shoulder. The corners of his mouth might have kicked up a twitch again. "I come to see both of you."

That earned him the rarest of things, a chuckle disguised as a snort, and between his smile and her snort, he counted the visit a success before it had even really begun.

She paused a few feet before the blue painted door that led to her fabled workshop. Fabled, because the pieces she displayed in her shop, so stunningly refurbished and restored, were never actually witnessed coming into the shop via delivery truck or any other method. And many of the pieces were far too immense to fit in the small confines of the tiny area at the rear of the shop dedicated to her workspace. There were almost as many stories about that as there were about the possible magic that resided in the tree. "Well, you've made puppy-dog eyes at the tree, so let's get on with the rest of your business. What do you need with me?"

"It's about Delia O'Reilly. I understand that she—" He broke off when Eula turned back. She clasped rawboned hands together in front of her waist, and pinned her gaze so directly on him that he stopped right where he stood, his hands instantly still by his sides, fingertips twitching, every fiber of his being fully aware and alert. Long years of training made such a move instinctive, though a reaction like that usually meant there was at least one gun barrel of some kind pointed in his general direction. Looking into her light gray eyes, he wasn't too certain that wasn't the case now. Double-barreled, even. "What's wrong?" he asked, without preamble.

"You've come to me. About Delia O'Reilly." She didn't make either sentence a question. Instead, she merely continued to observe him, quite sharply, for another long moment, before tapping one bony finger to the back of the opposite wrist, as if pointing to a wristwatch, only she wasn't wearing one. "I'd just about given up hope." She eyed him up and down once more, not bothering to disguise her disappointment. "Actually, truth be told, I had given up hope. Then Grace arrived, and managed to do what none of us could. She miraculously breathed life back into your sad, self-pitying state of affairs."

Ford knew his expression had shifted instinctively to the impenetrable mask it was trained to become when being questioned by the enemy. Not that he'd ever seen Eula March as an enemy, but there was no doubt he was presently under attack. Even for Eula, the words were unexpected, too close to home, and . . . hurtful. He hadn't thought himself vulnerable in that way, not with her. Apparently, his defenses had softened so gradually over time he hadn't even realized it.

"What is it you want from me regarding our Miss O'Reilly?" she asked briskly.

Ford couldn't jump conversational streams quite as deftly as Eula. He was still wading through the muddy one she'd so off-handedly jerked him into. "You think I'm self-pitying?"

She eyed him, seeming a bit surprised that he'd asked, possibly even approving of the fact that he had. It was hard to tell. "You've barricaded yourself out on that island, in a sky fort, no less, as if the island itself wasn't fortress enough. Cut yourself off from any and everyone who gives a damn about you—and you'd be quite surprised to learn just what that number might actually be. So, I don't know that it's so much what I think, as it is merely stating a fact."

"I'm not on that island because I'm feeling sorry for myself. I'm there to work."

She snorted again, though there was no trace of amusement in it this time. "Your work doesn't require year-round residence. You live out there because you don't trust yourself around other people. Not, as far as I can tell, because the scars you carry from your past have manifested themselves in some violent, post-traumatic whatnot sort of way that might be sprung all of a sudden on the unsuspecting. No, I think it's because you've decided you've been responsible for enough in this world, and you're simply not going to sign on for any more." She folded her arms. "Are you saying you disagree?"

"I don't see that as self-pitying." He'd been there when his own men, men who'd counted on him to lead them, had gotten blown literally to bits. Worse even than that had been the innocents. The little boy he'd watched kicking a ball around the dusty streets outside the shell of a building he'd made his temporary base, the little boy's even younger sister, who always looked up at him with that shy smile, the one who made him think about Grace, about family. The two children had been laughing as he'd driven out that morning on the sniper mission he was there to complete . . . only to come back several hours later to find half the village had been destroyed by a missile aimed at taking out his base of operations. He'd found the ball, and the lifeless body of the little girl, barely recognizable in the rubble. And that was just one day. One of many. So very, very many. Yes, Eula was right. He'd been responsible for enough in this world. He figured he was due a break from that.

"It is as if by doing so you intentionally cut yourself off from enjoying every other aspect of the rich and rewarding life you could be having, thereby also cutting off those who might be enriched and rewarded by knowing you."

Her words struck him like physical blows. "I've learned my limits, ma'am," he said, with every ounce of respect he had for her, which he realized now was quite a lot. Why else would he be standing in her shop in the first place? Why else had he turned to her for advice when faced with a problem he had no solution for? "I know what I'm capable of doing. And what I'm not. I've learned what I'm capable of giving. What I'm not. I'm a productive member of society, of Blueberry Cove's society and the greater society of Pelican Bay. The work I do is important. I think that is a very rewarding life, and I'm thankful for it. As to what people think about that? About me? About what I should or shouldn't be doing? Well, I don't give a good—" He stopped, ducked his chin, and bit off the rest of the words, even as they burned the tip of his tongue.

He tamped down the anger she'd triggered. "My apologies, ma'am." He lifted his gaze to hers, chin firm. "You would be right. I choose not to be responsible for anyone other than myself. You might see it differently, you might think it selfish, or cowardly. I don't. To me, it simply seems the best choice for all concerned. Not because people are not worth the time, effort, or energy, but because I simply do not have anything left in me to give."

"And yet you give, tirelessly, it would seem, to the creatures in need who populate your island."

"Because they don't have anyone else to stand up for them. I don't think the same can be said for the folks here. At the very least, they can stand for themselves, and each other. They don't need me."

"Grace needs you."

Another punch to the gut. He took it, absorbed it, swallowed tightly, but kept his gaze evenly, respectfully, on hers. "Yes. And I'm doing my best to be what she needs me to be."

"You are her brother. That's all she needs you to be. Do you not understand that simply being is enough? Being does not necessarily mean doing. Or owing. Or burdening yourself in some manner. Do you expect Grace to be something more, to do something for you, because she's your sister?"

"Of course not."

She merely lifted a pencil-thin gray eyebrow in response, and he swallowed another string of words unacceptable for mixed company. Except this time they were directed at himself.

"And now," she went on, "here you are, wanting to know what I can do to help you help Delia O'Reilly. My word, Dr. Maddox, aren't you worried that someone else might barge in on your private little sanctuary of one and expect you to just . . . be you?"

He wanted to turn and walk straight out the door, never to return. To never look into those all-too-knowing eyes again. "I can't help Delia. I know what's happening here, with her diner, with Brooks Winstock, but she won't accept my help and, frankly, I'm not sure what I could do even if she would. I just wanted to find out if you knew of someone who could help her."

"More's the pity. Perhaps if you joined the land of us self-sufficient folk who don't need you more often, you'd understand the nature of the fabric of her life. You'd know that it was once neatly and securely woven, but is now unraveling at an alarming rate around her. Maybe you'd even be able to figure out exactly how to stop it from happening, before it's nothing more than a pile of old thread left forgotten on the floor."

"Are you saying because you disapprove of the life I've chosen, that you won't help me? Or at least help her?"

"Did I say that? I don't believe I did. Here you are, finally asking for help. Why in the world would I turn you away? You might never ask again. What lesson would that be for either of us? What would anyone benefit from that?"

Ford closed his eyes against the dull throb that was forming behind his temples and rubbed a hand over the tight knot seizing up the muscles at the base of his neck. A conversation with Eula was always an unpredictable thing, but he hadn't expected anything like this.

He took a slow breath, and opened his eyes. "What can I do to get help for her? Who should I talk to?"

Eula looked heavenward and muttered something he couldn't understand under her breath. Then she looked back at him. "I should think the answer to that would be obvious. Talk to Delia."

"I already did."

That surprised her, and he shamelessly took a full measure of comfort in the knowledge that he could even do such a thing.

"And she told you to mind your own business." Again, not a question.

"More or less."

"Then you have a choice to make."

"I thought by coming here, to you, I already had."

"True. You could have returned to your island, tail neatly tucked, patting yourself on the back for trying, absolved of all further responsibility. After all, she said no thank you. No longer your concern. Instead," she went on, though his expression made it clear that he didn't appreciate the continued patronization, "you chose to step up. Now you're here, in the Cove, where your presence wasn't requested, your help not demanded, nor your protection overtly needed."

Then she managed to shock him all over again. She unfolded her arms, and her bony shoulders rounded, and something as close to compassion came into her expression as he'd ever seen. She didn't take a step closer, but in every way, she was simply closer to him, as she quietly said, "I realize this puts your neatly ordered life at risk. And I realize that the need for solitude, when you came to us, had to have been great, had to have seemed the only answer to your survival, for you to have cut yourself off so completely. But those needs, those choices, were based on things that have now happened a very long time ago. In some ways, a lifetime ago. You've made a new life here. For yourself. A good one. You are productive, you are working to do good, to quite literally heal, and be healed. Perhaps it's time to ask yourself if you're out on that island, up in that tree, because you still need to be? For your own sanity? Or because it's simply become the life you live because it's the only life you feel you deserve."

"Ma'am," he began, undone once more, but this time, not because she'd inflicted a hurt, but rather tried to lift one. "Eula—"

She raised the tips of her fingers to silence him, her gaze solidly on his, but there was a different kind of intent there now. He saw a depth of caring, and perhaps even concern, that stunned him even more than her blunt speech had earlier.

"That you're here, in my shop, asking me for guidance on what step to take next, should be all the answer you need to your question." She carefully smoothed her palms over her apron and pulled herself up to her full, starched, stiff-shouldered height. "It won't be easy. It won't be clear. It will be messy. And loud. And unpredictable. That is what life led among the living is all about. There is no map, other than the one directing you to stick by, and stand up. Do that. Stand up," she said, and Ford heard the echo of his own words to Delia the night before. *Stand up.* Had Eula known that? How could she have?

"I am standing up for her," he said. "I'm here."

She surprised him a final time with an actual smile. "Dear boy, I'm not telling you to stand up for her, but for yourself. Until you do that, you'll be of no help to anyone. Life doesn't make promises. But if you want to know what can be? You must first do that." And with that she turned and went through the blue door to her workshop, closing it behind her with a quiet, yet very final sounding, click.

Leaving Ford to stand there, feeling as if a giant sea squall had just blown up out of nowhere to batter him, inside and out.

He'd heard what she'd said, understood every lash, as well as every part that was meant to comfort, to guide him to a safe port. And at some point, when he'd recovered sufficiently, he'd figure out what he thought about it all. And what he was going to do about it. He looked up at the tree, into the branches reaching up to the eaves, feeling the pull, the promise it made. *Climb up, escape, never come down.*

"Wise words," he muttered to the tree. "I should have listened to them and never left the damn island in the first place." Then he turned and walked out.

Chapter 4

"I keep tellin' ya, come away with me on my fishing boat, leave all this behind." The creases at the corners of the old fisherman's eyes deepened with his toothy grin, his dark eyes twinkling above perennially tanned cheeks as he lifted his coffee cup for a refill.

"Stokey, my darling, be careful what you wish for," Delia said with a grin as she topped him off. "The way things are going, I might just take you up on that."

He clapped his empty hand over the napkin he'd tucked in the collar of his shirt. "I'd live out my years a happy, happy man."

"Don't kid yourself, Stoke," said Arnaud Pliff, his business partner and good friend of at least fifty of Stokey Parker's sixty-plus years. "She puts so much as a hand on you and you'd drop dead of heart failure. Then where would that leave her?"

"Why, on a fishing trawler alone with you, Arnie," Delia said with a wink and a nudge to his beefy shoulder as she moved on to the next table, leaving Arnaud waggling his bushy gray eyebrows to the hoots and hollers of the other fishermen who crowded several of the tables in the small, waterfront diner.

Delia expertly wove her way, coffeepot in one hand, tray balanced in the other, between the short row of heavily lacquered oak two tops wedged along the bay window at the front of the shop, and the trio of red-linen-covered four tops that filled the center space on wide plank hardwood floors.

Three booths with Wedgwood blue padded benches and oak tables lined a low wall on the opposite side of the room, with a narrow aisle on the opposite side, bracketed by a row of five barstools lined up in front of the counter that separated the eating area from the kitchen. Napkin holders, condiments, and the like were spaced evenly along the gleaming oak bar; at the far end, closest to the door, sat a mid-century, two-level glass dessert case she'd rescued and refurbished from Gran's restaurant after the fire. It had been the only thing that had survived, saved by a capricious arrangement of collapsed, charred beams. An antique cash register from Eula's shop sat on a small stand at the end of the bar, right behind it.

Delia glanced to the bells jingling on the door as Owen Hartley stepped inside. "Just the man I want to see," she said, and then smiled when Owen blushed to his ginger-haired roots. She'd known Owen her whole life. He'd been a few grades ahead of her in school, so they hadn't been close, but she'd always liked and respected him. He'd married young, taken over the family hardware store, so they'd had that in common, too. Then he'd lost his wife when their only child had barely been school age, and the whole town had come together for the two of them. Watching him over the years, seeing his sincere love for the town—he was a walking encyclopedia of Cove heritage knowledge—as well as how seriously he'd taken his role as a parent, her respect for him had only grown. She knew everyone in the Cove felt the same.

She gestured to the empty booth, then slid in on the bench seat across from him as he sat down, setting her tray on the table.

"Now, Delia, I know what you're going to say, and—"

"Have you talked to Lauren about it?" Delia asked, referring to his daughter. She turned over his coffee mug and filled it, then added the creamers to the tray she knew he liked and pushed it toward him. "She seems really happy with her decision to go to college closer to home. I'm sure she's excited about the idea of you running, isn't she?" Seeing Owen's face crinkle with real concern, Delia reached across the table and put her hand on Owen's wrist, keeping her voice low. "I know you have reservations about her wanting to come back to the Cove after she graduates next spring, but when she was in just before she went back for fall semester—Owen, she was just glowing with excitement. If it helps, I can assure you, it's what she really wants."

Owen's expression didn't smooth. "I know that's what she says, but I guess I'm afraid she's just coming back to take care of her old man, that she has some misguided thing about me being alone. That's not what I wanted for her."

"She's coming back because she loves her home here, and she loves Hartley's Hardware and the traditions built by you, your father, and his father before him." Delia beamed. "You provided that strong foundation for her, Owen. You gave her that sense of loyalty and pride. You did a good job with her: she's smart, she's happy, grounded. Trust that she's making the choice for herself, not because she thinks you need her, but because it's truly where her heart is. I saw her face when she talked about her plans. She couldn't be more thrilled about her goals."

Owen held Delia's gaze for a moment longer, clearly torn between wanting to believe her and being worried that his only child was making a huge mistake. He looked away, fidgeted with the creamer, then finally tore off the paper lid and added the creamer to his coffee, his thoughts clearly not on his meal. "I hear you, and I appreciate that you've been there for her. She—I've tried to be both mother and father, but I can only do what I can do and, well, you've—" He looked up at her again, sincerity and embarrassment making him flush endearingly. "You've been a good shoulder, Delia, and I should have told you sooner how much that's meant to me. She's always admired you, you know, running your own place. She trusts your judgment."

Now it was Delia's turn to blush. "That's—that's incredibly kind of you to say, Owen. I'm humbled, truly. I've always had a soft spot for her, you know that." Her expression turned serious as another thought occurred to her. "It wasn't me who was encouraging her to come back, I hope you know that. I just listened—"

"No, no. I know that. I—" He broke off, smiled, his soft blue eyes warming. "I guess it's just going to take me a little while to rearrange all those plans I had for her inside my head, try to see things from her perspective. I worked so hard to give her the opportunity to spread her wings and fly."

Delia squeezed his arm again. "I know you did, and she is flying, Owen. She's happy and she's focused and she knows what she wants. You can't be anything but proud of that."

He nodded, his smile growing wider, pride for his only child clear on his face. "Always."

Delia's smile widened to a grin. "So, you'll consider then? About running for mayor?"

Owen's smile fled and his pale skin paled further. "Now, now, I didn't say that."

Delia slid out from the booth and expertly propped her coffee- and tea-laden tray on her hand. "Talk to Lauren about it," she said. "Get her feedback. I'll be back for your order in a few minutes." Wisely leaving him to his own thoughts, she cruised the tables, topped off half-empty coffee mugs, left another creamer on the booth table for Old Lou, and took orders from a four top that had just filled up with incoming locals.

Lou lifted his coffee mug and she swung back to give him a refill. "You want some toast to go with your oatmeal today?" she asked him, glancing out the bay window to make sure no one had seated themselves outside. It was early yet, and a bit brisk with the wind coming in off the harbor, but that wouldn't keep die-hard Mainers from taking their first cup of coffee outside. "I have freshly made blueberry jam."

"Tempting," he said absently, his focus staying on the current issue of *The Blueberry Beacon* he'd spread over the table. He always took a booth so he could do just that. The *Beacon* was the Cove's one and only daily newspaper, which she provided for her regulars. "You read this yet?" he asked, nudging the paper toward her. "Says right there that Brooks Winstock is gonna build himself a yacht club in the Cove. Right here on this very spot, in fact."

"That's old news," Stokey said from his spot across the room by the front window, listening in, as was the habit of pretty much all of the diner's regulars. "Never happen. Delia's is a landmark. Can't go tearing down landmarks. That's not what we do." He smiled at Delia, and she shot him a wink and a smile, even as she prayed the clutch she felt in her gut didn't show on her face.

"I might be old, but that doesn't mean I don't keep up," Lou informed the room at large. "I know the rumors, but this here article says that Winstock told some news reporter down in Bar Harbor that it was a done deal." He stabbed a finger at the paper. "Right here. 'Done deal.' Quote, unquote. He goes on to talk about how the bay cruises on the new schooner will launch by Memorial Day weekend next season, and that he hopes to have the Half Moon Yacht Club up and running by July Fourth. Says he's already hired some big-name, hotshot architect who designed that new private resort down in the Hamptons." He looked up at Delia. "He even brings up Langston deVry, and how he's designing Grace's inn here, talking about how Blueberry Cove is the next Martha's Vineyard. 'The place where people will want to be.' His words." He snorted in disgust. "If a body needs some fancy club to want to be in the Cove, well then, we don't need them. That's what I say."

Somewhere during Lou's spiel, the chatter in the diner had gone from a sudden burst in response to Lou's revelation, to murmurs, to complete silence. All except for Lou, who continued on, seemingly unaware of the sudden silence, or thinking it was in deference to his ongoing commentary. "Of course," he said to Delia, "you'll be telling deVry about this, seeing as you two have been cozying up. Can't be too happy about these goings-on, especially after Winstock went after the Monaghan property."

The sound of the bell jingling as the diner door

closed had everyone turning their heads, everyone, that is, except Lou, who kept on talking. Everyone else watched Ford Maddox slide quietly onto a stool at the end of the counter by the register, his back to the room.

"When is he due back up here?" Lou was saying. "Soon I hope. He'll set this right for you." He gave her a wink, which she only caught from the corner of her eye.

Everyone's attention was currently playing ping-pong, going from Ford, to her, back to Ford.

"Good friends come in handy," Lou said with a bit of devil in his grizzled grin. "Good friends with deep pockets even handier."

"Lou, for the love of—" Stokey hissed. "Shut up already, will ya?"

Lou blinked myopic eyes through Magoo-thick glasses. "What?" He finally looked around the room. "What did I say? Everyone knows the two of them are an item. I was simply stating facts. Man like that isn't going to sit around is all I'm saying. He'll step up and—"

"Thanks, Lou," Delia cut in, smiling sincerely as she patted him on the shoulder, while simultaneously trying not to send everything on her tray crashing to the floor as she resumed her slide and glide through the tables.

Her jitters weren't because of Lou's public comments regarding her relationship with Langston. It wasn't as if she'd tried to hide anything there, nor was she about to start. Whatever conclusions folks drew, well, that was their business. She wasn't about to go around correcting them. No, her suddenly sweaty palms and jittery fingers had everything to do with the man presently staking claim to one of her counter stools.

She could feel Ford's presence in the room as if a giant live wire had just been plunged into the harbor, sending rippling waves of electric shocks straight up and through the town. Starting with her diner. Or maybe just with her.

Way back, when Ford had first come to the Cove to live, there had been speculation among the townies that perhaps a friendship—or something more—had formed between them when he'd brought Tommy O'Reilly home for his last services, a relationship that maybe had evolved over time and despite distance. Why else would he be back in the Cove? Speculation had run rampant as everyone waited and watched to see what would happen between the two.

Ford had spent a lot of time at the diner, which only fanned the flames of expectation. Though Delia had played it all down, the truth was, she hadn't worked overly hard to quash the chatter because she'd still been wondering herself why he'd come to the Cove. Wondering . . . and maybe waiting.

It had been clear early on, though, that he was there to heal, or maybe just hide—from the world, from himself—or a little of both. He wasn't looking for a relationship, or a repeat of the night they'd spent together. He was looking for sanctuary. So that's what she'd given him. Eventually, he'd started his college courses, going back and forth to Bangor, working for Dr. Pelletier. Summer came, went, other men were seen in Delia's company, Ford stopped coming to the diner as his work and schooling increased, then moved out to the island altogether when Pelletier took ill and passed away, and slowly the chatter died out.

Clearly, though, it had not been forgotten. Memories were long in the Cove. After all this time, Ford had returned to her diner. She was certain it wasn't lost on anyone, even Lou, when he finally spied Ford over the top of the booth, that Ford's arrival just happened to coincide with Brooks Winstock's well-publicized intent to demolish the diner and build his "foo-foo resort" as Stokey had taken to calling it.

It was like a collective holding of breath, as everyone watched her, then Ford, then her again, waiting to see what would happen next.

What happened next was she continued on with her job, hiding her uncustomary jitters and tummy flutters behind a bigger smile as she smoothly picked up where Lou had left off. "But since when have I counted on some big, strong man to save my bacon?" she said in response to Lou's rant. "If anyone's going to save my diner, it'll be me."

Stokey gave a hearty, approving laugh at that, and Arnie pumped a fist. "You tell 'em," he added. "That's what I've been saying. Nothing is going to happen to this place. You'll see to that."

"Saying to whom?" she asked Arnie as she slipped by for one last top-off before taking the new orders back to the kitchen. She was curious to know just how much of a conversation her situation had become, but mostly she'd asked to stall for another minute. Because to take the orders back meant going to the counter, and she needed another minute to regain her equilibrium. You'd think she was twenty-one, working for Gran, with Ford looking all hot and young and military sharp. A lot of life had happened since then, with a crucial bit more of it breathing right down her neck.

Arnie looked up at her, surprised by the question. "Everyone's talking about it, Delia," he told her.

"Well, I appreciate the support, guys. More than you know. You know I won't let you down." Silently, she prayed that wasn't a lie. Then, still not entirely ready, especially with a very interested audience, but knowing she had to put the orders in, she headed to the counter. Balancing the tray, she ducked behind the bar, and then slid the four top order through the window to the kitchen over the stainless-steel shelf. "Two specials, one over extra easy, and add extra pepper to the hash," she told Pete, who was handling grill duty that morning.

Then, with a short, calming breath, she put a smile on her face and turned to face Ford. She pulled out her order pad from her apron pocket and set it on the counter. "What can I get you?" she asked, as if he were a regular there. She couldn't help but think about the days when he had been. Her heart had fluttered its fair share then, too.

He glanced up from the menu. "You changed it," was all he said.

"I do that from time to time. Mostly to keep from being bored. But all the regular dishes are still there. Are you looking for anything in particular? Pete's in the back, so he can make whatever you want."

Pete was in his mid-seventies, Cove born and bred, and could run the entire kitchen with one hand tied behind his back. She'd often said he'd been born with a paring knife in one hand, a spatula in the other, and a mixing spoon in the third hand he obviously had and just kept hidden. He'd worked for Gran before Delia had started her own place, and though a gruff talker, when he talked at all, was as close to family as anyone she had left.

She looked up from her order pad, pen poised, to find Ford looking at her now, the menu forgotten. She could feel the weight of every pair of eyes in the place on the two of them, and thought it was a wonder Ford's plaid lumberman's jacket didn't have singe marks on the back from the intensity of their collective focus. In true small-town fashion, they weren't even trying to hide their rampant curiosity. It annoyed her and gave her a pang in the heart at the same time, because she loved them for it, too. Cove life was like that.

"What are you doing to save the place? Have you taken any steps?"

She blinked, not expecting that, but then, what she expected was that he'd gone back out to his island. Clearly, she'd gotten that wrong. "You mean since last night? I thought we had this conversation already," she said, keeping her voiced pitched low, as he had his. The last thing she needed to get out was that Ford had paid her an after-hours visit the night before. "I can't do anything until Mayor Davis decides to talk to me."

Ford cast a sideways glance toward the room, then back to her. "Your army awaits. They'd do anything for you."

Delia smiled, feeling heartwarmed and humbled at the same time. "I know they would. But apparently they need a better general, because this one doesn't rightly know how to harness their willingness and put it to effective use."

"I've been thinking about that."

Her raised eyebrow, along with what was likely a fair dose of skepticism in her eyes, had him flipping open the menu and breaking eye contact again. After a moment's browsing, he said, "They don't just hand out doctorates because they feel sorry for someone, you know."

Her expression was instantly abashed. "My skepticism wasn't regarding your brainpower, or possible lack thereof. Did you really think I meant that?" She just stood there, momentarily at a loss for words. She didn't know whether to be insulted that he thought so little of her, or a little heartbroken that he wasn't as confident as his demeanor would have her believe. *None of us are bulletproof.* He struck her as pretty secure in who and what he'd become, but could she be the chink in his armor, the way he was in hers?

She leaned her palm on the counter, and poised the pen over the order pad again, though she doubted a single person in the place thought their conversation had anything to do with the daily breakfast special. "You know, just because someone is surprised by something you do, doesn't automatically mean they assume you can't. The surprise is that you're bothering to try in the first place." She grinned when he shot her an aggrieved look. "See? Just like that. I meant bothering to try because you're not exactly known for your magnanimous gestures where the folks of the Cove are concerned. Not because you had no hope of succeeding, so why try. Sheesh." She flicked the end of her pen on his head. "I guess they don't hand out doctorates to guys with common sense, either."

Satisfied with his scowl, she pushed away from the bar as Pete slid the orders for the four top through the window. She propped the tray comfortably onto one palm and maneuvered around the bar, catching pretty much everyone else in the diner quickly looking anywhere but at her. But not in time for her to miss the grins on their faces. She probably shouldn't have tapped Ford on the head. But for a smart guy, he could have such a thick skull at times.

She'd finished delivering the tray of food and was taking Stokey's and Arnie's orders, along with those from another two top that had just filled, and noticed she had a pair sitting outside as well, when the door jingled again. She glanced over her shoulder with her customary welcoming smile and had already started to gesture to the booths, as those would be the easiest to serve now that the place was crowded, only to freeze, however briefly, at the sight of Camille Weathersby, standing just inside the door.

"Grab a booth and I'll be right with you," Delia said, quickly snapping back to action, hoping the woman hadn't noticed her momentary lapse. Cami was nothing if not . . . resourceful. If she was looking to stir things up, and she usually was, she'd exploit the tiniest weakness. Delia wouldn't put anything past her. She noted Cami's attention catch and snag on Ford. *But she would put just about anyone under her,* Delia thought unkindly, but not untruthfully.

The very married Cami—wife to head councilman Ted Weathersby—had a reputation for putting her wiles to work wherever it suited her needs. And, given her actions this last year alone, she was clearly a woman of many . . . needs. Of course, her husband was a born skirt chaser, so they were a match made, that was for certain.

"I believe I'll sit at the counter," she all but cooed to Delia.

Of course you will, Delia thought, working a little harder to keep her smile even.

Cami slid onto the stool next to Ford, a feat that seemingly defied physics, given the snug fit of her pencil skirt, and crossed her shapely legs, "accidentally" brushing the toe of one red, skinny-heeled pump against Ford's shin. Not that Delia was paying close attention or anything.

Who was she kidding? Every pair of eyes in the place was presently trained on Camille Weathersby and Ford Maddox.

In another act against nature, Ford laid his menu down and slid from the stool without so much as a glance in Cami's direction. Delia didn't think there was a man with a pulse who could have managed that particular feat, or one who would have even wanted to try.

Delia closed the distance between her and Ford before realizing she'd done so, then wasn't quite sure what to say to him when he paused at the door. He took care of that for her.

"When are you done tonight?" he asked, his voice carrying only to her.

"Close to midnight. Why do you—?" But he'd already nodded and pushed out the door. Delia turned back around in time to once again catch everyone reverting quickly back to their meals and conversation. She was surprised they didn't have neck strain from craning to hear what Ford had said. Did that mean she could expect another late-night kitchen call? She wasn't sure her sleep schedule could handle another hit of Ford pheromones so close to bedtime.

Shoving that out of her mind, she turned back toward the counter. And Cami Weathersby. Who, in addition to being Teddy the Letch's wife, was also Brooks Winstock's daughter. His only child. What she wasn't was a regular at Delia's. In fact, Delia couldn't recall that she'd ever seen Cami deign to set so much as a perfectly clad, designer labeled toe inside the diner. Had the village radar worked so fast that she'd somehow known Ford had shown up? Because he was pretty much the only bachelor under the age of sixty left in the Cove whom Cami hadn't already tried to seduce. And that was only because he lived in his ultimate tree fort out on an island.

"What can I get for you?" Delia asked, keeping her smile even and her gaze squarely on Cami's face.

"Is Ford Maddox moving back harborside?" she asked without preamble, then slid her business card across the counter. She was also, as her card proclaimed, the number one Realtor in all of Pelican Bay. Not surprising since her daddy owned most of it. "I think I have just the property for him, if he's interested."

I just bet you do. Completely renovated and fully loaded. "He still has his place on the other side of the harbor," Delia told her, putting down the tray behind the counter, and picking up a fresh pot of coffee. She left Cami's card on the counter.

"That's leased, isn't it? Has been for years. Some old professor of his or something is in it, last I heard. Hardly ever comes out, so I couldn't say for sure. Odd duck."

"I suppose you'll have to ask him," Delia said as she slid out from behind the counter and started on a fast round of refills. She needed to get outside and take orders on the deck, where all three tables were now fully seated. Another reason she couldn't let herself be distracted by Ford. It was bad for business.

"I didn't come here to talk to him," Cami said, executing a perfect swivel on the stool so she could continue the conversation. "I have some properties to show you." Her voice was modulated to carry easily over the conversations taking place around her, not that it was necessary, as the chatter once again dwindled to whispers and everyone turned their attention to the two women.

Delia's back teeth ground together a bit and her cheeks began to ache from the effort of keeping her smile looking easy, breezy, and unaffected. Giving the local grapevine a veritable carafeful of gossip was not exactly how she'd hoped to rally the troops, but it wasn't like she'd invited her two special guests this morning.

"I'm so sorry you went to that trouble, seeing as I'm not in the market for any property." Delia finished topping off Stokey's, Lou's, and the four top's coffee mugs in record time, then paused by Owen's booth to take his order, hiding her grimace when she noticed he'd slunk down in the booth, his expression making it clear he'd be under the table altogether if he thought he could get away with it. If he did make the decision to run, he'd be up against Cami's husband, and it was no secret that Cami terrified him, as she did most men in one way or the other. She leaned down and kept her voice low, pad propped to take his order as she said, "Now don't you let her get to you, Owen. She's all hot air and Botox. We can't let her and her father think they run this town."

"But they do," Owen said, furiously scanning the menu as if his life depended on it.

"Precisely why we need some balance around here. I'll bring you the special," she said. Then seeing Cami looking like she might head their way, Delia ducked out the door to the front deck before the blond menace could fire off another round. A chicken move, most certainly, and she was typically no coward, but she'd be damned if she'd give Cami a platform to talk about her father's big plans, right in Delia's own diner.

Not to be outmaneuvered, Cami simply waited for Delia to return, swiveling her tight-skirted backside around once again as Delia slid behind the counter to give Pete the deck orders. "Are you sure I can't get you anything?" she asked Cami as she turned back, smiling so brightly it was possible her eyes gleamed with it. "Pete's got a fresh batch of bacon coming off the griddle and the blueberry muffins are still warm from the oven." She paused, all but daring Cami with her over-the-top cheeriness to say or do something that would make her look like the killjoy she was to their avid audience.

Delia was quite certain Cami would do whatever it took to ensure that her father's plans moved forward, but the woman wasn't stupid. Far from it. Brooks Winstock's only daughter knew better than to risk turning Delia's regulars against her.

"That's okay," Cami said, then tapped a perfectly lacquered nail on top of her business card and slid it back toward her. "I'll go have a chat with Ford about that property I have in mind for him." She smiled easily at Delia, but the calculating gleam in her eyes, which only Delia could see as Cami's back was to the room, promised she'd be back.

"You take care then," Delia said, grabbing a towel to wipe down the counter as Cami slid off the stool and smoothed her skirt and matching mini jacket. Delia might have rubbed harder than absolutely necessary, as if Cami had left something contagious behind. A quick glance around the room told Delia that maybe Cami had been more successful than she'd thought. There were skeptical looks now, and furtive glances her way as conversation returned to normal once the door had jangled shut behind Cami's retreating figure.

Just then Peg came out from the kitchen in the back, tying on her apron as she did. "Sorry I couldn't get here sooner," she told Delia. "I swear Doc Fielding was behind schedule before he even opened his offices today. Kept me waiting almost forty-five minutes and I was first in the door. What's the point of living in a town the size of the Cove if you can't get seen by your own town doctor in a decent amount of time? Might as well live in the city, you hear what I'm saying?"

"I do indeed," Delia told her, smiling. Peg's nonstop chatter was to her what the sound of waves crashing on the shore was to other people: soothing in its dependable constancy. "I'm going to duck in the back and give Pete a ten-minute break. Orders are up for the deck tables."

Peg took over without missing a beat, like the seasoned pro she was. Delia would have to make time for a little chat later, see what the folks in the diner had to say about Cami's visit. Peg's status on the village grapevine wasn't head grape—that position belonged to pub owner Fergus McCrae—but she was darn near the top of the vine.

As much as Delia hated to admit it, she had to start thinking about strategy and figure out how best to use those she had supporting her. It wasn't that she minded asking for help; it was that she needed the help in the first place. Fighting Brooks Winstock made fighting city hall look like child's play. And she was fighting both.

But the first thing she was going to do was call Grace Maddox and gently explain why she needed to call off her big brother. If Delia had a chance in hell of pulling herself out of this mess, she couldn't have Ford fogging up her brain. And all of her other highly foggable parts along with it.

Chapter 5

Ford leaned his shoulder against the skinny white porch column of the saltbox house. The late summer night was clear, the moon high and bright, but there was a nip to the air. Fall would come early this year. He'd known it when the migration from Sandpiper had started earlier than usual.

He wasn't thinking about puffins and terns at the moment, though. There were far too many memories swimming around in his mind, taking up all his available attention. He realized he hadn't come by this house even once in all the years he'd been living in the Cove. When he'd spent time with Delia since he'd come to live there, it had always been at the diner, or sitting on her docks, just across Harbor Street. The tidy, nineteenth-century home had belonged to Delia's grandmother last time he'd come around. There had been a wake at the restaurant Mrs. O'Reilly had owned, but the immediate gathering after Tommy's funeral had been at her house. This house.

Even with the moon, it was hard to tell much in the dark, but he could see the Wedgwood blue paint was weathered, and the whole place was in need of a new set of shakes, maybe some fresh paint on the trim and the porch railing, but that wasn't out of the ordinary for any house in the Cove, given the severity of the winters. Otherwise, the place was well maintained, with a neatly trimmed yard, and equally tidy rosebushes lined up along the front of the porch. A short walk of carefully patterned pavers led from the front porch around to the side driveway, all much the same as it had been when her grandmother had owned it.

He wondered, idly, if Delia had changed anything inside, so the place would now reflect her tastes, her lifestyle, or if she'd simply left it as is, after Gran, as Delia had called her, had passed on. He guessed the latter. Delia didn't strike him as particularly concerned with being trendy so much as being practical. What would have been good enough for the senior O'Reilly was likely just fine for the current O'Reilly. Unless it broke down or wore out, he imagined she didn't try to fix up much. She had enough to do running the diner.

It was a simple life, unadorned by things, by possessions, much like the one of his childhood. Yet, in Delia's case, rather than being desolate or deprived, as his early life had been, her life was beautifully enriched by the people she'd surrounded herself with. As a kid, he hadn't—couldn't have—appreciated the importance of that particular kind of wealth, but standing there now, thinking about the great fortune she had amassed, the depth and breadth of it resonated somewhere deep inside him. And for the first time in a very, very long time, he felt something close to yearning.

Pushing that down, far down, he shoved the memories of his first time in the Cove, along with much, much older memories of his childhood, back up on that long disregarded shelf, and watched as she climbed out of her forest green Trail Runner, and gave her lower back a quick rub. She made the caring and feeding of people—a long and steady stream of them— look easy, but he knew it was damned hard work.

He stepped off the stoop and away from his past as she came around the front walk. "Hey."

She let out a short shriek. "Holy—you really have to stop doing that," she scolded him, rubbing the spot on her chest over her heart. "I swear, you're going to be the death of me." She squeezed her eyes shut as soon as she'd said it.

Ford swore under his breath. Maybe this hadn't been such a good idea after all. For a lot of reasons.

"Sorry. You know I didn't mean—"

"Stop," he said shortly, his tone a shade more abrupt than he'd intended.

She didn't so much as pause. "But—"

"Stop," he said again, more quietly than the first time.

She was standing a few feet in front of him. She didn't say anything, but her eyes were saying it all for her.

"It's no secret I was the death of a lot of people, Dee. It was my job, my duty. In service to this country."

She not only looked apologetic now, but completely ashamed. "You know I understand that. It's just, I know you . . . struggle. Or you did. It's been a long time since I've seen you, been around you. I don't know how you are with it all now, but when you first came back, you were dealing with a lot. With the demands of your service, what was asked of you. You wouldn't be human if you didn't."

"It was a long time ago. A lifetime ago."

"I know that, too. I wasn't apologizing because I thought you were all hair-trigger about it. I just—I didn't mean to be disrespectful. It was an unthinking comment. That's all."

He'd forgotten how direct she could be. Delia O'Reilly didn't mince words. He'd also forgotten how much he missed that. Actually, no, that wasn't exactly true. He'd intentionally not allowed himself to think about how much he missed that. Or her. A very different thing.

"It's a common enough phrase," he replied. "Don't tiptoe around me. You, of all people . . ." He drifted off, not even sure what he was really trying to say.

"Ford," she said, the single word thick with emotion.

"I'm not chastising you, Dee."

One eyebrow climbed halfway up her forehead. "Well, you sure have an interesting approach."

He felt the corners of his mouth kick upward. "Let me finish. Please."

She gave a little nod of acquiescence, and then added a deferential motion with her hand.

A real smile threatened then. Even humbled, she still had an attitude. "It was a request, that's all. And an apology."

That surprised her. "For what? Why?"

He wasn't even sure he could explain it to himself. He only knew that if he was going to find a way to help her, they had to have an understanding. And the fact that they didn't already have one was what he needed to apologize for. "Last night, when you fell all over yourself, worried that you'd said the wrong thing, I . . . it pissed me off."

"Ford—"

"And the fact that it did, well, that didn't help matters, either. But that's on me." He took a moment, searching for the right words, wanting to find them this time. He hadn't had to articulate thoughts of a personal nature to anyone in so long, he wasn't quite sure he knew how to do it. He'd tried, in recent months, with Grace, but the truth was, when they spent time together, she did most of the talking. And he let her. He'd told himself that listening was what she needed from him, that taking in what she had to say to him, learning from it, apologizing when necessary, wishing he had all the answers she sought with her endless questions was what he had to give her, all the while knowing that he deserved far worse than her periodic frustration with him.

He glanced away, looking out from where Delia's house was perched on the side of the hill leading down to the waterfront to the twinkling lights in the harbor below. The right words weren't magically forming in his head. So, he just went with the ones he had. "You're right. It has been a long time. You can't know where I am now, because I haven't been around to let you know it. I hated that you imagined I was still so screwed up that the least little inadvertent reference or stumble over a sensitive subject would send me . . . I don't know. Somewhere. I was angry with you, that you didn't know me better than that." He looked back at her. "Then I realized how completely full of shit I was."

Now both of her eyebrows climbed. She straightened her stance, folded her arms. "Go on."

He shook his head briefly, but the smile was there now, and it wasn't going away. She confused him with the conflicting emotions she so effortlessly evoked. She had from the moment he'd met her. Some things didn't change with time, or with reflection. Possibly, he admitted, because he'd avoided doing just that. *No time like the present.* A lesson Grace was teaching him. Daily. "I wanted to blame my reaction on you. I was mad that your opinion, after all this time, all I've done for the Cove, was still so piss poor."

"It was never—"

He didn't let her finish. It was either say it now, or forever leave that unspoken gap between them. He might not know what to say to his only sister, because words alone—well, there weren't enough of them in all the world to make up for what he'd done to her or, more to the point, not done for her. If he'd learned anything from all that listening he'd been doing, it was that he could expect no one else to step up, speak, make his thoughts known. He understood now that he'd stopped sharing himself because he hadn't wanted to risk the possibility that there wouldn't be anyone who wanted to listen.

"That 'after all I'd done for the Cove' bit was a bunch of bullshit, too. All I did was bury myself on an island, isolated myself away from everyone, and most particularly you. What the hell else would you think?"

"You isolated yourself from me? Specifically?"

That caught him up short. He hadn't meant to say that. Or maybe he had. Christ, it had been too long; he was too old to tiptoe through the minefield that was someone else's emotions, someone else's needs. Yet, taking in the stricken look on her face—not angry, or annoyed, or even exasperated, but truly hurt—told him he was already standing in the middle of the minefield. Hell . . . maybe he'd been standing there all along. That would explain why he'd refused to take a single step. In any direction.

"Why?" she asked, and he could hear the emotion thickening that single word.

He swore under his breath. Leave it to him to fuck up a simple apology and make her feel even worse.

That was precisely why he shouldn't be trying to insert himself into her present difficulties, or any part of her life. Even after all the listening he'd done, the self-recrimination, he wasn't any better at relationships now than he'd been when he'd enlisted at the age of eighteen, and left his five-year-old sister behind, with what turned out to be no one to properly see to her care.

He searched for better words, with no confidence he'd find them. *So much for that doctorate you were touting back there.* "Two days ago I'd have said that my decision to live my life out on Sandpiper had nothing to do with you, and only to do with me. And two days ago, that would have been a lie. But I'd have likely convinced myself otherwise."

"And . . . now?"

"When Grace asked me to come in to help you, my first reaction was . . . not to. To keep my head down, do what I do best. Or what I do now, at any rate. You and I . . . we hadn't crossed paths in a long time. I know you've gotten close to Grace, and that is a good thing, a very good thing. She . . . she trusts you, counts you as a friend, almost like a sister, though maybe that's overstating it. Still, having you in her life, that's a very big thing for her."

Delia dipped her chin, and though it was hard to tell by the porch light, the moon was full enough that he thought he saw the flush of emotion rise to her cheeks. "She's very special to me, too," she said, emotion still there in her voice.

"I didn't know why I was so resistant. If there was nothing between us, nothing except—" He broke off.

"Tommy," she said, filling in the ensuing silence. "It's okay." She looked up at him now, held his gaze squarely, but kindly. "It's not an eggshell topic with me, either. I put my brother to rest—*we* put him to rest—a long time ago, and he earned his eternal peace."

Ford nodded. "I thought I'd put all of it to rest, too, at least as much as it ever can be."

"That's good," she said. "Really good." She studied his face now. "You know, no one in the Cove holds your reclusive lifestyle against you, or thinks less of you because you—" She broke off, swore. "What I mean to say is they know what you did for Tommy, for me, for Gran. They know you were a ranger, special forces, so they have a pretty good idea of what you sacrificed for our country, at least as much as anyone who hasn't done the same can."

A flash bang of images punched through his mind, some more gruesome than any human being should have to witness. He wanted to tell her that no, no one could appreciate the sacrifice unless they'd been there. And even then, the repercussions, the true nature of the sacrifice made, wasn't a fully known quantity until later. Much, much later.

"They have great respect for what you've done. We are simply thankful for your service, and happy you've chosen to live your life here." Her lips curved briefly. "Still in service to others, only now they have wings and flippers." She smiled truly then, and the moonlight danced in her eyes. "Mainers are a pretty pragmatic folk. Not to mention none of us are particularly normal. The fact that we willingly put ourselves through Maine winters, year after year, is proof enough of that."

"I—thank you, for saying that," he said, shoving the rest back, listening to her words, appreciating the sincerity behind them. "That's why I'm here." He rubbed a hand over the back of his neck. "Part of why I'm here, anyway."

"What do you mean?"

"I mean if things were so square between you and me, and I'm in such a good damn place with my past, then I'd still be dropping by your diner from time to time, listening to you chatter on—"

"I do not chatter," she said, with mock affront. She added a little sniff, smoothed out her blouse, rumpled by the steam from doing dish duty again. "I make charming and witty banter with our colorful town folk."

A smile flashed over his face. "Is that what they're calling themselves?"

She knocked her elbow forward, bumping his arm. "What do you mean? You're one of the most colorful ones we got."

He let out a short, surprised laugh at that. Why the hell *had* he stayed away so damn long? What had he been afraid would happen?

Eula's words echoed through his mind. *Perhaps it's time to ask yourself if you're out on that island, up in that tree, because you still need to be? For your own sanity? Or because it's simply become the life you live. The only life you feel you deserve.*

He hated to admit the old woman might have a point after all.

"So, I was trying to apologize," he said.

"And I still don't understand what for."

"That's what I was trying to say. You were a friend to me when I needed one, and we're not square, because I haven't been one to you in return."

"What you did for Tommy—"

"Was for Tommy," he interjected. "What you did when I came back, you did for me. You provided a bubble for me, where I could exist without having to interact. I understood that, and I took full advantage."

Now it was her turn to duck her chin, only he wasn't

exactly sure why, or where that embarrassment he'd seen flash over her face had come from.

"Maybe I did that for Tommy, too," she said, quietly.

"That's how I added it up. But that's wrong." He waited a beat. "You did that for me, because that's who you are."

She took a breath, and he was surprised to hear a thread of shakiness in it. But when she raised her gaze to his again, she stood a little straighter, and there was no trace of uncertainty on her face. "So, bottom line it for me, Maddox," she said, injecting some of her well-known sass into the words. "It's been a long day and I've been on these feet for all of it."

He felt a little jerk on the knot inside his chest at that tone, that amused look on her face. So many memories tumbling through his mind, all good ones. How had he managed to make himself believe there hadn't been so much good? And that the good hadn't been worth sticking around for? "You were there for me," he said simply. "I want to return the favor."

She folded her arms, regarding him, not so much with skepticism as simply trying to read him, figure him out. *Good luck with that,* he wanted to tell her. He didn't know himself.

"What?" he was finally forced to ask when her silent regard continued.

"I've heard you use more words in the past twenty-four hours than I have collectively in all the years I've known you." She lifted a shoulder. "Hell, maybe you've been out there chatting up those seals and seabirds all day long like a regular Chatty Cathy. How would I know?"

"You wouldn't," he answered, quite sincerely, even though he knew she was ribbing him. He swallowed, heard Eula inside his head again. *I'd think the answer is obvious. Talk to Delia.* And Eula was right again. It was remarkably obvious. So why didn't understanding that make it any easier to actually do it? He held her gaze, and took the first step. The first real step out of his self-imposed solitary confinement. And it scared the ever-loving shit out of him. "I'd like to change that."

He'd expected a smile, or even just a look of surprise, maybe a dose of friendly sarcasm. God knows he'd earned those reactions and more. Instead, that embarrassment flashed back. And maybe the flushed cheeks, too. She started toying with her collar. "And you needed to tell me that now? In the wee hours?" There was the note of dry humor he'd expected, but he couldn't help hear the note of strain as well.

He stepped closer. "I didn't want an audience. I just wanted to talk to you."

"I—after what you said earlier, at the diner, I thought you were going to drop by the kitchen like you did last night."

"I did. Your crew was there."

"I could have stepped outside."

"Dee—" He broke off, swallowed another string of swearwords, then stepped back. "You're right. I shouldn't have come here. You put in long hours, the last thing you need—"

"That's not what I meant. You're always welcome here. Or anywhere that I happen to be." She paused, seemed to gather herself, then let out a short breath and looked up at him again. "You matter to me. Because of Tommy. Because of . . ." She glanced down again, then resolutely back up. "Just because, okay? So, you're always welcome. You're right that I'm a friend, that you can trust me. I know this wasn't easy and I really respect you coming forward, out of your comfort zone. I know Grace would be—"

"I didn't do this for Grace. Come here, I mean. Tonight. This is just between me and you." He thought he saw her shake a little, or tremble, and that set off all kinds of alarms, the kind that had put him out on Sandpiper Island in the first place. He didn't know why she was reacting like she was, or what she was feeling, or what he'd done or said to make her so uncomfortable. Delia was always so supremely confident, so sure, so certain.

Flashes of that long-ago night stormed into his mind. She hadn't been confident that night, or sure, or certain of anything. Neither had he. She'd never once mentioned that night, not in all the years that had followed, not even now, so neither did he. Maybe she was afraid he would, afraid that he knew a side of her that no one else did, when quite clearly she wanted to pretend otherwise.

I'm a friend. Those were the words she'd used. He'd do well to remember that was all she would be to him. And that was fine, because he wasn't even sure how to be a friend to her in return. He wasn't looking to complicate things any further.

He curled his fingers into his palms to keep from reaching for her, to pull her in close, to offer her comfort, a little shocked to find how badly he wanted to do that. He didn't know what he'd done, what he'd said, or simply what was wrong, or how he could help fix it. He kept from reaching for her, though, because, in that moment, staring down at her bowed head, he understood why he'd stayed out on that island well past the time when his battered soul needed to be exiled. Because she mattered to him, too. In ways he didn't understand, and ways he understood all too well. Ways he didn't think he could trust himself to live up to.

"I'm your friend, too, Dee. At least I'm trying to figure out how to be that."

"You don't owe me—"

"Stop," he said again, gruffly again, though without the impatience it had had before. "Look at me."

She lifted her gaze to his, and he wished like hell he could decipher all of the emotions he saw swimming in those pretty blue eyes of hers. He was trained to do a lot of things, to rely on his instincts, go with his gut, and that had saved his life, and the lives of others, on more occasions than he could count. But on this kind of playing field? He had no idea how to operate, no idea how to read the opposition. For that matter, he had no idea how to not look at the person—any person—standing in front of him as anything other than "my side" or "their side." He had no tools, no training, for when "my" and "theirs" became "ours."

"Friends, Dee. We are that. But I'm rusty at it. Or maybe I always sucked at it. Maybe I always will. But I'm trying. We share a bond. You say I matter. Well, the truth is, you matter. You always have. I shouldn't have forgotten that, or pretended otherwise."

She just continued to stare at him, and suddenly she didn't seem so all-knowing, the confident, ballsy, smart-assy, outspoken woman who had single-handedly taken on the care and feeding of an entire community, with the caring part just as important as the feeding part, and made it look like it was just another thing she did. No biggie.

And then he was doing instead of thinking, acting instead of analyzing. Maybe that was the only way it worked. He reached for her, pulled her into his arms, and hugged her, held her. "I'm sorry," he said, lips pressed against her hair. "Grace shouldn't have had to call me. I should have already been here."

She let him hold her, but kept her arms folded between them.

"I'm here now," he said. "I hope it's not too late." He rested his forehead against the top of her head. "You helped me, Dee," he said quietly. "I'm not sure how I would have transitioned from my life before to this life, without you. That's why I came back here. I . . . I didn't know where else to go. Who else to turn to. There wasn't anyone else." He paused, felt his heart racing in his chest; the rush of adrenaline punching into his system almost made him feel sick. None of this was easy, far from it. He wondered whether she understood that. And, if she did, whether she cared. "You were my lifeline," he said past the knotted ball in his gut. Every one of his instincts screamed at him to shut up, curl up, pack up, to head home. Lowering guards, allowing anyone to look in went against everything he'd been trained to be, to do, to feel.

But, goddammit, this wasn't war, this wasn't a battlefield. No one was trying to kill him, or anyone whose care had been put in his charge. What the hell did he have to lose? If his life was the most important asset he needed to protect, well, that wasn't in danger here. So why was this so fucking hard?

He lifted his head slowly, and then tipped her chin up when she didn't look up at him. His fingers weren't steady. Nothing about him was steady. Unsteady got you dead, so he instinctively fought to control the fine tremor, mostly because he couldn't seem to control anything else. He stared down into her eyes, and willed his heart to slow, to return to that place he'd left behind a long time ago, that place where he could retreat inside himself, where he could focus, aim, and pull the trigger. Only he couldn't seem to find his way in. He was in uncharted territory, with no clear path through the minefield surrounding him.

"I don't know how to help you," he said. "Like you helped me. You need to tell me what I can do." He slipped a hand to her cheek, pressed the flat of his palm to the warmth, the softness of the skin there, and realized how very long it had been since he'd allowed himself even the simple pleasure of touching someone else.

"I don't need you to help me, Ford," she said in a shaky whisper, her eyes searching his, boring into his. "I can't need you."

If she'd unsheathed a hidden knife and plunged it deep into his belly, he couldn't have been more surprised, or more stunned by the sharp, hot pain her words caused. An excellent reminder that well-constructed walls existed for a reason, and should never be lowered in the first place. Because there was more than one kind of dying.

In tandem with the pain came blinding understanding. Of course, she didn't need him, couldn't need him. He wasn't to be blithely given something so precious as her trust simply because he asked for it. What in the hell had he done to deserve that gift? Nothing, that was what. Not a damn thing. Words were empty, hollow things when not backed up by deeds. She might respect him, she might even call him friend, she might care about his well-being, because of who he'd been to her brother, but that didn't mean she'd trust him with anything having to do with her own self. And why should she? Why the goddamn hell should she?

He let her go and abruptly stepped back. "Right. And smart," he added. The desire to turn away once more, to escape the look in her beautiful, sad eyes, was thwarted by the echo of Eula's words. "You may not want my help, I get that. But you want to save your diner, don't you?" He didn't wait for her answer. "As much as you might want to do that alone, I don't think it's possible. You're going to need help, somehow, from someone. Maybe a lot of someones. I understand why you don't trust me to be that someone for you. You're probably wise to avoid leaning on me. But I do know how to get things done. And I was never handed a mission that I didn't complete. So if I say I'm going to find a way to help you keep your place, then that's what I will do."

Her eyes widened at the intensity, the force of his words. "Ford, this is not your problem—"

"Delia O'Reilly, you don't have to trust me, you don't have to need my help, or even want my help, but you've got it all the same. All you have to do is take it."

She straightened and her arms unfolded as her hands dropped to her sides. He saw defensiveness and pride flash across her expressive face.

So, he cut that off, too. That's what a good mission commander did. "If it makes you feel any better, let's just say I'm doing this for Tommy. He'd want me to help his sister out, and there's nothing I wouldn't do for him. I owe him my life."

Chapter 6

"**D**on't start," Ford said when Grace burst through the door of his office without knocking. "I'm already working on it." He dragged a big text on Maine property law on top of his stack of research on business licensing. There had to be some kind of loophole. He wasn't a lawyer or an accountant, but after cramming eight years of college into slightly less than five, he knew a thing or two about studying and research. "Did you talk to your friend in DC about getting Delia some local legal help? I think we're going to need it. Some of these laws haven't been changed since the Penobscot and Passamaquoddy tribes ruled the area." It occurred to him then that maybe that's why she'd come bursting in, and he looked up. "Did they find something out we can use?"

"No. I mean, I don't know. Delia won't talk to them. But you can stop." Grace braced her hands on the desk, leaning over, as if she'd run all the way there.

There being his office on the second floor of the small shop space the Project Sandpiper foundation used as its local, open-to-the public headquarters, located not too far from the diner up on High Street, which ran along the hill above Half Moon Harbor. He'd been bunking on the couch in his office.

The shop space below was open daily from Memorial Day weekend through Labor Day and on weekends the month before and after, weather depending. He staffed it with interns and volunteers who helped coordinate various fund-raisers, set up the intern schedule for the summer, and basically got the word out about the work being done on Sandpiper to encourage folks to donate to the cause. The whole enterprise was funded by grants, donations, and the dedication, blood, sweat, and interest-free tears of the interns and Ford himself.

With nesting season over and tourist season pretty much done this far north, there was just one intern and a few volunteers running the shop now, and he was on the island alone. The bulk of the off-season work would be on Ford's shoulders, so with Labor Day less than a week off, he'd gone ahead and sent the last remaining intern home early and kept the volunteers on a will-call basis for the following few weekends before they closed up for good for the winter. The office had a big, old leather couch that doubled nicely as a bed. God knew he'd slept on far worse. He looked at it now and thought a nice long nap, possibly a weeklong one, was looking mighty appealing.

Instead, taking in the anxious look on Grace's face, he slid off his glasses, rubbed the bridge of his nose, and then ran a wide palm over his weary face. "Why?" he asked simply, holding her gaze.

"I—I don't know if Delia wants to save the diner."

He had no idea what had sent Grace racing up the stairs and bursting through his door like a banshee, but that was definitely not on any list he might have come up with. "Say again?"

Grace turned around, hefted the stack of folders and binders off one of the two leather seats facing Ford's desk, and then slumped into it. "Delia stopped by the inn today. George—Havens, my lawyer friend from DC—did come through. He sent me two recommendations for lawyers who might represent Delia in her fight to save the diner. Only . . . when I told her, she changed the subject, and so I asked her why she wasn't fighting harder. And . . . well, we had this conversation that was . . ." She trailed off, lifted a hand and waved it helplessly, before letting it drop back to her lap.

"Was . . . what?" Ford demanded.

"Odd." She shrugged. "And kind of sad. I—she's been ducking me, and I thought maybe it had something to do with you being back in the Cove—"

"Why would that matter?"

Grace gave him that *Seriously?* eyebrow, but didn't bother trying to explain and since he wasn't sure he really wanted to know, he didn't push. "Turns out it wasn't you, or well, not only about you. Anyway, as we talked, I realized that my other suspicion, which was that she was too proud to accept help from anyone, or was just in some kind of denial, wasn't it, either. I told her she struck me as the kind of person who would be mad as hell, storming city hall, or something of that magnitude, and how surprised I was that she wasn't doing that and, well, she is definitely mad about the whole thing, and she thinks it's every kind of wrong. So I was brainstorming possible options, and sort of pushed her to think about a real, workable solution, and—Ford, her eyes welled up, and she said she didn't know if she really wanted to fight, just that she felt she had to. I asked what it was she did want and—"

Ford lifted a hand and Grace fell silent, looking relieved to not have to explain any further.

"I feel awful," she said in a hushed whisper. "It's none of my business—our business—really, but I barged in anyway. She knows I'd do anything for her, but I shouldn't have pushed when she made it clear she didn't want the help. I should have respected that. I know she didn't want to talk about it, but I kept pushing. . . ." She propped her elbow on the arm of the chair and dropped her forehead into her open palm. "I probably shouldn't be telling you. I feel like I'm breaking a confidence." She looked up again, clearly miserable. "But she is my friend—our friend—and I just . . . we have to do something, Ford. She's really upset, and confused, and . . . I don't even know. You've known her longer, a lot longer. And the two of you share this . . . thing." She let that drift off. "I just think she'd listen to you, or maybe you could just let her know you're there for her. Be an ear, and a shoulder. You give really great shoulder."

He'd squeezed his eyes shut as he rubbed his hand over his face, trying to figure out what the hell she was talking about, but opened them again when she said that.

"What?" Grace said. "Don't look so surprised. You're not much in the way of advice, but you listen like no other. Because you do really listen. I just think she could use that right about now. I'm not so sure she'd let anyone else get close enough to do that."

What the fresh hell? was all that kept going through his mind. The crick at the base of his neck that had settled in from sitting hunched over the desk for hours on end expanded to include a dull throb in his temples.

"Has she . . . said anything to you like that?" Grace asked, when he didn't respond to her emotional outburst.

He shook his head. But Grace had made a very good point. Delia was a fighter by nature, and it didn't make any sense that she wasn't doing whatever she had to in order to save her livelihood. He'd chalked it up to pride and stubbornness, but he'd seen the emotions simmering close to the surface, too. He'd put that off to his own overactive imagination and the memories of their past . . . activities, which had been regularly besieging him during his waking hours, and the sleeping ones, too.

"What exactly did she say?" Ford asked. Maybe Grace was confused, or had read the situation wrong. Although her ability to read people, himself most disconcertingly included, was uncanny. She'd just proven that with her concise little synopsis of the connection he had with Dee. "Did she come out and say she didn't want to run the diner any longer?"

"She said she wasn't sure she wanted to fight to save it, but she got real emotional when I asked her what she did want to do. She said she didn't know. She sounds . . . I don't know. As I said, I haven't known her as long as you have, but she doesn't sound like the Delia I've come to know over the past summer. Not even close. Has something else happened to her recently?"

You mean other than me showing up in her life again? He shook his head. "I've been out on the island more than not, for a long time now. So Dee and I . . . we haven't really been in touch. I don't know what might have happened in her personal life." He paused, not because he had any reservations about mentioning it, but because the next part bothered him more than it should. "I understand she's been seeing your architect friend. Socially, I mean. Maybe you should ask him. Seems she'd confide in him, if anyone."

"Langston?" Grace laughed and waved the suggestion off as if it was the most ridiculous thing she'd ever heard.

The fact that that pleased him as much as it did made him scowl. He had no claim, none whatsoever, on Delia O'Reilly, and wasn't looking to stake one. Never had before and certainly didn't intend to now. *Someone's sure protesting a whole hell of a lot.* He ignored his inner voice. Annoying little bastard. "If she's dating him, she'd talk to him. I know he's like some kind of uncle to you, but that doesn't mean she sees him that way."

Grace had explained how her unusual friendship with the exceedingly wealthy, world-renowned architect had developed when she'd represented his estate after the death of his wife. Ford was grateful Grace had such a solid, wise, and well-connected mentor. He was also grateful, given the guy was decades his sister's senior, that their friendship had always been just that. Maybe she couldn't fathom that Delia felt differently about the older man.

"Oh, I didn't mean it that way. Langston is like the guru of getting people to tell them their deepest, darkest secrets. He's just got this way about him. You trust him, you can't help it."

Ford slid his hands to his lap, and forced his fingers to remain relaxed on his thighs. He'd seen pictures of the flamboyant deVry and the very last thing he wanted to imagine was Delia with—he closed his eyes briefly against that very thing. Only that just made it worse.

"So, if he's God's gift to confessionals," he managed, proud that he'd done so without gnashing his teeth, "why the laugh?"

"Because, while Langston is a dear, and he'd do anything for anyone he cares about, he's been in Tokyo for the past month."

"They have phones there, too."

"It's not that, it's just—well, Langston loved his late wife very much, and he hasn't been really . . . focused, since she passed away. He has the biggest heart in the world for everyone else, but for himself, well . . . he's been very guarded. Anyway, he was only supposed to be in Japan for a weekend, on business, but that was ages ago, and he's still there. He doesn't have the kind of schedule that comes close to allowing that, so I got curious, and I finally pried it out of him. He's met someone. And he's smitten. Very smitten. So much so he's still in Tokyo. And since all this happened with Delia just in the past week or so, I doubt seriously they've talked."

This time Ford's anger came from a very different place. "Does Delia know about it? If not, you need to—"

"Calm down. It's not like that with them." But her expression made it clear she thought it was interesting that he had thought as much. "Delia knows. I told her when I found out, because I knew she'd be happy for him. They're close, good friends, but it never really went anywhere. Not, I don't think, because they weren't interested, but between his schedule and the demands of her life . . ." She shrugged. "When he left the Cove this last time, I think they'd both decided that anything more was too complicated and both seemed happy to have found a friend out of the deal. If anything, I believe Delia was the one who made that clear. She's even less long-term a person than Langston is. Or was, anyway. Like I said, Delia is happy for him, but I don't think they've talked."

"I get the picture," Ford said, shortly. So shortly that his sister raised a speculative eyebrow, but wisely said nothing. He had every intention of changing the subject back to the diner and what should or shouldn't be done about this latest curveball, but what came out of his mouth instead was: "How do you know? You've only been here a few months," he clarified, already thinking he should just sew his mouth shut, and then take his boat directly back to Sandpiper.

"How do I know what?" Grace's mouth curved in that knowing way again and it made him want to fidget in his seat. He, who was so expertly trained in the art of being completely still that he did so as second nature. His interns commented on it all the time. Not always to his face, but his ability to be still was envied. Of course, his interns envied it as it applied to wildlife observation. No need to explain that the training he'd received had been for the purpose of human observation. And not as it pertained to helping preserve life. At least not the lives of the ones he'd been ordered to observe.

"Do you mean, how do I know Delia's not an LTR type?"

"LTR?" He instantly hated himself for asking.

"Long-term relationship. You know, you do get the Internet out on that pile of rocks. You should look into social media."

He merely scowled at that, which perversely made his sister grin. "Yeah," she said, "on second thought, maybe not." She cocked her head. "Although, women do like that bad boy thing. All alpha and angry at the world. You put that face and the fact that you have a PhD on a dating profile and you'd have women swimming out to the island. Your screen name could be Crusoe. Leave the Dolittle off," she advised, far too blithely, enjoying herself way too much. "Too many negative connotations." She made a gesture with her forefingers, putting them close together, and then making a sad face.

He simply stared at her, unable to believe they were even having this conversation. All parts of it.

"You're very cute when you're annoyed with me. And I love that we've come far enough where I can tell you that. Of course, you're annoyed with everyone, or so it seems. We still need to work on that. That's not as cute."

"I'm here," he reminded her. "Not out on my pile of rocks, where I should be, and oh, so desperately wish I was."

"Buried in binders full of nesting data. Sexy." She feigned a yawn.

"At least binders of nesting data don't talk back." He flipped the top legal tome closed.

"Wait," Grace said, instantly alarmed, her smile erased as she sat forward. "Don't go off in a huff because I'm giving you a hard time. This is about helping Delia."

"Who you just told me doesn't want our help. Doesn't, in fact, want to save her diner."

"I said she wasn't sure she wanted to save it. And that just means we have to figure out what she does want, what she needs, and shift our help accordingly."

Ford knew better than to argue. He'd learned enough about Grace to know that she liked to work things through, puzzle out problems, by talking about them. Initially, he'd pressured himself to step in and offer solutions, thinking that's why she'd come to him with whatever problem she was having. Only he'd quickly learned that the last thing she wanted was advice or, God forbid, actual help. She just wanted him to listen. She just wanted him to be . . . him.

Out of nowhere, Eula's words came to him. *Do you expect Grace to be something more than simply your sister?*

It was a lesson he was still having a hard time learning. He'd been nothing to his sister; he'd abandoned her, so of course he had to be more than just her brother. Up to that point, simply being her brother hadn't meant shit. But the way Eula had phrased it had had him thinking about it in an entirely different way. He had to be present. He had to be open. He had to be willing. To listen when needed, help when asked. Nothing more, but nothing less. The crux of it was he had to be there.

So, that's what they needed to be for Delia. Only he wasn't sure, in her case, that simply being present, being willing, and in Grace's case, listening to her vent, or cry, was enough.

"So," he asked, wondering for the hundredth, the thousandth time how, exactly, he'd ended up in the position he was presently in, "how do we do that?"

His mind spun to how and where they should talk to Delia. It should be both of them, he thought, him and Grace, so it was more like family than it was like . . . whatever that had been in front of her house. She hadn't felt like family then. She'd felt like . . . heaven.

He abruptly steered his thoughts away from that, as he had every minute of every hour since he'd left her place. It would be him and Grace, for certain. They'd need somewhere private, quiet, where Delia would feel comfortable, secure, not ganged up on. No locals listening in. Maybe her house, her own turf. Grace could get her to relax, to open up, and he could . . . well, he wasn't sure what the hell help he could be, but he knew Delia needed to have them both there, see them both there in front of her. Present.

"I think maybe she just needs to see how much she's loved, how much the folks here really do want her to fight, not for them, but for herself. But she needs to really get it. Feel it. I think it will ground her again, renew her sense of purpose. I know!" Grace's delight brightened her pretty face. "We throw her a huge, save-the-diner block party!"

Chapter 7

Delia climbed out of her car and hefted the strap of the backpack that did double duty as purse up farther on her cramping shoulder. She was so tired her bones ached. If she had to drink herself stupid to make the constant hamster wheel of thoughts racing through her mind shut down, she was going to find some way to sleep tonight. Only, no, she decided, no alcohol. She couldn't afford the hangover. Charlie had already called to ask for the next day off, so she was short a short-order cook. She'd have smiled at that, but even the muscles in her face were too tired to move. Something she'd have to rectify as Fridays were always busy days, and Friday nights even busier. Fergus attracted the happy hour and TGIF crowd, but she had the family night and teenager hangout crews which, even without the alcohol, could get rowdy.

Normally, she enjoyed the weekends. As exhausting as they could be, they were also the times when she caught up with most of the locals. She enjoyed the weekend-is-here energy; it sparked her, rejuvenated her, even if weekends in her world meant her busiest workdays.

At the moment, however, the idea of facing a long Friday and two even longer days after that, made her want to kneel down, weep, and beg for mercy.

She'd like to think it was because she had her act *that* together, but it was utter exhaustion that kept her from squealing like a girl when Ford stepped off her porch and into the pool of moonlight. "We *really* have to stop meeting like this," she said, her heart thumping. She paused, waiting for him to respond, but even the brief delay in forward motion was enough for her body to decide it was all done for the day. Her shoulders and calves started to cramp in earnest. She swallowed the grimace—she didn't want a lecture about her work habits, or anything else for that matter—but ended up letting her backpack slide to the ground by her feet to relieve some of the burden.

His handsome face creased in concern as he stepped forward and snagged the nylon strap in those big hands of his. "You okay?"

She might have weaved a little on her feet. Delia knew she was made of some pretty stern stuff, even by New England standards, but averaging sixteen-hour days on less than two or three hours of sleep a night for the past few weeks had finally caught up to her. "Fine," she bald-faced lied. A two-year-old could have picked up on that. "Just need to get inside. Long day."

"And I doubt that's anything new," he said. "Come on." He kept the backpack when she reached for it. "I got it."

She said nothing to that and merely trudged by him, wincing as her tired feet and cramping calves protested every step to the front porch. She was beyond caring what anyone thought at this point, even Ford Maddox. She climbed the porch steps, swallowing the sigh as her lower back joined in on the aching and cramping chorus, then paused and stared dumbly at the door. *Keys. What did I do with my keys? Oh, right. Backpack.* She turned . . . and smacked right into Ford, her nose grazing his hard chest. It took enormous self-will to keep from turning her head and resting her cheek there, just for a moment. "You smell really good," she thought. Or maybe she'd said it right out loud. Didn't matter. She breathed in, and discovered her lips could indeed still curve. With proper motivation.

"Where are your keys?"

"Jump ring," she murmured. "Loop. Side of the bag." She realized as the soft flannel of his shirt rubbed against her lips that she hadn't exactly straightened. Yet. She was working on it, though. Any moment now she'd get her second wind. Or her hundredth. Whatever. She'd lost count.

She heard a jingle. Her keys. Good. Almost there. She doubted she was going to need any help in the sleep department tonight. She just needed to get horizontal, and all would be right in her world. Or, at least unconscious. At the moment, that was good enough. The door swung open and she came perilously close to swinging in with it. Then a strong arm was wrapping around her waist.

"Hold on," he instructed.

She had every intention of looking him straight in the eyes, telling him she could get inside her own house all by herself, thankyouverymuch. But that would mean opening her eyes. Which at some point . . . well, they weren't open now. And, at the moment, it was beyond her to do anything about that. It made more sense to simply do as the man asked. Hold on. So she slid her arms around his waist. Yes, that was much better. He smelled good, and he was warm. Sturdy, too. *Just give me a few seconds of this, and I'll be good to go.*

She thought she heard some muttered swearing; then she was suddenly airborne, or at least not on her feet any longer. "Don't," she protested with zero conviction. "I'm—"

"I've got you," he said gruffly, and she could feel the words vibrate deep in his chest. Which was conveniently pressed against her ear. "Don't wiggle like th— for God's sake—just hold on."

Delia gave up trying to pretend she was even in the realm of fine and allowed herself to enjoy the ride. Not that she had any choice in the matter. And that was okay with her, too. She was tired of choices. So many of them had to be made, too many things to figure out. What did she want? What didn't she want? Who did she want? Who did she want to not want? And, most important, how did she stop wanting him?

If she hadn't been so wiped out, she'd have been amused by the fact that she was presently trying to figure out how to stop lusting after the man who, at that very same moment, was carrying her into her house and, presumably, up to her bedroom.

"Wait," she said, only, again, there was no real heat to it. Nope, all the heat she had was presently pooling somewhere else. In the one place that apparently still had some life left in it. *Didn't that just figure?*

He ignored her. She let him. She'd make sure he understood that this whole carting-her-bodily-around thing was just a onetime occurrence due to extenuating circumstances. She'd spell it out for him, if need be, in explicit detail. Later. Just as soon as she got her second wind back.

"Hey."

Delia smiled. She knew that voice. What she didn't

know was why she'd been so annoyed by the dreams she'd been having about that voice. And the extraordinarily complex and handsome man who was attached to it. They were nice dreams. Okay, who was she kidding . . . they were scorchers. But life was hard at the moment—with so many things happening, possible huge life-changing things, didn't she deserve a little fun? Especially the kind that couldn't hurt anyone. Namely, her.

She snuggled in more deeply. Maybe he'd do that thing he'd done last time, where he started with the tip of his tongue on the curve of her shoulder . . . and worked his way down. Slowly. With incredible, dedicated focus. Like he was cataloguing every freckle for future study. Who said scientists couldn't be hot? Yeah, she'd liked that thing he did a lot. Or maybe he wouldn't be so patient. Maybe he'd be demanding and intent on getting what he needed, and giving her what she needed, no waiting, no wooing, just straight up against the nearest wall, clothes stripped from her body, lifting her up, on . . . in. She squirmed, moaning softly, thinking Ford unleashed would be spectacularly satisfying. They could save the slow savor for the second round. Ford had remarkable stamina. Dream lovers were like that. Although she happened to know in reality he had incredible staying power. And so . . . *so* much more.

Sure, having these lengthy, incredibly detailed, highly erotic dreams about him made dealing with him now that he'd left his island for a stay in Blueberry a bit of a challenge. Every time she laid eyes on him her mind had the most disturbing way of flashing immediately to the most vivid scenes of them doing . . . oh, so many delicious and delectable things. She sighed. Even when she wasn't laying eyes on him. Just knowing he was in town, that he could show up at any second, was keeping all of her nerve endings—the good kind—at a kind of fever pitch. So, yes, at some point, she should probably work on curtailing them. Every toe-curling, heart-pounding moment of them. And she would. Just as soon as she got a few other things off her plate.

"Dee."

She wriggled down even deeper, wanting him like she wanted her next breath and damn the consequences. She liked it when he called her that, though she'd never tell him. Would make them both uncomfortable, probably. Except in her dreams. In her dreams, they were never uncomfortable. In her dreams, they both wanted the same thing. And they wanted it often. She let her eyes drift open. Yep, there was that face. Those eyes. They haunted her sleeping hours and a goodly number of her waking ones, now, too. "Hey, yourself," she said, her smile warming, her body flaming hotter. Oh, yes, she needed these dreams. Sometimes she thought they were the only things keeping her from losing it altogether.

"Feeling better?"

Better? Had she been ill? She didn't remember that part of the dream. Usually, when she dreamed about Ford, neither one of them had any, um . . . weaknesses. Well, except for each other, of course. "Mmm," she said, wondering whether he'd mind if she pulled him down on top of her this time, beg him to take her and take her hard, and fast, and fierce. What was she thinking? It was a dream. Of course, he wouldn't mind. In dreams she could have whatever she wanted, and dream he wanted it, too. And often. Oh, if only life were that simple.

Her lips curved as she dropped her gaze to his

mouth, thinking—knowing—exactly how it was going to feel. Here. There. Everywhere. "Much better."

"Good. Had me worried there, have to admit."

She frowned, seeing the clear concern in his eyes. That wasn't part of the dream. Well, whatever. Dreams weren't supposed to make sense, anyway, right? His expression would change soon enough, she thought, twisting farther down and turning toward—her elbow hit something soft. In fact, the whole length of her body was wedged up against . . . something. Only it wasn't Ford, because his gorgeous face was on the other side of her. She looked to her left. She blinked once, twice, even as her body stiffened. She looked down at herself. She was lying on her couch. Fully clothed. She looked back at Ford, who was squatting beside the couch, wedged between it and Gran's spindly old tea table, which he'd moved back a bit to accommodate his size. "You're real," she said, dumbly. Then she closed her eyes in hot mortification when she saw surprise, then a wink of humor flash through his dark eyes.

"Last I checked."

She could never look at him again. "What time is—"

"Six."

"In the morning?" She was alarmed, and all her fears of looking foolish fled. She started to sit up, only to have a very strong, well-muscled arm block her move.

He kept his palm planted on the back of the couch, just inches above her midsection. She looked from his arm to him. He was really close. And, dammit, he still smelled good. That part was very real.

"I have to get to the diner. I'm minus Charlie today, he had a dentist appointment," she said, remembering. "I should have been in there an hour ago doing prep." She glanced back at his arm, and then shot him an implacable look. "I appreciate your helping me last night. I mean that," she added when he merely cocked a brow. "But I have to go to work." Then another thought occurred to her. "Did you stay here? Last night?"

"You were pretty out of it."

Oh, she'd been rather into it, actually. She forced that thought and every last image of what she had been into straight out of her mind. "That's not an answer."

"As I said, I was concerned. You work too hard."

"I work hard," she corrected him. "It's what I do. What I love. I—I wouldn't know any other way. And I've never needed a babysitter before."

"You've never been in danger of losing what you love before." The moment the words came out of his mouth, he frowned, looked away. "That was—I'm sorry. Thoughtless."

"You told me not to tiptoe around you. Well, same goes. I can't say I think about Henry, but I miss Tommy and Gran every day, in some form or fashion. I remember them fondly, happily, not mournfully. Life's too short for that."

"Wise words."

"Where did you sleep?" She shook off the last of her dream daze, but she didn't want to think about the loss he'd actually been referring to, either, much less talk about it. Back to business.

"I was going to move you to your bed, but you were sleeping so soundly. I figured you needed that more than anything, so I thought it best to leave you to it."

"My bed, then."

The look he gave her was inscrutable. She liked knowing she could read people. She prided herself on it, in fact. It made it easier to take care of them when she could tell what it was they really needed. So, she was not a fan of inscrutable. He was one of the only people in her life who could pull that off. She'd forgotten how inscrutable he could be.

"It was available," he said, at length.

"Okay." He'd done her a favor. Like the old friend that he was. So what if she'd been lying a mere room away from him, having dreams that, if he knew his role in them— She cleared her throat, looked down at her still-clothed self. "Well, you're right. A good night's sleep is never a bad thing. So, I'd better get up and put it to good use." She eyed his braced arm pointedly.

"You've got the morning off," he said, looking less inscrutable now, and perhaps a tad uncomfortable.

"Do I now?" she asked, surprised—no, shocked—by his apparent high-handedness. "And how would that be?" She started to sit up again, but flopped back when she hit the arm. "You didn't close the diner, did you?"

He raised both eyebrows, but otherwise kept a smooth expression. "Would the world as we know it end if that were the case?"

"Just the Cove. So . . . same thing."

"Dee—"

It shouldn't annoy her when he called her that. In her dreams, it was the exact opposite of annoying. Probably there was a connection there, but she was too distracted by the diner situation to worry about it. "The same folks have been coming in for breakfast, coffee, lunch, and the like for—well, between Gran and me, longer than I've been alive."

"I assume they won't die of starvation or from shock if they were left to fend for themselves for a morning."

"That's not the point."

"Then what is the point?" He cut her off before she could tell him exactly where he could take his point and put it. "I know folks like having their daily routines, and you're a big part of the day-to-day fabric of this entire community. Not the food, or the shelter, but you."

She—had no response for that. She hadn't been expecting it. "All the more reason for me to get up and get my fanny in to work."

"What I'm saying is you've banked a lot of goodwill in these parts. You take care of everyone. They would be fine with a small break in the routine if they knew that it was a chance to repay the favor."

Yet another Maddox frustrating her with making logic seem all . . . logical. "Ford—"

"I called Peg," he said, ending the discussion. "She opened. You're trading your shift with hers. So, you're not due in until the lunch shift."

"Peg is not even remotely a morning person. That's why she never opens. Ever. How on earth did you—"

"I asked."

The repercussions of Ford calling Peg at God knew what time of the morning to ask her to open the diner, and what possible reasons he could have given Peg for why he'd been the one doing the calling—Delia groaned. "I can never step foot in there again."

He merely gave her a questioning look.

"What did you tell Peg? About why she needed to open? And why you were doing the asking? What did she say? And how did you even know to call her? Or what her number was?"

"I said you were exhausted and needed some sleep. She said fine, she'd cover for you. I found her name, along with everyone else who works for you, on an old typed-up list tacked to the corkboard next to the phone in the kitchen. And I knew to call her because, though it's been a while since I was a regular, she worked for you back when I was. Just because I moved out to Sandpiper didn't mean I lost all memory of what came before."

And just like that, a very specific memory of what had come before—most specifically the two of them, well . . . coming—flashed into her brain. Like a heat-seeking missile. Seriously, she really had to find a way to make that stop. She looked away, forcing the images out of her overly fevered, clearly undersexed brain. "Thank you."

He looked sincerely surprised at that.

"What?" she said. "I'm not—I was just surprised. It was a nice thing you did. Above and beyond the call of friendship. I'm sorry I wasn't more . . . immediately grateful. But I am. Grateful. I'm more of a morning person than Peg, but that doesn't usually involve dealing with people until I've had a few hours with a sharp knife in my hand."

Now a smile played around his mouth. *Oh, that mouth, and the things it did for her, had been doing to her, less than an hour ago in her dreams.* She shifted her gaze to his arm. To the rumpled, sleep-creased shirt she was wearing. Still wearing. Anywhere but at that mouth.

"Good to know," he said, with an edge of humor that buzzed right along her nerve endings, like the caress of a broad, warm palm across her skin.

"So . . . can I get up now?" She really needed some alone time. Or, more specifically, some away-from-him time.

"There's something else I need to talk to you about."

She frowned and tensed. "What now?"

"I didn't come over last night to play white knight. I had a reason for stopping by."

"Oh. Right. I forgot about your stealth visit. And what's up with that anyway? It's becoming a habit."

"I wanted to speak to you alone. That's the only time I know for certain you're away from the diner and all the listening ears that go with it."

"Okay. So . . . what's up?"

"It's about Winstock. And Grace."

Her gut squeezed on the first name, her heart on the second. "Maybe there should be coffee before we go any further." The moment she said the word *coffee*, her stomach growled in clear agreement. She gave him a wry smile. "The ayes have it, then." She finally pushed at his arm. Hard. "Let me up."

He didn't budge.

"Unless you want to be in charge of the percolator, let me up. And by percolator, I mean the real deal. It was Gran's. Brews the best coffee you'll ever taste. Even better than what I brew at work, which is pretty awesome, but doesn't touch my homemade. Sometimes the old ways are better. Don't tell anyone, though, or they'll start dropping by."

"Dee, there's something I need to tell you—"

"Let me up," she repeated with an edge, damning her own heart for fluttering every time he said her name. Add him needing her, for any reason, and well . . . she was hereby officially never sleeping again.

He lifted his arm, but clearly against his better judgment. She kicked off the old quilt he'd tossed over her, then immediately grabbed it back. "You—" She peeked under the quilt again, but she definitely wasn't dreaming now. "You *took my pants off?*" She looked at him accusingly.

"About that."

She was confused, because she very clearly still had on her bra and shirt—what the hell? So it took her a moment to see his face had reddened. "About that," she repeated. "Enlighten me. Did we have a sudden storm I don't remember? Where only my pants got soaked? What?"

"You . . . uh." He broke off and looked away. "You don't remember then."

She'd already opened her mouth to prod him to explain himself in a more stringently worded demand, only to snap her mouth shut. A heat she hadn't felt in a long time crept up the back of her neck. It was the heat of embarrassment. Not the typical day-to-day, do something dumb embarrassment. Everybody had those, and she was no exception. No, this was looking to be the kind of embarrassment that made lists. Specifically that Most Embarrassing Moments Ever list that everyone kept tucked away somewhere on a mental tally sheet. She could only assume, given the nature of her dreams, that perhaps she'd removed her own pants—she closed her eyes against the images of what that striptease had looked like, given her overall appearance at the time.

"No," she finally managed, in a much smaller voice. "I don't suppose I do." Before he could say another word, and to spare them both what was sure to be further embarrassment all around, not to mention a dash of total humiliation tossed in for grins, she said, "You know what, it doesn't matter. You stopped by to tell me something and I all but passed out dead at your feet. You did a very kind—if unnecessary—thing," she added, "by staying to watch over me, even making sure I could get more rest than usual. Like I said, above and beyond a good friend gesture. I slept here, you slept there—" She gestured in the general direction of the narrow, cypress plank steps that led up to her second-floor bedroom. "All's well that ends well. I don't think any further explanation is needed."

He nodded and looked as relieved as she felt. Which was no small amount.

"So, uh, where are my pants? Actually, never mind." She pulled the quilt around her, feeling silly as she bumbled upright. It wasn't like he hadn't seen her bare legs before, though that had been in the very distant past, but what were bare legs anyway? Nothing. It was the sex dreams making it all seem more . . . suggestive. Besides, she was still wearing underwear. At least . . . *dear Lord. Am I?* She didn't dare wriggle to find out. "I'm going to go shower, change clothes. Then coffee. You—can you wait just a little bit longer? God, I'm being a lousy hostess and even worse friend. Why don't you go on with your day and we'll figure out another time to chat."

"Go shower. I have the time."

Awesome. Dammit.

He straightened his long frame and shifted to the side, away from the spindly tea table. She pretended not to notice him reach a hand to help her maneuver the bulk of the bundled quilt between couch and table, and busied herself scooping the corners of it up off the floor as she managed to get herself past him without tripping. Or touching him.

"Ten minutes," she said, not bothering to add she had no intention of waiting until lunchtime to go in to work. What the hell else would she do all morning? She'd already set up a time with Blue to look at the fresh catch that afternoon and she'd gotten in the veg and meat order the day before. She had paperwork to do. There was always paperwork to do. But otherwise . . .

She felt the newly familiar clamp start to tighten around her heart. It didn't help matters any that as she climbed the stairs, she could feel the quilt rub across her very bare fanny. But she had bigger concerns than the fact that she'd quite possibly flashed her lady parts at Ford the night before. Who had not accepted the invite. *Don't even go there.*

She flipped the shower on, waited for the steam to rise, then stepped in and hoped the beastly hot spray would bake the worry and the indecision right out of her. She stuck her head under the streaming water, then tilted her chin down and let it beat on the tight muscles of her neck and shoulders.

The diner wasn't just her job; it was her home, the place she felt she most belonged. Her little cottage was the place she and Tommy had lived for most of their childhood, at least all that she could remember of it, and yet, it was pretty much just the place where they'd slept, showered, changed clothes. Gran's restaurant was where they'd lived. Where they'd gone every day after school and stayed until bedtime, oftentimes past bedtime. The restaurant was where they'd done homework, had their sibling squabbles, and existed in the bosom of what was the Cove. The regulars were their extended family, and waiting tables, washing dishes, their version of family chores.

Delia's Diner had quickly become to her exactly what O'Reilly's had been. Her home. Where she belonged. Where she lived. Ford was right in that she gave to the community, but they gave back tenfold. They were and always had been her very large, very extended family, with all the love, friendship, support, and yes, dysfunction, that went with it. She owed them everything. In the Cove, at her diner, was where she felt her worth, where she felt valued, loved. All for doing something she loved to begin with. Who could want anything more than that? She had no regrets about the choice she'd made not to follow Henry's dreams but to stay in the Cove and follow her own.

But there was still a future ahead of her, and more choices to be made. Choices she hadn't seen coming . . . and the feelings those choices had evoked had been startling and unexpected. The little trickles of unease, of dissatisfaction she'd been feeling, made her feel ungrateful and . . . well, scared. She didn't want anything more, at least not in the way of having a life that was bigger or broader than life in the Cove. Her place was here and that knowledge, that certainty, were both comforting and fulfilling. So . . . why the unease? Why the sense that there should be something more . . . somehow?

It would be easy to blame Winstock. But, truth be told, the niggles had started before all this. Thinking about what might happen to her diner, and what that would mean to her, to her life, had only underscored the unexpected thoughts she'd already been having.

She'd never had a family of her own, but she wasn't yearning for some late-in-life child. She'd long since made peace with the fact that children were not in the cards for her. She liked no strings. No strings meant no pain, and she was perfectly fine with that. But no strings also meant no husband or partner, and, therefore, no kids.

Single parenting wasn't for her, either. She wasn't going to force a kid into her chosen way of life, nor was she going to farm out child care and be a stranger to her own child. Besides, the locals were her children. She nurtured, fed, settled squabbles, gave advice . . . and then locked up and sent them all home every night. What wasn't to love about that?

But there was still a feeling she was missing . . . something.

Her thoughts went to Grace. Delia had tried to hide from the fact that her inner turmoil, the yearning for something . . . more, had started right about the time Grace Maddox had relocated her life to the Cove. Delia had initially thought about the fact that she had no immediate family. That was natural, watching brother and sister reunite. It emphasized the part of her life she was missing, the part she could never get back. Tommy.

That had also been when she'd started dreaming about Ford. Also not a big surprise, given his sister's arrival had triggered all kinds of memories about her past experiences with Grace's older brother.

Except, instead of getting herself back to normal as Grace found her own niche in the Cove, Delia felt a greater sense of . . . dissatisfaction. Then Winstock had failed in his attempt to buy Brodie's property out from under him, so he and his conniving daughter had started looking for the next best thing. And Delia had unwittingly handed it to them on a platter by failing to pay attention to the end date of her decades-long lease agreement.

She had wondered if her screwup had maybe been some kind of subconscious thing, a sign of how deep her life-questioning truly ran. But the truth was, she'd always paid her annual dollar at the end of the year, and she hadn't thought to make this particular year any different, even though she had been very well aware it was the twentieth one. She'd have had a talk then about what was to happen next, with that most likely being her buying the property.

She forced herself to shift mental gears, to what it would take now to save the diner, if that was indeed what she wanted. She didn't see how she could. She supposed she could sue the town if Davis ruled against her, but she didn't have the kind of resources needed for the very protracted court battle that Winstock would no doubt push her to. He could ruin her financially, and then she'd lose what viability she did have to take out loans and start over.

Her entire body tensed almost to the point of physical pain at the thought of having to do that. Start over. From scratch. Yes, she'd have the built-in customer base, but it wasn't succeeding once she was open that filled her with dread. It was all the rest of it. Taking out loans and being heavily in debt—again—after working so hard to get out from under that. Only this time she was twenty years older, and not all that excited about spending another twenty under that kind of burden.

Then there was the real estate search, which was finite in a place as small as the Cove, or it was if she wanted to be successful. Folks might love her, but they weren't about to drive ten or fifteen miles out of town to grab their morning coffee or a late-night burger. Even if she was fortunate enough to have the perfect location open up, there was the building or renovating, and all the incredible amount of work it took to launch a place. She could certainly gut her current place and take everything she possibly could, but it wasn't a plug-and-play kind of deal. It was rare that two spaces would have the same kind of layout, the same equipment requirements, the same— She broke off as a gulp of unexpected tears rushed up and closed her throat over, spurting out of her eyes before she could stop them. She leaned her forehead against the cool tile as the shower beat on her back, trying to choke them down. Failing. *I'm so sick and tired of feeling like this. Wrenched and gutted. All the damn time.* She just wanted it to stop, wanted to wake up and have it all be clear, the answer right there in front of her. Then she would know what to do, what it would take to make her feel like herself again, and she'd do whatever that was, whatever it took, happily, because she'd know the outcome would all be worth it. Her problems would be solved.

Only the answers weren't there.

"And if you can't even figure out what the hell to do with yourself for one morning, what exactly did you think you were going to do with yourself for the rest of your life if it's not starting over with another diner?"

"Dee?"

She startled, swore, even as she hiccoughed through another clutch of tears.

There was a pause, then, "Sorry. I just—you'd been in there a long time. Are you okay?"

"Fine," she snapped, more annoyed with herself, with her uncustomary and very frustrating inability to find an answer. She'd never once questioned who she was, what she was meant to do. She felt lost in a way she'd never been in her entire life, and as it became more and more clear that it wasn't simply going to figure itself out, the reality of that possibility terrified her. "I'm fine. I'm always fine." Horrified, instead of the anger giving her a handhold on finding her control, she felt fresh tears rising.

He opened the door a crack. "Maybe that used to be true. But you're not fine now, Dee," he said quietly but with an edge to his tone. "You need to get it out, talk it out, something. Keeping it bottled up isn't working. You're running yourself right into the ground."

She didn't respond, couldn't, not because he wasn't right, but because he was. And it unraveled what little control she had left.

"What you say to me stays with me, stays right here.

I won't tell Grace, I won't go behind your back to try and fix it. I'll just listen." He paused, waiting.

Tears were already streaming down her face, and she had to work not to fold over in two and let the sobs take over. She was so tired. Just so . . . tired.

"Deal?" he said, when she hadn't replied.

She tried to tell him to go away, to let her finish her shower, give her time to get her shit together. Ten more minutes and this would pass. She would find a way to be the strong, solid, always-in-control Delia everyone knew her to be, counted on her to be. Instead one sob escaped, then another.

A second later the curtain was being ripped back, and she couldn't find the breath to so much as squeak in surprise, much less order Ford to get the hell out. And then he was in the shower with her, fully clothed, and not caring, pulling her into his arms, keeping her there, with the hot water beating down on her back as he tucked her face against his chest. She didn't even try to fight him, was too far gone to be mortified—it wasn't anything he hadn't seen before and she couldn't bring herself to care enough to be embarrassed.

If he'd said a single word, she—she didn't know what she might have done. But he didn't. He didn't try to soothe her or stop her crying or sympathize, or . . . anything. He just held her, so strong, tall, sturdy . . . all the things she wasn't at the moment, so she could finally, safely, utterly, fall apart.

Chapter 8

There was nothing remotely sexual, much less arousing, about holding a naked, sobbing woman in his arms. And yet, his heart was thundering so hard it was all he could hear, even with the shower pounding down on them.

He'd heard that first sob, like someone had reached down inside her and ripped a vital part of her out, and had simply reacted. He wanted to be annoyed with her for pushing herself so hard, to the breaking point physically and, worse, it seemed, emotionally.

He wanted to be angry as hell, but what he felt was . . . something very close to fear. Not the kind that happened when his life was in jeopardy. That kind of fear he actually knew how to handle. But this . . . this was precisely the kind of fear he'd buried himself out on that island in order to avoid. The fear of caring, the fear of being needed, then not being enough, of doing the wrong thing . . . or worse, doing all that he knew how to do, only to find it wasn't enough. Failing. Failing someone who mattered.

He didn't want to care. Didn't want to feel . . . anything.

So . . . why was he standing, fully clothed, in Delia O'Reilly's ancient claw-foot tub, getting soaked, while holding her as she sobbed her heart out? What had possessed him to think that was a good idea? For either of them?

Grace's face chose that inopportune moment to flash into his mind. Not thirty-two-year-old Grace, but five-year-old Grace smiling through tears as she waved him off to war. Then nine-year-old Grace, clutching at him, scared, as he explained that he couldn't stay, that he had to go back, that she'd be better off without him. That was who he was, what he'd done with the person who had mattered most to him.

He squeezed his eyes shut against the cavalcade of guilt that rushed through him, threatening to crush him, squeeze his heart to a standstill, every time he let his mind go there. What the hell made him think he'd do any better this time?

The water started to turn cool, mercifully pulling him from that mental path. He had no idea how to go from where they stood, to getting her out, dry, and dressed, in a way that was anything less than awkward. *But what the hell, Maddox, you're in it now.*

At some point, the sobs had quieted to hiccoughs and raw, catching breaths, but she still had her face buried in his chest. He lifted one sodden, booted foot to toe-nudge the white porcelain handles off so the water stopped, all while keeping her naked form pressed against him with a strong arm around her back. He let go with one arm long enough to shove open the curtains an inch, reach out, and grab for one of the thick, green towels that hung on big silver-and-white porcelain hooks that had been screwed into the whitewashed plank wall.

He wrapped it around her from the back, and

nudged her away just enough so that she could grab the corners and wrap it around the rest of her. He grabbed another towel for her hair, and then had no real idea what to do with it. He could hardly rub at her curls like one would a family pet.

"Ford, I—"

"Shhh," he said, reflexively. Her throat had to be raw, the words were so hoarse. But he'd quieted her as much because he wasn't ready for whatever she was going to say as he did to save her the pain of talking.

"I'll—let me step—" She stopped, keeping her chin down, her hair dripping in a dark, auburn halo around her downcast face.

He helped her step out of the tub, then lamely handed her the other towel. "Your hair," he muttered.

She took it, but didn't look at him. Her breath was still hitching badly, and he doubted she was enjoying any part of this, either.

"You're . . . soaked," she managed. "Towels. You need—"

"Just—will you be okay to go change? Can I do something, get something—?"

"I'll be fine."

He didn't challenge her on that point. She wasn't, and neither was he, but that wasn't what was being debated at the moment. "Okay. Go change . . . I'll take care of me." That, at least, he knew he could do.

She nodded, hiccoughed again, and clutched the spare towel to her chest, where she was still clutching the towel closed around her body with her other hand. Hair dripping, she moved to the bathroom door, which still stood open from when Ford had barged in. "I . . . thank you," she said, without looking back.

"Anytime," he said lamely, telling himself to be thankful it hadn't been any more awkward than that.

Then, as the door closed behind her, he looked down at his soaking wet self and thought, *Well, maybe there's still some awkward to get through.*

Just as he'd convinced himself it was best if he simply took his soaking wet self back to the foundation offices to change, giving Delia some time and space to regroup, there was a knock on the door.

"I—here's some clothes. I put them by the door. Sweatpants, T-shirt, old hoodie." Her voice was deep, hoarse, and he could hear the embarrassment. "They were Tommy's," she added. "I—I don't know why I kept them—but he always wore things three sizes too big, so . . . anyway."

"Thank you," Ford said. *Yep, not done with the awkward.* There was no sign of Delia when he opened the door and snagged the neatly folded stack. Unbidden, memories snuck back in and flash-bombed him as he dragged off his wet clothes, and dragged on dry ones. Nine-year-old Grace, mortally wounded Tommy, grief-stricken Delia . . . Too many memories. Maybe he still needed Sandpiper more than he realized. He felt like being here in the Cove was sucking him back in, back to where he'd been in his life when he'd first arrived. He didn't want that, couldn't do that.

In the past thirteen years, he'd learned that while physical wounds could and did heal, some of the emotional ones never would. He'd also learned he did still have something useful to offer, and where best to offer it. But maybe that best place was only on Sandpiper. The longer he was in the Cove, the harder it was to pretend otherwise.

He might want to help her, but the bottom line was, even thirteen years later, Delia O'Reilly still deserved better than him.

She was in her tiny kitchen, in front of the infamous

percolator, when he came back downstairs. He'd put
his wet clothes in the trash bag she'd left under the
stack of dry clothes and had set that and his wet boots
on the front porch on his way to the kitchen. "I'll get
the clothes back to you," he said.

She startled at the sound of his voice, bobbled the
old tin coffeepot, and then set it gently on the heating
pad she'd placed on the small table positioned in front
of the bay window. The far side of the table was pushed
up so the base of the curved window formed a bench
seat for two, while two additional chairs had been
pushed in on the near side.

Ford glanced around, noting that the kitchen appliances had been updated at some point since he'd
been there for Tommy's funeral, but everything else
still looked as he remembered it, from the glass front
cabinets, with the old red metal door handles, to the
wood trim, all painted white, as were the drawers and
cabinets built in below the counter. The countertop
had been updated from when the house had first been
built, but still pre-dated him by a good twenty to thirty
years. It was blue-and-silver speckled linoleum, the
white background having long since yellowed from
years of use, with the occasional cracked edge and
peeled-up corner showing the plank wood under-
neath.

The curtains over the sink and framing the bay window were different, brighter, a cheerful blue-and-white
checkerboard pattern, with yellow flowers, bright green
leaves, and ladybugs stitched all along the bottom edge.
He wasn't sure what he'd have guessed as being Delia's
personal style, but the ladybugs and flowers wouldn't
have been his first choice. They definitely brightened
up the place but, though charming, seemed unneces-

sary, given the energy and life force that always emanated from her in a seemingly inextinguishable flow.

Or perhaps that was just how she was at the diner, feeding off the energy of those she cooked for. Maybe here was where she recharged that endless supply, and she needed fanciful, black polka-dotted bugs and yellow daisies to help her do it.

At the moment, whatever energy she might have left was subdued, at best, and his concern for her returned front and center. Because whatever she was going through, it was going to take a lot more than time spent staring at embroidered curtains to build herself back up again.

He looked back at Delia. She was dressed in dark blue, comfortable slacks and a pale blue polo shirt with the name of the diner stitched over the pocket in red, in the same font and style as the signage for the place. There was no actual uniform for the diner that he'd ever seen. Actually, he could only recall the youngsters she hired for the summer crush wearing the polo shirts and slacks combo. The guys in the kitchen wore the traditional white jackets, black pants, but nothing stiff or starchy.

Peg favored floral dresses, style-appropriate to her age, which was somewhere between sixty and, well, he didn't rightly know. She paired them with fifties-style white aprons that had her name stitched over one bountiful bosom, and kept her dyed chestnut hair pulled up in a small bun near the crown of her head, always tucked under a little net with lacy trim, usually with something festive tucked into the bun on a stick. On anyone else that affectation would look silly, but on Peg, he'd always thought they looked just right. Like her boss, she always had a knowing smile, advice whether requested or not, and a way about her that made her feel like family, both the kind you loved and the kind that occasionally made you wish you had a different last name. She reminded him of the housekeeper on that old TV show he'd seen as a child: *Hazel.*

Back when he'd regularly spent time at the diner, Delia usually wore khakis, whatever blouse she'd pulled out of her closet, and a kitchen apron knotted around her hips and a kerchief tied around her neck. He knew she tied her hair up in it when she cooked or did kitchen duty, knew her crew called her Lucy, and had always been privately amused by that. Both she and the famous character might have had red hair, but the similarity ended there. Lucy Ricardo was something of a shortsighted klutz, and the Delia O'Reilly he knew was anything but.

"They fit," she said.

He realized Delia was staring at him expectantly. He looked down at the clothes he was wearing. "Yes. Thank you."

"Tommy wouldn't like it that I kept some of his stuff; he'd have seen it as maudlin." She didn't smile, but honest affection warmed her red-rimmed eyes. "He'd be happy knowing he did something for you, though. He thought the sun rose and set by you." She lifted the mug she was holding, "One sugar, no cream, right?

He jerked his gaze from her face, from the slippery slope of memories to the coffee. "I—yes. Good memory."

"Just doing my job," she said, quickly turning back to the counter.

He took a seat at the table, nursed his first sip, and thought his eyes might roll straight up into his head because he'd surely just died and gone to coffee heaven. "This is . . ." There were no words, so he took another sip instead, and thought he might have groaned.

She spared him a quick glance. "Told you so."

He was relieved to hear the thread of wry humor in her tone. She wasn't one for wearing a lot of makeup, just the basics, but even to his untrained male eyes, in just that quick glance he could see she'd put some effort into trying to mask the ravages of her crying jag. He wanted to tell her she didn't have to do that around him, that he understood and accepted her as she was: human. Then he took in the whole outfit again, and realized she hadn't tried to improve her looks for his benefit. "You're not taking the morning off." He didn't make it a question.

She finished stirring a dollop of real cream into her coffee, then finally turned and leaned back against the counter, meeting his gaze for the first time since she'd clambered off the couch. "I have work to do. Peg can run the front and I can catch up on some paperwork before taking the afternoon shift. I also need to call Blue and reschedule, since I'll be working. I'd send Charlie, as I trust his judgment with the daily catch, but he's off, so . . ." She lifted a shoulder, her expression implacable, as if it were simply the way it had to be. No discussion.

Since it wasn't his life, it wasn't his call, so he didn't offer an objection she most certainly wouldn't want to hear anyway. Even if he felt that holding her while she fell completely apart due to stress, exhaustion, and who knew what else might have at least earned him the right to offer some advice on the subject. *Fat lot of good that would do.*

"What brought you over last night?" she asked, sounding for all the world as if that scene up in her shower had never happened, or the one on her front walk the night before, for that matter.

But the way her blue eyes bored into his said otherwise, as if she was still trying to hold on to him, to something stronger, sturdier than herself, and using any conversational gambit she could grab hold of as a way to do it.

He'd promised her several times now that she could talk to him, open up to him about what had turned her so upside down and inside out. Perhaps the best way to do that was to let her steer the course to getting them there.

"Grace is worried about you," he said, without preamble. On the one hand, he hated to pile on when she was obviously in an overwhelmed place, but he didn't want her blindsided by his sister's well-meaning actions, either.

"I know she is," Delia said quietly. "Everyone is worried about what's going to happen with the diner. I wish I had an answer for them. I just . . . need some time."

"Grace thinks what you need is a party."

Delia all but spit her sip of coffee back in her cup. "She—what? Why?"

"She thinks you need to see that the people in the Cove are behind you and will support you. She thinks something public like that will also make Winstock and the mayor see that they're messing with a local icon. I guess it's really more rally than party, but her intentions are good."

"And so you're, what? Warning me? Why?"

"I'm not sure it's a good idea. I mean, it's a solid approach. But only if . . ." He trailed off, unsure if he should be the one to put it out on the table, and risk putting her on the defensive, which could very well make her clam up. *Jesus, you still suck at this.*

"But only if what?" she asked.

He looked up from where he'd been contemplating the flat, black surface of his coffee, as if there were answers to be found in its aromatic depths. He looked at her standing there, spine straight, still pretending she hadn't just had a complete emotional breakdown not fifteen minutes ago. All prepped and ready to step back into the fray, without resolving a single damn thing that had gotten her into that state to begin with.

"Only if saving the diner is what you really want to do. Grace says you're not fighting Winstock because you don't want the diner. That you don't know what you want to do."

Delia didn't so much as blink. If anything, her eyes went flat, and he swore he could see her pulling her battle armor more tightly around her with every blow. Or every perceived one, anyway.

Ford set his coffee mug down and straightened in his chair. This was what he'd been hoping to avoid, but he wasn't convinced it hadn't been the right thing to do. He wasn't sure she'd ever open up about what was eating away at her if he didn't reach in and grab it out of her.

"I guess sibling bonds trump friendship confidences," Delia said tightly.

Ford frowned. "That's unfair. She's worried about you. Deeply worried. Grace is loyal, to a fault. You know that better than anyone. She only came to me because she thought it was the only way to help you. You can trust her, Dee." He would have added that she could trust him, too, but that wasn't necessary now. She'd trusted him with quite enough already that day.

Either she knew her instincts about him were right, or she didn't.

"I'm sorry," she said, and despite her flat tone, she did appear contrite. "I'm just—I'm not used to trusting people." She shook her head. "That didn't come out how I meant—what I meant was I'm not used to having to trust people. I know I have a lot of support, and I'm grateful for it. I know if I need my driveway plowed out or help with taking an old tree down, I have a couple dozen people I can call, any time of the day or night. I'm thankful for that, too. They know they have the same assist in return, if needed."

"But the kind of trust we're talking about here is different," he finished for her. "You don't usually need that. Because you're usually the one providing the safe place for others. You're the one they come to, but when push came to shove, it wasn't a situation where you felt you could do the same in return. Not when the problem was personal."

She simply stared at him, and then finally, she gave him a quick nod, a mere jerk of the chin. "It's not because I'd doubt their sincerity, or their loyalty, or even their willingness. It's just . . . not how things are. They confide, they share, they seek advice. I know everything about them, but I don't do the same, share the same, so there's no foundation going that direction, you know?"

He saw her shoulders stiffen, her spine straighten, and recognized them for the defense mechanisms they were, only this time he was pretty sure she was putting them up to defend against herself, against her own fears. It was the briefest of moments when her bottom lip quivered, that had him putting his coffee down, sliding his chair back, and very deliberately closing the short distance between them. He took the mug from her hands before she sloshed the contents and burned herself, and set it on the counter behind her. Then he closed his hands around hers, and drew them up between them, and waited, until she lifted her gaze to meet his.

"Talk to me," he urged her. "I know you don't want to talk about it at all, even with yourself. I know you wish you had a better sounding board, but I'm the one you've got. I don't know that I'm any good at finding answers to your problems, even if you want me to. But I know I can listen." The corners of his mouth kicked up. "Grace says I give good shoulder."

Delia's eyes were huge, luminous pools of sapphire blue, glistening with the threat of tears, like sun dancing along the surface of deep waters . . . even as a storm brewed just below. Even so, her lips quirked at that last comment.

His own smile surfaced fully. "So, I have that going for me. And I know I can offer honest opinions when asked." When her eyebrow arched at that, he let out a short laugh. "Okay, maybe even when they're not requested." He held her hands more tightly in his and both of their expressions grew more serious. "We helped each other through a hard time once. And . . . maybe we were more than that, briefly, when we needed to be." It was the first time he'd ever alluded to that night, but there was no point in picking some parts of what they'd meant to each other, and discarding others. It all mattered. "You can't keep going like you're going. Even you have to see that. You trusted me once. That's all I'm trying to say. At one of the toughest times in your life."

"I—" The single word was hardly more than a rasp. She stopped, and he saw her throat work, saw the tension tighten across her shoulders, could feel the flex of it in her hands, and knew she was going to pull away, going to refuse. Politely, perhaps, but still . . .

"We all need someone sometime," he said quietly. "I've screwed that up in the past. With Grace. I know you know that, too."

Her gaze flew to his. "I wasn't—that's not why—" She choked the words out hoarsely, eyes still glassy, the soft skin around them still puffy.

"Who knows, I could screw it up again this time. But it won't be for lack of trying to get it right. The way I see it, the only person you don't have to worry about, the only one you can be completely yourself with . . . the only one you can say anything to, scream, shout . . ." He ducked his chin down, kept her gaze when she would have let it slide away. "Cry," he added, "is me."

"Ford . . ." she began, but trailed off. Then he watched her regroup, pull the armor on, and his disappointment was so keen it was a physical hurt. She looked directly at him. "I—thank you, truly, but—"

"No thank you?" he finished for her, feeling the first bite of real frustration. "You know, I can understand you not wanting to deal with the possible sudden loss of the diner, but why in the hell won't you at least try to help yourself?" She looked away, but he shifted so his gaze was still on hers. "Dee—"

"Stop calling me that!" she erupted, apparently as surprised by the outburst as he was, if her widening eyes and stunned expression were any measure.

"Okay," he said slowly, after a brief pause, truly confused now.

"I'm sorry," she said. "I'm . . . tired. And, as you've so unfortunately seen firsthand, my head's not exactly screwed on straight at the moment. But it will be." She was talking faster as she went on, using speed to create an aura of confidence.

Not that he was buying it. "Delia," he said, deliberately enunciating the syllables, and earning a scowl from her for the effort. "At least be honest enough to just up and say what it is you do want. Whatever the hell it is, however off the wall. It doesn't matter. Just *say it already*. No judgment. No advice. Not from me. I get that you want nothing to do with me, but I'm here for the moment, so just put it all out there, use the moment, use me."

She swore under her breath, and muttered something else that sounded a lot like "if you only knew how I've used you already," but since that didn't make any sense, he ignored it.

"Do you want out from under the diner? It's a lot of work, you've devoted your whole life to it, so it wouldn't exactly be a big shocker if you wanted to move on and do something else, spark a new fire, find a new passion."

She looked away then, but not before he saw her cheeks turn bright crimson.

"Dee—I mean, Delia—shit."

She swung her gaze back up and blurted out, "I dream about you. Okay? About us. About . . . back then. That night. When we were briefly . . . more, as you said. You called me Dee. You were the only one who ever did, except Gran. And I didn't correct you, because . . . I didn't. Only it's now, in the dreams, not then. I can't seem to stop. I don't know why. There, I said it. Okay? Humiliation complete. Now maybe I can get past it and get past you, and figure out what the hell I'm going to do with the rest of my life. But I can't do that *with* you, because—" She tugged a hand free, waved it around her head. "Understand?"

If she'd kneed him, he couldn't have been more astonished. She . . . dreamed about him? Sex dreams?

He flashed immediately back to the moments when she'd first woken up on the couch, had been all soft and open and . . . he felt a little heat rise up the back of his own neck. Well . . . damn. He didn't know how he felt about it, but his first instinct wasn't to be upset, while hers clearly was all that and more of the same.

"I'm—" He lifted his shoulders, a shrug of defeat, tried like hell not to smile. "Yeah. I got nothing."

Her gaze narrowed. "You think this is *funny*?" She tugged her other hand free. "Well, of course you do. You're a man. And you want me to trust you with my deepest, darkest, and yet the first thing you do is smirk because I dream about you? *Really*, Ford?"

"In my defense, I said I wasn't sure I'd be any good at it, but—" He snagged her fist as she aimed it for his shoulder, wrapped his much bigger palm around it, and lowered it, then took her other hand, just to be safe, and held on to that one, too. "I wasn't laughing at you. I was . . . hell, I guess I was flattered." He still couldn't quite wrap his head around her revelation, or the myriad of other things it might imply, much less how he felt about them.

He thought he might have spied steam starting to leak from her ears.

"There's nothing wrong in my being flattered about you dreaming . . . you know, about us," he said. "You caught me off guard, okay? I—it wasn't something I'd have guessed."

The pink in her cheeks went straight back to a mortified red again, causing him to quickly play his words back. "No, that's not—not that I wouldn't think about you the same way, I just don't—I haven't—well, shit." He risked letting go of one hand and cupped her cheek, brought her face back up until their gazes met again, then wove his fingers through her hair and tipped her face back when she tried to look away. "Actually, since we're being honest . . . I have. Thought about it. That night. When Grace messaged me, told me you were in trouble, my thoughts went . . . well, there." He let that trail off. "I don't even know why, exactly. I haven't let myself think about that time at all really. I spent so much time thinking about my life back then, my service, what I did, analyzing, reliving . . . at some point, when I'd done all the work I could do to fix myself, I made a decision to look forward, not back. So, it's not an insult, or even personal, it's just—"

"Survival," she managed.

He nodded. "Yes. Then Grace came back into my life and . . . well, it's not surprising that it's dredged things up."

"Dredged," she echoed. "Lovely."

He gripped her hand more tightly, and tipped her chin up. "Stop it," he said, frustration back. God, she was the damnedest woman, made him feel the damnedest things. Hell, she made him feel, period. He'd gotten pretty damn good at not doing that. "I don't mean it that way, and you know it."

"I don't know anything, Ford. You came back to Maine, and you were around all the time; then you started school, and you pulled away, and well . . . I knew you weren't in great shape." She lifted her free hand. "In here." She tapped the side of his head. "Or in here." She curled her fingers, pressed her knuckles to his chest. "I tried not to take it personally, told myself you needed to do whatever you needed to do. I knew I hadn't pressured you, or pushed you. I just let you come into my orbit, and exist, because I thought— hoped, anyway—that it helped some. If I wanted anything more, well, I knew right off that wasn't on the menu." She tried a dry smile, but her eyes were still wary, and maybe a little sad.

"Did you—want more?" *Why the hell are you asking her that? Let it go, man. She's having an emotional life crisis and has twisted you up in it somehow, so don't press her about it, for God's sake.*

"Maybe," she said, surprising him with the directness, though why anything surprised him at this point, he hadn't a freaking clue. "Okay, not maybe. I did. At first. Because you came back to Maine, and I couldn't figure any other reason for you to do that than that I was here. I was the only connection left. But, like I said, I realized, pretty much right away, that you'd come here looking for . . . well, safe harbor. And while that security or grounding or . . . whatever you needed included me, it didn't include any other kind of entanglement. I got that, too, understood it. I understand it now. And that's okay, Ford. I was a grown woman by then, not a young, naïve girl." She let out a short laugh. "Any naïve I had in me was wiped out when Henry left, then Tommy died, then the restaurant burned, then Gran . . ." She let the words trail off, shook her head slightly, as if brushing away past memories. She looked up at him. "Life happens and you learn from it. I did. So I was okay with whatever you needed from me. I just hope it helped."

He searched those blue eyes and found he was no longer thinking of the young woman she'd been, the one grieving the loss of her brother, and the abdication of her young husband. . . . Now he was looking at the woman she was. And he didn't need flashes of a long-ago stormy night to feel the things he was feeling. He realized now what some part of him had realized in the shower, when she'd come undone all over him and his heart had pounded as if something completely different was happening. Their bond wasn't just one of shared tragedy, or a friendship forged under trying circumstances, then deepened during a time of healing, but more . . . a lot more. There were many reasons, good, solid reasons, behind his choice to live his life out on a solitary spit of land, but he could no longer pretend that one of them wasn't avoiding having to deal with what was truly between them.

"It did help," he said, the words a little gruff because his throat had tightened up. "Even more than you know."

"I'm glad," she said. "I thought when you moved out to the island full time . . . well, I guess I was more worried than anything. I wanted you to be okay. I worried that you weren't."

"I don't know how you define okay, but if that means finding your place in the world and being at peace with it, then . . . yes, I'm okay." He reached up, stroked a still-damp tendril of hair from her face. His fingers were steady, his heart was anything but. It had been a very, very long time since he'd been so intimate with someone. Even longer with someone who mattered. And there was no one, save Grace, his only family, who mattered more.

"You're not okay, Dee," he said, unaware he'd used the nickname until her pupils punched wide with instant awareness, the kind of awareness that made him all the more sensitive to just how close he stood to her, how he could feel her breath on his chin, her pulse leap where his fingers brushed against her temple. And that opened up something inside him he couldn't seem to slap shut again. Wasn't sure he wanted to. "Something's going on inside you and you have to let it out."

"I know you've seen me at my absolute worst," she said. "At my lowest points. I—back then, we were both grieving, we both needed. It was easier, because there was give with the take." She searched his eyes. "It's not just trust, Ford. I do trust you. It's about taking. I'm . . . not good at that."

"I took from you," he said. "When I came back. You said it made you feel good, to offer help. So, let me have that same pleasure. Or just consider this evening the score."

A ghost of a smile hovered over her lips. "Somehow, I don't think me falling apart all over you in my own shower was all that pleasurable for you."

"If it helped, I'd do it again," he said, and realized he meant it.

She looked away, clearly abashed.

"Don't be embarrassed, it's human, for God's sake. We're not perfect and we're not impervious."

"That's just it. I don't fall apart. I don't. Not even in private. I work things out, I find solutions, I keep a cool head. I'm the rock, I'm the one who tethers others to shore." She shifted, so her cheek was no longer in contact with his hand, then sidestepped out of his personal space, but no farther. Didn't matter, it was a distinct divide, no matter how narrow. "I don't know how to tether myself to someone else's shore. But you're right. I need to learn, because I feel like I'm losing it. And I don't think I can do that with anyone but you." She broke off, looked down again. "I'm not sure what the dreams mean, or why I have them, but that's all they are, Ford. Maybe it's some kind of mental retreat, to a safe place, a place that feels good, where there's only pleasure. I'm not a shrink. But I do know that's all they are. Harmless fantasy." She looked up at him and a hint of that saucy smile of hers hovered at the corners of her mouth. "I'm not going to jump you is what I'm trying to say."

"Dee—"

The smile ghosted away, and she looked as serious as he'd ever seen her. "But I appreciate the offer of an ear. Your ear. Hopefully, not your shoulder. I think I'm all cried out. God, I certainly hope so, anyway. I think it was just fatigue and worry and uncertainty that made that happen. I feel better for the release, maybe a bit hollow." She shook her head again. "I don't know what I feel. Except grateful for the offer." She looked directly into his eyes, then. "Of an ear. Of help. Of friendship. I guess I do need it. I know I need something."

"Well, for whatever I might be worth, you've got me."

"You're worth a lot."

He nodded, surprised that what he felt wasn't abject fear, or the urge to run and hide . . . but relief. Relief she'd finally accepted that she shouldn't struggle through this alone. Relief that he wasn't going to be removed from her life again, this time by her choice. There were some other, stronger emotions swirling in there, too, but she'd made it clear she was only looking for—could only handle—friendship. So he thankfully, mercifully, didn't have to examine them too closely. As it was, he was already hoping he didn't let her down.

She picked up her coffee mug and stared down into the dark depths for a long moment. When she finally looked up at him again, she was smiling, as if she'd come to a decision, and was good with it. Her gaze was open, all the way down to her heart. No walls. And it was as if all the time they'd spent apart had simply gone away, leaving them once again at the core of what they truly were, what they'd always been. Two people joined in a unique bond. A team, a duet, a pair. Partners. Just the two of them against the world. In her eyes he saw relief, and trust, and . . . hope.

And, just like that, in this moment that felt separate and apart from all the moments that had come before it, he actually felt his heart . . . click. As if, after all this time when he'd thought it was better, a blessing even, to not feel at all . . . his heart had, in reality, just been tucked away. Healing. Hibernating. Waiting. Grace had opened the door a crack, letting the light back in, proving to him there was still life there. But it was only now, seeing the light shining in the depths of those beautiful blue eyes that he felt his heart come all the way back to life.

"So, about this rally circus your sister wants to throw," she said, lifting her mug in a silent toast to their partnership. "How can we stop that from happening?"

Chapter 9

Delia turned from her street onto Hill Road, and then let her SUV roll to a stop as she looked out over the harbor below. Peg had more or less put her foot down and insisted she swap shifts with Delia for one more day, and Delia had been too tired to argue. That meant she wasn't technically due in for hours yet, but . . . what else was she supposed to do? Besides, she had a mountain of office work to do. She always did, so she'd go hide in the back, get some work done, pull her thoughts together, then relieve Peg when the time was right. Sitting in her little house was just making her think of Ford, and she really didn't need to be thinking about Ford.

Instead, she looked at the harbor, and thought about her other problem. What she was going to do about her diner. Below, she could see the frame of the immense, real-life replica of the eighteenth-century tall ship that Brodie Monaghan was building, on the very same site his ancestors had built those very same vessels hundreds of years earlier. She spied the workers going in and out of the boathouse on the other end of his property, which hugged the heart of the harbor, the one Grace was renovating into her gorgeous, unique little inn. Beyond that to the east was Blue's, the largest of the fishing companies in Half Moon Harbor, employing a healthy percentage of the men in town, continuing the tradition of one of the Cove's founding industries.

Just beyond that was her diner, perched on the high side of Harbor Street, with the deck out front, and her own dedicated dock across the road, where folks could tie up their boats, and come in for a bite, or wander Harbor Street and the shops that dotted the road, up and down, on either side of her place.

No one was behind her, so she took a moment and tried to imagine how the landscape before her would change with a yacht club wedged smack in the middle of it. The clubhouse would sit on her lot and the adjacent two empty lots that were presently used for general harbor parking, but for which Winstock had already gotten promissory notes of purchase.

She did the best she could to clear her mind of sentiment and prejudice and simply imagine how it would look from Winstock's viewpoint. It would be beautiful, of that she had no doubt. The man might be a snake when it came to getting what he wanted, whatever method he had to use, but there was no denying he had good taste when it came to his possessions. His palatial estate on the edge of town was testament to that.

Sitting up on a rocky promontory, you could look out over the Cove from the sweeping front porch. She imagined that positioning had been intentional. King of all he surveyed. But despite the immensity and scope of the place, which was really more compound than simply a mansion, the design and landscaping were surprisingly warm, inviting. Not that anyone just felt free to drive up the long sweeping road that led up the knoll to the home. It was gated, for one thing. But Delia happened to know firsthand what it felt like to stand on that porch. Not because she'd been invited, but because as a teenager, she had been hired, as had Gran, to work the Winstocks' seasonal parties. Back before Mrs. Winstock had taken off for greener pastures, their parties had been legendary, despite the fact that very few folks who actually lived in the Cove were invited.

Delia thought about how she'd felt sorry for Cami back then, a little girl who never had the attention of her mother, raised by staff, spoiled to an embarrassing degree by a doting father with more money than sense. Then later, after Brooks's wife had taken off, she'd felt a kind of kinship, since she'd lost her mother at a young age, too. Delia snorted. "Yeah. That didn't last."

Even when Delia was a teenager, the stories about the philandering Mrs. Winstock had been legion. Delia had seen her at the parties, always leaning on the arm of someone else's wealthy husband, but rarely her own. She supposed Brooks spoiled Cami in some misguided attempt to make up for either his poor choice in a marriage partner in the first place, or her absence later on. Probably it was both. It was odd then, and sad, Delia thought, that daughter had taken after mother, at least in her insatiable need for attention. Only, in Cami's case, like seemed to have married like, as Creepy Ted was even more handsy than his wealthy wife.

"Gah," Delia said with a little shudder, trying to shake off those thoughts, but memories of the past lingered. Though she'd never thought less of herself for having served at the Winstock estate, she had to consider that because she had, Brooks Winstock quite likely still saw her as nothing more than the hired help. "The uppity hired help, at that," she said, a wry grin twisting her lips. It explained a lot about his patronizing condescension whenever he'd spoken to her, though he always delivered any statement he made to her with a broad smile.

She pulled her gaze back to the central part of Half Moon Harbor, back to her part. Or the part she'd always thought of as hers. Would the yacht owners and club members see the whole of it the same way she did? As charming and traditional, historic and purposeful? Would they see it the way the others who had made their living there did?

Or would they not want to be so up close and personal with the "local color" of fishing trawlers and working shipyards? Would they only be willing to join Winstock's little club if maybe he "spruced up" the rest of the harbor by doing to, say, Blue's what he'd done to her? Would Winstock and the town politicians think that bringing in money from the rich and powerful yacht owners would make it okay to push out the largest employer of the Cove's core industry, the same one that had been the town's economic base since its founding three centuries ago?

She had to get Owen to reconsider. It wasn't so much about saving her diner—she was getting more and more convinced that they could only thwart Winstock's plans for so long—but at the very least they needed to have some checks and balances.

She was startled from her thoughts by the sudden blaring of a horn just behind her. She had no idea how long she'd been sitting in the middle of road, staring at the harbor. She lifted her hand automatically in a gesture of apology and pressed on the gas. Once underway, she glanced in her rearview mirror to see who'd laid on their horn. A tap would have been more than enough to alert her, and more typical of how locals treated locals. So it came as no surprise when she spied Cami in a big, black Lexus SUV the size of a small tank.

"Wonderful." Hill Road ended at the intersection with Harbor Street. She braked at the stop sign and flipped on her right blinker. The sole traffic light in town, at the other end of Harbor Street, must have just turned green so, as she waited for a few pickup trucks and a couple of cars to file by, Cami pulled up next to her and lowered her passenger window.

Reluctantly, Delia lowered her own window and turned an expectant gaze toward the brightly smiling blonde. Camille Winstock Weathersby was a tiny thing, and Delia thought she looked like a kid driving her daddy's car, wondering—unkindly, she knew—if she needed a booster seat to reach the steering wheel. Delia also knew not to mistake diminutive size for diminutive power.

So, though she was tempted to say something provocative and unwise, she instead clamped her back teeth together and kept her expression carefully blank as she waited for the younger woman to say whatever was on her mind.

"I thought you'd be on your way over to the county building," she chirped.

"Why would that be?" Delia replied blandly.

"Why, Daddy is over there talking to Mayor Davis and I just assumed that you'd be in on that little meeting, too." Her smile turned a shade nasty. "Guess I was wrong. Maybe they didn't feel the need to include you, seeing as you don't really have a say. Still, I'd think you'd at least be courteous enough to allow Mayor Davis to let you down privately, saving him the embarrassment of having to publicly explain to you what everyone else already knows." When Delia didn't reply, the gleam in Cami's eyes turned a shade more malicious. "Your little handout from the city was all fine and well and certainly more than generous given how long you've been, well, squatting there. But it would certainly be refreshing to see that you understand that lending one poor person a hand up is only a worthwhile endeavor for the city when it's not otherwise hindering real growth. I'm sure you're thankful to have gotten what you did." Cami said this as if it was understood that that was far more than Delia had actually deserved.

At Delia's continued silence, Cami's ever-so-gracious smile returned. "I still have those listings to show you. You just let me know when you're ready to go looking. I'm sure I can get you a good deal. Not for a dollar a year, you understand," she added with a little laugh. "You'll have to pay actual rent, but folks here will feel sorry for you, of course, because that's their nature when it comes to the downtrodden. We can work that sentiment in your favor. Explain how your sacrifice is making it possible for Blueberry Cove and Half Moon Harbor to reach new heights of growth to benefit everyone. So, you see? There's a silver lining to everything. Well, maybe more silver for me than for you, but still. Win-win. Winstock!" she added with another gleeful little chirp, then pulled her behemoth of a vehicle out onto Harbor Street with a punch of gas, leaving a little spray of gravel in her wake as she headed in the opposite direction.

Delia yanked her head back to keep from getting road grit in her eyes, and punched the button to raise the window. What she wanted to punch was a lot softer, and wore too much foundation and mascara. She couldn't guarantee that if Cami dared to come within fifty yards of her person, ever again, that she wouldn't follow through with the impulse.

"Take a breath," she schooled herself, gripping the steering wheel with both hands. Then she let go and smacked it with her open palms. Hard. "Dammit! Now I'm finally mad enough to fight and there's nothing left to fight for." She left a little spray of gravel herself as she whipped her vehicle onto Harbor Street, pulled a U-turn, and headed back up the hill and over toward the county municipal building.

Blueberry Cove didn't have a town square, per se, but it did have a three-square-block section of town nestled on the north side, above the harbor, that housed some of the oldest buildings still standing and still functioning. Most of them were commercial, a series of small shops and services, with a few residences tucked in between on the side streets. Near the center of it, on Front Street, sat the old stone building that housed the county courthouse, along with the somewhat newer brick and clapboard buildings—newer meaning only a hundred years old—that housed the mayor's offices, the tax assessor's office, the zoning commissioner, along with those used by the various town council members who requested a public office, all of which comprised what the townsfolk called City Hall.

She pulled up to the curb alongside the small park that sat between the clapboard building on the end, and the courthouse, with old cobblestone walkways meandering through it, circling the large fountain at the center. She left the engine idling while she tried to get herself under control, before she went and made an even bigger fool of herself.

She didn't know anything more about what she wanted than she had yesterday morning, when she'd fallen apart all over Ford, but one thing she had figured out was that she couldn't just sit idly by and let it happen to her. She might not have a leg to stand on legally, but the very least Mayor Davis owed her was the courtesy of a decent explanation.

As if on cue, the double doors opened, and out stepped Mayor Davis, Brooks Winstock, and Ted Weathersby.

"The evil triumvirate," she muttered, half surprised the ground didn't quiver when she said it.

Mayor Davis was a short, rotund man with perpetually flushed cheeks, thinning hair, and an insincere laugh always ready to trip off his tongue, as if he was always a bit nervous about something and tried to hide it by being extra jovial. He didn't run in quite the circles that Winstock did, but he wasn't one to drop by the diner, either. If anything, he liked to imagine himself running in circles bigger than the ones he actually inhabited.

Brooks Winstock was tall, lean, his white hair always neatly and expensively cut, elegant in designer casuals that made him look like he'd just stepped off the eighteenth green. "Or out of his yacht club." And with that thought propelling her, she was launching herself out of her car and walking across the small park, directly to where the three of them stood.

They were all smiles and shoulder claps, clearly quite happy with themselves. Mayor Davis spied her first and looked instantly uncomfortable. His overly loud chuckle was testament to that. "Well, well," he said, looking to Brooks for support. "Look who is here. I was just telling Brooks—er, Mr. Winstock here, that I was going to call you." He chuckled again. "Looks like you saved me the trouble."

"Yes, Mayor, it appears I have." She smiled brightly at Brooks and Ted. "But that's me, always wanting to save folks some trouble."

Ted glanced at his father-in-law, as if looking for guidance, but Brooks didn't so much as blink. Instead, he extended his hand, all suave smoothness and benevolent kindness. "Ms. O'Reilly, a pleasure to see you as always," he said, despite the fact that he rarely, if ever, actually laid eyes on her. He paused, and with fake concern, added, "My apologies. Did I get that right? You did take back your maiden name after the unfortunate circumstances leading to your divorce, am I correct?" He glanced at Mayor Davis with a patently false look of self-deprecation. "Can't keep up with these modern women, but I certainly applaud their right to do what makes them feel best."

Delia shouldn't have been surprised by his gall, but it admittedly caught her off guard enough that it took her a moment to regroup. She ignored his proffered hand and instead looked at the mayor. If Brooks was going to use him as his foil, then Delia felt perfectly within her right to follow suit. "You men are so lucky," she said, her bright smile dripping with just as much sincerity as Winstock's. "You don't have to wear your marital failures on your sleeve . . . or typed on your business license," she added pointedly, looking directly at the mayor. "Your name stays the same regardless of the—I'm sorry, what did you call it?" She glanced at Winstock. "Oh, right. 'Unfortunate circumstances.'" Delia wanted to throw up in her mouth a little, just for being reduced to saying that. She swallowed the bitterness and looked back to the mayor, but Winstock spoke before she could say what she'd come to say. Whatever the hell that was going to be.

"Some of us learn and grow from past mistakes," Winstock said, patronizing smile curving to reveal his perfectly white, perfectly capped teeth. "Others seem doomed to continue to learn things the hard way." He placed his hand on her arm and it was all she could do not to snatch it away. "I'm terribly sorry about how this all worked out for you, but I believe my daughter has spoken to you about some other properties you might be interested in. Around the other side of the harbor, of course." He said that last part as if it was clear to all that her diner would have no business being in the same part of town as his high-and-mighty, exclusive little club.

"Ms. O'Reilly," the mayor broke in, a fine sheet of sweat beading on his wide forehead as he sensed the direction the swiftly deteriorating conversation was going to take. "Why don't we step inside and have a little talk. I need to go over some paperwork with you, as well. I'm sure Martha can bring us in some coffee and we'll have ourselves a little chat. We'll work things out for you."

He said this as if she were one step from living in her car, and not the proprietor of one of the most successful businesses in Half Moon Harbor. All of the Cove, for that matter. "I can take care of things myself, Mayor, but thank you for being so thoughtful." She smiled as he looked confused as to whether she was being sincere or not, then he chuckled, just in case.

"Yes, well, we all need to look out for each other in Blueberry."

Delia had to curl her fingers into her palms, but then Ted finally spoke up.

"Let's cut the bull, shall we?" He turned and looked

at Delia, the most ingratiating, openly condescending smile on his lean, handsome face.

Delia had always thought Teddy the Letch was the living embodiment of the word *smarm*. *Lounge lizard* also came to mind, his dark eyes being more than a little . . . reptilian.

"You've had your turn milking this town dry, camping out on a vital piece of harbor real estate. The free ride is over. I'm sure you'll land on your feet. Your family seems to have a knack for that. Well, except for your brother."

Delia snapped. She got right up in his face, and to his credit, his eyes did dart a little as her gaze bored into his. "You can take all the little potshots you want at me, though if I were you, I'd have a hard time saying the things you do and looking at myself in the mirror each morning. But to each his own. My brother died a hero, with a silver medal. They don't just hand those out to anyone, Ted. He gave up his life in service to his country, while you sat on your ass in your imagined little fiefdom here and let your father-in-law buy your future for you. So be very, *very* careful—"

Ted lifted his hands in surrender and took a careful step back, but wisely remained silent, though as he gained his space, his expression returned to one of smug righteousness. "I know this is a sensitive time," he said, once he was safely beside the mayor, though Delia could have told him nothing would save his sorry ass if he dared say another word about her family.

"Why don't we head inside," Mayor Davis said with a chuckle, then dabbed at his forehead with the handkerchief he kept in the breast pocket of his suit jacket. "Sun is making us all a little overheated."

"Thank you for the offer, Mayor, but I'm sure I will

hear about your decision and the reasoning behind it when you announce it publicly to everyone in the Cove."

He looked surprised by this, and his gaze darted to Winstock, then to Ted, then back to her. "But, I wasn't planning on—"

"Oh, I would make a plan." Delia took a step back and looked at all three men. "After all, this is a momentous time in Cove history. The day when, after hundreds of years of priding ourselves on our self-sustaining livelihoods, our grit, and fortitude in the face of all adversity, our strength that has always come from banding together, family to family, to see each other through . . . we finally cave and allow the wealthy few to make decisions for us all, and sit by and idly watch as we give in to the greed of the almighty dollar. Although I'm sure you'll find a slightly more palatable way of putting it." She grinned. "Gosh. Think of what an excellent exit speech it will make."

She looked at Ted, her grin still pasted on her face. "Speaking of that, I know you've got your suit all picked out for the swearing-in ceremony, but, word to the wise." She looked him up and down, as if imagining him in that suit, then stared him in the eye and continued. "It might be a day that's more about the swearing part for you." When Ted opened his mouth, she cut him off. "My gran always told me not to count my chickens before the eggs have hatched. She was a wise woman. You're so good at listening to your elders, I'm sure you can appreciate that." She smiled at the three of them and thought she did pretty well considering her clenched jaw. "Good day . . . gentlemen." She said the last word somewhat sarcastically and was certain from the way Brooks frowned that he hadn't missed it.

She managed to make it all way to her car without breaking into a run or breaking down into tears. In fact, her eyes and throat felt dry as dust.

So, that's it then, she thought as she climbed back into her car. *No more diner.* She stared, unseeing, out the front windshield. "Now what?"

Chapter 10

———

Delia pulled into the gravel lot of the diner and parked around the back, but didn't immediately get out. She couldn't remember a single part of her drive there. She was still trying to absorb what had happened. Not the potshots and condescension, but the reality that, at the bottom of it all, the mayor had apparently made up his mind. She had no idea when things would happen, when the diner would close, any of that. She'd have to call . . . someone at the county courthouse. Someone she could talk to without feeling the need for firepower, to get the answers she needed. And she needed that information before she told anyone else.

It was all . . . too much. She didn't know what to do first, or next, but she knew she needed to calm down before she went inside. She imagined she looked like a raging virago at the moment. Red hair and a pale complexion made having any kind of poker face an impossibility. She palmed her cell phone, but didn't punch in the number that had immediately come to mind.

She wanted to talk to him, but was it because she

really thought his listening to her try to put into words what was going on inside her head would actually help . . . or because it was simply an excuse to hear his voice?

She'd learned that apparently there was no level of mortification grand enough to stop the dreams from happening. She'd had one again last night, and felt her face warm as she thought about the fog of pleasure she'd still been feeling when she'd opened up her eyes that morning. Right before she'd blinked wide awake, looked wildly around to make sure she wasn't on the couch, half naked, or that Ford wasn't somewhere in the house, waiting for her to wake up. Again.

No, she shouldn't call him. Besides, now she had her answer. Or one of them anyway. She was going to lose the diner.

She stilled, waiting, as if half expecting to either burst into tears or fly into a fit of rage. But neither of those things happened. *Still numb.*

She didn't look at the diner, she noted. Not directly. Not yet.

There was an avalanche of things that would happen, swiftly, once the axe actually fell. Things that would need to be done, not the least of which was finding a way to explain to her crew and to her customers that they'd no longer have a place to work, or a place to come and eat, pass the time, catch up on the latest Cove gossip and news. No, Delia decided. Mayor Davis could explain to her crew, to her customers, why there would be no Delia's Diner. And she was damn sorry if that made him uncomfortable. She was sure he would get over it while enjoying his free yacht club membership. Or whatever perks Brooks had promised him.

A light rap on her window had her jumping and guiltily snatching her phone up and holding it to her chest. As if she'd been doing something she shouldn't. *Like your sex dreams about Ford are, what, somehow broadcasting themselves on your phone screen?* She turned, scowl at the ready, because she'd just about had it with folks sneaking up on her, only to go still when she saw it was Ford. A frowning Ford.

She instinctively started to lower the window, and then realized that was stupid and just opened the door. He had to step back as she got out.

"I tried to get your attention, but you were really lost in thought," he said by way of apology. "Everything okay?"

"Define 'okay'?" she said sardonically, and then noted the concern on his face, which didn't seem to be aimed at her. "Everything's not okay with you, though. What's up?" It was a relief of almost giddy proportions to put her thoughts apart from her own problems and onto something, someone else. Even if that someone was her sex dreams co-star, Ford Maddox.

"I have to head back to Sandpiper."

"Oh," she said, surprised, though not sure why. She'd known all along his time back in the Cove would be short-lived. In fact, given how much his news disappointed her, it was probably just as well he was leaving sooner than later. "Is something wrong? I was going to call you and tell you to go on back. I mean, we'll talk at some point, about . . . things. But I'm just back from city hall, and it looks like the decision has been made."

The distracted look in Ford's eyes vanished and he focused instantly on her with laserlike precision.

Wow. No wonder he was good at the special forces thing. She felt like he could have pinned her in crosshairs at three hundred yards without needing a scope, his focus was so intense.

"Mayor Davis announced he's accepted Winstock's

offer?" he said shortly. "Did you at least get the chance to talk to him first? What did he have to say?"

"Cami found me and told me Brooks and the mayor were having a meeting, and by the time I got there they were already out front, hearty handshaking and backslapping."

"Did you talk to them anyway?"

Delia's smile was rueful. "We might have exchanged a few words." When Ford's concerned expression didn't change, she said, "Davis wanted to drag me inside and make it all go away over a cup of coffee, but I told him he'd have to announce the yacht club news and, by default, the closing of my diner news to the town himself."

"Good," Ford said, though he didn't look all that appeased. In fact, it looked like it was a good thing he didn't have any firepower on him. At least, she didn't think he did. "When is he going to announce it?"

Delia shook her head. "I have no idea. I left and came back here."

She looked up into those gunmetal gray eyes. "The bottom line is, I'm going to lose my diner. Now I have to figure out what comes next. And . . . I'll need a little time on that. There are a lot of other things that will need to get figured out first." She looked over her shoulder at the back door to the diner's kitchen, and felt the first real knot of dread work its way past the numb. "Like how to tell everyone," she said, the words a little rougher.

Ford took hold of her arms and gently turned her back to face him. "I know you don't want to hear this, but it sounds like you're just giving up without a fight."

"You weren't there, Ford. The decision is made. There's no wiggle room." She felt a little mad coming on. It wasn't as good a feeling as numb, but it was a close second. And it beat the living hell out of despair and anguish, which she was pretty sure were her next stops. "And so much for only offering advice when asked."

His lips twitched, but the concern in his eyes remained. "I said I'd try. And I personally don't care if you fight or not. But it's one of those things you can't go back and do over. You need to make sure you're okay with it."

"I don't think me being okay with it or not being okay with it is an option. I don't get to choose. It's being decided for me."

"Let me put it this way," he said, not backing down in the face of her growing anger. In fact, he remained infuriatingly calm.

Note to self: never argue with an army ranger.

"Will you regret not having at least voiced your opinion?" he asked. "Not knowing for certain that you did everything you possibly could?"

"Oh, I voiced my opinion. But it was after the fact, so while it felt good, it wasn't exactly taking a stand because there was nothing left to stand for. Beyond that, I try not to live with regrets. They're a nonstarter."

"What are you going to do? Start over?"

She raised a palm, lifting that arm out of his grip. Her anger evaporated as her stomach balled up in earnest. "Don't you have some kind of island emergency you need to go deal with?"

"Yes. But you're more important."

Her knees might have gone a little weak at that. Then her face crumpled.

"No crying," he said, an edge of panic in his voice. "I told you I'd be here for you, and I am." He tugged at the arm he still held, pulling her a half step closer.

"Were you really going to call me and tell me to head on back to the island? You just found out you're going to lose your diner and what, you didn't think you could turn to me with that?"

"Turn to you for what?" she said, exasperation and fear lacing the words in equal measure. "It's over. Done. I can't change it. What could you do?"

"This." He pulled her against him, wrapped those big strong arms around her, and held on.

She'd fallen apart on him before, not two days ago in fact. He'd carried her into her house the night before that, too. But she'd already been a wreck in both of those cases, not able to fully appreciate or recognize what it was that was happening. This time she was exceedingly aware. How the sturdy wall of chest felt against her cheek, how the steady thump of his heart was so reassuring, the feel of his arms, banded around the small of her back, supporting her, no matter what. She was also very aware of how her body lined up with his, how his thighs felt pressed against hers, how her hips tucked in perfectly between his. She trembled, and knew the reason for her unsteadiness reached far past the emotional trauma that was most certainly heading her way.

"It works better if you hug me back," he murmured, his lips brushing her ears.

Her knees actually knocked at the velvet gruffness of the words, and the feel of those lips on any part of her anatomy made certain muscles between her thighs clench so tightly she might have moaned a little. Her hands slid around his torso and up his back, where she grabbed fistfuls of plaid flannel and held her face against his chest.

He pulled her in closer, tucked her into the frame

of his body. "Just hold on to me," he said, the words hard to hear over the pounding of her heart. "You can always hold on to me."

She didn't cry. *Thank God.* She just did as he asked and held on, and gradually allowed her body, and perhaps her mind, and more important, her spirit, to be braced, supported by his strength. It had been a long time since she'd been hugged, she realized. She handed hugs out often, but giving comfort was not the same as receiving it. How was it she could have forgotten the unwavering power there was to be had in simply being held in another person's arms?

She felt him run a broad palm over her hair, smoothing it down, keeping the steady harbor breeze from snatching at it. She shivered at the sensations that rippled through her at the pure pleasure that came with having any part of her stroked. She lifted her cheek from his chest, and he cupped the back of her head as she tipped her face up to his. "Thank you," she said, emotion thickening her voice. "I'd forgotten how much good a hug can do."

He ran the side of his thumb along the outline of her cheek. "Me, too."

It took every scrap of willpower she had to keep her gaze on his eyes, and not lower them to his mouth, not lean in, just that tiny bit of space, so she could taste them once more. It had been so very long ago. A lifetime. They weren't even the same people.

And yet, looking into his eyes, he was still exactly the same. Rock steady, instinctively protective, spectacularly focused.

Somewhere in the back of her mind, she knew they were standing in the middle of her parking lot, in broad daylight, in full view of anyone going in or out of the diner. And it was unlikely anyone would think, looking at them, that he'd merely been offering her a hug of comfort and support. She wasn't sure she cared what anyone thought they were doing, but he might.

His gaze dropped to her mouth just as she opened it and said, "You—don't you need to go take care of something on Sandpiper?"

Instead of bringing his gaze immediately back to hers, he let his eyes linger on the movement of her lips for another endless second or two afterward.

And suddenly it didn't feel as if he thought it was just a hug of comfort, either.

Her body shifted of its own accord, coming into fuller contact with his, and a soft gasp escaped her lips when she felt him very specifically twitch in response. "Ford—"

He lifted his gaze slowly, almost lazily back to hers, and her throat went dry as she noted his dilated pupils, and the light of a very different kind of focus entering their dark and stormy depths. He let his thumb slide over her cheekbone and slowly drew it to the corner of her mouth.

She was a split second away from turning her head and nipping the tip of that thumb, pushing them squarely past the edge of the cliff they were both dancing along, when the slap of the diner door had her leaping back as if she'd been scalded by him.

Not exactly an inappropriate comparison, she thought, resisting the urge to fan herself.

Whoever had exited the diner didn't come around the side of the building, but she smoothed her hair, straightened the front of her shirt, and then rubbed her damp palms on the sides of her thighs anyway. "What's wrong—" She had to stop and clear her throat. "What happened? On the island."

He hadn't moved, hadn't blinked, hadn't so much

as turned his head to see who had left the building, and apparently didn't care if they had bleacher seats full of spectators.

Which somehow made the whole moment they'd just shared even hotter. If infernos could be hotter.

"I've got a possible puffling rescue," he said, at length. His tone was normal, maddeningly calm. But the look in those still black eyes was anything but.

"Did you just say . . . puffling?" And how was it possible that made him even hotter?

"We had that nest marked DNS. Did Not Survive," he explained. "But we have a cam on that burrow and I saw movement. So I need to go check it out."

"Okay. I'm sorry. I mean, for the puffling being in dire straits. Your interns are gone now, right?" She paused, and then blurted out, "Do you need any help?" *What on earth are you asking?*

He looked surprised by the offer, but said, "Yes, they have, but that's okay. I just—" Now he did finally break the laser-beam gaze he'd set on her to glance across Harbor Street to the water beyond. "I need to get going if I'm going to beat the tide."

"Yes, I didn't think about that. I guess you do," she said. "How long?"

He looked back to her, lifting an eyebrow in question.

"Will you be gone," she added. *In case I need another hug. Or . . . something.*

"Till tomorrow at the soonest." He didn't add anything else, and she wasn't sure if he wanted her to ask him to come back, or . . . probably his thoughts were on where he should be right now, and that wasn't staring all enigmatically at her.

Now it was her turn to look away, and glance at the diner. "I don't think I'm going to do anything—say anything—right away." She pulled in a breath and let it out slowly, hoping the pheromone fog would dissipate along with it. "I need to make a few calls. I didn't grow up in this town and feed almost every mouth here without making a few contacts. I have a few in the mayor's office, so maybe I can at least get a heads-up on how he's going to handle everything. And when."

"That's good. No more blindsiding." He finally took a step back. "If you're sure—"

"I'm sure. Go, go," she said, and meant it. "I can't take being responsible for letting down everyone here in the Cove *and* a dying puffling. It would put me over the edge."

He smiled briefly at that. "Not everything is on you, you know."

Oh, I know. Her body was already protesting the protracted distance she'd put between it and the very nice other body she'd had it pressed against not minutes before. *Boy, do I know.*

"What can I say? I'm a caretaker by nature."

"There are worse things," he said, appreciation now in his gaze.

That warmed her, too. "Being taken care of wasn't exactly awful, either," she said, offering another smile, this one of thanks.

She got a smile back for her efforts. She had the stray thought that maybe she should do whatever it took to get more of those.

"I have my phone on me," he said. "I won't be near the computer until late tonight." At her frown of confusion, he said, "In case you need to talk." He stopped when she simply stood there, staring at him. "It's that thing two people do when they're trying to work through issues and find solutions. Amongst other things."

"Right," she said, thinking that somehow they'd gone from him popping back suddenly into her life, to being . . . friends. Only, this time, he was giving as much as he was taking. Actually, he was doing more giving than she was. "Yes," she said, still distracted by the realization. "Thanks."

He shook his head, clearly thinking she was a lost cause. "And I thought I was the one cut off from all humanity," he said, but there was a gentle dryness to the jibe. "I can't figure out how it is that you've spent your whole life in the middle of this tight little community, but still managed to stay so far outside the circle when it comes to sharing who you are." He'd clearly meant it as a rhetorical statement, because he turned and walked toward his truck.

She didn't take it as one, though. In fact, for her, it was something of a profound lightbulb moment. "I guess because I didn't think anyone really wanted to know," she said slowly, wondrously, but to herself, not loud enough for him to hear. "My job is to listen to them, not the other way around."

It hadn't always been that way. Growing up she'd had dozens of close friends, confided every last thought, dream, secret, and hope. Hell, Gran used to say she could befriend a kid while handing them a menu and be their bosom buddy by dessert. And she wouldn't have been far off the mark. Later, Delia had dated Henry all through high school and they weren't just sweethearts, but because they'd known each other all their lives, they'd also been the best of friends. If she had a problem, big or small, she'd bend his ear, or Gran's, or Tommy's, whoever was best suited to help her with whatever issue was bothering her.

When had that changed?

The day Henry told you he was going to move to Alaska whether you wanted to go with him or not. That's when.

It had been a long time since Henry had had the power to hurt her, but in that moment, it felt fresh all over again. He hadn't just broken her heart, he'd shattered her trust, and her belief that what they had between them was bigger than, stronger than, anything that happened outside it. Only that wasn't true. Not for Henry. And as she was later forced to admit when she chose her family over her best, most trusted friend and husband . . . not for her, either.

After that she'd opted out of sharing confidences and seeking counsel, not wanting to risk building bonds of trust and respect when they were ephemeral at best. She had her family to turn to when she needed help, needed guidance. Family was the only bond she could trust, the only bond that couldn't be severed.

Only it had been, though not by choice. Tommy was taken from her. Then Gran. From that point on, she'd relied only on herself, because she was the only one left who wouldn't let her down.

She looked at Ford's retreating back, heard his words echo through her mind. *For whatever I may be worth, you've got me.*

And another lightbulb fired off. She'd instinctively pulled back from what he was offering her because, well, he'd vanished before, hadn't he? She shouldn't let herself want what might disappear again. Should she?

But . . . so what if life was ephemeral? So what if there was no guarantee that what was offered today would still stand a month from now, or a year, or a lifetime? Should she go a lifetime excluding herself from something so basic, so pure as a hug of comfort, just because those same arms might not be available sometime later? Did that negate the value of all the hugs that might have come before?

She honestly didn't know the answer to that. With Tommy, with Gran, the answer was clear. She'd treasured every moment with them, every hug, every bit of their support, and her only regret was that she hadn't been fortunate enough to have more of them. But trusting in your family wasn't a choice you made, it was a gift you were given. At least it had been for her.

Ford paused by the door of his truck and looked back at her. Maybe his super-spidey ranger senses told him she'd been staring holes in his back.

People you chose to bond with, however, people you chose to trust, could, in turn, choose not to honor that bond, could willfully betray that trust. Or worse, they could be taken from you altogether through no fault of their own, leaving you with no one to turn to. Except the only person who could never leave you: you.

Was that risk worth the reward? Worth the possible pain and anguish?

She could rely on herself, could trust herself . . . but she couldn't wrap herself up in strong arms, couldn't be an objective sounding board, couldn't push herself when she didn't know she needed pushing.

He turned back and opened the door of his truck.

"Ford!" she blurted out. Then, before she could think better of it, or think at all, she was running across the parking lot toward him.

He was half in the driver's seat when he jerked his head around and slid back out again. "What's wrong? What happened?" He reached for her arms and caught her, steadying her as she all but skidded to a stop in front of him.

"Here," she said, pushing her backpack into his chest. "Hold on to this. I'll be right back."

"What? Wait, what are you doing?"

"I'm coming with you. I just need to tell Peg."

"Coming with—why?"

She leaned past him, through the open door of his truck and tossed her cell phone on the passenger seat. "Two minutes," she told him as she maneuvered herself out of his grasp; then she was running back across the parking lot.

"Delia!" he called out. "Dee!"

She only realized she was grinning like a loon when she looked back over her shoulder. "I'm taking you up on that offer."

"What offer?"

She turned and trotted backwards a few steps. "To be my friend." Her grin split her face wide. "I'm officially stepping inside the circle."

Chapter 11

Ford bumped the boat against the dock and opened his mouth to call to Delia to step back so she wouldn't get her fingers smashed against the piling, but she already had the nylon line looped and in her hand. She tied off neatly and expertly, so he stepped aft to do the same.

He lifted her backpack off the console and handed it to her as he met her by the ladder that led up to the dock. "I guess growing up on the coast, you've done that a time or two."

She smiled. "Once or twice. Been a long time, though. Guess it's like riding a bike. Or sailing a boat."

He reached to help her up the ladder, but she slung the pack over her shoulder and was halfway up before he could pocket the keys to the boat. "Well, okay then," he murmured. He grabbed the small cooler Blue had stowed on the boat for him, along with a gear bag, and then climbed up after her.

"What do you need to do first?" she asked anxiously, as he stepped onto the dock next to her. She was already wearing one of his old sweatshirts, which hung down to mid-thigh. Fortunately she was also wearing jeans rather than slacks, although he wasn't too sure how her shoes would fare on the rocks.

"Keep the sweatshirt," he told her. "And put this on." He slid two hard hats out of the gear bag, handed one to her, and popped the second one on his own head.

She eyed the green plastic helmet, clearly confused. "Just how deep are the puffin nesting burrows?"

"It's not to protect you from what's underground, but what's overhead."

She looked up and he snatched the helmet back and stuck it on her head about a second before she ducked, a laugh spluttering from her as the first splat hit the dock beside her. "Holy cow. I mean, I saw that there were a bunch of birds flying around as we were heading into the cove here, but—is it always like this?" She chanced a half glance upward.

Ford didn't have to look up; he knew the sky overhead was filled with a variety of seabirds. Dozens and dozens of them. "No," he said. "Over most of the summer, it's worse. Far worse." He smiled briefly. "Or better, depending on your perspective."

"Right," she said. "A good migratory news, bad poop news kinda deal."

He let out a short chuckle. "More or less. Hold on." He climbed back down to the boat and pulled a pair of scuffed-up black wellies from one of the storage bins. He climbed up till he could toss them on the deck next to her. "Might want to slide your feet in those."

She tugged them on over her thin-soled leather flats as he climbed the rest of the way to the dock. "So, this wouldn't be considered a lot?" she asked. "Birds, I mean." She gestured overhead as she hopped on one foot to get the other all the way into the heel of the boot.

He steadied her, then reached down and gave the loops on the sides a good tug, and her heel popped right in. "Well, it will dwindle pretty dramatically come winter, but there's still a good number, and we get drive-bys of other species who stop off on their way south over the next few months. The arctic migratory birds, like the Atlantic puffin, only come on land once a year, for ten weeks or so each summer, for the sole purpose of procreating. Once that's done, succeed or fail, they head back out to sea for the oncoming winter season."

"And they don't go on land again until . . . the next summer? At all? Really?"

"Really. That's why it's such a challenge to gather information about them. They spend the bulk of their time out to sea in some pretty unforgiving areas of the world. Makes it difficult to establish range, much less various behavioral patterns."

"I would guess so. I had no idea. Even the babies go out to sea?"

"Yep. And they don't come back until they're old enough to breed. A few years at least. They spend most or all of that time solo."

Delia made a sad face. "Poor pufflings."

He smiled briefly. "It's just how they roll. And float. And fly. Makes finding a good nesting ground that much more important."

"They all leave at the same time?"

"You mean the different breeds? No. It turned cooler earlier than usual, so many of them fledged earlier this year. Left the nest earlier," he explained. "The last of the razorbills and puffins left a few weeks ago—

well, except for one, apparently. There are still a few guillemots waiting to fledge, but none with cams on them. They don't migrate south, so getting them off island is not a big concern. I'll check on them as well."

"I thought you said they were all arctic."

"Not all. The puffins are. They winter up in and around the Arctic Circle. But other seabirds, like the common terns, for instance, head down to South America, and the arctic terns go all the way to Antarctica."

"Seriously? Why?" She shot him a wry grin and adopted a New York accent. "Couldn't they just winter in Miami, then come back to Maine in the summer, get a nice condo on the beach?" When he rolled his eyes, her grin only widened, but her next question was serious. "Do they come all the way from Antarctica to Maine every summer?"

He nodded. "When they're old enough to breed, yes. Most will come back to whatever place they were born. It's instinctive."

"You're like the Jacques Cousteau of birds. Jacques Crusoe Dolittle."

She looked entirely too pleased with herself. He just shook his head, took her elbow, and guided her down the long pier toward the boulder-strewn shoreline. But a smile was hovering, all the same.

"And the babies, what do they do when their parents fly off?"

"Depends on the species. Pufflings go solo. Terns follow their parents."

She goggled. "All the way to Antarctica? But didn't they just get their feathers in? How can their little wings do that?"

"Well, they either migrate or perish. Most of the chicks fledge at night to keep the chances of predators to a minimum, but it also makes getting out to sea a bit trickier." He walked down the ramp that sloped to shore at the end of the dock. Then he held up a hand to help her navigate the few steps over the rocks, before they both jumped down to the scrub grass and undergrowth that edged a thin line between boulders and forest. There was no beach or sand.

He started down the trail that would lead eventually to the tree house. Delia had to walk a little faster to keep up with his long-legged stride, but Ford saw the hand she waved in front of her face. "I don't want to hear the tragic stories about the ones that don't make it. I mean, I get that it happens, more often than is good, or you wouldn't be out here studying them, but that's why I'm a cook and not a scientist."

He paused, turned, and she stopped and looked up at him, her hard hat sliding down over her forehead when she did. His lips curved as he bumped the brim back up again, until those startlingly blue eyes of hers met his once again.

"I'm such a fashion plate, I know," she said, dryly. She struck a pose. "Seriously, you're so lucky. You always manage to see me looking my absolute hottest."

"You do the helmet proud," he said, and meant it. With her red curls, still a bit wild from the boat ride, sticking out from under the band of the hard hat, all curling and whipping around in the breeze, and the pink in her cheeks from the wind, her eyes the deep blue of the ocean in Maine, and that wry smile curving her lips . . . he found her utterly captivating. "You do know that there might not be a Disney ending to our little trip out here."

She nodded, putting on a brave face and giving him a little salute, even as her bottom lip stuck out in that little pout. "Aye, aye, captain. I know."

His gaze dipped to that pout, and got all hung up there. He had the sudden, intense, and clearly insane desire to lean down and nip the lush little bow of her bottom lip. The urge was so strong, and caught him so off guard, he actually took a full step back. "Just . . . fair warning," he said, more gruffly than necessary, and then continued on down the dock.

It was the damn dreams, he thought. She never should have told him about that. He'd spent an inordinate amount of time thinking about it or, more to the point, forcing himself not to think about it. "The male razorbills will actually teach their young to fish," he said, inanely, groping for any topic to get him off his current mental track.

She was silent for a moment, and then asked, "Are the males involved like that with all of the species?"

Relieved, he said, more easily, "Pretty much. The same pairs will return and mate every season."

"Aw," she said, "I love that."

"Good pairs who work well together have a better chance of producing healthy chicks."

"Such a romantic," she said sardonically. "What happens if something happens to one of them? Do they mate for life?"

He shook his head. "If one mate doesn't return, the other will eventually find a new partner, though usually not that first season. Both birds take responsibility for the chick, even before it's hatched."

"So they just have one?"

He relaxed further, back in his element, and warmed to the subject. "Most of the smaller seabird species, yes. But some of the bigger species have more. Osprey, eagles, gulls to name a few. The black-backed gull is the world's largest, and a major predator for the alcids."

"El Cids? What, like little Charlton Hestons and Sophia Lorens"—she snapped her fingers over her head as if she had castanets and did a little dance in her rubber-boot-clad feet—"Castilian knights of the eleventh century kind of thing?" she said, with a heavy Spanish accent.

"Alcid," he enunciated, but he chuckled all the same. "Means burrowing seabirds."

"Ah," she said, her smile still wry, as she dropped her arms and resumed her place behind him when the trail narrowed. "What do you do about that? The predators, I mean."

"Nothing. It's part of the life cycle. But we observe, monitor the behaviors and general numbers." Steering the conversation away from the predator aspect, he paused and pointed toward a tumble of rocks just down the coast. "We have other guests, too."

Her face brightened. "Harbor seals! I love them," she said. "Their pups are adorable."

"Most will head south for the winter, some only as far as Long Island; some will go as far south as the Carolinas. And a few hang out here year-round."

"All the way out here?"

He nodded. "A few might head in closer to land, but generally they prefer more remote, less populated locations. Safer that way. Grey northern seals will start showing up over the winter months and have their pups. There are a few well-established bald eagle nests, too."

"So, it's not just what's happening in the summer," she said. "I didn't realize how year-round the life cycle was out here."

"Well, most of the work we do takes place over the summer months with the seabird nesting, but yes, being out here all year does afford me the opportunity to observe the migratory and breeding patterns of a number of other species, too."

The trail had wound between the boulder-strewn shoreline and the edge of the pine forest, but now took a turn inward. Once they stepped in among the thick stand of tall pines, he took her helmet off and tucked it back in the gear bag, along with his own. "Keep the boots on; you'll need them to navigate the rocks when we get to the other side."

She reached up self-consciously and fluffed at the wild tumble of curls. "Helmet hair." She rolled her eyes. "It just gets better and better."

"Your hair is beautiful." He'd spoken without thinking, simply being honest, but when her eyes widened a bit and her wind-pinkened cheeks took on a slightly deeper shade, he suddenly felt awkward. "Always does," he added, lamely. "Look good, I mean." *Stop talking, start walking.*

"Why, thank you kindly, Dr. Maddox," she said, adopting a fluttery Southern accent this time.

He tossed a "give me a break" look over his shoulder, but she just laughed. And God help him, he loved that laugh of hers, rich and full, without a lick of self-consciousness. It bordered just on the edge of brassy but was deep enough to be sexy as hell. It had always caught at him, but at the moment, it made the fit of his khakis a bit uncomfortable, which in turn made him uncomfortable. Seriously, he wished to hell she'd never mentioned those damn dreams. *Don't worry, I won't jump you.*

Only it wasn't her he was worried about doing the jumping. "Don't you already know a lot of this stuff?" he asked, forcing his brain back to the topic at hand.

The one he was comfortable with, at any rate. "Growing up here, I'd think you'd know most of this by osmosis."

"You'd think so, but no, not really. Not in that kind of detail, anyway. I grew up feeding fishermen, and I was busy helping Gran, then, later on running my own place, so I never really get on the water much myself. And the fishermen weren't talking about migratory patterns and breeding habits of seabirds." Her voice dropped to a more sultry tone. "I could tell you more than you want to know about the mating habits of lobsters and eels, though. If you're interested."

The path had widened a bit and she'd caught up to him. He glanced down in time to see her bat her eyelashes at him, and chuckled. He'd forgotten how outrageous and funny she could be, always a laugh and a smile on her animated face. She hadn't been like that since he'd come back to try to help her, and it was good to see the real Dee finally coming back out to play. "Thanks, but I think I'll leave that to the marine biologists."

"Suit yourself," she said. "It's pretty steamy stuff. Especially the lobsters." She nudged him with her elbow. "Get it, steamed? Lobsters? Diner humor. I crack myself up."

He let out a short laugh. "You need to get out more."

"You said it, sailor," she replied, only more to herself than him.

"You tied up the boat like you grew up on one. You've obviously spent some time on the water."

"I sailed in the summers when I was younger, school age, but that's it, really. I mean, I know the general nature stuff we all learned in school, and what I see with my own eyes around our docks. We have those same birds hovering all over the harbor, but—" She gestured back toward the rocky shoreline, now hidden from view by the trees, and laughed. "Nothing like that."

"You've never been out here? What about the other islands in the bay?"

She shook her head again, and shrugged. "Like I said. Busy." She smiled. "As my Gran used to say, 'I clean fish, I cook fish, so someone else can do the catching. Keeps us all in business that way.' Well, that's ditto for me."

"Makes sense." Ford continued to lead the way deeper into the woods. The trail moved upward toward the higher ground that formed the central part of the heart-shaped island. The footpath was still clearly visible, but that would change once the pine needles started to carpet the forest floor, and then the snow would come and pile on top of them. That was another month or two away still. He hoped.

They fell into a companionable silence, and his thoughts went back to the boat ride out. There had been no conversation then. His old trawler was loud and the ride had been bumpy over choppy waves. He'd manned the boat, so Delia had gone up and perched herself on the foredeck. He'd watched the wind whip her red curls into a wild mass as she turned her fair face toward the wind. She'd looked all but lost in the folds of his old green university hoodie.

She'd looked contemplative as they'd chugged out of the inner harbor and he'd left her to her thoughts. He figured she was having second thoughts about her impulsive decision to join him. He still didn't know what had possessed her to do that. Escape? She'd said she was stepping inside the circle, accepting that she needed a friend, needed to talk. Maybe that was all it was. A chance to get away from everything, to clear her head and get a handle on what she was going to do next.

He, of all people, could respect the need to do that. *Hell, you've turned it into an art form.*

It had been closer to five minutes than the two she'd promised, but when she'd come running back across the parking lot, she hadn't looked upset. In fact, she'd been smiling. The kind of smile he hadn't seen since their little midnight reunion in her kitchen. She'd said "Shotgun!" as she climbed into the passenger seat and pulled on her seat belt, and he hadn't had the heart to question what the hell she was doing. When he'd asked about her getting coverage at the diner, she'd told him that Peg would call a few of the local girls who waited tables for Delia in the summer, fairly certain at least one of them would be happy to earn the extra pocket change now that the high season was over. Delia had made a call on their way to where he'd docked his boat at Blue's and secured coverage for kitchen duty for the early morning crowd. She assumed they'd be back tomorrow and that was likely the case, but if he felt he needed to stay on Sandpiper longer, he would do that, and he'd told her so. She'd shrugged and said she'd deal with that if it happened.

He hadn't asked her if she was concerned that her sudden absence would create an alarming buzz among her regulars. He hadn't asked her what would happen if Mayor Davis chose that afternoon to announce his decision while she was a forty-five-minute boat ride away. She was a grown woman who could make her own choices. That, and when they'd cleared the inner harbor and he'd opened the engines up, he'd watched the tension roll right out of her shoulders and off her back. Didn't matter how hard the boat bottomed out after cresting the heavier rolls, or that the salty sea spray was making her hair and her hoodie damp: She grinned like a kid on holiday.

When was the last time she'd done something as simple as take a boat ride? he'd wondered. Given their brief conversation since landing, he'd guess a very long time. That had surprised him, but maybe it shouldn't have. Other than Tommy's funeral, and the night that had followed, every single moment he'd spent with her in Blueberry Cove had been while she was working. Hell, he'd had to ambush her at her house in the middle of the night just to get a minute alone with her. He'd never really thought about that, assuming, he supposed, that she must take time off to do something other than run the diner, but if she did, he'd never witnessed it. But then, he'd been wrapped up in his own stuff.

He recalled the comments he'd overheard when he'd stopped in at the diner, about Delia and Langston de-Vry being an item. Grace had made a point of saying they were merely friends, but surely someone of Langston's resources could have wooed Delia out for an afternoon sail. Or a hop across the pond for dinner in Paris, for that matter. His pockets were that deep.

Given the sobbing heap of exhaustion she'd been in his arms in the shower, though, if deVry had gotten her to take any kind of occasional break, it hadn't made much of a dent in her work routine. It was no wonder that Winstock's pulling the rug out from under her diner had turned her world a bit more upside down than folks really understood. Something like that would have to make a person take stock, question what it was she wanted, reassess her life. And she'd already been taking stock, apparently. She'd alluded to that by mentioning that Grace's coming to the Cove had been when she'd started dreaming about him.

He nimbly sidestepped a protruding tree root at the last second, and forced his mind away from that part. Again. She'd been more carefree, more, well, more herself, when he'd come back to Maine all those years ago. He had to wonder how long she'd been so tense, so emotional, so exhausted.

For the moment, he decided it was enough that being here on the island, away from the Cove, had lightened her up immeasurably. He knew a short boat ride wasn't going to fix anything, but for now, it was a start.

"What is the plan?" she asked, breaking the long silence. "For the baby puffin, I mean."

He lifted the cooler he carried. "Blue packed away some fresh herring for me. That's high on their preferred diet menu. I'll go out to the burrow and check, firsthand, see how it's doing. I can put fish in the burrow, and then monitor to see if the chick eats. If it appears too weak for that, then I can pull it out, hand-feed, take more direct care."

"You can do that? I mean, it won't screw up its instincts, or whatever, to go back to sea?"

"I'll release it to sea myself, when it's ready."

"So, you've done this before."

"Every season there are some who simply don't make it out past the rocks and into the sea without the tides or waves thumping them back up on the rocks, and sometimes they're too weak to attempt it again. My interns will judge if they're able to be saved, or if an attempt should be made, and in some cases, they have done that."

"Isn't that interfering with the cycle?"

"Yes, but puffins in particular have suffered a decline in recent years and so if the chick has made it as far as fledging, and it just needs a little nudge to get back out there, then if we can, we will. We won't interfere beyond that though, as far as predators who may be—"

She lifted a hand. "Let me have my Disney visual, okay? You releasing the chick into the wild, and it flapping its way to freedom and a life of happiness and herrings."

Ford grinned. "Well, the ones that do make it wouldn't have otherwise. Just think of it that way."

She smiled up at him. "I like that way."

He caught himself lifting his hand to push away a stray curl that had caught on the tip of her eyelashes. The bay breezes still managed to find their way through the tall pines. It was a simple gesture, one a friend would do for a friend. But the fact that he caught himself, that he'd paused, thought about it, told him more than he wanted to know about what had motivated him. He wanted to touch her. And, God help him, he was dying to taste her.

He'd held her naked against his body not forty-eight hours earlier and had not a single recollection of what she'd felt like. The time spent under that hot shower had been fraught with a lot of things, a lot of racing thoughts, but her being naked wasn't one of them. Now he might as well be fifteen again and a twisted mass of raging hormones. Or twenty-three, he thought darkly, bringing home the body of the battle buddy who'd died in his arms . . . then drowning his grief in the soft, willing, and oh-so-pliant body of his slain buddy's sister. Even making himself think about it like that couldn't taint the memory of that night. Nothing ever would. It had been mutually consented to, and mutually therapeutic. He hadn't regretted it then, or a single day since. For a long time, he'd felt like she'd saved him that night, proving to him that beauty and kindness, passion and pleasure could indeed coexist in a world that was also harsh, brutally unfair, and deadly. Maybe he still did.

His thoughts were all caught up in the past as he tried to put the feelings he was having now in some kind of perspective that would make it easier to deal with her being in such close proximity. Out in the middle of nowhere. Alone. On an island. His goddamn island. So he wasn't thinking, wasn't aware, when he walked into the clearing below his tree house, that she'd stumbled to a stop behind him, gaping upward at his home in the sky, until she gasped.

"That's . . . incredible."

Ford stopped and looked back to where Delia stood at the edge of the clearing.

"I mean, I knew you'd built a tree house, but I guess I thought, well, I don't know that I thought anything, really. Not specifically." She took slow steps forward, her face still upturned, as she spun in a circle, taking in the octagonal main structure with the pointed dome roof, the ladders and rope that provided access from deck to ground, then on to the rope and plank bridges and pierlike walkways that connected the main structure to various outbuildings built around and supported by other nearby trees. "But I definitely didn't picture anything like this." She finally stopped and lowered her wide-eyed gaze to his.

Her gaze grew wider still when he put down the cooler and gear bag and said, "Wait here. I need to grab my notebook for that burrow," and then took the fastest way up, which was hand-over-hand on the heavy knotted rope.

He glanced down as he levered his legs onto the

deck platform in time to see a grin split her pretty features. He swore he could see her eyes sparkle all the way from where he stood.

Her expression was one of pure delight. "My God, Ford," she called up to him. "You're not just Cousteau-Crusoe-Dolittle, you're freaking Tarzan!"

Chapter 12

Barely two minutes after he'd disappeared inside, he shimmied back down, dropping to the ground in an easy crouch once he was about five feet from it, then quickly scooped up the cooler and gear bag before turning to face her. The late summer sun speared down between the towering pines, highlighting the streaks of blond in his shaggy brown hair, the shadow of a beard on his cheeks and chin, while casting those gray eyes of his in shadow. Which was apt given he was a man made of shadows, Delia thought.

He'd changed into old jeans that hung low on his hips and showcased his long, leanly muscled legs just like God and Levi Strauss had intended. What she'd come to think of his standard uniform of faded tee and plaid jacket emphasized his flat stomach and broad shoulders. The wire rim glasses he'd shoved in the chest pocket along with a small, dog-eared, rolled-up spiral notebook were paired with aviator sunglasses dangling on the front. Big hands gripped the cooler, stocked with food for the endangered little puffling, and the black canvas duffel, stuffed with survival gear for adults. She'd teased him about those iconic hero labels, but damn if he didn't embody every single one of them. She could toss in Indiana Jones and Mac-Gyver while she was at it.

He stood there with his amazing tree fort lair, built by his own two hands, dominating the airspace over their heads, yet not diminishing his stature one iota. If anything, the whole setting only served to enhance it. He was the very embodiment of survivalist doc. All he needed was a big knife sheathed on his belt and a stethoscope hanging from around his neck. And she wasn't too sure that both items weren't on his person somewhere.

Delia's heart pounded and her palms grew damp. The enormity of the landscape that towered over them, dwarfing them, evaporated from her conscious awareness like so much sea mist, leaving only the two of them, and the pine-needle-strewn carpet that stretched between them.

She wanted to stay in that moment, inside that fantasy bubble, where the need to have him was so keen, so sharp, it heightened every nerve ending to a crackling snap. Hell, even her pores ached for him. What made the moment so intense, so pulse-pounding, was that she could swear the expression on his face mirrored her own need. *Such a wonderful fantasy bubble. Please let me keep it.*

She'd known even as she'd called shotgun that impulsively getting on Ford's boat like a borderline stowaway was the most irresponsible thing she'd done in a very long time. Maybe ever. She had no business leaving the diner. Most especially not now, with Davis's announcement bomb ready to drop at any moment. She'd told Peg. She had to do that much. The older woman wasn't surprised, and had taken the news in stride, which Delia supposed shouldn't have surprised her, either. Peg was as stalwart as they came, and she'd seen the writing on the wall, too. What had surprised Delia was when Peg had pulled her in for a short, fierce hug, then gruffly told Delia to go off and do what she had to do, promising she'd hold down the fort.

"About time you looked after yourself," she'd said. "Past time, you ask me."

Two hugs in the span of ten minutes and both had rocked Delia in different ways. She'd paused at the door, and Peg had threatened to chase her out of the kitchen with a butcher knife. Delia wasn't so certain the older woman wouldn't have done exactly that, which was why she'd been grinning as she hotfooted it out of the back door. That didn't mean she hadn't spent every minute of the boat ride out worrying that she should never have put Peg in that position in the first place. She'd picked pretty much the most horrible time ever to essentially run away from home.

The thing was . . . it felt freaking awesome. Free. Away. Solo. She could exist inside a single moment, this exquisite moment for instance, without a dozen other somethings or someones simultaneously clamoring for her attention. Standing in the woods, staring at Indiana Maddox there, was its own little ecstasy. *Why in the world don't you do this more often?*

Hell, maybe if she had, she wouldn't be so screwed up in the head about her diner, about . . . well, about her whole life.

"Well, if you're planning on playing doctor's assistant, then we need to keep moving," he said. "The puffin burrows are on the far side." He lifted the gear bag to indicate where the trail picked up just beyond the cleared forest floor beneath his treetop home.

She looked to where he pointed, then back at him,

and felt the bubble pop and fizzle away. *Ah, well, that's what fantasies are, after all, right? Just so much sea mist.*

"Thanks, I'd like that," she said, half wishing the mist would return. Okay, maybe more than half. She forced her gaze away from him and back upward once more. "After we're done, will you show me the place? I can't believe you built this. Hell, I can't believe you even imagined this."

She lowered her gaze and found him still staring at her, not all that differently than she'd imagined him looking at her during her little fantasy bubble moment. *Must be a trick of the sunlight.* But tell that to her pulse rate. "Of course, I'm going to have to use an alternate access route." She lifted her arms and flexed. "I've got some pretty good girl arms, but that?" She pointed to the knotted rope he'd climbed like he was part marmoset. "Would be embarrassing. I've managed to embarrass myself quite enough in front of you lately, so I'll just take the long way up, if that's okay."

"Sure," he said, but it wasn't the heartiest of assents. In fact, it seemed as if he'd opted to go with the polite response, meaning what he'd wanted to say was no. The inscrutable expression was back, too.

Double yay.

He turned and crossed to where the trail picked up, and then continued on without waiting to see if she followed. She should have been annoyed at the sudden lack of manners, but it wasn't as if she'd been invited on this little scouting trip. So she hustled and caught up with him, but not before taking one last look back at Swiss Family Robinson Wonderland. She wouldn't have thought he had a romantic bone in his body. And while it was true that the overall design was functional in appearance without any frou-frou design-y elements, which definitely reflected the Ford

Maddox she knew, it seemed to her that a person didn't—couldn't—dream up a place like that unless they had a little dash of romance and a healthy dollop of wonder in their soul.

A shame he keeps that all to himself.

The forest ended rather abruptly and she all but burst from deep shadows to blazing sunlight. She immediately bracketed her forehead with her palm to cut the glare caused by the beams of sun bouncing off the deep blue waters of Pelican Bay. Her breath caught as she looked left, then to her right, and realized they stood on a promontory of sorts, a spit of grass and rocky ground that comprised the point of the heart-shaped island. The view was stunning. The coastline angled back on either side of them, and every bit of it as far as she could see was made up of a steep tumble of boulders and rocks, then water. No beach or sand on this side, either.

"It's beautiful," she said, lowering her hand as a few clouds drifted by and blocked the sunlight. She took another one of those freedom moments to simply enjoy the salty tang of sea spray as it misted her face, the feeling of the much stronger sea breezes whipping her hair into a frenzy. Remembering, suddenly, the last time she'd been out in the open on the island, she abruptly ducked her head and glanced up. "Helmets?"

"Not on this side, not now anyway," he said, glancing back from the spot where he stood, a few feet in front of her, right at the edge of the hard-packed dirt ground before it became a surge of rock.

He took her breath away, standing there with that amazing backdrop framing him. His expression was all business now as he scanned the shoreline and she shamelessly took the opportunity to enjoy scanning him.

"Where do the puffins burrow?" she asked, as she came to stand next to him. His taller, broader frame blocked the wind, but the lack of direct sunlight due to the cloud cover still left her feeling a chill, even with the sweatshirt on.

He pointed to the rocky ledges and jumbles of rock on either side of them, up above the waterline. "They like crevasses and tucked-away places to have their chicks. Helps to protect against elements and predators."

"Also against invading humans, I'm guessing. Pretty inaccessible unless you can fly in for a landing." She wrapped her arms around her waist, willing the clouds to pass. It wasn't surprising how much chillier it was out in the middle of the bay, but there was a marked difference even between this side and the side of the island where they'd landed. Probably because the natural cove created by the top of the heart provided it with a bit of protection from the elements. "How can you tell where the burrows are?"

"They tend to use the same ones every year, but we also keep a lookout when the birds first come in, to see if we spot comings and goings from any new locations." He pointed again. "See the pink and orange marks on some of the rocks? Those are our marks, so we know where each burrow is."

Delia immediately saw the spray-painted numbers and scanned the ledges and tumbles for more. "There's a lot of them," she said, surprised.

"Not all puffins. Some are razorbills, guillemots. The terns like the grasses, and overgrowth, so they prefer to nest around the southerly turn of the island coastline, where there is a wider band of growth between rocks and trees."

"So many different species, and so spread out. I

don't know how you keep up with it all," she said, her teeth just on the edge of chattering now. One of the downsides of playing stowaway was the lack of time to prepare for the potential consequences of said stowage. Thank goodness he'd had the hoodie to loan her or she'd be more frozen than the herring Blue had packed in that cooler.

"At times, neither do I," he replied, setting the cooler down, pulling his notebook out, and sliding free the pen that he'd tucked in the coils. "Thank God for enthusiastic interns with indefatigable levels of energy." He'd slipped his glasses on and was quickly thumbing through the notebook, keeping it half curled to prevent the wind from catching the pages.

He was all scientist now, and even sexier for it. PhD brains and military brawn. *Professor Rambo. Lethal, lethal combination, that,* she thought, mentally fanning herself.

In an effort to keep from jumping him where he stood, she nudged him with her elbow, and went for friendly. "You say that like you're ancient."

"Spend a summer crawling around on these boulders and then report back to me on that." He glanced down, a surprising hint of dry amusement in his expression, given how distracted he seemed.

Her gaze might have drifted to said mouth, lingering there for a moment longer than was wise. So much for the friendly banter remedy.

He looked away first, back to his notes, though he suddenly seemed to have lost his place and spent a few moments flipping pages forward, then back again.

She cleared the sudden dryness from her throat, and shifted her gaze back to the rocky tumble. "Where is the burrow with the chick?"

He continued consulting his notes, then motioned

to his right. "Number thirty-two. Orange paint. The pair using that burrow have been here every year since Claude—Dr. Pelletier—started monitoring the island and have successfully fledged a chick in all but two of those seasons, which is a remarkable statistic. The final notes from the interns monitoring that burrow say that their chick seemed to do well this season. It wasn't one that was banded so I don't have more specific data. Just that it didn't make it to fledging. It's not surprising, even given their success rate."

"Is that common? I mean, do you go in after the fact and do any kind of, whatever they call a bird autopsy?"

"If there's been a dramatic change in fledging that doesn't seem related to weather or food supply, yes, we have. But in general—"

"You let nature takes its course," she finished for him. "So, some . . . thing will come along and . . . you know."

He looked to her again, all wire rim glasses and stubble and lumberjack plaid jacket. *Oh, my.* "It's the life cycle. Even predators have to eat. All creatures are hunting something for their food supply."

"I know, you're right, just . . ." She rubbed at her arms, not wanting to think about anything called a puffling being snatched out of its nest. "So, what do we do now?"

"My notes say the parents hadn't left the nest as yet when the last interns were done for the season, but there had been no activity with the chick for the previous forty-eight hours that they could see on the monitor. Since both parents were still actively attending the nest, they didn't interfere. That's why the monitor was still active, but with the chick marked DNS, I wasn't watching it closely."

Because he'd been called in to watch her closely,

she thought, feeling even more miserable about that if it cost some poor baby puffball its life. "But you didn't see the parents on the monitor?"

He shook his head. "I'm pretty sure they're gone. The fact that they stayed after their chick passed isn't abnormal. Some parents will still attend a nest even after a chick has successfully fledged." He paused, looked at his notes again.

She knew he was probably thinking the same thing she was thinking. "I'm sorry," she said. "If your coming back to Blueberry took you away from the final nest checks, or whatever it is you do. I feel awful if—"

"I made the decision to come back," he said, cutting her off. "And let's shelve the rest until I get out there and see what's going on."

"Can I help? Or will I just get in the way?"

"The tide is out, which gives us a few more paths in to the burrow that aren't as strenuous as having to go down over the boulders from the edge where solid ground meets rock." He looked down at her feet. "You going to be okay in those?"

"These feet haven't let me down yet."

He nodded, but still looked concerned. "Just be careful, pick your spots. There's a lot of kelp and sea-weed on the rocks exposed by low tide, and it's very slippery."

She smiled up at him. "I might not have spent much time on the water as a kid, but I did spend my fair share climbing all over the shoreline of Blueberry Cove, including rocks, boulders, beach, in low tide, frozen winter crust, you name it. Of course, in my case, there was usually food involved. Clams, blueberries." She could see by his expression he wasn't convinced and put a hand on his arm. "You saw me tie off the boat, right? Some skills you don't forget. If I feel like I can't keep up, I won't hold you back waiting for me, I promise. Deal?"

"Deal," he said. He opened the cooler and took out a short stack of fresh herring, then stuck them in the pocket of his jacket. He followed her gaze to his pockets, and the barely concealed grimace. "Pufflings don't have a five-second rule," he said.

"I wasn't thinking so much about the puffling as the jacket."

He shrugged. "That's what washing machines are for."

"Remind me if we're ever stuck using the same one to do my stuff separately."

He'd already begun making his way over boulders and down closer to the exposed sea bottom. "Because diner owners never get anything on their clothes," he shot back over his shoulder. "I'm thinking a little herring slime would be nothing compared to what you come home with."

She laughed at that. "Point to you. I guess I wasn't thinking about my work clothes when I said that."

He shot her a fast glance over his shoulder, and then paused to reach a hand back and help her jump down from one particularly large rock. "I wasn't aware you had any other kind."

She could feel the warmth in her cheeks, so she gave him an exaggerated cheeky smile, and said, "I tend to keep what I wear under my aprons in a separate wash load. That's all I'm sayin'."

His lips twitched at that, but he quickly turned back to the matter at hand. He'd slung the gear bag over his back with the strap diagonally across his chest, freeing up his hands to help with balance. She wasn't carrying anything and still wasn't close to half as graceful in her maneuvers as he was. "So, maybe some bikes take a little bit of getting used to when you get back on them again," she muttered under her breath, huffing and puffing slightly as she scrambled and crawled.

He glanced back again, and paused when he saw she was quite a bit behind him, but she waved him off. "I'll catch up eventually. I'm fine. Just trying not to break anything I might need later," she called out good-naturedly.

He paused for another second, observed her less-than-graceful clamber over a few more boulders, then apparently satisfied she wasn't going to break her neck, he continued. She smiled in relief, liking that he credited her with being able to take care of herself. *Not that you mind it too much when he steps in to help if he thinks you can't.*

From the promontory the orange-painted burrow number hadn't looked all that far away, but she felt as if she'd been scrambling up and down rocks forever and it was still a ways off. She turned around at one point, to use the divots in a smooth boulder as handholds, as there was no other down route from that particular rock, only to turn around . . . and find that Ford was nowhere to be seen. How was that possible? They were, for all intents and purposes, at sea level, and the boulders were not so big that she couldn't see his tall frame more often than not.

She waited a moment, but he didn't magically reappear. She scanned the rocks again to orient herself, looking for the orange-painted number thirty-two, and didn't see that, either. "Don't panic. It's not like they both got beamed up or something."

Then she saw movement. To be exact, she saw Ford's

ass. Wriggling. He was on his belly, shimmying over the edge of a rock, she assumed to get down as far into the crevasse where the burrow was as he could, so he could look inside. His body had been blocking her view of the painted number and his clothes made him sort of blend in with his surroundings. "Pretty nice ass, though, as it turns out," she murmured, thinking she'd spent so much time focused on the front side, she'd somehow missed a very fine backside. "And you shouldn't be thinking about either of his sides. Focus, for God's sake."

She continued her quest to reach the burrow while keeping all of her bones and joints still functioning properly. How had he scampered over them as quickly as he had? And he was older than she was. *And you thought running your own butt off while taking care of an entire diner's worth of people was hard work.*

When she finally reached him, she wasn't sure whether to say something so she wouldn't startle him, or if speaking would somehow disturb the poor chick.

Then he was edging backwards, back out of the crevasse he'd been leaning half into, and she scrambled out of his way. Once out, he rolled over and sat up. He held some kind of device on the end of a wire, which was attached to a cord that ran into some other device she now saw sticking half out of the gear bag he'd propped on the rocks.

"So? What did you find?"

"I poked the camera in first," he said, waving the wandlike device in his hand, "and we do have a live chick, only not doing all that well at the moment."

Her expression had brightened and collapsed within seconds of each other as he finished the sentence. "So, what do you do next?"

"It's managed to get its foot wedged between two of the rocks. I'm not sure what kind of damage it's done to itself trying to get unstuck, but it's worn itself out."

"Didn't anyone see it flailing or something, on the cam?"

"The cam doesn't expose every inch of the burrow, and the chick is on its side, below the rock where the cam is positioned, so movement was only seen when part of the feather fuzz lifted above the rock edge as it moved. No one watching could see what was going on, or enough of the feather fuzz to tell there was distress. I'm guessing it wore itself out to the point of exhaustion and was likely still so long, the interns marked it DNS."

"Did you give it some fish?"

"Not yet. Can't reach in that far from this angle. We went in from a sliver between the rocks over the burrow to insert the cam. I can try to do it that way, but the angle would make it hard to get the fish close enough for the stuck chick to reach it. I don't want to torment it with food out of reach. Even if I can get some herring in there and the chick does eat it, that's only going to prolong the inevitable."

She gaped. "You're going to leave it in there to die?"

He shifted and dumped his gear in the duffel, then propped his forearms on his bent knees and looked up at her. "Not if I can help it. Just not sure what options I have at the moment. This is one of the trickier burrows to get access to. We lucked out with the sliver in the rock to get the cam inserted. The only reason we even went after it is because of the success rate of the pair that nests here. Cams aren't cheap and monitoring and maintaining them in the weather conditions out here takes a lot of time, so we only have them in a very few burrows, one or two per species. Most of our data comes from firsthand observation, taking detailed notes on the comings and goings of the parent pair. We can tell a lot by their actions." He rubbed a hand over his face, and she could see that his mind was spinning out possible scenarios, so she stayed quiet, and let him think.

"The thing is, even if there's a way to move some of the smaller rocks without collapsing anything, it disturbs a burrow that has been a very successful nest."

"So you save one chick at the risk that the parents might not want to nest there again? Or find as good a nest elsewhere?"

He nodded. "Nature happens and disturbs burrows all the time, so it's not something they don't deal with, even without human intrusion. But one of the reasons we think this burrow has been so successful is that it's tucked in a natural crevasse between two pretty big boulders, which protects the nest from the elements, the kinds of things that can change rock formation, et cetera."

Delia sank down to sit cross-legged next to him. "I feel awful. For both of you."

"New meaning to 'between a rock and a hard place,'" he muttered.

For all his calm recitation of various and sundry scientific facts, she could see that he was very concerned. Upset, even. She knew it was part of his job to witness, routinely, the unsuccessful breeding attempts of the seabirds he studied. Given his previous life as an army ranger, his long tenure in special forces, and the things he had to have seen—and done—during that time, she'd assumed he was the perfect guy to handle the harsher aspects of his new career.

Looking at him now, she wasn't so sure of that.

He was looking out to sea, maybe gauging the time

they had before the tide came in and blocked their most direct path back to the promontory. Then he looked directly at her. And not just her face, but at all of her, as if taking inventory. He turned around, still seated, and looked back down into the crevasse. Then he looked back at her.

"What?" she asked, not sure she liked where his thoughts seemed to be going.

"You might fit."

Well, so much for easing into the subject. "Might?"

"Might," he said, either completely missing the overt skepticism in her voice, or simply not caring. He turned away and grabbed his notebook again, only to set it aside to dig farther into the gear bag.

Indiana MacGyver to the rescue. She had no idea what he was rooting around for, but would only be half surprised if he pulled out something that magically became a crane, complete with pulley rope to lower her, headfirst, into the crack between the two boulders. The two big-ass boulders.

Turned out she wasn't far off. He came up with a harness, a length of nylon rope, and carabiners, the hook links that hikers used. "I'll keep you tethered to me the whole time," he said. "We have a head strap that the camera device hooks to. You'll wear that, and I'll keep the base unit and help to guide you in. There's a little light coming in from the sliver in the rocks over the burrow, but it's going to be shadowy, and though you'll have the cam on you, I'll be the only one seeing what it's sending back."

He hooked the camera into a nylon strap that had Velcro on one end, then handed that to her, along with her green helmet and a pair of leather work gloves.

She took the strap and wrapped it around her forehead, pulling it snug before overlapping the Velcro end piece. Then she propped her hard hat on, this time taking the chin strap out from where it had been tucked up into the dome and clicking it shut beneath her chin. She smiled and struck a pose. "I'm sure it's going to be all the latest in island wear next season."

She looked at the gloves. "I'm not worried about my manicure. I run a diner." She flashed her fingers. "Short nails, no polish."

"Peg has nails. Talons, actually."

"Peg is bionic. Or she's part Borg. I've thought so for years. I look at the talons as proof of that."

Ford chuckled. "Well, the gloves are not just to keep your hands protected while I lower you in, it's also because the chick—"

"Ah. Right. Beaks and claws." She hadn't thought about that part. It wasn't like rescuing a person who would be so thankful for the save they'd simply go along with the extraction plan. The poor little guy they were after was probably hurting and scared. Not a great combination for the rescuer. "Won't the gloves scare him—or her—further, though?"

"It's a risk we'll have to take. It's not like the puffling can go anywhere."

"What do I need to do? I mean, free the foot—claw—first. But then what?"

"They're a pretty docile breed, as birds go. And you're right, it will be scared and is also probably hurting, but it's also exhausted, so I don't think there will be much of a fight, or a flight, for that matter."

He went over the best way to hold the bird, once she'd freed it, both to calm it, and protect her hands. "Keep it away from your face. You'll be on your belly, so you won't be able to tuck it to you, you'll have to hold it extended in front of your head, pretty much the whole time. So make sure you have a good hold on it before I pull you out."

"Oh, God," she said nervously. She slipped the harness belt on, then stepped into the beltlike getup he'd made from the nylon rope and linked that to her waist, then around each upper thigh as he directed, before running it back through the hooks. She looked down at her bunched-up pants and the way the rope sank into the soft parts between butt cheek and thigh and sighed. "Seriously, the fashion don'ts here are epic."

She got on her hands and knees and started toward the edge, only to feel a tug on her waist. She looked back and realized her ass and rope-creased thighs were more or less aimed right at his face. *Yeah, and so not in a provocative way.* Any latent fantasies she might have had about her getting to play Jane to his Tarzan as he carried her up to his treetop lair to have his way with her died a quick death.

"You don't have to do this, Dee," he said, his gaze mercifully on her face and only her face. He looked very serious.

"I want to do it. I'm only nervous that I'll do something wrong. I don't know anything about how to handle birds. What if I hurt the chick? Or worse?" The very idea that she'd be face-to-face with this poor creature and not be able to do the right thing for it agonized her. "What if I can't free it? I mean, there's no way I can just back out and leave it there." She felt a little tremble in her limbs, and not because the ropes were cutting off her circulation. "I'm scared, Ford."

"I know," he said quietly. "We have to make choices out here all the time that don't have great odds, but all we can do is try our best. If I could fit—"

"No, I know. And I agree, it's just . . ." She looked down into the crevasse. She didn't know what she'd thought her role would be when she'd offered to come and help. Okay, insisted on coming and helping. But never in her wildest dreams would it have been this. "Let's just—" She broke off and finished the thought by turning back to face the crevasse. It wasn't all that deep, just narrow, with no direct view of her end goal. Much less the poor thing inside it. "Do this," she whispered to herself as she got on her belly and braced her gloved hands on either side of the boulder.

"Just start edging down. Once your weight is more over the edge than on it, I'll anchor you. You don't have to worry about falling. Just ease down, angle yourself as needed so you have as much upper body freedom as possible. Then when you get to the burrow, stop and call up before you reach in."

"Okay," she said. Then repeated that word about a dozen times under her breath as she started inching downward.

"Thank you, Dee," she heard him say, just as her fanny was bent over the edge, an inch away from where she would lose control of balancing her own weight. "For doing this. I'm glad you came along."

"All in a day's work," she grunted, as she eased past the point of no return.

She felt him pull on the ropes, and though it made things more uncomfortable—a lot more uncomfortable—she relaxed a little, feeling more securely anchored now. "And stop staring at my ass," she called back, in hopes of relieving her nerves with a little humor.

She could have sworn she heard him chuckle, but it was hard to tell over the rapid tattoo of her heartbeat thumping in her ear.

"What," he called back, "and let you have all the fun?"

She grinned at that, and calmed another notch. She made her way to the bottom more easily than she'd expected. It wasn't that far down, or it didn't feel like it now that she was wedged into the crevasse. It helped that she had total trust in the rope handler back up top.

She rolled to her side so she could slip the camera prong thingie out of its pouch on her forehead and poke it into the burrow opening ahead of her. "I'm only going to be able to get my hands inside. I can't get an angle where I can look in," she called back, trying not to shout any louder than she had to so as not to completely freak the baby chick out. "I'm sticking the camera thingie in there so you can guide me." Which meant Ford was going to have to guide her on where to reach and how to free the bird's leg. She'd be doing it all by feel.

"Got it," he called down. "Ready?"

"Ready!" She edged back so she could slide her hands into the burrow. "Okay, little puffling," she said softly. "Super Delia is coming to the rescue. Just don't beak the hand that frees you. Deal?"

Chapter 13

"She's to the left," Ford called down, watching the scene unfold inside the burrow on the screen on his mini-sized tablet. "Push the camera in that direction so I can see better."

He had no idea if the chick was a she or not, but figured that would make the baby seem less threatening to Delia. "Okay, that's good. You're going to need to reach under her belly and get to her right foot. I think if you turn it a little to the side, it will come out. You may have to work to nudge the front claw under as you do. I think that's what's got her stuck, but she's got webbed feet, so it's not going to be comfortable for her. Just go slow, be gentle, but do what you need to do. We can repair the damage after if we need to."

He saw Delia's hand go still at his instructions; then after a brief moment, she began to move her hand forward. She kept her gloved palm to the floor of the burrow, moving it slowly over the rocks. The camera had a small mic, which was mostly picking up the rustling sounds of her gloved hand rubbing across the floor of the burrow, but over that he thought he could hear her calmly whispering into the burrow, talking to the puffling.

Ford didn't realize he was holding his breath until she reached the chick, who was on her side now, and breathing rapidly, but shallowly. Scared, but exhausted. The latter would be a good thing for them.

Delia's soft murmurs continued as she gently moved her hand under the chick's belly. There was a sudden squawk and flurry of feathers, but to Delia's credit, she didn't yank her hand back out. She stiffened, and the camera bobbled as she pulled her head back, which tugged on the camera cord, but she kept her hand where it was.

He could hear her saying, "It's okay, it's okay," softly, over and over again, and smiled briefly, thinking the soothing words were as much for her as for the injured chick. He didn't call out any further instructions, wanting the chick to calm down as much as possible. Another tense minute passed, and she began to move her gloved hand a bit farther under the chick's body. There was another round of squawking, more flapping, then a sharp cry of pain, followed quickly by "Ooh, ooh, it's okay, it's okay," from Delia. "Good girl," she cooed. "Look how brave you were."

Then, to his shock and delight, Delia moved her hand out from under the bird, wrapped both palms around the body, holding the wings in, and slowly began to extricate the puffling from the nest.

He didn't say anything; she seemed to have things well in hand, literally. Once she'd moved her hands past the camera, he began to pull her body back up to the cliff. She couldn't use her hands to propel her body upward, so he worked slowly.

Once her lower body was completely back topside, he scooted forward and put his palms over her calves.

"I've got you now," he said, keeping his voice low as her head was just over the edge now. "Keep her snug. I'll get you back over the edge. As soon as we're past your hips, roll to your left and pull her in to your chest."

It all went as smoothly as he could have hoped. He reached down and pulled the cord to retrieve the camera that still dangled from Delia's headband down into the burrow crevasse, unhooked it, and scooted back, staying in a crouch as she rolled to her side; then he helped her to an upright seated position, while she held the baby to her body like a very coddled football.

"Great job," he said, so incredibly proud of her. He frowned when he glanced up to see tears sliding down her cheeks. Instantly alarmed, he said, "What's wrong? Are you okay? Did she get you?"

"No, though she definitely gave me a moment. I'm fine, good," she sniffled. "Happy tears. I've never been so scared. I think I was more scared than she was."

"Do you want to give her to me?"

Delia shook her head, sniffled inelegantly, her helmet sliding over to one side as she snuggled the baby chick a little more. "Just . . . another minute."

Ford smiled and rolled back until he sat on the ground, knees bent. "Another minute would do both of you good."

Delia peered down at her little bundle, who was still breathing rapidly, but appeared content to stay where it was, securely bundled. "Her beak isn't bright and colorful." She glanced at Ford. "Are you sure it's a puffin?"

"That comes later. She looks to have shed all her fuzz though, so that's good. She'll be ready to fledge as soon as we see to her foot."

"I haven't looked at it," Delia said. "She tucked it up

under her when I took her out. Do you have stuff to take care of that kind of thing?"

"One of the tree huts is for rehab. A few of them actually, but one is set up to do observation, minor first aid. Generally, I think we do more first aid on us than them," he added with a smile. "But, if she tucked it in, that's a good sign. Means the movable parts are working. She didn't injure anything too severely."

Delia drew in a shaky breath, and let it out slowly, then finally seemed to pull herself together. Rescue was an emotional thing, he knew, so he let her take whatever time she needed.

She looked out over the rocks, toward the promontory. "How will we get her back there?"

Ford reached in his gear back and drew out what looked like a colorful fabric sling. "Papoose," he said.

Her face crumpled again and he looked alarmed, but she just sniffled and said, "That's the sweetest thing I've ever seen. A little baby birdie sling."

"Well, actually it's a baby human sling, but it does the trick when we need to transport fragile things over the rocks."

"I'd do it, but I'm apparently the worst klutz on those rocks—"

"No, that's okay," he said, already slipping the pouch over his shoulder. "I've got it."

Once situated, he moved over to Delia and undid as much of her harness gear as he could in her current position. "When you stand up, it should slide off into a pile. Just step out of it, and then pack it into the gear bag. You can put gloves, hat, whatever in there, too."

"I could carry the gear bag if you want me to," she said, with a last sniffle, even as she gave the size of the bag a dubious look.

He grinned. She was a mess, and he'd never thought her more beautiful. "That's okay. I've got it. Ready?"

She looked up at him, then down at her little black-and-white feathered bundle. The chick was so small, its body barely the size of soda can, with its wings and feet all tucked up. She sighed. "I suppose."

They made the chick transfer without disturbing it too greatly. That it didn't flutter much told Ford just how exhausted the little thing truly was.

"Will you be able to feed it when we get back? Won't that help her recover faster?" She lifted a shoulder when he just smiled. "I can't help it. Feeding things is what I do."

"They don't eat much before they fledge, but we'll definitely hydrate her, offer her some herring if she wants it, see what needs to be done with the foot. Her body weight is good, so her parents must have left her in good stead with fish within reach before they left." Privately he thought how lucky the chick was that no predators had found it, but he kept that to himself.

Once he had the chick situated at the front of his body, he reached to help Delia up. She made short work of stowing all the gear, and then zipped up the bag, but he reached for the handles before she could try to pick it up.

"It's okay. I have it. I'm going to take a slightly longer way around, keep the footing more level." He looked out to the water. "We've got time."

"Okay," Delia said. "I'm going to follow you then, if that's okay."

"More than."

She sighed, and it sounded a little shaky. Probably the aftereffects of the adrenaline punch leaving her system. He knew what that felt like. He touched her arm, turned her to face him. "You did an amazing job. Like a pro." He smiled down into her tear-streaked face. "If you ever want a summer job, I could use a good intern like you."

Her response was another inelegant sniffle, which made them both chuckle, though hers was a bit more watery than his. "Yes," she said, "just what you need. A blubbering intern who can't scale a simple pile of rocks."

He tipped up her chin, and then brushed away the curls that were blowing into her face. "You did what needed to be done, and that's all that matters."

"She'll be okay?" Delia asked.

"Pretty sure. She's a fighter to have made it this long."

"So . . . Disney ending?" Her smile was quavery, and he'd never wanted to kiss her as badly as he did right then.

"Good chance."

"All right then," she said, and squared shaky shoulders before pointing toward shore. "Lead on, Professor Rambo."

"Professor Ra—? You know what, never mind," he said with a disconcerted chuckle. "Follow me, careful of the sea kelp. There's more of it the way we're going, but less climbing."

"I'm all about less climbing," she said, and fell into step behind him.

It took longer than he'd thought it would to make it back to flat shoreline. Not because of the baby chick. It was dozing soundly, as far as Ford could tell, which wasn't surprising. He'd slowed his pace so that Delia wouldn't fall behind. It was slippery, and the clouds had begun to bank, which didn't bode well, and the tide was almost on their heels now.

He reached down to help her up and over the last rock, so she was standing next to him on the grass spit promontory.

"Thanks," she breathed, letting go of his hand once she was up and next to him. "And thanks for slowing down for me." She looked up at him, wry smile in place. "Don't even bother pretending you didn't," she added. "Me and my forty-three-year-old legs are too appreciative to be insulted."

Before he could think better of it, he glanced down, then back up. "I see absolutely nothing wrong with your forty-three-year-old legs."

She laughed and blushed at the same time. "Well, let's just say I'm a lot more sympathetic to the need for those indefatigable interns you spoke of than I might have been a few hours ago."

He chuckled. "Come on, we'd better get back to base camp before—" He looked up at the slowly darkening sky.

She didn't. "Yes, I noticed. Looks like we're in for a little storm."

Or a not-so-little one, he thought warily. "You might want to put a call in to Peg when we get back, or send an e-mail, just in case."

"I was thinking the same thing, but—" She palmed her cell from her pocket and wiggled it. "No service for me out here. What do you use?"

"Satellite phone," he said. "I just forward the cell calls to it while I'm out here."

"Smart." She nudged. "I guess they don't just hand out those doctorates, after all."

He smiled, but felt a bit of heat climb his neck at the reminder of his less-than-stellar commentary that first night back in her kitchen. "It's just a different kind of learning," he said, realizing that in addition to coming off like some self-important ass, he'd probably insulted her as well. "If they handed out degrees in running diners—"

"Stop while you're ahead," she said on a burst of laughter. "My ego isn't the problem."

His neck got a little warmer, and he took her advice. Then he spent the rest of the hike back wondering what her problem really was. She'd told Grace she wasn't sure what she wanted to do about the diner. Build a new one, do something else entirely. But while she might be at some kind of crossroads, self-imposed or Brooks Winstock–imposed, or a little of both, he'd noticed that when she talked about the diner, it was always with sincere love and affection. He didn't get even a subconscious hint of burnout or dissatisfaction. So . . . where did the floundering she seemed to be experiencing stem from?

They finally reached the base camp clearing and he motioned to the ramp to his left. "We'll go up that way, then back in to where the rehab huts are. I initially thought to put them up front for easiest access, but the difference in time to reach them is minimal, and the activity level is substantially reduced. And if we're keeping birds for observation, or tagging, or in fewer cases, rehabbing, quieter and calmer is better."

"Makes sense." She paused, looked around again, still clearly awed. "It all seems pretty peaceful, though."

"For most of the year, yes. But if we've got patients in residence, then that means we also have interns and volunteers in residence. Summertime is active, noisy, and pretty much nonstop."

They started up the first ramp, which angled off to the side and below his central building, then angled up with the next section, then switched back, and up again, until it met the series of swing bridges and walkways that were level with his main floor and headed back into the forest, with no clearing beneath them. Definitely more secluded and tucked in.

"Is that why you called it base camp?" she asked, taking it all in as they made their way through the treetops toward the biggest circular hut in the center of three others.

"What? Oh," he said, surprised by the question. "I guess so. What else would you call it?"

She turned to look at him. "Home?"

"Well. Sure," he said, completely disconcerted now. "It's that, too, of course."

"Of course," she murmured, and edged past him to open the door of the largest of the four med unit huts as they stepped up on the last landing, which was built of solid, stable board planking, as was the base of the hut, both attached directly to and around the tree itself.

He stepped inside behind her, intending to ask why it mattered what he called the place, but she'd already taken a quick look around the small structure and turned back to him, that amazed expression on her face again. "I don't know what I was expecting, but something a lot less state of the art than this."

He glanced around at what looked a lot like a vet's examining room, with a steel table in the center, kennels of varying sizes lining one wall. There was an industrial sink, next to a counter with cabinets above and below it. All were glass fronted and well stocked with a variety of necessary first aid and other supplies. There were even a few pieces of equipment to provide rudimentary assistance—microscopes, stethoscopes, beakers, and Bunsen burners.

"We've been fortunate enough to be awarded several really useful grants over the past handful of years," he said, carefully setting the gear back inside the door and closing it behind him. "And technology has come a long way in enabling remote-outpost setups like this."

"It's impressive, truly." She looked at him, smiling. "I'm glad the foundation is getting the support it needs." Her gaze dropped to the bundle on his chest. "So, what do we do with her next?"

"Take a look at her foot, do what we can there, offer food, hydration, then set her up for the night."

Delia glanced at the wall section of little kennels. "In one of those?"

She looked like he'd said they were going to tie the chick to a stake in the yard. "Yes," he said, trying not to smile. "There will be appropriate lighting and the place is heated. She'll do okay."

"They just look so . . . sterile," she said of the stainless-steel enclosures.

"That's because they are. Keeps that whole germ thing down to a minimum."

She rolled her eyes at him. "It just seems, I don't know, cold, after the little burrow she had."

"Well, if you want to go down and get rocks and twigs and dirt and make her a little home for the night, be my guest. But her foot would do better in a more sterile environment. She'll have bedding."

"I know you think I'm being ridiculous."

"No," he said, his smile gentling. "I think you're just being a concerned intern."

She gave him a little smirk at that, but her heart was in her eyes as she looked at the chick nestled in the pouch.

He got a clean towel from one of the cabinets and demonstrated to her how to best hold the chick so he could have the freedom to examine her feet and claws.

"I'll wrap a towel around her body to hold her wings down and tucked in. Then you gently grip her this way." He showed her by modeling with the towel and his hands in the air. "So the beak isn't where she can snap at anything, but she can't flap and get away. Just make sure to keep your face back from her face."

Delia smiled, nodded, but he could see she was nervous again.

"The hard part is over, you know," he said.

"I know," she said, shaking her arms and rolling her shoulders. "I'll just be happier when she's all cared for and tucked in for the night."

"Me, too," he admitted. "Okay, let's do this." He carefully unwrapped the papoose from his body, and then set the entire thing on the stainless-steel table. There was a little rustling as the baby chick woke up.

"Poor thing, she was enjoying her little hammock time," Delia said as Ford lifted the folds of fabric away from the now disgruntled-looking chick. "Aww, look at you. You don't know where you are, do you?" Delia cooed. "Well, Dr. Rambo here is going to get you all fixed up, don't you worry."

"I thought I was Dolittle," he muttered as he laid the last fold of the fabric flat on the table, leaving the baby sitting in the middle of it.

"That was before I grabbed those biceps," she shot back with a grin. "Besides, the only one talking to the animals around here seems to be me."

"You talk, I'll doctor."

"She's sitting on her feet, how are we going to—"

"Just like I showed you."

Delia pulled a sad face and looked at the chick. "But look, she's sitting there all tucked up, getting her bearings."

"Yes, which is why we need to do our job before she

does. We'll be done before she figures out how to thwart our efforts." He handed her the towel.

"Well, at least it's soft," Delia said, folding it the way he'd showed her. The baby chick took that opportunity to let out a little grumbly squawk. Delia laughed. "I couldn't agree more, sweetie." She stepped around to the other side of the table. "Okay," she said, taking in a breath. "Here we go."

As it had been out on the rocks, her anxiety proved to be unnecessary. She might be an outdoors and wildlife novice, but she was a smart, sharp, competent woman, and that strength served her just as well during the bird examination as it did in running a diner.

Ford did his examination and could all but hear the sound of Delia's racing heartbeat filling the room. He'd barely let the bird's foot go and motioned Delia to set her back down on the table again when the questions started.

"So? How is she? Is the foot okay? I mean, she won't lose any of it or anything awful like that, right? Because I know there was a Disney movie where they made that dolphin a fake tail, but that's not the Disney movie I had in mind when—" She broke off and snapped her mouth shut when he simply lifted his gaze and stared at her.

"I babble when I'm nervous." She lifted a finger. "Don't say it. And no cracks about knowing the Disney movies. They help me unwind."

Ford held her defiant gaze for another long moment, and then smiled as he looked back down at the chick. *Just the damnedest woman.* "Well, it looks like she's torn up this foot pretty well, and the claw is broken off. We'll need to file it smooth, clean up the damage to the foot, give her some antibiotic. Then it's bed rest. I'll put some food in with her."

"And then?"

"And then we wait to make sure there's no infection in the foot before she goes and plunges it into ocean water for the next three years. Make sure she can walk on it. The fact that she's settled down on it and doesn't seem to be favoring it is good, but she could just be in shock. So, we'll keep a close eye." Before she could ask what he knew was her next question, he said, "Yes, there is a cam in here, so yes, you can sit up and watch her all night if you want."

"Okay," Delia said, looking too relieved to give him an aggrieved look. "That's good. Really good." She looked at the chick and he could see she wanted to reach out and pet it by the way she curled her fingers inward against the temptation.

"Once I get her fixed up, you can get her settled if you want." He explained what the puffling would need in the kennel. "If you want to get that done, I'll work on her."

"Don't you need me to hold her?"

He nodded to the chick, who was already dozing again. "I don't think so. She's wiped out. I'll clean the open wounds and get the gunk out of the end of her claw, but we'll leave filing it down till tomorrow."

"Gunk," Delia said, her smile returning. "Medical term?"

"Yes," he said, in an overly serious tone. "Only those of us with doctorates are allowed to use it."

Delia bowed in mock deference but her grin when she looked back up had her eyes twinkling. "I will see to setting up the queen's quarters, then."

He smiled and shook his head as he went about collecting the things he'd need to see to the bird's wounds. They did make a good team. And not just in the ways of emergency wildlife rehab.

It took another half hour, and Delia did have to hold the chick for some of the treatment, but all in all, it went as well as he could have expected. Once they got the puffling settled into the kennel, she tucked up immediately and went to sleep.

"She didn't even look at the herring," Delia said, concerned.

"Rest is more important," Ford said, removing the fish. "We'll try again tomorrow, but for now, this is what she needs most."

He moved away to take care of the fish, but Delia remained looking into the kennel, which was chest height. "She's going to be okay," Delia said, but it was more an affirmation to herself than a question to him.

He came to stand beside her again. "Thank you. Again. For coming out. I don't think she'd have made it if you hadn't. I couldn't have gotten her out of there. Not without destroying the burrow."

Delia leaned against his arm, just a little. "We did a good thing."

"Yes," he said, curling his fingers inward now, not trusting himself to touch her. "Yes, we did." His resistance, what little he had left, was crumbling. The first rumble of thunder overhead had him stepping away. "We should get over to the main building before the skies open up. I need to make some notes, make sure the cam is up and working."

"I can put together something to eat while you do the paperwork."

"I thought you jumped in my truck to get away from having to feed people for a bit."

She looked up at him. "I'm still not exactly sure why I jumped in your truck." She smiled. "But I'm glad I did."

Jesus, he was doomed. How on earth he was going

to get a wink of sleep that night, he had no idea. And it wasn't going to be from worrying about a baby puffin. *It's going to be figuring out how in the hell you're going to keep your hands off your temporary intern.*

More to save himself than to give the recuperating chick some peace and quiet, he stepped over to the hut door and opened it so Delia could precede him back out onto the deck. He noticed her looking around with avid curiosity. He glanced up at the sky through the treetops. Not as ominous as he'd thought. "You probably have a good ten or fifteen minutes. I can figure out the food situation and make notes if you want to go take a quick look around. None of the huts are locked." He nodded towards the network of bridges, ramps, and the treetop buildings they led to.

Her face immediately lit up in pure delight, but then she said, "No, I'm the one who barged in. The least I can do is feed us while you do your highly educated, advance degreed scientist . . . stuff." She gave him a sidelong glance as she stepped onto the first rope bridge that led diagonally across, directly to the main hut. "That is the technical term, right?"

"Yes. I won't tell anyone you used it."

She laughed and he watched as she walked in front of him, his attention not on her body, but on the way she swiveled her attention left and right, then left again, taking in his setup, obviously charmed by the whole thing.

It wasn't his first time seeing that reaction. Many of his interns and volunteers—most of them, actually—went through pretty much the same thing. Though many of the guys pretended to be way cooler about it than they actually were. He smiled at the memories, all of them good ones, of the people, most of them a great deal younger than he, who had come out over the years to learn from him, from the island, from life, much as he had with Dr. Pelletier. On the one hand, that made him feel old, but then he looked at Delia, and he felt like that twenty-three-year-old soldier coming to the Cove for the first time, and falling under the spell of a redheaded angel.

It was his first time having someone here who wasn't an intern, or visiting professor, or from this funding organization or that grant committee. He supposed what he was really thinking was that this was the first time he'd brought a woman here. But Delia wasn't just some woman.

No, he thought a bit more shakily than he'd have liked, *she's definitely not that.*

Chapter 14

"I feel like I've fallen down a rabbit hole," Delia said upon entering Ford's sanctuary. "If a person can fall up into a tree, that is." She took a slow turn. He'd called it base camp, and she supposed that wasn't far from the mark. It was basic, utilitarian, and uncluttered with the sorts of personal items or décor bits and pieces that put a character stamp on a place. But the richness of the open beam construction, and the tree trunks forming the corners, the inviting heat of the potbelly stove planted in the middle of it, the overstuffed cushions on the couch—she didn't even want to know how he'd gotten that up there—and the old quilt thrown across the back combined to create a warmth, a coziness, that pulled her in.

The octagonal shape of the place made her feel that she was being hugged inside its warmth. The stack of books on the floor next to the couch looked quite serious and stuffy in nature, as did the stack of magazines they sat on. There were a multitude of binders and spiral-bound notebooks stuffed on a small set of handmade shelves that backed the couch. *I'm not the only one who lives her job,* she thought. On the antique banded barrel he used as an end table, there was a lamp and what looked like a few dog-eared detective novels. She smiled. All in all, he'd put his stamp on the place anyway, whether he realized it or not.

She looked back to find him hovering at the base of the ladder that led up to a loft space above, watching her. She could still see him with that brightly patterned pouch slung across his chest, the injured chick nestled inside, and her heart bumped hard against the inside of her chest. She thought about the family she'd created for herself among the folks of Blueberry Cove, and realized Ford had done the same out here with the seabirds and the seals. Whether he fully understood that or not, she didn't know, but seeing firsthand how truly connected he'd become to his new path, how sincerely passionate he was about the work he was doing, made her feel good . . . and less regretful about the time they'd spent apart.

Delia wondered, now that Grace was in his life again, and he'd spent some time back in the Cove, if they'd keep their renewed friendship active. *And, if so, how I'm going to keep it just as a friendship.* It was hard not to want more, but what more could they really have? And was it worth jeopardizing the renewed bond they did share?

She glanced at his face and was surprised to find him looking a bit uncomfortable, then realized she hadn't said anything. "This place is amazing," she reassured him, then grinned. "Walt Disney himself would be proud. I can't believe you not only dreamed it up, but made it happen."

"I can't take that much credit," he said. "You'd be surprised how much literature there is out there on this kind of thing. I just took the bits and pieces that worked for me. It's basically cobbled together from other people's ideas. With space at a premium, functionality was key, so I decided not to reinvent the wheel but go with what worked for others."

He spoke comfortably about the place, almost offhandedly, so being worried about her impression of it wasn't what had made him uncomfortable. "If you need to go up and write your notes while today's adventure is fresh in your mind, or set up the cam for baby puff, don't let me keep you," she said. She glanced in the other direction, at the kitchen area that took up most of the other side of the main floor. "I really don't mind cooking dinner. In fact, I'd enjoy it. It'll be nice just to cook for two for a change. Especially since one of them is me." She smiled back at him, but he still looked a bit out of step or something. "Is everything okay?" Another thought occurred to her and her smile faded. "Is there something wrong that you're not telling me about the baby, because—"

"No, the chick is fine. Will be fine. I'll just—" He put one foot up on the ladder. "If you really don't mind putting something together, that would be great. Don't go to any trouble. I think there's lunch meat in there, so sandwiches—"

"Ford," she said, "it's all good. Go."

He held her gaze another moment, then climbed the ladder. She watched him go up, took a moment to shamelessly admire his very fine backside once again, then, with a sigh, turned back to the kitchen area. Maybe he was just uncomfortable having someone in his private space. Although she had a hard time believing that since he'd made it sound like the place was overrun with interns and volunteers at all hours every summer. She glanced back up at the loft when a light flicked on, and thought, *Or maybe it's because the someone in his private space is me.*

Maybe he was worried about where to put her up
for the night. Her body leapt to attention with its own
solution to that, but she ignored it. Or tried to. She'd
just ask him where the interns stayed and bunk there.
Or she'd take the couch. It looked quite comfy, actually, right there in front of the potbelly stove. It all felt
very wee-cabin-in-the-woods cozy. *Just up a few dozen feet
in the air.*

Then another thought occurred to her. Where did
he sleep? Certainly not the couch. There was only one
part of the main floor that appeared to be boxed out,
and had a door leading to it, but it was small, so she assumed bathroom. Yet another marvel of treetop living
she didn't want to know the physics of, if that was indeed the case. So . . . *where* do *you sleep?* She glanced
over at the ladder, then up to the loft ledge, but that
wasn't a broad enough floor area. If he had any kind
of office set up there, there would be nowhere to
sleep, too. Then she turned and looked farther up, on
the other side. She'd thought the flat top was the ceiling of the space. There was a hole in the middle where
the long pipe stem from the potbelly stove went up
and out. Only now she recalled, from the outside, the
top was domed, up to a point at the peak of the roof,
so . . . She stepped around the stove, over to the ladder, and looked up the other way, across from the loft.
From where she stood, she realized that there was another ladder from his loft that led up to what she'd
thought was the ceiling, but was in fact another platform. The ladder in this case ran up through an opening in the platform, meaning the entire upper section
of the domed building was on yet another floor.

Smiling at the whimsical concept of having a bedroom at the top of a tree house, wondering if that felt

like sleeping up among the stars, she walked back over to the kitchen before he looked down and caught her spying up at him.

She took a moment to check out the kitchen itself, marveling that it wasn't some kind of abbreviated camp stove kind of thing, but an actual fully functioning kitchen. "The wonders of modern technology," she murmured. She supposed with the right kind and number of generators and gas-powered gizmos, a person could build anything, anywhere. She paused beside the door that led out to the deck and her smile widened at the small, red-and-yellow-striped pot buoy that hung there, with various and sundry key rings hanging from the hooks. Pot buoys were how lobstermen marked their pots out on the water, but they'd also become a symbol of the fishing traditions that were such a big part of Maine's history. You couldn't drive a block through town without seeing a cluster of them hanging here or there, as kind of a talisman of that proud heritage.

She wondered if there was a story behind Ford's buoy. She'd have to ask him. She reached out and rubbed her hand over the heavy trunk of the pine tree that formed one of the corners. She supposed if she'd pictured his place, she'd assumed the tree would run up through the middle with the house built around it, something, she supposed, like Eula March's shop, built around her oak tree. But she saw now the wisdom of using naturally spaced trees as he had to distribute the burden of the weight of the structure itself, along with the people and things that were inside it.

She was quite certain if she asked him about any aspect of the construction of the place, he would be able to give her the same in-depth, encyclopedic rundown of what was entailed in much the same way he'd told her about the seabird colonies and their mating and migratory habits.

Her smile widened at the thought, and she went back to the kitchen to start on the evening meal. She started with the fridge, opening the door of the small unit. Bigger than dorm size, it was as tall as she was, but narrower. "And no freezer," she noted, when she opened it.

"I have a freezer chest built into the shed that sits below the house," Ford said, and she whirled to find him standing behind her.

"I swear I'm going to hang a bell around your neck," she said, "and don't think I won't."

"Yes, ma'am," he said, in his best military polished tone. "Begging your pardon, ma'am."

She rolled her eyes at that, which made his serious soldier face break into a smile, and she was happy to see him look a little more relaxed. So what if his smiling soldier face made her heart do that little stutter step inside her chest again? She'd just have to find a way to manage that. At least for the next twelve or so hours. *Good thing you'll be sleeping for most of that time.*

"I could say I'd like to see you try," he added, "but if there's anyone who could accomplish that it would be—well, you know, now that I think about it, I'd have to say Peg maybe—probably—then Eula; Grace would just wheedle me until I begged her to put it on me; but then you next after that. Definitely."

Delia laughed. "I'd say I was insulted at not even breaking the top three, except I'm pretty sure you've got the pecking order right on that one."

He flashed a brief smile, and she realized that he'd smiled more today with her than she could remember him doing, well . . . ever. It did put that bit of light in his eyes she'd wondered about, and the effect was downright mesmerizing. So much so she got caught up in them for a moment, then blinked and quickly turned back to the open fridge door. Because it was that or run across the small kitchen area and jump him. *Come on, cold refrigerator air, cool me down. Cool me way down.* "So," she said, probably a shade too brightly, as she rummaged. "You know Eula March? How did that come about?"

"Maybe I was in the market for some nice antiques," he said, trying to sound insulted by the question, but there was obvious amusement in his tone.

Which was another new thing. A new thing that also increased his jump me quotient. By a lot. She started moving things around on the narrow shelves so she could see what was behind them, praying for something to distract her. "I'd say okay, except I don't know that I recall Eula having old oak wine barrels as part of her inventory."

"Well, she should. I think they'd be a big hit in coastal décor."

She laughed again, and thought, *I am such a goner.* Unless he did or said something incredibly insensitive or stupid, it was only a matter of time before she did something embarrassing.

As a young soldier returned from war, he'd been all alpha strong, with tragic grief giving him that vulnerable edge that had made him irresistible to her oh-so-young, recently broken heart. As a special forces veteran of the kinds of missions she'd never be able to fathom, even if she tried, he'd been reclusive, wounded, but searching, and her thirtysomething heart had melted once again.

Now . . . now, however, he was a man more fully evolved, one who'd managed to put his life into sharp perspective, and had come out the other side with a new path, a new mission. He was a man who knew what he wanted, and—more important—was sincerely good with what he'd found. He was solid, and strong and, to her surprise, a lot more open and relaxed with her than she'd ever anticipated him being. Rather than making him less interesting, or less desirable, it made him quite the opposite. He was more even keeled, steady, and stable, yes, but he still had an edge, still exuded that raw masculinity, that instinctively protective, I'll-do-battle-for-you vibe. And that particular combination was . . . well, it was perfect. To her.

You are in so much trouble here.

She realized then just how true that was. She didn't merely want Ford in the jump-his-bones, no-strings, casual, let's-not-get-too-serious kind of way she'd turned into an art form. Maybe it was finding out that a lasting friendship with Langston deVry was even more satisfying than a short-lived physical fling would have been, but her concept of relationships with the opposite sex had started to undergo a change over the past summer. Grace's coming to the Cove, and pulling Delia into her reunited family situation had started to change things, too, especially since the other part of that family unit was Ford. The dreams had started. So had that little seed of disquiet. And with that, everything else had started to change, too, she realized. Winstock's devious end run to steal her diner out from under her had just brought it all bubbling to the surface where she was forced to confront it, forced to figure out what the hell it was she really wanted.

She just hadn't known what was wrong, what that disquiet was all about, the internal sense of something . . . missing. Not a family of her own, she'd determined, so she'd assumed it had to be professional, that maybe she needed to rethink what she was doing with her life, and what, maybe, she should be doing instead. Something to fill that sudden emptiness she felt growing inside herself.

Now as she looked at Ford, an entirely different realization started to blossom. Maybe what she was missing wasn't family, wasn't a new occupation, or hobby or . . . anything like that. Maybe it was something as simple, and as terrifying, as wanting there to be someone in her life to share the journey with. Wherever that journey might lead.

She closed her eyes and pictured Ford Maddox as he was now, as he'd been with her today, and knew that the possibility of actively wanting to develop something more with him was very much up for consideration. And she honestly didn't know what to do about that. She had spent her entire adult life actively avoiding such connections.

"Actually," he said, completely unaware of the profound epiphany she was having while moving milk cartons and sifting through wrapped packages of lunch meat. "I went into her shop when I got interested in building a tree house. I wanted to see how she'd built around the one in her shop."

Delia forcibly shut down the mental track her brain had taken, and tried to ignore the slight tremor in her hand as she moved a bottle of salad dressing. She jerked herself back to the conversation, proud of the sardonic look she managed to shoot him over her shoulder. "And how'd that work out for you?" *See? Friendly banter. That's what they were. Friends. Who bantered. She should be thankful to have that much.* Was *thankful.*

"About as well as you can imagine," he said sardonically. "She actually accused me the other day of dropping by to make 'googly-eyes'—her words—at her oak tree."

Delia smiled, having no problem whatsoever imagining the eccentric shop owner saying exactly that. She moved a pitcher of iced tea, frowned at the bottle of what looked like green juice that was behind it. *Juice should never be green.* Then smiled again when she found a half carton of eggs. She added it to the wrapped block of sharp cheddar cheese and another of mild Swiss she'd already moved to one side to start her meal-making stash. *Food, just focus on the food. You can analyze life epiphanies later. Food you understand.*

Then his exact words sank into her brain and she straightened and looked over her shoulder at him. "So you've been by Eula's shop since you came back to the Cove to help me? Still trying to lure magic oak tree secrets out of her?" She'd added that last part so he'd think her interest was casual, and . . . she wasn't sure what her interest was, to be honest. It just seemed an odd pairing, the two of them.

He held her gaze for a disconcertingly long moment, and she'd turned back to the fridge when he finally said, "Actually, if you want to know the truth, I went there to talk to her about you."

Delia had just slid open the small plastic bin drawer and found mushrooms and green peppers. She said "Bingo!" as her brain scrambled to figure out what she should say to that little revelation.

"There's some bacon under those, I think," he said.

"And there is a God," she breathed as she did, indeed, find a half a rasher of bacon under the peppers. She straightened, juggling her bounty against her chest. "I'm about to whip up an omelet that will make you rethink everything you thought you knew about breakfast food. Do you have corn meal?"

He stepped forward to help her with her stash, and frowned at the question. "For an omelet?"

"No, for the corn bread I'm going to make to have with it." At his continued skepticism, she added, "Bacon corn bread."

His eyebrows rose. "I make it a rule to never say no to bacon."

"Right?" she agreed. *And we're bantering. But . . . God, he smelled good.* She noted he'd changed clothes, and wished she could have done more than just pull off the hoodie she'd worn while scrambling over rocks and bellying into a puffin burrow. *There will be no more taking off of clothes. Smell the bacon if you want, but leave the man-smelling alone.*

He took the eggs and the bacon from her grasp and let her juggle the cheeses and vegetables to the short butcher-block counter that was wedged between the sink and the stove. "Where did you find these not quite miniature but not quite full-size appliances?" she said, striving to say something, anything, that would take her mind off how close he stood . . . and, dammit, he really did smell amazing.

"Houseboat manufacturers," he said. "You'd be surprised how similar houseboat living is to tree house living."

"Hunh," she said, wondering if he'd mind if she just leaned into him and took a deeper whiff. "Never thought about that, but I guess it makes sense. Handy market for appliances. Smart thinking." She smiled at him as she took the bacon and eggs from him with her now empty hands. "Did they teach you that in doctorate school?"

He rolled his eyes. "I'm never going to live that down, am I?"

"Only until I say something that hands you similar ammo, and then we'll draw up a treaty and never speak of either again."

"Something to keep in mind," he said dryly.

She started going through cupboards, pulling out a mixing bowl, a cutting board, a cast-iron skillet. She felt her nerves calm as she gathered her tools, sort of like getting into the zone. "Knives?" she asked. "Sharp ones?"

He gestured to a drawer, but let her have room to work.

"So," he said at length. "You're not going to ask me why I went to Eula to talk about you?"

"Well," she said, finding matches on the back of the stove and lighting the pilot light so she could turn on one of the burners. She coated the cast-iron skillet with oil and put it on a low flame to temper it, then pulled the cutting board over and started going through the mushrooms and green pepper. "I'm not sure I want to know, to be honest. That's between you and her. Do you have a grater? A potato peeler will do in a pinch."

Instead of telling her where it was, he stepped over and opened another drawer, then moved next to her and set it by her cutting board. Then he didn't move away. She slowed her chopping before she clipped off something important. Like all four of her fingertips.

"I wanted to know how to help you," he said quietly. "It was the morning after I first came back, after we'd talked in the diner's kitchen. I guess I thought maybe she'd know someone I could call or ask to step in and fix the lease thing."

Delia stopped chopping. "That was . . . incredibly

kind of you. Above and beyond. Especially considering I wasn't exactly welcoming."

"You were . . . overwhelmed. Have been for a while now. I told myself I pushed because I didn't want Grace hassling me, but the truth was I didn't like seeing you that way." A note of amusement crept into his tone. "So, in typical male fashion, I wanted to fix it."

Delia smiled a little, then let out a sigh, and caved. "So, what did Eula say?"

"That the person I needed to talk to was you. I told her I had. So she told me I had to stand up. I said I was there in her shop because I was standing up for you. She corrected me and said I had to stand up for myself."

Delia looked up at him then. "What do you mean? Or . . . what did she mean?"

"I wasn't exactly sure at first. She said a few other things and managed to piss me off a little, which is pretty much par for the course for our conversations." His expression grew more serious. "She cares about you. A lot."

"Me?" Delia was honestly surprised. "I don't even know her all that well. Gran spent time with her over the years, I think, but I only know her in passing. She's only occasionally come by the diner. She's not all that social, really."

"Maybe it's more that she respects you, respects what you've done with yourself, with the diner. I'm not sure. I think what she was trying to tell me was I had to stand up for what I wanted. Not for what I thought other people wanted. That, I guess, it wasn't what Grace wanted me to do, or even what you wanted me to do, or not do, as the case may be. But what I thought it was best to do."

"And what was that? I mean, I know you stayed in town, but—"

"Grace and I scoured legal texts and more town documents than I ever want to see again. Then she had that talk with you, and came and told me that you weren't sure what you wanted, and I wasn't sure then what we should be doing. I didn't want to be out there trying to save the diner if what you were looking for was a way to get out from under it. So I did what Eula told me I should do. I went to talk to you."

"And I fell apart all over you." Delia didn't know what to say about all that he'd done for her. She felt humbled, and grateful and, well, stunned. "I didn't know—you shouldn't have gone to all that trouble, not when you have so much work—"

He took her by the elbow and gently turned her to face him. "I wasn't doing it because I thought you wanted me to, or to score points. Or because I owed you a debt. I did it because I thought it was the right thing to do. I did it because I care what happens to you."

She dipped her chin and felt her heart start up a good tattoo inside her chest. "I—thank you."

"You'd have done the same for me," he said. "At least, I think you would. So look at it like that."

"I would have, and . . . you're right." She glanced up at him, a hint of a smile cutting through the seriousness their conversation had taken on. "I'm thinking you'd have given me an even harder time than I gave you, so suddenly I'm not feeling all that bad."

If her humor registered, it didn't show in his expression, which was still intent, still serious. "Well, it didn't matter in the end, because it looks like there is no loophole." He ran his hands up her arms and a shiver of keen awareness raced down her spine. "And you've got more on your plate than worrying about your diner."

If you only knew, she thought, and hoped he didn't feel the tremble that had started to shake her legs.

"After you went renegade and hitched a ride out here, I could see the tension leaving you the farther out to sea we got. I hoped that maybe coming to Sandpiper would be a chance to take a step back, find some perspective. I'm guessing with rescuing the puffling, you really haven't had much chance to—"

"Actually, I have," she said, nervous now, unsure whether she should take even the smallest step in that conversational direction. Her realizations were still fresh and unexamined and he was standing so close, the feel of his warm, wide palms circling her arms was sending a riot of sensation through her body.

He lifted a questioning eyebrow, but said nothing.

"Not about the diner," she said. "Actually, until I got back here and started looking into what to make for dinner, I realized I'd gone almost the whole day without thinking about it." A smile wavered on her lips. "I wouldn't have thought that possible, probably because I spend most of my waking, breathing moments there."

"So . . . maybe you need to schedule more stowaway time on my boat," he said, a hint of something lighter in his tone, but his gaze searching hers, still quite serious.

"I . . . don't know, maybe I do," she said, trying to joke, but she was too hung up on the message she thought she might be seeing in his eyes to think straight.

"You know, one thing I've noticed, if it helps—" He broke off, and there was a brief twist of a smile at the corners of his mouth, a mouth she was trying desperately not to look at. "And yes, I'm aware I'm about to offer unsolicited advice, but this is actually more of an observation."

"Well, doctor, you're paid to observe," she said, grappling for the same light tone, even as she felt as if the very ground was shifting beneath her feet. "What did you notice?"

"What you said to Grace about not being sure what your future held, if you wanted to save the diner. For what it's worth, as overwhelmed as you've been, stressed out, exhausted, by whatever questions you're trying and failing to find answers for . . . I just thought you should know that every time you've mentioned your diner, or cooking, or the townspeople who are your regulars, well . . . you beam. Hell, you almost glow." He gently squeezed her arms, his gaze so intent it felt like an additional caress. "I guess what I'm saying is, it doesn't look like you've lost the desire to do what you do best. Maybe that's the place you start, and figure out what's next from there."

"I . . ." She had no idea what to say to that. Or how it felt to know he'd paid such close attention to her, that he was so aware of her. She'd been kidding about him being paid to be observant, but the truth was that was his field of expertise, so maybe she shouldn't be surprised after all. "Thank you," she said, softly. "I think that does help." At least as it pertained to what her next step might be professionally. All it did was muddle her brain further about what steps she might want to take personally.

Maybe it would have been better, or at least easier, if he had said something insensitive or stupid, instead of something so thoughtful and insightful. Then she could convince herself she'd been foolish to consider, even for a second, that she might want to risk the one part of herself that she had permanent, incontrovertible rights to: her heart.

"Good," he said. And she swore he gave a little sigh of relief, as if he'd been worried she might take it wrong.

"I am grateful," she said, needing him to know that. "That you stayed. That you tried to help." She tried to keep looking into his eyes, but it was all too much, so she darted a look downward, but got caught up with looking at his big hands, so gently holding on to her arms. And how close they were standing to each other. "That you stood up for what you thought was the right thing to do, and that was to help me . . . thank you for that. I wish . . . I'm sorry I don't have my act more together, so your efforts weren't wasted."

He jerked a little on her arms, surprising her with the sudden tension she felt in his fingertips. She looked back up to find those dark eyes of his so intent on hers that she thought she'd simply fuse to the spot where she stood.

"It wasn't time wasted. Any more than your time was wasted out here today."

"But here we did something, fixed something. With me, I'm just—"

"Worthwhile," he said. He let go of her arms and tipped her face up to his. "You told me my friendship was worthwhile. Spending time trying to help you, whether or not it gets immediate and direct results, is worth it because you're worth it. Do you think that if that baby chick hadn't made it today, I'd just write off your help and assistance as worthless?"

"No," she said, eyes widening. "That's not what I meant, I just—"

"You just try to downplay yourself right out of the

conversation, but for the life of me, I can't figure out why. And it's not just about giving and taking and needing all things to be equal. You make it so damn hard for anyone to get close. Maybe it's just me you don't want help from. If so, just tell me to back the hell off."

"I thought I did!" she exploded, in utter terror that her worst fear was about to manifest itself before she'd even figured out how to go about trying to reach out to him in the first place.

"Well," he said, then lifted his hands from her and took a step back. "Pardon me, then. Pardon the hell out of me."

"Ford," she said, when he turned away. "I don't even know why you're mad. We were just talking about what I could do next and I thanked you—sincerely—for helping me, for your observations. I meant that. And I'm glad I came out here today, glad I helped. And I'm sorry if I seem at a loss about why you're so intent on helping me. It's not that I'm not grateful. I am. How many times can *I* say that? I'm trying to be your friend, step inside that circle, trying to figure this whole thing out, be more open to taking help when it's offered, and to—to—" She flailed her hands, as if that would fill in the blanks.

"To what?" he asked, spinning back about. "You can't even say it."

"Say what?" she asked, truly bewildered. "What do you want me to say? What do you want from me?"

In an instant he closed the short space and all but jerked her into his arms and up against his body. "I want this, Dee." He cupped her face, slid his fingers back through her hair. He pulled her mouth, still open from her gasp of surprise, up to his own.

He paused for a heart-stopping moment, his lips a

mere breath away from hers, and searched her eyes like he was hoping to find the answer to all of life's mysteries in them. Then he took her mouth in a kiss that turned her world on its side, and her heart right over along with it. He didn't so much kiss her as lay claim to her.

His lips were hard but warm, and fit hers like they'd never left. She thought she'd romanticized him, how he'd felt, how he'd tasted, how he'd made her feel as he'd taken her. She knew she had turned that night into a fantasy, where every touch had been electric, every sigh had been perfect. She'd been right. This kiss wasn't the one from her dreams.

It was so . . . *so* much better.

There was no ambivalence, no distraction of grief. His intent was specific, and focused, and all about her. She felt the calluses on his thumb as he stroked her cheek, tilted her mouth up into his, so he could open it, sink inside, and claim her all over again. It wasn't just her mouth that parted to him; it felt like everything inside her opened as well. He said she didn't know how to take, but, oh, if this was what he was giving . . . she'd take all that she could get. And the giving she wanted to share in return was going to make it twice as amazing. But before she could gather her senses enough to reach for him, he was lifting his head, and her heart tripped. *No, not yet.*

"I want you," he said. His chest rose and fell, and there was ferocity and fear in his eyes. "Dammit, I just want you." He let her go, as if suddenly realizing what he'd done, and started to turn away.

It hadn't been the ferocity in his eyes that decided her. It had been the fear. She grabbed his arm and yanked him back. "Then do like Eula said. Stand up for what you want," she said. "For what you think is right." She reached up on her tiptoes and took his face in her hands, pulled him down to her. "But there's no turning back, Ford."

"No," he said, hauling her up off her toes, and against his body, wrapping his arms around her. "No turning back."

Chapter 15

The moment his lips had touched hers, his need for her, to have her, take her, to finally, dear God, bury himself in her, was mindless in its all-consuming intensity. Her words jerked some nascent part of him back to the forefront. *There's no turning back.*

No. One night, twenty years in the past, cloaked in grief, then left behind to stand on its own. That's the only intimacy they'd ever shared. So, no, whatever happened, wherever it led them to, this . . . would not be that.

From the moment she'd entered his tree house, he'd felt he was climbing out of his skin. He'd all but hidden upstairs in his office, but when that didn't help, he'd come back down to the kitchen. She made him laugh, made him think, made him want to wring her neck. Sometimes all in the span of a single sentence.

And he'd never wanted anything or anyone as much as he wanted her. Now. Here.

Now that he had his hands on her, he was so caught up in wanting her soft skin bared to his touch, open and willing for him to taste, he couldn't decide where to begin, where to start. He wanted to strip them both down and take her right where they stood.

Needs unmet for so very, very long would be an easy excuse for his uncontrollable desire to have every part of her, all at once, and yet he was very well aware that it wouldn't matter if he'd availed himself of every woman he'd ever met since that single, stormy night. None would be Delia, none would bring him to the brink of what was surely insanity. The demand to sink himself into carnal oblivion with her was so white hot he thought it might just burn him alive.

He drew her legs up over his hips, groaning when she pressed so intimately against every last straining inch of him. How on earth had he thought he could go the rest of his life without having her again? And how was it he hadn't known that she was the one he'd been waiting for, the only one he'd ever wait for?

"Hold on to me," he said gruffly, moving his mouth from hers, nudging her chin up so he could move his lips from the soft lobe of her ear, to the sweet throb of the pulse just below it.

She crossed her ankles behind him and he moved his arms to support her, wrapping them lower on her back, shifting her up so she could wrap her arms around his neck. She buried her face there, and then started to nibble her way along his jaw, as she raked her fingertips up the back of his head, over his scalp. The sweet pressure of her body against his, the sharp nip of her teeth, the scrape of her short nails, all combined to create a jolt of pleasure so intense, it was like simultaneously putting each one of his nerve endings against a live wire.

A crack of thunder outside was followed by a tree-shaking bolt of lightning, making the house sway, as it was built to do. Delia froze, her hold on him tightening to a clutch. "Holy—did that strike the house?"

"We're fine," he murmured, continuing to drop kisses along her neck, nudging her shirt collar open so he could move to the curve of her shoulders. He was so used to the vagaries of the weather on the island, they didn't intrude on his single-minded task of tasting each and every inch of her.

"Ford—" She gasped as he nipped at her shoulder, and groaned when the muscles running along her inner thighs reflexively squeezed around him. "The house. It's—moving."

He was dying by inches, wanting more, wanting it all, wanting it now.

"The house is built to move with the trees," he murmured between kisses. "Storms can be intense, sound intense, but we'll be okay." He moved back to her mouth, his lips hovering just over hers. "I seem to remember another storm, another night . . . you weren't so bothered by the sound and the fury then."

He could feel that the tension, the fear hadn't left her, but she smiled against his lips. "Was there a storm that night?"

She kissed him, and he groaned, deep in his throat. Playful Delia, with that throaty laugh of hers, just might kill him where he stood.

"I must have been distracted," she went on, nipping his bottom lip, making his body leap to painful rigidity.

"Well, then, let's see if I can . . . distract you again." He turned and carried her toward the couch, thinking he'd be fortunate to make it that far when he would have been happy pressing her up against the wall in the kitchen.

But she wrapped her arms around his neck, broke their heated kiss long enough to press her lips to his ear. "Would you . . . take me upstairs?"

The hesitant catch in her voice did him in. He'd been so intent, so caught up, he hadn't thought . . . "I would take you anywhere."

He felt her tremble, and swore silently that he hadn't made her feel she was worth cherishing, worth the comfort of a bed.

He nudged her face back to his as they reached the bottom of the ladder. "Grab the ladder," he said, turning so she could slip her legs free and take hold of the ladder. As soon as she did, he turned and offered his back. "Climb on."

She laughed. Actually, it was more of a giggle, which was incredibly endearing, and just as sexy as her laugh.

"I may be a disaster on the rocks, but I'm pretty sure I can handle the ladder," she said.

He could hear the breathlessness in her voice, and smiled, knowing he'd put it there. "But then I wouldn't get to keep you wrapped around me," he said, and turned to glance at her just in time to see the pupils in her eyes shoot wide and her lips part on a soft gasp. It gave him immeasurable pleasure that he was apparently affecting her every bit as much as she was affecting him. He turned back once again. "Hold on to me, Dee."

He might have gasped himself as she slid the palms of her hands over his shoulders, taking the time to run them down over his chest before looping them lightly there. He reached back and ran his hands up the sides of her legs, then all but growled as she began to do amazing things to the nape of his neck with her tongue and teeth. He leaned his head back, giving her greater access, and slid his hands a bit farther up her legs than necessary to get hold of her thighs in order to lift her so she could wrap her legs around his hips.

His fingertips slid between her thighs as he lifted her and pressed, briefly, between them. She cried out, the sound muffled against his neck, and he felt her muscles clench under his fingers. His own knees lost a bit of their stability in that moment; then her long legs were wrapping around his waist, her hands splaying across his chest, sliding inside his open plaid jacket, grazing across the front of his T-shirt, over his nipples.

"If you don't stop that," he ground out, "we'll never make it to the first landing."

"I'm thinking now that maybe that's not such a bad thing," she murmured, then traced her tongue along the side of his neck. "We can work our way up there."

And that was all it took.

He gripped her thighs, held them, and pressed her back against the ladder. "Tuck your hands under one of the rungs," he instructed hoarsely, then turned within the circle of her legs as she did. "Hold on," he said. Saying a silent message of thanks that she'd taken off his hoodie, he gripped the front of her blouse and ripped it open. "Sorry about the buttons," he said, already leaning in and cupping his hands over her breasts, rubbing the taut nipples between his fingers through the thin silk of her bra.

"I'm not," she breathed, sounding a bit stunned, but her blue eyes all but glittered into his now. She let her head tilt back to rest on one flat rung, sliding her hands behind and around the one over her head, and relaxed into him as he pressed his hips into hers, pinning her there.

He gripped her hips, forcing her legs to unhook and drop from his hips, then shifted her up a rung so he could lean in and take one nipple into his mouth, suckle it, then the other. She writhed under his tongue, panting soft little gasps as her heels sought purchase on one of the lower rungs.

The moment they did, he slid his hands from her hips, under her open shirt, and unclipped her bra, then pushed it aside so he could taste—"Ah," he groaned as he finally closed his mouth over bare, heated skin, tasting her, drinking her in. She arched against him, her hands gripping the ladder rung as she twisted under his tongue, his teeth. He slid his hands down, around, to the front of her pants, grappling now, wanting, needing—he freed the button, the zipper, and shoved pants, panties, down her legs. She took over, kicking off her leather flats, wriggling, writhing, to fling the garments free as he undid his own belt, his own jeans.

"Ford," she cried, and it was a keening demand as she arched her hips, bared to him now, looking to him like a pale, perfect, porcelain Venus.

He grunted when he finally got his pants undone, shoved down, freeing his rigid, aching—"Jesus," he breathed, as she hooked her heels around him, drew him in.

He gripped her hips, lifting her onto him, pushing into her slowly, then fully in one life-releasing thrust. She growled this time and her heels dug into him as she locked him between her thighs, greedily keeping every inch of him inside her. He thought if a man could die from the intensity of pure pleasure, he'd have gone straight to his great reward right in that instant.

He steadied himself, or tried to, then lost what little control he had when she tipped her head forward and nipped his bottom lip again. He claimed her mouth like a man starved, letting her take his tongue just as her body was taking the rest of him. She didn't wait to let him establish the rhythm; she just met him thrust for thrust, no slowing down, no effort to make it last, just a furious, frantic race to nirvana, which was surely right there . . . right *there,* just one . . . more . . . thrust.

They both groaned, grunted, shouted, uncaring how loud they were, heedless of any force but the one that bound them together. The fury of the storm outside had unleashed itself in full. Thunder boomed, lightning rattled, but all he heard was the storm going on inside his body, his head . . . his heart.

He could feel himself gather, feel her shuddering, trembling, and knew the instant she peaked and went over the edge, she would rip him rocketing right past it with her. Some sliver of sanity wormed into his brain as he sought to control the climb, focus on her. "Dee," he panted against her mouth. "I—we're not—we didn't—"

She shook her head, apparently understanding his meaning. "It's okay. I'm—it's—" She let her head tilt back and lifted up just enough that he slid in a fraction deeper. "You can—" She panted, lifting her hips another fraction, then opened her eyes at the last second as he felt the tremors race straight up her legs, and looked right at him, into him. "Trust me, Ford," she said.

Then he shuddered, pushed, and she cried out, shattering all over him, her body wracked with almost convulsive spasms, squeezing him so hard he let out a long, groaning shout and went over with her.

He lost track of how long they clung to each other. He slid his arms around the small of her back, holding her to him, holding himself to her. He wasn't sure who was holding up whom as they both shuddered through the first wave, then rode the first twitch of aftershocks, then the next, then the next, until she finally relaxed, her body no longer bowed. She let go of the ladder rung and slipped her arms around his neck as he pressed her back against the ladder and buried his face in the curve of her neck.

"Dee," he breathed, but that's all he could manage.

"I'm sorry," she said, when she finally could control her breathing.

That had him frowning, tensing, and lifting his head. "For?"

"I should have—I mean, we should have talked, discussed—I know you think I must, that I'm—that I have had—" She stopped, closed her eyes, clearly trying to draw her scattered thoughts into order.

He gave her the space because he honestly had no idea where she was going with this.

She opened her eyes, and found his gaze, held it, then finally got her breath back. "I know there wasn't really time to talk about protection. I'm on the pill," she said. "But, more than that, I know I have a reputation, for dating. A lot. And I have."

"Dee," he said, relief washing through him, even as his heart squeezed just a little, that she thought she had to confess anything to him. "You don't have to—"

"I do for me," she said, so he fell silent, and nodded at her to continue. She lifted her hand, pressed her palm to his cheek, and took his gaze just as intimately into her own.

The squeeze in his chest became a pang. The way she looked at him should terrify him, but it did the exact opposite.

"I haven't," she said. "In a long time. But when I did, I always used protection." She drilled those beautiful blue eyes into his. "Always. And I make sure I'm healthy, annual checkups. Because I'm not stupid. And . . . when I told you not to . . . that was a first for me. I wanted you to know that." Now the red climbed into her already flushed cheeks and a smile hovered at the corners of her mouth. "It seemed important. At the time." She dipped her chin and he slid his hand up and tucked her cheek against his shoulder, then leaned down and kissed the top of her head, keeping his hand on the back of her neck and shoulders, just holding her to him, not sure if the trembling was her, or him, or a bit of both.

"I appreciate," he said, at length, "that I mattered enough for you to feel the need to explain." He pressed his lips against her hair. "That I mattered enough for you to want me, like that. I do trust you. More than you know. More than I even knew I had it in me to trust." He nudged her until she turned her face to his, until he had her gaze fully on his. "And I'd have taken you if you were going to die tomorrow and doing so would have taken me with you. Do you understand that?"

Her lip quivered, and her eyes went all glassy. "Ford . . ." she said, on a choked whisper.

"You said no turning back. I couldn't turn back, because there's nowhere else to turn, no one else to turn to. Just you. It's always been you."

She opened her mouth, closed it again, looking stunned as a single tear tracked down her cheek.

"Don't—" He stopped, then pressed her cheek against his shoulder again and wrapped his arms fully around her, holding her tightly against him. "You don't need to say anything to me. I just . . . needed you to know. You needed to know."

Chapter 16

Delia stood alone in Ford's little circular shower in the main floor bathroom, which was the only bathroom in the central tree house, she'd found out. Her legs were still shaky. As much from Ford's declaration as from what had happened up against that ladder. She closed her eyes as the hot water beat down on her head and shoulders, willing the steady sound of the water, both inside her little cubicle and the greater rushing sound of the rain now thrumming heavily on the roof of the tree house, to find its way inside her head, and calm her rampantly racing thoughts. *What in the hell had she done?*

She hadn't thought any of this through. *Jesus, Delia.* She hadn't just stepped inside the circle, she'd gone and taken a flying leap off a cliff. Ford's words, so many of them, all of them, played through her mind over and over. And they were just as beautiful, just as powerful, just as devastating, every time.

How was it that she'd earned something so ... incredible, so worthy, from a man like Ford? That she felt all those same things in return, could have said all the same words to him, only served to heighten the panic that threatened to send her into a hyperventilating mess.

She understood, intellectually, what her deal was with relationships. It was a bargain she'd struck with herself a very long time ago. And she'd been quite comfortable with it; that deal had stood her in good stead. She hadn't suffered the slings and arrows of heartbreak, hadn't had to pull herself from the depths of despair, to repair her heart, or find the grit, the determination, the idiotic foolishness that would enable her to go right back out and risk it all over again.

Oh, no. She'd been far too clever for that. Life had handed her a nasty platter of betrayal, tragedy, and loss at a tender age, but she'd learned from it, hadn't she? She hadn't marched out there only to suffer through it again and again.

Only, all along, the joke, apparently, had been on her. She'd spent all that time congratulating herself on avoiding the pitfalls of love and relationships, and somewhere along the line had completely forgotten about the benefits she was also missing out on. It wasn't that she hadn't borne witness to countless happy couples, wasn't that she didn't believe in a happy ever after. She had, in fact, quite sincerely rooted every last one of them on. Because that was for them, and all the power and joy of it to them, too. It just wasn't meant to be for her. It was a risk she chose not to take.

It was true that watching the particularly heart-tugging and grief-surpassing love blossom between her friends Alex and Logan had reached some heretofore hidden spot inside her heart. She'd been thrilled for them, still was, but would be lying if she said that there hadn't been, for the first time, a little twinge, the tiniest bit of envy. Then Grace had come to Blueberry, and not only had she brought out an entirely new side of their brash Irish import, Brodie Monaghan, she'd introduced the gallant and incredibly sweet and wise Langston into Delia's life. She'd even forged her own path into Delia's day-to-day life, as a friend. And then there was Ford. Grace had come to the Cove to reunite with him, had wanted to know all about him, and who better to ask than Delia? Who else could she have asked if not Delia?

In doing so, that chapter of Delia's life, so long ago closed and tucked away, had been reopened. Not just the part where Ford had played a starring role . . . but all of it. Losing Henry, losing Tommy, then Gran. Even Ford. How had Delia not seen that that was the beginning, that it was that series of events that had sown the seed of her discontent? How could she have possibly been so blind not to have seen that that was when the hollow ache inside her had begun to yawn wide?

She understood now why she'd been so resistant to Ford, and it wasn't the stress, the fatigue, the creeping uncertainty about her life, much less about her diner's future. It was the opposite. It was that somewhere inside her, she'd known letting him in would mean letting down her walls. And that would lead to her having to confront what was really going on, what it was she really wanted. That what she wanted . . . was him.

"And now . . . here he is," she said, squeezing her eyes shut. She should be delirious with joy. She should be doing a little tap dance of glee right there in the shower. She'd gotten what she wanted, hadn't she? And so very . . . very much more. To want and be wanted in equal measure. "Who could ever ask for more than that?"

There's no turning back.

How prophetic her words were indeed. No turning

back, no more being just friends, no more keeping her heart safely tucked away.

And the very knowledge of that, of the step she'd taken, scared the living bejesus out of her. She'd managed to go all this time, living by her personal code, a code that had worked for her, and then what did she go and do? Hand her heart over to the one person who didn't just have the ability, the power, to hurt it, or break it . . . oh, no. She'd handed it to the one man who could shatter it. Into a million tiny, irreparable little shards. She wouldn't recover from losing Ford Maddox. Not like this, not now. Which meant not only was there no going back . . . if she lost him, there would be no going forward, either.

The shower started to grow cold. "You really have to stop having breakdowns in hot water," she told herself, and shakily turned off the spigots, then grabbed the towels he'd given her before going out into the storm.

Because that's who he is. The man you just up and surrendered your heart to. The kind of man who goes out in a thrashing lightning storm to check on a wounded baby bird. How could I not love a man like that? Dear God, I'm so incredibly doomed.

Ford's foray into the thunderstorm had come about after he'd gone to find her something to change into, because her blouse wasn't exactly wearable, and her pants had seen better days as well. First he'd offered up another one of his well-worn, freshly laundered hoodies and a pair of heavy socks.

"How many of these do you have?" she'd asked, as he'd handed her the faded navy blue sweatshirt.

"I live out here year-round. That includes Maine winters." He'd smiled. "I could probably open up my own secondhand shop."

Then he'd gone up to his office and rummaged through boxes of promotional samples that routinely showed up at the foundation offices from companies hoping to solicit souvenir and advertising business. He'd come up with a pair of women's black sweatpants and a bright green T-shirt, each with a different version of the foundation logo silk-screened onto it, both still in their original plastic wrappers. He'd handed them over, and then announced he had to go out to the hut to check on the puffling. When he'd gone up to his office, he'd noticed that the cam had cut out, and a quick look through the porthole window he'd put in at the office level showed that all the lights had gone out in the rehab hut cluster. "The generator flickers sometimes, especially in hard weather. I just need to check on it, make sure the generator shed is closed up, kick it back on again."

He'd pulled on a tarpaulin coat and dragged the hood over his head, and then out the door he'd gone.

Damp and shivering, Delia tore the plastic wrappers off the clothes and pulled everything on, then toweled her hair a little more. She didn't look in the mirror, because then she'd never leave the bathroom again. He'd seen her at so many levels of awful by now, crazy hair was the least of her worries.

She heard the door open and close, and stilled in the act of gathering up the wet towels and the remnants of her previous outfit. She wasn't ready to go back out there, to do or be or say whatever it was she was supposed to do, or be or say. That was yet another reason why she shouldn't be doing this. Why she should have kept things casual, easy. *Why couldn't you have stopped at friendly banter? Huh? Why?*

Because when he'd looked at her, so fiercely, so intently, then yanked her into his arms, the first thing

that had gone through her stunned mind had been . . .
finally! Like after all that time apart, after all the life
that had been lived, they'd finally made it to that right
place at that right time.

But now that we're here . . . what the hell do I do about it?
She really needed more time to think, more time
to analyze and sort through and figure out what this
was going to mean and what choices she was going to
have to make. Only there was no more time and she
couldn't hide in the damn bathroom forever.

She opened the door, thinking she'd start by asking
where he put dirty laundry, maybe offer to do a load,
then hotfoot it back to the kitchen and start the meal
they'd never gotten around to having. In fact, it had
been the damn cast-iron skillet she'd left on the low
burner to temper with oil for the corn bread that had
jerked them out of their little postcoital conversation.

At least in the kitchen she'd have a chance to further collect herself, collect her thoughts. Kitchens were
her safe spots, her havens.

Only she stepped out of the bathroom to find Ford
standing just inside the kitchen door, jeans soaked to
the skin, tarpaulin coat dripping wet . . . and the baby
puffling once again strapped to his chest, under the
coat, in the bird sling.

And any hope she might have had of salvation was
lost as her heart tumbled, utterly and completely, right
at his feet.

Delia rushed across the room, setting her damp
towels and clothes on one of the kitchen chairs so she
could help Ford disentangle himself from wet canvas
coat and birdie sling.

"What happened?" Delia asked. "Is she okay?" She
glanced up at him and saw the wind had been at him
along with the rain because even with the canvas coat

and hood, his hair was damp and his face ruddy from the wet and the wind. "Are you okay?"

"Yeah, just frustrated with myself. I meant to check the gas level for the generator but forgot. We didn't use it much this past season, and it ran out."

"Do you need to get more then?"

He shook his head. "No, it's fine now, I have it running. But the combination of the light and heat going out and the sounds of the storm must have panicked her pretty good. It's nothing she hasn't heard before—"

"But not while in a metal cage in a strange place by herself." She leaned down as he unhooked the harness, wrapping her hands around sling and bird so the straps could slip from his body. She pulled the baby bird into her body, but left it tucked in the fabric.

"I couldn't calm her down and I was afraid she'd injure herself further, so I figured I'd bring her back here. Maybe we can get her to settle down. I've got a few boxes that I think will work up in my office. Just need to dump some stuff out of them."

"I'll hold her," Delia said, already murmuring to the frightened bird. "She's scared. You can feel her heart drumming, but she's not panicking, so that's a good sign, right?"

"Yes," he said, sliding his coat off and hanging it on a peg so that it dripped onto a large mat that had been placed under the row of pegs apparently for that exact purpose. The wellies she'd worn, along with a pair of his hiking boots, were lined up on the mat. "Hopefully after a night or two she'll be good for release. Did you get hold of Peg?"

"I did. Thank you for the use of the phone. The storm hit there just a bit ago and she said it was pounding the harbor pretty good. No one is going out in that tonight, so I told her to close up shop and go on home. I don't know the forecast and didn't think to ask, but tomorrow is Sunday, so we won't be busy until after morning services let out, and probably not really busy until closer to dinnertime. Do you think . . . ?"

He picked up on where she was going before she finished. "Depends on the surf. Even if the storm blows out of here by morning, the surf is likely to be pretty rough for a while due to the wind. I'll check for small craft warnings in the morning. I'll know more then. I know that might not be—"

"No," she said. "It's okay. Stowaways don't get to pick and choose their boarding times. I'll just need to know for Peg, that's all. She can handle it. And I seriously doubt Mayor Davis is going to make an announcement of any kind on a Sunday. I happen to know he's a big football fan and preseason games start airing tomorrow. Most everybody will be home or at the Rusty Puffin all afternoon. It's more important to make sure we do what needs doing for our little feathered friend there."

"Well, I'll hold out for that Disney ending for you," he said, an amused smile coming naturally to his face.

She noted there was a definite light in his eyes, too. Even with the damp hair, the weather-reddened cheeks, and soaked jeans, he looked . . . happy.

Which made her insides get all jumbled up, so she looked toward the kitchen, used it as kind of a grounding visual spot, and said, "I was going to get the meal going. I, uh, ended up in the shower longer than I thought. I'm really sorry, the hot water is gone. I should have realized your supply wouldn't be big—"

"It's okay. By the time I get her set up, it'll be good to go again." He took the bird back from her in his big, capable hands.

She'd been in the direct care of those big capable hands and though that baby bird couldn't know it, she'd lucked out in who she'd gotten as her rescuer. *Maybe the same could be said for you,* Delia's little voice added.

"As for dinner, as long as it's something hot, I'll be forever grateful," he said, turning toward the ladder and his office.

"That I can do." She watched him cross the room. "Do you need help navigating her up the ladder?"

He looked back over his shoulder at her and Delia was pretty sure her heart bounced once, and then came to a complete stop. She'd never seen Ford grin like that. It was pure sex with a little devil on the side. Okay, maybe not so little. There was nothing little about Ford Maddox. *Seriously, just go ahead and beg him to take you right here, right now. You know you want to,* her little voice taunted. *Boy, do you ever.*

"I think if we want to get her set up before sunrise," he said, a bit of an edge to that voice, just to make the whole package completely lethal, "you and I should probably not be near this ladder at the same time." It was possible his grin turned a shade more devastating. "Fair warning."

"Warning taken," she said, not at all surprised to hear the breathlessness in her tone. More surprising was that she'd formed words at all.

He navigated the ladder easily and gracefully, like the overgrown marmoset he was, while Delia gripped the back of the closest chair and tried to put her pheromone-overloaded brain cells back into her head.

"So," she murmured, as she made her way to the kitchen counter, then stood there staring dumbly at it. If she'd had any questions about whether or not Ford had been having second thoughts, she supposed she had her answer. "I guess that means I'm not going to have to worry about where I'm sleeping tonight."

She glanced upward briefly, and thought about what the top level of his tree house might look like . . . and what it would be like to spend time up there with Ford. Any hope she had of making smart, clearheaded choices would likely be gone completely if she spent the night in his arms. In his Disney tree house bedroom.

But . . . then what? She had to go back to the Cove and sort out pretty much her entire life. He had his work out here. Sure, he had Grace also living in the Cove, but ever since her arrival, Ford's sister had always come out to the island to see him. Delia figured that could change, but to what end? His work was on an island at the farthest reaches of the bay. Hers was in the Cove.

Well, it always had been in the Cove, she thought. It wasn't quite the same as Henry asking her to go to Alaska with him, and it wasn't as if Ford had actually asked her to do anything, make any choices . . . but the fact remained her life would have to change if she wanted Ford to be part of it. She tried to see the end of her diner as some kind of sign, that maybe fate was taking away one thing in order to force her to look at what else there could be. Like when Tommy had been taken away from them, then O'Reilly's had burned to the ground, forcing her to regroup and make a new plan.

Except it didn't feel like that. Ford was right. She did love feeding people, and a big part of that was because it put her directly in the midst of the energy and life that made up Blueberry Cove. Ford hadn't asked her, but living out on Sandpiper with him, while wonderfully intimate, would eventually suck the soul from her. She needed people, and noise, and the general chaos that was day-to-day life in a small town, not the solitude that he craved. Sure, there were the ten weeks in the summer when the island was crawling with interns, but that left the other forty-two weeks. . . .

She paused in the midst of chopping up a fresh batch of vegetables to go in the omelet and looked around her again. Everything had happened so fast, she hadn't had time to really think about what the possibilities would be for her, could be for her, in terms of starting up a new place in the Cove, but her gut was telling her one thing for certain. "I don't know if I could live out here," she murmured. "Not full time."

She forced her attention back to the food, took solace in the rhythms of chopping, sautéing, whisking. She scratched the corn bread idea and whipped up some cheddar bacon drop biscuits instead. She searched and found plates, silverware, glasses, and by the time she heard Ford coming down the ladder, she had their meal set up on the small kitchen table.

"That smells incredible," he said, coming straight to the kitchen.

He'd changed into fresh jeans and another T-shirt with an open flannel shirt over it, his wire rim glasses tucked in the chest pocket. His hair was toweled, but his face still bore a bit of redness from the wind and rain. He'd shaved, too, she noticed. He looked big and warm. And happy.

She turned back to the kitchen and retrieved the basket of biscuits, ignoring the pang in her heart.

"How is our patient doing?" she asked, searching for a comfortable subject, wanting—needing—to calm her nerves. *Just let it all go for now. Sit and eat a meal. It's not like he asked you to run off with him.*

"She's still nervous, but a great deal calmer overall.

You'll be happy to know she rethought her position on the herring and made quite a pig of herself. She's back asleep."

Delia smiled at that, sincerely pleased. "I'm relieved. Now it's our turn to pig out." She pulled out a chair and he did the same. She served and they both ate in silence, with Ford making the occasional appreciative groan over the omelet and the biscuits.

When she reached to start clearing the table, Ford surprised her by placing a hand on her wrist. She looked at him questioningly. "I can make more biscuits, but the eggs are gone."

"No, that's not it. I can clear the table; you cooked."

"I don't mind—" she began, but he moved her hand to the table, and then put his hand over hers. His expression was serious, she noticed, and he wasn't paying the least bit of attention to the empty dishes and platters. His attention was focused entirely on her.

Her body was confused. It didn't know whether to go all fluttering hearts or knots in the stomach. So it did a little of both. For that matter, so did her thoughts. She settled in her seat. "I really don't mind," she said, stalling.

"When I went to check on the puffling, it gave you time to get in your head, start to have thoughts."

She blinked. She was not used to being around a man who was so damn perceptive and observant. And so focused. It was impossible not to respond, but her brain was scrambling at the sudden shift to serious discussion. "Well, I just, we hadn't really even talked about—I mean, I hadn't given any thought to—I wasn't expecting us to—"

He mercifully cut off her stammering by saying, "I did some thinking, too."

The flutters in her chest fell silent, but the knot in

her stomach pulled tight. This was why she didn't do relationships. Too many chances for the other person to make painful choices that she'd have no control over. "Okay," she replied, unsure what else there was to say.

"The look on your face right now is exactly why I wanted to have this conversation."

The wonderful meal she'd just prepared and eaten started to make her feel not so wonderful. "What look would that be?"

"Utter panic."

She immediately looked affronted. "I am not panicking. What would I panic about? I mean, I get it, we lost our heads, hormones got the better of us. Who knows, maybe we're just triggered by storms or something. It's not like I'm going to get all clingy and start making demands, if that's what you're worried about. I know you like your alone time. I'm not exactly—"

"What I'm worried about is that you won't. Make demands. Or want to make any kinds of plans. What I'm worried about is you'll do exactly what you're doing right now."

"I'm being rational, calm, practical—what, were you expecting some kind of emotional—"

He squeezed the hand he'd covered with his own. "I'm expecting you to assume the worst. And I understand, completely, why you would."

She opened her mouth, already prepared to refute anything he might have said. Except, perhaps, that. She snapped it shut again.

"When I said I'd been thinking, why did you automatically assume it was something bad?" He shook his head, then picked up her hand, and wove his fingers through hers, which scrambled whatever brain cells she had left. "Because that's where your thoughts had already gone," he answered for her.

"Ford," she said, completely abashed. "It's not what you think. I just—"

"I understand," he said again. "You've done what I've done. We've both kept certain parts of ourselves apart from everyone else."

From somewhere inside her panicky, jumbled thoughts, she managed a sardonic smile. "In your case, that would be all parts."

He smiled briefly. "True. I get that your default position is to pull back. So is mine."

"So you're saying . . . what, exactly?"

He held up their joined hands, propped his elbow on the table. "That I don't want to do what I've been doing. I don't want to pull back."

Her heart crawled out of her knotted stomach and started fluttering again. Only it might have been more accurately described as a kind of rapid thumping. "Meaning . . . ?"

"I don't know. I mean, like you said, it's not as if we thought this through." He tightened his fingers when she would have slipped her hand free, certain he could feel the tremble in them. "But I want to," he said. "I think we need to. Only not while you're in the shower and I'm out fixing generators. I think we'd do better if we thought it through together." He grinned again, and it rocked her even harder this time, because it was even more unexpected. "I figure if we have any chance of not reverting to form, we need to be each other's backup." He pulled their joined hands closer to him and leaned forward, until he could press his lips against the side of her bent fingers. It wasn't exactly a kiss, more of a plea. "That is, unless you want to go back to keeping yourself apart."

"I—" She broke off, her mind spinning, heart thumping, body clamoring. It was all too much, and he was right, her first instinct had been to prepare herself for the worst, to retreat.

"Answer me one thing," he said, "and be brutally honest. Because that's also what we'll need to be, for ourselves, and for each other."

"O-okay."

"When I asked if you wanted to go back to keeping yourself apart, what was your very first gut reaction? Not what you thought after feeling it, just that immediate reaction. Was it relief? Or was it dread? Or panic? Or some other feeling like 'Please, don't let this be over?' "

Delia was surprised by the question. Surprised to realize what the answer was. She looked at him, her eyes widening. "Please, don't let this be over," she said in a hushed whisper.

His grin this time was so wide, his smoky gray eyes all but glittered with it, and she thought if there had been any chance whatsoever that she might have found a way to avoid whatever lay ahead between them, good or bad, that chance had just passed her by. Snuffed out by the all-consuming need she discovered she had to get as many of those heart-stopping grins directed her way as humanly possible. A lifetime of them would be like winning the biggest lottery ever.

"So . . . now what do we do?" she asked, no longer panicked so much as finding herself in a place she'd never been before. A place where two people wanted each other, and were willing to figure it out. Together. Henry hadn't done that. He'd issued ultimatums, putting his happiness above hers, above theirs. To be fair, she'd done the same. Putting her family's needs above her own, and above those of her husband.

She'd been so young then, so inexperienced in how to handle herself, her fears, life in general.

A lot of life had happened since then. So why was she still playing by rules she'd established when she'd barely been past the verge of adulthood?

"We figure out what we want to do, about us," he said. "Whatever that is. Then we'll talk about what we need to do about everything else. And how we can make the two fit together."

"How is it you have such a clear way of looking at things? And where were you when I needed this kind of clarity four months ago? You have a way of putting things in perspective that makes it so much easier for me to figure out what's what."

He pushed his chair back and stood, pulling her around to his side of the table and into his arms. "I wish I could say I learned it in doctorate school, just to make you—" He broke off, and smiled. "Give me that look," he finished, and she stuck her tongue out at him. "Careful where you aim that," he said.

Delia was pretty sure that when she'd wondered what Ford would be like when the lights twinkled back on in his eyes, and inside his heart, she'd had absolutely no idea just how dangerous a combination that would be.

"It came from my time as a ranger," he said, surprising her, both with the serious shift, and the comfortable way he'd said it. "I learned to look at things differently, assess situations with a very different kind of clarity. Observe, understand, solve. Emphasis on the *solve*. There was no time to get bogged down in what-ifs, or analyzing things to death. I learned to go with my gut, to live by my gut."

"And what is your gut telling you?" she asked, still a bit shaky. "You asked me what my reaction was . . . what's yours?"

He smiled and slid his hand under her hair at the

nape of her neck, and lifted her mouth to his, so naturally, so simply, that she felt her nerves smooth out, and the edge of panic skitter away.

"My gut is telling me that these dishes will wait until morning." He grinned against her mouth, then kissed her until she wasn't sure which way was up. "Want to see if we can make it past the ladder this time?"

Chapter 17

They made it past the ladder, but it was touch and go. Mostly touch. Ford watched with barely restrained hunger as she climbed the ladder from his office loft up to his bedroom. Hunger, hell, he was starving. He wondered how long it would take before he didn't feel the need to have her wrapped around him with every breath he took. This was when he wasn't wondering why the hell he'd waited so long to go back to her in the first place.

They had managed to take their hands off each other long enough to check on the still-dozing puffling. Although, come to think of it, they hadn't actually stopped touching each other then, either. Her hand had found his and held on as he knelt and checked on the sleepy chick. He smiled at that, liked that she felt the need to stay connected to him, prayed she didn't let go of that need once they were no longer cooped up in his tree house together.

The puffling was happily nesting in a box tucked into the recessed foot space under his desk in the makeshift burrow he'd constructed. The storm had dwindled to a steady rain, which he hoped was more soothing to the healing puffling than alarming.

Now it was time to take Delia up to his own nest. That would be a first for him. He'd come to Sandpiper to heal, and to be apart while he did so. The summers were a frenzy of activity and, over the years, his tree house had become frenzy central. It wasn't something he naturally loved, but he'd come to terms with the hubbub; it was productive and he wouldn't have to use two different office spaces. But his nest, his aerie at the top of the tree house, was his sanctuary and his alone. The very few times he'd given in to the impulse for female companionship had been while he was traveling on foundation business. And while his body might have been okay with that arrangement, his soul had always felt a little more hollow afterward. After a while, it had been easier, or at least kinder to himself, to ignore the impulse.

It was too late to ignore what he'd gotten himself into now. Nor did he want to. Instead of leaving him feeling hollow and less of who he'd been than before, losing himself in all the wonderment and fire that was Delia O'Reilly hadn't felt like revisiting the past in some sort of empty reach for a long-ago moment. No. It had felt like coming home. Like he was exactly where he was supposed to be, after having been lost somewhere along the way. Really lost.

Oddly, it was Delia's own struggle to come to terms with what she wanted—him, thank all merciful gods— and what she'd always told herself was better for her— being alone—that had clarified for him what he wanted. It felt utterly wrong to him, like a giant backward step, for her to shy away from what they had done, from where it could take them. Which meant it was equally wrong for him to do the same.

That she was willing to try, that she was climbing the ladder upward, literally and figuratively, was no small miracle. He knew that. She might be struggling with a number of things in her life at the moment, but she was not a wishy-washy, ambivalent sort of woman. Once she decided on a track, she was strong, committed, and loyal. He realized now that was why she'd been so uncharacteristically subdued regarding her diner being in peril. She hadn't decided on her track.

He was smart enough, knew her well enough, to know that a simple conversation over a single meal was not going to magically change Delia into someone who would allow herself to run willingly toward something she'd been actively running away from her entire adult life.

There was also the not-so-little matter of the rest of her life being upside down. He wasn't sure if that was a blessing in disguise for them, if the great probability that her diner would be taken away from her would allow her to rethink everything, including the possibility of something long term with him. Or if, with everything else going on, she'd feel overwhelmed, making her that much more determined to control the things she could, namely, not dealing with him or the demands of trying to have a life together.

Because it wasn't going to be some kind of Disney movie fairy tale. It was going to take a lot of discussion, of being bluntly honest with each other and with themselves, about what they could and couldn't handle. Each of them would have to make considerable adjustments in order to be together. And she was already facing the mother of all considerable adjustments with Mayor Davis's impending decision regarding her diner. He knew she wasn't just going to pack up and move to Sandpiper. She wasn't a loner, and she certainly wasn't the sit-around type. She was the antithesis of that.

Which was where his major adjustments would come into play. Her life, as she knew it, was going to evolve into something else completely, because of the diner, because of him, but whatever that life was, a good part of it would be spent in the Cove. His life would evolve then, too, because he wanted one that included her and, he realized, included Grace, too, which meant he'd also be spending time in the Cove.

He would have to come to terms with having someone invade his world, his space, wherever that space happened to be. That it was Delia, that he wanted her like he wanted his next breath, was a good thing. A great thing. An amazing thing. But that didn't negate the reality that he was going to have to get used to an intrusion into his day-to-day world unlike any he'd had since moving to Maine. If he couldn't get used to Grace popping up on his laptop screen whenever she felt like it . . . how was he going to handle being available to someone twenty-four/seven?

"Oh, Ford," Delia gasped as she climbed up through the opening, and then stepped off the ladder, which ended a few feet up above floor level. "This is incredible."

He finished the climb and stepped off the other side, flipping a switch to illuminate a small lamp by the queen-size bed that dominated the room. He watched as she took in the last part of his home. He recalled her comment about him referring to his place as base camp. Maybe he'd spent too long on military outposts and in science labs and his brain was utilitarian-wired, but that's how he'd always seen it. It wasn't some psychological thing. At least, that had been his reaction to her comment. But seeing her standing there in his bedroom . . . he realized this was the first time he'd naturally thought of it as home.

"I didn't see the skylights from outside." She looked at him. "Is the snow a problem on them in the winter?"

"It can be. The trees deflect a fair amount, but I also built the roof with solar panel stripping and additional generator-powered stripping designed to heat up and melt the bottom layer, causing the snow to slide down and off. That's why they're on that side and at that angle. It's the one side that doesn't lead down to a deck, where an unsuspecting head might be located when the avalanche occurs." He noticed she'd stopped looking at the pair of skylights that angled on the opposite side of the roof from where his bed was positioned, and was looking instead at him, highly amused. "What's funny?"

"I was thinking earlier that if I asked you about this house you'd be able to give me the scientific rundown about it much the same way you did about the migration and mating patterns of your seabirds."

"Nailed it, huh?" he asked, smiling briefly. It was disconcerting to be read so easily, not that he'd taken great pains to mask his thoughts or feelings. It was enough, though, that he had a better appreciation of how she felt when he passed along one of his many insights into her behaviors.

"Pretty much," she said, grinning. "I was going to say it was a cool design feature that seemed almost whimsical in a home that's otherwise very function-over-style oriented. But I'm sure you'll tell me there is some scientific reason for the skylights that has nothing to do with their aesthetic value."

"Only if you ask me," he said, lips twitching, but otherwise taking the fifth.

She laughed outright at that and, as her laughter always did, it caught at that place in his heart that was hers. They'd spent less than a full day together as something more than friends, but he was rapidly losing whatever remaining piece of his heart he could call solely his own. He wasn't as poleaxed by that realization as he'd thought he'd be. In fact, it was his lack of alarm that should be most alarming to him.

He credited his sister with being the one to crack open the heavy vault door he'd kept that particular piece of himself locked behind all these years . . . not that he planned to share that information with Grace. In the brief time since he'd been reintroduced to what life was like when there was a member of the opposite sex in his day-to-day orbit, he'd utilized his special forces training in ways he'd never thought he'd have to.

Never divulge secret information. Mission planning is strictly need-to-know basis, and the other side never needs to know. Of course, he'd also been trained to never surrender, but that had gone out the door the first day Grace had pulled up to Sandpiper's only dock. It occurred to him that the fast friendship Delia and his sister were forming would likely test him in ways the rangers had never even anticipated, and he might have silently groaned. A little.

He watched Delia look over the rest of the octagonal room. The walls were only four feet high, and then changed to ceiling, which was of exposed beam construction and pitched immediately inward on all sides, rising up to the point at the top. Industrial-strength skylights had been installed in two of the roof sections. His bed was tucked against the wall diagonally below, so the sun rose behind it, and set over the skylights. He'd built drawers and shelves into the walls on the far side of the bed, and a cedar chest into the remaining unused wall section on the near side. Delia had been right when she'd said that functional use of space in a tree house was key.

He also had a taller, narrow rack space boxed out on the office level, which held the few suits he owned, as nothing longer than a shirt could be hung up on this floor. Not that he had any other clothes that required a hanger. At least, he didn't think they did. He wondered what Delia would say if she knew that the hoodie collection she'd been seeing was pretty much the beginning and end of his sartorial choices.

She turned back to him and he stepped into the room, delighted when she didn't hesitate but simply moved naturally into his arms and smiled up at him. "You know, I'm thinking when Grace and Brodie have kids, you'll be like the coolest uncle ever."

Now *that* poleaxed him. He'd never even considered the possibility. He was still getting used to having his sister around.

Delia laughed again. "If you could see the look on your face right now." She slipped her arms around him and hugged him tightly. "I'll protect you from the rug rats, I promise. I have special forces training of my own when it comes to crowd control and unruly tykes."

He wrapped his arms around her and pressed his lips to the top of her head. "I am not too proud to accept any and all assistance in that area," he said, still feeling a little shaky at the very idea of having nieces or nephews romping about. Okay, maybe a lot shaky. "In fact, it's possible there could be begging involved."

She snickered against his chest, then reached around and pinched him right on the ass, which surprised a wide grin out of him. "Didn't they train you in ranger school never to show your weaknesses?"

"I thought we were allies?" He lifted his head and

leaned back just enough to look down into her face. "Don't you have my back? You clearly think you have my backside."

Her teasing expression immediately softened and she tipped up on her toes and planted a fast kiss on his mouth. "Always," she promised. Then she grinned up at him. "For both parts. Doesn't mean I won't work things to my advantage whenever possible. That's what I learned in street-smart school, doc."

He chuckled. "On the mean streets of Blueberry Cove?"

"You've lived through Maine winters, right? I know a whole new level of mean."

He had to nod at that. "I concede the point." He started backing her toward the bed. "But I reserve the right to take advantage of your weaknesses then as well." He levered her off her feet and onto the bed, following straight down on top of her and pinning her hands beside her head before she knew what had happened. "I mean, fair's fair."

She smiled up at him, but he hadn't missed how her gaze had already dipped to his mouth . . . and neither had other parts of his anatomy. "That is true," she said, then closed her eyes and faked a martyr's expression. "Just, go gentle with me."

He leaned in and caught at her bottom lip, suckled it, then moved around and nipped her earlobe, making her hips instinctively arch up into his. "You sure about that?" he murmured against her ear.

"How about—" She broke off on a gasp as he lifted up just enough to strip her sweatshirt straight up and onto her arms, but not off altogether, leaving her hands and wrists bound by the twist of heavy cotton. Her eyes were wide, but her pupils had almost swallowed up all the glittery sapphire surrounding them. "Fine, just do your worst then," she said, but her faux defenseless victim ploy was ruined by the way her gaze kept getting all tangled up on his mouth, then his eyes, then his mouth again. "I'll never crack."

"Oh, I don't want to make you crack," he said, then started working his way down her torso. "There is something else I'd like to make you do, though."

He was drawing the tip of his tongue in a line straight down from her navel when, between gasps and the sweetest little moans he'd ever heard, she managed to say, "Please tell me . . . they didn't teach you this particular . . . kind of torture . . . in ranger school."

He glanced up as she writhed beneath him. "Some things just come naturally."

"Please God," she panted, pressing her head back hard against the bed, "let me be one of them." He chuckled, and then she let out a long groan that ended in a hot little growl as the tip of his tongue found nirvana.

By the time he'd driven her up, slowly and quite deliberately to the edge, considering every one of those growls his reward for a job well done, he'd lost control of his own hips, which pressed repeatedly into the mattress, getting little to no relief for the effort.

"Ford," she gasped, wriggling under him.

Then her hands were on him, her fingers weaving through his hair, and he realized she'd been wriggling her hands free from the sweatshirt sleeves. She tugged him gently—well, maybe gently was underselling her urgency a bit—and prodded him upward.

"Please," she said, and the rough need in that one word was all he needed—or, more to the point, all the more needy parts of him required—to abandon his current post and move on to a new mission entirely.

So intent was he on enjoying the trip from base

camp number one, to base camp number two, with a decided and intensely pleasurable layover in the hills he had to cross in between . . . the opposition pulled a surprise attack.

One second he had his lips wrapped around the most deliciously hard nipple, and the next he found himself flipped to his back and a wild, red-haired virago straddling his hips and pinning his wrists to the bed. His CO would have drummed him right out of the rangers for it, but he gave up without making even a token struggle. His wide grin was a further indictment as it indicated his complete lack of remorse on that matter.

"My turn," she said, releasing his wrists and sliding her soft palms along the undersides of his arms.

He considered making it at least a little more challenging for her, but then she slid her palms to his chest, shifting back a little, before sitting upright . . . and sliding right down onto him in the process. So his countermaneuvers would have to wait, until his eyes stopped rolling back in his head.

She began to move on him, and he decided surrendering completely wasn't entirely out of the question, either.

Her little gasps every time she moved her hips downward finally had him opening his eyes, and then cursing himself for missing even a second of the incredible view before him. If she'd been a pale Venus before, this time she was a virago goddess. In command, if not entirely in control, as her own body challenged her with every shift and slide to keep her focus on anything other than her own pleasure.

He watched her take her pleasure from him, working herself higher, then higher still, and thought his heart might explode from the thundering pace she'd driven it to. He was torn between the gift it would be watching her fall apart all over him when the inevitable climax ripped through her . . . and rolling her to her back right that second and claiming her like the wild animal she was turning him into, not certain he could survive both.

But then she let loose a keening wail as the edge was reached . . . and raced right over, followed by the intensely satisfied pants and groans that followed as her body rode out the wave, milking it for every last ounce of pleasure that could be had from it.

By some miracle, she didn't rip him straight past the edge with her, but his control had frayed beyond his ability to hold on any longer. And when she pressed her thighs to his hips and let loose with the most incredibly satisfied laugh, he rolled her to her back and pushed every last inch of himself into her so fast, so hard and deep, they almost moved past the edge of the opposite side of the bed. She didn't even pause, her smile turning to a delighted if devilish grin, her eyes back to glittering sapphires once more as he took her again, and again . . . and again, until it was his turn to groan and growl.

When his body finally slowed, finally stopped convulsing, he was so utterly spent, he barely had the strength and wherewithal to shift to the side and pull her to him rather than simply collapse the entirety of his weight on top of her.

"You don't have to do that," she murmured into his chest, then pressed a kiss over his still thumping heart. "I like the feel of your weight on top of me."

"Good . . . to know," he managed. "Next time."

She kept her cheek pressed to his chest, but slipped her hand up and cupped his cheek, then drew her fingertips along his jaw, across his lips, and down over his chin in a gesture that was both sweet and intensely erotic. That he could even register the latter in his current state spoke volumes about the impact she had on him.

"Deal," she said drowsily, then tucked her foot between his calves, and relaxed into sleep.

Ford dragged the heavy down comforter over them, then slipped his arms around her and let his head sink back farther into the pillow, every protective instinct he'd ever owned all but raging inside him. Only this time, the instinct wasn't to protect himself. It was for the woman he held cradled to his chest.

"Please, God," he prayed, never more sincere in his life, "don't let me ever let her down." Only he knew, even as his eyes drifted shut and he slipped into slumber, that the only one accountable for not letting that happen was himself.

Chapter 18

Delia was awakened by the pitiful bleating sounds of a hungry puffling.

She blinked her eyes, or tried to, and pushed haphazardly at the hair that had tumbled into her face, trying to figure out what that sound was and, more important, where she was.

The warm skin under her cheek would have resolved the second question, but she'd already breathed in the distinctly pleasurable scent that she was happily and swiftly becoming quite attached to. "Ford?" she murmured, untangling their legs and managing to shift so she could prop herself up on one elbow and stare down into his beautiful sleeping face.

The dim light coming through the skylight proved they'd slept straight through the night. It also proved that while the rain might have stopped, the skies were still quite overcast. "Like having your own little weather station right over your head," she murmured to herself.

Ford didn't so much as grunt at the sound of her voice, so a delighted Delia took the opportunity to drink in her fill of his face. She might have peeked at the rest of him while she was at it. *Island living might have its challenges,* her little voice said, *but it certainly does have its benefits.* His body couldn't have looked any better if he'd still been undergoing the daily rigorous routine of a special forces operative.

She smiled and had to stifle an utterly smug little giggle when she thought about the rigorous routine they'd put each other through. *Twice.* She wasn't as successful at hiding the wide grin that came with that, but there was no one around to see, so she took the opportunity to simply revel in the moment, to soak in all the goodness and joy she was feeling. Who knew what the day would hold, much less the days that were to come. Right now, in that spot, for that space of time, Delia O'Reilly was happy. Stupidly, giddily, perhaps-even-foolishly-but-who-cares, deliriously happy.

Her self-satisfied little moment was cut short by another pathetic bleat from below. "Poor puff," Delia whispered. She started to turn with the intent of sliding as quietly from the bed as possible to go check on the little thing, but stopped, looked back at Ford, and then dropped a short, sweet kiss right over his heart. Feeling the smug smile again, she returned to her initial intention, only to have a strong arm clamp up and around her waist.

Her gaze flew to Ford's face, but his eyes were still closed and he appeared for all the world to still be deeply asleep. Not another muscle in his body had moved other than the arm he'd quite swiftly and most decidedly wrapped around her. She'd just begun to wonder if perhaps it was some latent instinct from his ranger training and if she had anything to be concerned about, when he slid his other arm around her, then let the flat of his palm trace the curve of her waist, her derriere, and down to where that curve met her upper thigh.

"One more," he murmured, the rough gravel of his voice doing delectable things to all of Delia's most pleasurable nerve endings.

So, okay, his hand on her ass might have had a little bit to do with that as well. "One more . . . ?" She braced herself, preparing to find herself on her back any second; then, when it didn't happen, she smiled and leaned down again. "We have a hungry puffling to feed." She kissed his chest again.

He made a deep, happy groaning sound, and his lips curved upward. "Thank you," he said. "Those are nice."

She was briefly confused. "Those . . . oh," she said as comprehension dawned. She was surprised to feel a little blush steal into her cheeks. She'd thought he wanted to start the new day the same way he'd ended the last one . . . when what he'd wanted was another little heart kiss. Which was possibly the sweetest thing ever. *Ford Maddox, stop making me fall madly in love with you,* she wanted to beg him. Or she should have been wanting to beg him. Somehow she was still smiling and not feeling at all panicky. *What was up with that?*

There came a more demanding bleat from below, and she stifled her laugh against his chest, but looked up to see him grinning, too. He finally opened his eyes and dipped his chin to look down at her. *And dear Lord help me, those eyes are only making the fall an even more rapid descent.*

Gone was inscrutable Ford, or Dr. Rambo Ford, or exasperated Ford, or even grinning, calculating Ford. She knew exactly what to do with those Fords. The eyes she was staring into now, if she wasn't mistaken, looked like a whole new Ford she'd never met before.

Affectionate and open Ford was a complete and total stranger.

But every fiber of her being yearned to do whatever it took to get as up close and personal to that Ford as was humanly possible.

He drew his hand what felt like reluctantly back up her body, and then paused to play with the ends of her curls as he continued to regard her with that new Ford expression of his.

"We should probably feed the poor little thing," she said.

"We should." His stomach chose that moment to growl and she snorted a laugh, and then laughed even louder when she saw him look a bit chagrined at himself.

She poked a finger in his flat belly. "We should feed you, too, apparently." She started to sit up, but he simply shifted her body so she lay completely on top of him.

"I have a particular menu in mind," he said, and the grinning, calculating Ford returned.

Delia's body was perfectly willing to welcome him back, too. "You know, you can't just manhandle me because you're bigger and stronger than I am," she said, trying, and epically failing, to sound aggrieved at his high-handed maneuver.

"If I let you manhandle me back, would you consider it a fair division of power?"

She laughed and rolled her eyes. "How about you go feed the puffball and I'll go make us some breakfast? That's a fair division of labor. We can discuss division of power later."

He let his gaze drop and linger on her mouth, then rise ever so slowly back to her eyes. Her entire body trembled as it remained pressed to his.

"You sure they didn't teach you this stuff?" she said faintly. *Wow, but you pack a pure, carnal punch when you put your mind to it,* she thought. Hell, just breathing and doing absolutely nothing, he was pretty damn hard to resist.

He stopped toying with her hair and pressed his fingertips to the back of her head, pulling her slowly down until her mouth met his. Her eyes drifted shut and she moaned as he kissed her slowly, thoroughly, and deeply. As if he had the rest of the day, possibly the rest of his life, to get it right.

She was ready to clear her calendar, too, when he ended the kiss and rolled them both to their sides.

"You'd better go first," he said, "or I'll never get out of this bed."

She looked at him, and then laughed. "You just want to watch my bare ass."

He tried and failed to look affronted by the accusation. "That's not true." Then the grin crept back across his handsome, morning stubbled face. "I also wanted to watch these bounce a little as you climbed down the ladder." He slipped his hands up to caress the sides of her breasts.

"Men," she said, but her matching grin pretty much erased whatever exasperation she was able to inject into the single word.

"Guilty as charged," he said, then propped his hands behind his head.

Delia knew he expected her to give him a hard time, or wheedle him into climbing out of the warm cocoon of the bed into the chilly morning air first. And being predictable would never do. He was so observant and all wise, it would be good to shake him up whenever the occasion presented itself. Otherwise, he'd just be insufferably smug.

Her grin might have turned just a shade malicious, right before she yanked the heavy down comforter they'd burrowed under at some point during the night straight off them both—what was good for the goose, after all—and dumped it to the floor. Then she jumped off the bed, swung her backside in an exaggerated wiggle as she went over to the ladder, turned, and shimmied her shoulders for all she was worth as she carefully climbed down through the opening in the floor.

And she was rewarded with yet another new Ford— the gob-smacked Ford—for her efforts.

Her smile of victory faded a bit when she made it to the office level and realized she was cold, naked, and all of her clothes were back up in the bedroom loft. She moved on tippy toes to the chair behind his desk, snatched the sweatshirt draped across the back, and pulled it on. As it passed over her face, she paused in the act of pulling it on to take a deep whiff. *Delia, honey, you've got it bad.* Seriously, though, was it his fabric softener or what? Would a man like Ford even use a fabric softener? She had no idea, but damn, even his day-old hoodie smelled good.

She yanked it the rest of the way on, past her hips, before he came down the ladder and caught her mooning over his old sweatshirt like a college coed who'd just scored the quarterback's jersey. She bent down and took a peek in the box under Ford's desk and melted at the black-beaked face looking up at her. Baby puff let out the most soulful bleat ever and Delia made apologetic noises. "He's coming down to feed you, I promise. If I had some fresh herring on me, I'd feed you myself. Aw, you poor little sweetheart. How is your foot?"

In response, the baby chick let out an even more pathetic bleat, then turned her back on Delia and settled down with a huffy little fluff of its feathers.

Delia grinned. "Well, I guess I've been told." She tiptoed on the cool wood floor back to the base of the ladder and called up to Ford. "Fair warning, the patient is in a mood."

"Good," he called back down. "Means she's getting her fighting spirit back." A moment later, a pair of thick wool socks were pitched down through the hole in the floor, causing her to duck and cover her face.

"Nice aim."

"Nice ass."

She laughed at that. "Thanks." Then, "For the socks, I mean." She pulled them on, and then paused before climbing down to the main floor and said, "Okay, and for the ass compliment."

"The pleasure was all mine."

"Not true," she called back as she climbed down the ladder. She might have paused about halfway, thinking about what had happened the day before on that very ladder rung. "Not true at all," she whispered as she climbed down the remaining rungs. She hurried over to stoke the potbelly stove, which was sputtering out nothing more than ember heat, then peered outside the deck doors before heading to the kitchen to see what there might be to rustle up for breakfast. She wasn't particularly heartened by the overcast skies or the dearth of anything breakfast-food-related, but found herself smiling as she heard the floorboards creak overhead. "Life could be a lot worse."

She finally decided on another batch of cheddar biscuits, sadly without bacon this time, but there was a jar of blueberry preserves and she could put together a small fruit and cheese plate. Once she got the biscuits in the oven, she would tackle the dishes left from the evening before. Funny how she didn't mind the chore so much because she was too busy grinning like a fool recalling why it was they'd been left overnight in the first place.

She'd just washed the mixing bowl and utensils she'd need to make the biscuits when she heard the phone chirp up in his office. A moment later Ford called down, "It's Peg."

Delia looked at the clock on the stove and saw it was just after seven. "Why would she be calling this early on a Sunday?"

Ford climbed down the ladder—sadly, he'd found his clothes—and brought her the phone. "I have no idea. Why don't you ask her?" He handed her the phone, but didn't let it go when she reached for it. Instead, he used the leverage to tug her in for a fast, knee-knocking kiss.

He lifted his head, smiled down into her face, then went and grabbed the cooler that held ice packs and herring off the deck, and headed back up to his office. All the while Delia stood on unsteady legs and watched him dazedly through hormone-fogged eyes.

"Delia?" came a squawk from the phone.

"Oh!" She put the phone to her ear. "Peg, hi, sorry. I was . . . distracted."

"And no one's more glad to hear that than me," she said in all sincerity, but Delia heard the edge to her voice and the fog cleared instantly.

"What's up?" she asked.

"Well, remember you told me to pack it in early yesterday?"

"I did. I mean, I do, yes. Did something happen at the diner while it was closed?"

"You might say that."

Delia's stomach knotted like an anxious parent getting bad news about a child. Then she remembered that whatever had happened would be moot to her if the town was selling it to Winstock. "Hopefully something that's only toxic to the development and building of a yacht club," she replied.

"Actually, it is about that."

Delia straightened, worried all over again. "What happened, Peg? Just tell me straight out. No sugar coating required."

"Well, I came by this morning to do some early prep before going to church and found a notice tacked to the door."

"A . . . notice? On the door? What kind of notice?"

"An eviction notice."

"What?" Delia had all but screeched the word, and took a moment to pull herself together and tamp down her anger. "Are you telling me that Mayor Davis couldn't even be bothered to inform me directly, or send a letter, something? Really? I can't believe he'd do that."

"Well, I'm sure we can blame him for making the decision to go with Brooks Winstock's offer on the property. But the signature on the notice is Ted's."

"Weathersby." Delia swore under her breath. "Still, that's pretty shitty. Excuse me for saying," she added, knowing how Peg felt about swearing.

"Actually, I would have to agree with you."

"And he did that on a Sunday? How low can they stoop? And why? I mean, they won. I lost." She shook her head. "I just guess I thought I deserved better than this."

"No guessing about that. You do, honey, you bet you certainly do. Small consolation, but just so you know, according to the time and date on it, they came by yesterday when we would have been open, but—"

"I had you close early due to the storm. Still, I'm not

sure that would have been any better. Serving me with some kind of legal papers in front of my customers. Everything about this stinks."

"Well, honey, as I say, if it acts like a pig, rolls around in the muck like a pig, you can't rightly expect it to come up smelling like a rose, now can you?"

"No. I suppose you're right." *Still*, she thought, it didn't just make her mad. It stung. It wasn't as if she'd even actively opposed or tried to shout Winstock down. Hell, she'd been so wrapped up in her own worries, she hadn't said boo to Winstock, or his hateful daughter for that matter.

"I'm not sure I can get back there today, Peg," she said with a resigned sigh. "I honestly didn't expect anything to happen this weekend."

"Might be why they did it like that." She paused, then said, "Might be that most anyone in the town who matters knows you're out on Sandpiper with our Dr. Maddox."

Delia started to ask her how—or why, for that matter—anyone knew or cared where she was, but she knew the answer to that. A town the size of the Cove thrived on local gossip. She'd have to get used to being part of that for a change, she guessed. And fast, too, considering she was about to hand them the mother of all grapevine special bulletins when word got out about the eviction notice. She sighed at the thought, and then smiled briefly. She'd liked hearing Peg say "our Dr. Maddox," so there was that.

"Mayor Davis never exactly struck me as the type to have any starch in his shorts, if you know what I mean," Peg continued.

Delia spluttered a surprised snort at that. "I do, and I concur. Good thing he's not running for reelection, the weasel. Not that his replacement is going to be any better."

"Worse, I'd say. Especially given what his father-in-law is doing."

"Sure wish I could get Owen to reconsider running against Ted so we'd at least have a fighting chance before Brooks Winstock steals the whole town out from under us."

"I know, honey. I've talked to him, too. He'd be such a good candidate. Honest and fair."

"Well, maybe we need to bend his ear again. When word gets out about this, maybe it will light a fire or something."

"Maybe," Peg said, sounding doubtful. "And don't you worry about getting back here. It's not like they're going to come dragging me out by my hair."

"Peg," Delia said, instantly alarmed. "You don't think—I mean they've already stooped this low. Is there a date saying when—" Out of the blue her voice caught, broke. She took a breath, then another when the first one hitched. *They're going to tear my diner down.*

"I'm so sorry, Delia. I truly, truly am. You know if there's anything we can do, some petition we can sign—"

"It's over, Peg. I think we need to face that and—" She broke off again as the enormity of what was happening started to crash over her, the horror of it and the pain combining to make her gulp back a wave of fresh tears. It wasn't just the mayor making a chicken-shit move on her while she was gone. It was also the fact that word was going to get out swiftly, people were going to be upset, and she was stuck out here on an island in the midst of heavy seas that were going to last for God only knew how long.

"I'll hold down the fort here. You just get back when you can."

"I appreciate that, but I'm not going to put you through any more than I already have. I want you to put a sign up saying we're closed. Put the damn notice on my desk, call Charlie and whoever you got to cover for Pete—how is his hand, anyway?"

"Old coot," Peg grumbled. "Ask him, all he needed was a little crazy glue and a Band-Aid. I told him his brain was held together by crazy glue. I did manage to keep him from coming in though. I got Charlie for today and Kevin is on board if we need him."

"Well, call them and tell them I decided to close today. I'll pay him anyway, and you, of course, then—I'll figure something out," she finished, her brain scrambling but not pulling things together very well.

"I'm not worried about my paycheck and neither is Charlie. Don't you risk coming back right away. Small craft advisory is in effect today. Stay out there. Take advantage of that strong pair of shoulders you've got with you and lean on 'em a bit. You hear?"

Delia felt like she was walking into a thick haze. Stumbling, was more like it. She'd known at the courthouse it was going to happen. Had that just been yesterday? Seemed impossible. A lifetime of things had happened to her since then. But there was a whole new lifetime waiting to unfold as soon as she set foot back in Half Moon Harbor. And she wasn't ready for it. Plain and simple . . . she wasn't ready.

"I thought I'd have more time," she whispered, her voice tight with unshed tears. "I mean, I knew it was coming, but it wasn't even two weeks ago that Brooks made his snake-in-the-grass move in the first place. How much time do we—?"

"Notice says September fifteenth."

"But that's just a little over a few weeks—" She stopped, realizing that it was exactly thirty days after her lease had technically expired. "What a rat bastard," she muttered. "What does Brooks Winstock think he's going to do in the month or so we've got before the first snowfall hits? Does he really need me to be gone this instant? What the hell? I mean, I know he's an aggressive businessman who doesn't hear the word 'no' too often, or ever. But I guess I never thought he'd do something this . . . well, this mean. Doesn't he realize that a little goodwill would go a long way with the townsfolk? He's going to make a lot of enemies kicking me out."

"It's just business to a man like him. He doesn't really care what we think. But I'll tell you this. His smarmy daughter even thinks about stepping one foot in this place, and I'll take a frying pan—"

"I'd say I'll promise to bail you out," Delia said with a watery laugh, "but honestly, Peg, she's not worth the effort." The haze wasn't lifting; instead, a nice headache was settling in right along with it. She wanted to tell Peg just to lock the place up and walk away, that she'd deal with it when she got back, whenever that turned out to be. Sixteen days might as well be no days. But that meant her employees would be immediately jobless, and she couldn't do that to them. Two weeks wasn't much, but they could at least be earning a wage while looking for new—her face crumpled and that thought trail went right along with it.

"You go have yourself a good cry," Peg said, sounding miserable. "Maybe I will, too. I'd say we've earned it. I'll close up today if you insist, but we'll be back tomorrow, I'm telling you that right now. We're not just folding up the tent and going quietly into the night."

Delia didn't have it in her to argue or overrule.

"Okay," she said. "Thanks, Peg. I appreciate everything you've done. Are doing. You know that, right?"

"We've all got each other. That's what matters. That's what's important. I'll call if anything else pops up."

"Thank you, Peg," Delia said, tears burning the corners of her eyes. She clicked off, then stared unseeing at the phone.

She jumped slightly when broad palms bracketed her hips. Then she immediately slumped against Ford as he pulled her back against his chest, reached for the phone, set it aside, and wrapped her up against him with his cheek pressed to the top of her head.

"How much did you hear?" she asked thickly.

"Enough."

She opened her mouth, and then closed it again. There was nothing to say. No point in raging against Winstock, or Ted, or the mayor. They weren't worth the energy. The grief, however, wasn't going to be so easy to duck out from under. "Twenty years," she whispered shakily, and then dissolved completely as the tears finally burst forth.

Ford turned her in his arms and wrapped her up tightly against his chest. As before, he said nothing, just held her, her rock in the storm, steady and unwavering, trusting that she could fall apart without needing any guidance on the subject from him.

When the worst of it had passed, he let go with one arm long enough to grab paper napkins off the table and press them into her hand.

"Thank you," she said, sniffling. "I haven't cried in so many years, I can't remember when I did last. Yet that's all I seem to do around you."

She blew her nose rather inelegantly, and his hold on her never wavered.

"We all need to let it out from time to time," he said.

"Not me," she said.

"Even you," he said more quietly, tucking her cheek back to his chest. "You just keep it bottled up. Probably why it's shaking you so much now. Maybe all you needed was a port in the storm."

"A place to tether to," she said, and slipped her arms around his waist.

He held her as her breathing slowed, hitching less. At length, he said, "None of this is going to be easy, Dee. Not the situation with the diner. Getting through the next few weeks. Or figuring out what comes after." He snuggled her a bit more deeply into his arms. "I know this isn't going to be easy, either," he said, and she knew he was referring to whatever it was they'd begun since coming out to the island.

She nodded against his chest, knowing he was right.

He leaned back until she tipped her chin to look into his eyes.

"Just promise me you won't pull away. Won't think this is something you have to do on your own."

"Ford—"

"I mean it," he said. "We've spent a lot of years hard-wiring ourselves to go it solo. I imagine when the going gets tough, either one of us might opt to rely only on ourselves so no one else gets caught in the crossfire. If we go down, at least we only take ourselves out in the doing."

She just stared at him, and was surprised to see one corner of his mouth briefly kick upward. "How'm I doing so far?"

She surprised herself and him by finding a rueful smile of her own. "Remind me not to fall for a guy who thinks just like I do."

He cupped her cheek then, tipped her face up to his. "Are you, Dee?"

"Am I what? Going to duck? I—I can promise you I'll at least tell you what's going on, but if you're out here and I'm in the Cove, then I'm going to do whatever I think needs doing."

"I'm coming back with you."

She lifted more of her body away from his and stared fully into his face. "But the chick—"

"Is good. I'm going to file the nail down today, do a closer examination of the foot, but the damage is surface; nothing important was injured or broken. I think she could be released in the next day or two."

"But—"

"I'll radio Blue today and see who he's got coming out to this area. He puts boats out in weather that would terrify a Norse warrior. One of his guys can come by. We can meet him out at the edge of the harbor in my boat, and they'll get you in. I'll follow as soon as our B&B guest up there is ready to check out."

Delia smiled again, and realized there was something to be said for having a shoulder, and not just to cry on. "It helps," she told him. "A lot. Just being able to talk about it. It makes me feel . . . proactive." She looked up at him. "And less alone."

"Good." He smiled. "Even if I can't get back for some unforeseen reason, the phone works. Grace even taught me how to videoconference one-on-one, or whatever it's called."

"Skype."

"Right. So we'll talk, and . . . do that. Whatever we need to do."

She rose up on her toes, and pulled his head down for a hard, fast kiss.

"What was that for?" he asked, looking a little stunned. "Not that I'm complaining."

"I know I've managed to look out for myself for a lot

of years. Most of them, in fact. And I've been good with that. So, I'm not saying I can just flip the switch and suddenly turn to you for every last thing. But . . . when I pulled up to the courthouse to speak to the mayor, and ended up seeing the writing on the wall, the first instinct I had was to pick up the phone and call you. It shocked me, to be honest. But . . . that's where my mind went. So, it will be a process. For both of us. But I . . . I just wanted you to know that."

"Thank you," he said. "That does mean something to me." He paused, and then said, "Why didn't you? Call me, I mean."

She surprised them both by smiling. "Well, I sort of thought that all but fainting in your arms, apparently flashing you and unsuccessfully trying to seduce you, then not only admitting my lascivious nighttime thoughts about you, but falling completely and utterly apart in your arms, in my shower, with you dressed, would be enough to shame my subconscious into never dreaming about you again."

Ford's lips twitched, but he said nothing, forcing her to finish with no help from him.

"I would have been wrong about that," she said primly. "So calling you seemed . . . imprudent. I mean, was I calling for help, or was it my sex-addicted subconscious essentially begging me to drunk dial you?"

His mostly stoic soldier face broke at that and he let out a short chuckle. "Well, if it makes you feel any better, thinking about your admission—which was more a revelation, if I'm being honest—distracted the ever-loving hell out of me. If you had any idea what an impossible time I had trying to force my thoughts anywhere but there, and then you go rogue on me, leaping into my car, begging me to bring you out on my boat—"

"Whoa, whoa there, sailor. There was no begging."

"Only because I graciously allowed the damsel clearly in distress to stow away on my boat."

"So, it was simply a charitable gesture on your part."

"Yes. Compounded by the fact that I was already struggling to get my thoughts about you under control, so—"

"So you're looking for what, double Good Samaritan points?"

"Then you go and admit you have this sex-addled subconscious, so we may be talking more than double here as I see it, because—"

"Because you're so full of it. You know that?" Her laugh turned into a short squeal when he lifted her up off her toes. "Careful, you know where this led last time."

He closed his eyes for a moment, his face a picture of reverence. "I do indeed. I can't decide whether to have that ladder christened with some kind of plaque memorializing the date, or to replace it completely. The latter, I think, if I have any hope of ever getting any work done around here."

"Decisions, decisions," she said in mock sympathy. "I might have to replace Gran's claw-foot tub. For mortification reasons, of course. So it's not just you, bub."

He let her slide down until her toes grazed the ground, but kept her wrapped up against him as he dipped his head. "We could always reprise the shower scene, only with fewer clothes on my part, and fewer tears on yours."

"Mmm," she said, sneaking a kiss from him. "Maybe falling for a man who thinks like me isn't such a bad thing after all."

He looked into her eyes. "That's actually what I was asking earlier. You thought I was asking if you were going to duck and run, but . . ." He trailed off, suddenly looking as if he wished he'd never opened his mouth.

Delia played the conversation back through her mind, then her eyes widened as she looked up at him, and her heart bloomed even bigger. So big, so strong . . . she couldn't forget that didn't mean he wasn't vulnerable, too. "I am," she said, softly. "Falling. If that's what you were asking."

She saw not so much relief in his gaze as the comfort that came with acknowledgment. "Good," he said, his voice a bit gruff. He leaned down and kissed the corner of her mouth, then her lips, once, twice, then simply sank in.

Delia moaned softly and moved more deeply into his arms.

"Glad I'm not the only one," he said against her mouth as their lips finally broke contact.

She smiled, feeling her lips curve, still pressed against his. "Yeah, whose brilliant idea was it that going solo was a better deal?"

He chuckled, and then kissed her again.

Delia was pretty sure they wouldn't make it past the couch this time, only the phone chirped again. Ford was going to ignore it, only Delia broke their kiss just long enough to say, "I told Peg to call. If there was anything else that—"

Ford nodded and kept one hand on her hip as he stepped away to grab the phone from the table. He looked at the digital display, and then handed it to her without answering. "Peg," he said. "I'm sorry."

Delia understood what he meant. If Peg was calling again so soon, it probably wasn't with good news. She clicked the response button. "Hi, Peg, what's up?" She listened for a moment, her eyes growing wider with each passing second. "But how did they—" She broke off, and listened some more. "No, no, I understand. Yeah. We have a plan. I'll let you know."

Ford took the phone from her when she clicked off.

"I think you need to call Blue," Delia said, still trying to digest what was happening back in the Cove.

"Okay. What happened?"

"Well, seems as if Peg wasn't the first one to find the eviction notice."

Ford's eyebrows climbed up a notch. "Who else knows?"

"Old Lou came by. Lost track of the days, I guess. He does that. He didn't realize it was Sunday and we weren't open yet. Saw the notice, and . . . it only takes one grape on the vine to alert the whole Cove." She looked up at him. "And well . . . it seems that they've staged a protest in the park by the municipal buildings. According to Peg they made some signs and they're marching around and yelling at the mayor."

Ford's lips twitched. "How many is 'they'?"

"I don't know," Delia said. "I didn't think to ask." She shook her head, smiling just a little. "I'm really touched, but I can't let them do that. At this point, I wouldn't put it past the mayor or the town council to call Logan and have them arrested or something."

"Would Chief McCrae do that?"

Delia shrugged. "He might not have a choice if they're breaking the law." She looked up. "So much for that Disney ending, huh?"

Ford smiled. "I don't know. Having the townsfolk picketing city hall to save the town diner does have a certain Hollywood ending feel to it."

Delia smiled, too, but it was short-lived. "It does. But it will only make matters worse if they go and get themselves locked up."

Ford turned her into his arms and pulled her in close. "You going to be okay?"

"I have to be," she said. "What they're doing is the sweetest thing ever, but I can't—"

"I don't mean are you going to be okay for the town." He tipped up her chin. "Are *you* going to be okay? This is your diner. Your life. You've barely had time to catch your breath since this started."

"I know. You're right. I—I guess I don't know how I am." She smiled bravely. "But it looks like I'm not going to have to wait long to find out."

Chapter 19

Ford helped Delia down the ladder onto one of Blue's big trawlers. He handed down the kennel containing their disgruntled houseguest, and then climbed onboard himself.

"Ford," Delia said, holding the kennel with the puffling against her body. "You don't have to do this."

"Sure I do," he said. "She'll be fine," he added, nodding to the baby chick. Before Delia could protest again, Ford turned to the captain. "Thanks, Robbie. I appreciate this."

"Happy to," he said, "but you might want to strap in. It's going to be a bumpy ride, doc."

Ford slung his pack and Delia's backpack off his shoulders and stowed them in a console bin near the prow, then followed Delia and their resident patient aft. Delia hadn't said much once he'd made the call to Blue. They'd lucked out and Robbie had been about ten minutes out. Ford had made sure Blue explained to Robbie that he'd pay him well to make up for the lost time on the water. At the moment, he was more concerned about Dee.

She was clearly moved by the townsfolk's reaction,

but she was worried, too. He'd tried to explain that they were grown adults who were responsible for their own actions, but he understood why she'd feel a certain responsibility for what was going on. He was glad he could be there for her, but the hardest part was not being able to step in and fix it. Whatever "fixing it" might imply.

There was no doubt she was crushed at the thought of losing her livelihood, but he was certain she'd figure out how she wanted to resurrect herself and her business. He'd do whatever he could to help her. And it was clear the townsfolk, or a goodly number of them, would support whatever her new endeavor might be.

But saying that and actually going through the steps of dismantling the business she'd spent half of her life building, then figuring out how and where to move on, was not going to be a simple task. Not physically, and most definitely not emotionally.

"I don't want to watch," Delia said.

They were both sitting on a bench seat inside the wheelhouse, out of the direct wind. He looked down at her and saw she was staring out at the horizon line, though he doubted she truly saw it. He wasn't even sure if she knew she'd spoken out loud. He'd tried to take the burden of the kennel from her, but she'd just tightened her hold on it, and he'd understood that, too. He put his arm around her shoulders, though, and pulled her close.

"I watched O'Reilly's burn. The last of it, anyway," she said. "I'm not going to watch them tear down my diner. Once in a lifetime is enough."

His heart squeezed for her. He debated saying what had been going through his mind, then went ahead and said it. "It's a plot of land and an old building that you brought new life to, making a whole lot of wonder-

ful and lasting memories for a whole lot of people."
He looked down at her until she glanced up at him.
"They might be tearing down that building, but the
heart and soul of Delia's Diner is here." He tapped her
chest. "That means wherever you go, whatever you do,
Delia's lives on. No one can take that away from you,
for any price."

Tears glistened in her eyes, and her smile was
tremulous. "What did I do to deserve you?"

"You're my home, Dee," he said simply. "It wasn't
the Cove I came back to. It was you."

She pulled in a shaky breath, and then pressed her
head against his shoulder. He pulled her in more
tightly, careful to keep the kennel and its houseguest
stable on her lap as they braced themselves against the
rough pitch and fall of the boat as it trundled over
open water, cutting through the waves.

Robbie had explained he was going to take a longer
route back to the harbor, weaving through some of the
small islands to lessen their time on open water, where
the waves were the heaviest.

"We'll figure this out," she said at length and another little part of his heart settled at her use of the
word *we*.

He still didn't know how he was going to reconcile
the daily routine change he was facing, but what he
wouldn't lose sight of was the truth he'd just given her.
She was home to him. Any changes he had to make,
any adjustments they might require, would all result in
his having this woman next to him. Those changes
seemed suddenly insignificant, given the payoff.

He left her to her thoughts for the remainder of the
ride in, content that she stayed in the shelter of his
body, drawing from him whatever strength she could.
Once they got back to the Cove, he'd contact a few of

his volunteers and have them meet him at the foundation offices to set up puffling care. There were a few who lived in town, or close enough to it, who knew how to take care of injured seabirds. It might mean keeping the chick a day or two longer than was strictly necessary for her to heal, and he knew it was critical to get her out to sea before the summer turned any closer to fall so she could start her northerly migration. But it would all get done. They'd given the baby chick her best chance for survival. Now it was time for him to do the same for Delia.

Upon docking back at Blue's, he helped her up the ladder, then passed her the kennel and their packs once she was dockside before turning back to Robbie. He shook the older man's hand. "Thank you. If there's anything I can ever do—"

"Just keep up the good fight, doc. Blue said to give him a shout when you're ready to go back out."

Ford nodded, then climbed up to the dock and helped Robbie push off again before turning back to Dee. "My truck is in the lot, so I can take you wherever you need to go first."

"What about the chick?"

He explained his plans. "Why don't I take you to your house first? I'm guessing you want a change of clothes. I'll go by the foundation offices and do what I need to do, then meet you wherever you are by then."

She nodded, still looking a bit lost in thought. "Sounds good."

"Dee—"

She looked up at him. "I know I seem out of it, but I'm just . . . thinking. Planning. Not about what's next. I . . . I honestly don't know what I will do, but I do know that I want to keep doing what I do. I just . . ." She blew out a long breath. "It's the where and how that are a little overwhelming. The idea of starting completely over, building a whole new place. I guess it should sound exciting or something, but it just sounds . . . exhausting. And that's assuming I can even find a place that's worth putting the effort in on."

"You know you want to cook, to feed folks, give them a roosting spot," he said. "That's the biggest part of it. What, how, where . . . that will come."

She nodded. "I know. That's what I was thinking. I wasn't focusing on that, really."

Surprised, he said, "So, what were you thinking about?"

She surprised him again with a smile. "How to reward my champions down at city hall with a little support from their up-till-now somewhat shaky leader."

Ford grinned. He knew she'd find her footing.

"City hall handed me a pretty crap deal. I didn't deserve that, and neither do those folks who have supported me all these years. So, the very least we can do is give back the same." She handed Ford the kennel, then pulled her phone from a side pouch on her pack and scrolled through her contact numbers. "Winstock might have money, but I have wealth, too. Only mine comes in the form of folks I've kept fed and happy over the years. I think it's time to see if I can get that investment to pay out a dividend or two." A particularly satisfied smile curved her lips as she punched the button and held the phone up to her ear.

Ford wasn't sure he wanted to know, but his own smile matched hers as he heard the voice that answered on the other end.

"*Blueberry Beacon,* this is Brenda."

"Hi, Brenda," Delia said to the local newspaper editor, as she and Ford started the trek up the dock to the lot where his truck was parked. "I have a story for you. Yes, over at the courthouse. You already have someone there? Excellent. Hey, listen, do you still go to Mary-anne down in Machias to get your nails done?" She lis-tened. "Good, good. Her brother works for the local news station headquartered in Bangor, right?" Delia grinned as she listened to Brenda pick up that ball and run with it. "I was thinking the same thing. And any-one else he wants to bring along with him."

She hung up; then Ford watched as she scrolled, found, and punched in another number. "Hi, Sam," she said, when another woman answered. "I know it's a Sunday and you're not exactly close by but—yes, it is true." She listened some more. "Thanks. I appreciate that. Your mom is the sweetest. Yes, I'll tell her when I see her. No, no, there's nothing we can do to save it. But I was thinking you have media contacts there in Bar Harbor, right? Where Brooks Winstock has his yacht club membership? Well, maybe the local paper there would be interested to know he's trying to start up his own little club up here, and that might have a negative impact on the club there if he's thinking about culling some of his buddies from their member-ship roster to fill up his own." She paused. "Yes, sounds like it might make a great local story. If someone wants to get up here, I can promise that by this afternoon, there might be a little local color going on here involv-ing Mr. Winstock as well." Her smile spread to a grin. "Well, that would be fabulous. Yes, I believe he does have a golf membership there. I'm not sure what his plans are for adding any kind of pro level course here, but nothing would surprise me at this point. The more the merrier."

She clicked off as Ford stowed their gear in the back

of the truck and secured the kennel on the bench seat, wedged between the driver's seat and the passenger side.

"Do you—"

She held up a finger, stalling him, and he realized she'd made another call. "Yes, hi, Owen. Yes," she said. "It's true. I know, I—thanks. I really appreciate that, it means a lot. Listen, I'm going to be heading over to the park in the next half hour. Could you meet me there? There's something I want you to see." She grinned. "You rock. See you then."

She climbed in the passenger side and pulled her seat belt across her lap with a sharp little click. It took her a moment to notice that Ford was staring at her from his spot on the driver's side.

"What?" she asked when he simply kept staring.

His smile was slow, and wide, and he was surprised again by how good something as simple as a grin could feel. "You've found your track," he said.

She looked at him quizzically, but smiled along with him. "I don't know about that, but I do know that Mayor Davis will have to own up to what he's done, and the good folks of Blueberry Cove are going to see firsthand how their town council golden boy plans to do business if he's elected mayor. Also, everyone is going to know that Brooks Winstock might have a vision of a better Blueberry Cove, but he's not going to get any support if he plans to completely ignore the folks who already live here by stomping on them to get his way. And if a few other news outlets happen to spread the word of his plans to folks who might not be as happy with his expansion ideas . . . well, that wouldn't break my heart."

Ford grinned. "Like I said. You've found your

track." *About time,* he thought, relieved to see the Delia he knew come fully back to the forefront. He put the truck into gear and pulled out of the lot. *Look out, City Hall. You're about to find out what happens when you mess with a local icon.*

Chapter 20

Delia's palms were sweaty as she steered her SUV onto Front Street, toward the park. She wasn't second-guessing the little maneuvers she'd pulled earlier, when they'd docked at Blue's. She understood business was business, but she'd been raised to understand that treating people with decency and kindness was the best way to do business. It was time someone reminded the mayor, town council, and even Brooks Winstock of that little fact. She was just nervous about facing everyone, having to tell them that the good fight was over.

Her nerves were forgotten a moment later as she slowed to a stop a good block away from the park. Not because she'd changed her mind, but because she simply couldn't get any closer. The streets were jammed with cars, media trucks, and people. So many, *many* people.

When Peg had called her out on the island, Delia had had a vision of some ragtag group of her most loyal regulars, sporting homemade signs as they marched in a little circle in front of the courthouse.

She'd pictured Old Lou, Stokey, Arnie, maybe even Peg and Pete out there. But that vision paled, significantly, in the face of reality.

She pulled onto a side street and parked, and could hear the shouts even as far away as she was. Was that— was that Peg? Using a bullhorn?

Delia clicked the remote lock, stuffed her keys in her pocket, and hurried toward the courthouse. She had to duck and weave through people in order to see what was going on. A murmur started in the crowd around her and suddenly, like a magical parting of the seas, folks moved back as word spread that she had arrived.

Then, quite abruptly, she was almost stumbling out the other side of the crowd and into the small park. Which was filled, body to body, with people from the Cove. Faces she recognized, people she'd fed, listened to, grown up with, for God's sake. Every last one of them had signs waving in the air, most saying things like SAVE THE DINER and NO YACHT CLUB! Though she did particularly like the one that said, DELIA'S HAS HEART! MAYOR'S GOT NO SOUL!

They were all shouting "Save the diner!" and her heart swelled almost to bursting with the love she felt for each and every one of them. Fruitless as their endeavor was going to be, it was still a good thing that the town's constituency was being heard, that Ted and Brooks realized they couldn't just bulldoze the whole town the way they were going to bulldoze her diner. The townspeople had woken up now, seen what was going to happen firsthand, and they weren't going to just roll over and let Winstock do whatever he wanted. And if Ted had his eyes on anything bigger than being mayor, he was going to have to win back the people whose trust he'd lost the moment he'd tacked that eviction notice on her diner door. *And that,* she thought, *is the victory I'll take with me from all this.*

She spied Owen over by the courthouse doors, talking to Peg, who had mercifully put down her bullhorn for the time being. But before Delia could make her way over there, or figure out how she could address the crowd and let them all know how deeply touched she was by their support, a news reporter shoved a microphone in her face.

A perky brunette in a navy blue suit asked her, "Ms. O'Reilly, is it true that local magnate Brooks Winstock is forcing you from property that the city encouraged you to build on twenty years ago? The same property that you've run a very successful business on for all of those twenty years?"

"The city has decided not to renew my lease," Delia began, speaking the simple truth. "So as of the fifteenth of next month, the property will no longer be mine and the city can do what they want with it."

"And why did they decide to shut down a prosperous business, one I understand is a favorite of many of the locals here?"

"Mr. Winstock made them an offer that I can't come close to matching. It's almost triple the current market value."

"Why would he do that?"

"He wants to build a yacht club, bring in deep pockets to help grow the economic foundation of the town. My property—I mean the town's property, where my diner is located—is the only prime spot left on the harbor with deepwater docking suitable for such a club."

"So, he pushed you out."

Delia shrugged. "I was informed by a letter from the land manager's office two weeks ago my lease would not be renewed. And this morning there was an eviction notice on my door. I have sixteen days to vacate."

There was a collective gasp and mutters of disgust from the crowd.

"So, you're telling me that after operating a business here for twenty years—two decades"—she intoned, with the kind of gravitas only a seasoned news reporter could—"they are forcing you out and didn't even have the decency to inform you in person? Pick up the phone and make a call?"

Delia smiled thinly. "It would appear so, yes. The mayor is retiring this fall and from what I understand, he didn't wish to end his tenure by making an unpopular decision. However, as I imagine he also wants to be a charter member of the new yacht club, his hands were somewhat tied. The notice on my door, though, was signed by our mayoral hopeful, town council leader, Ted Weathersby. Who also happens to be Mr. Winstock's son-in-law."

The folks from the Cove booed that comment loudly, and all those who had come in along with the news truck caravan gasped again and started a murmur running through the crowd.

Delia had said all she needed to say. The media could take that and run with it, or not. She wasn't interested in getting folks any more worked up than they already were; she'd just wanted the truth out there. "Thank you," she said politely to the news reporter.

The brunette tried to collar her for a few follow-up questions, but Delia had already ducked away, intending to find Owen, and Peg, too. More microphones were stuck in her face, but when she kept on moving, those reporters turned to other locals to get their reaction to what their local politicians and business magnate had done.

Delia lost count of the number of hugs and hand-shakes she accepted and offered as she made her way closer to the courthouse. She was glad she'd done what she'd done. It wasn't about changing the course of things. The yacht club was going to happen; she was resigned to that, and she'd done a lot of thinking about it on her way back into town. Once again she'd found herself at a crossroads on her life path, but this time she was much better prepared to make decisions on what to do next. Her thoughts went to Ford, and she smiled. She also had a lot more to consider this time, too.

Before she could figure out the next step, however, there was one last thing she had to do, or at least try to do.

She found Owen still by the courthouse doors, but Peg had lost herself back in the crowd. Delia gave a quick scan, and then grinned as she spotted her faith-ful employee sharing her two cents with one of the re-porters. "You want your reaction sound bite, you'll get it from her," Delia murmured, and then said, "Owen," before he could turn away and be lost from sight again.

"Delia!" he said, looking relieved and a bit over-whelmed.

"Hi," she told him, and then gave him a quick hug. "I really appreciate your coming. I had no idea—" She waved her hand behind her at the crowd. "I mean, I knew there was a little demonstration going on, but—"

"I'm so sorry," he said, "about what the town coun-cil is doing. It's not right."

"Thank you," she said. "It's just how things go, I'm afraid. But they should have handled it better."

"You think?" Owen said, sounding uncharacteristi-cally worked up. "I mean, I think about if someone did something like that to me, to the hardware store. It's not just a store, it's part of Cove history. I mean, I know change has to happen, growth, but it needs to be responsible. Or at the very least handled with dignity and compassion."

"Fortunately," Delia said, happy to hear him say that, "you own your property, so you can rest easy. But you're right about the rest. Some of us, most of us—shopkeepers I mean, business owners—rent or lease our property. Many of us have done so for generations. In some cases the sons and daughters are leasing their shops from the sons and daughters of the original owners of those same shops. It is important that we pay attention to what's happening, that we speak up, not just when we disagree with what is being done, but how it's being done." She held his arm. "What did Lauren say? About you running?"

"She's for it," he said, looking both sheepish and proud. "I'm still getting used to her coming back. Wanting to come back. I had sincerely hoped she would take this degree and do something with it. She's the first one in my family and her mother's family to get a degree and, well—"

"But she is doing something with it, Owen. She's coming back to the Cove and bringing all those book smarts with her. We can't stay the same, but when we grow, we need to grow responsibly. Lauren will be ready to do that. I think you should be proud of her. It must be a wonderful feeling, knowing she loves you and loves what you've built, what her ancestors built."

"It is," he said, pure pride shining in his eyes. "And thank you. I am proud of her, don't get me wrong." He smiled. "And I'd be lying if I said I wasn't happy to have her back home again. I've missed her. So much."

There might have been a little shine in his eyes behind his glasses, and Delia wanted to hug him all over again. He was honest, sincere and, most important, real. "Now that you've seen what's gone on here today, and heard how city hall has handled things, are you sure I can't convince you to reconsider running for mayor? We need you, Owen. You're the perfect person for the job. You've done what we business owners have done and, just as importantly, you have a real and abiding knowledge and respect for the history of this town, while at the same time being young enough to see the potential it has, too. You've got Lauren to help you with the store, and being mayor isn't a full-time job, unless you want it to be."

His cheeks had taken on a ruddy hue at her effusive praise, but she'd meant every word.

"Peg already cornered me and gave me pretty much the same speech."

"Owen—"

He raised his hand. "And I told her I'd think about it."

Delia's face lit up. "You will?"

He nodded. "No promises, but—oomph!" Whatever else he'd been about to say was cut off by Delia's tight hug. And his ruddy face went deep red when she gave him a resounding kiss on the cheek.

"That's all we can ask, Owen. I'll cater meetings, whatever you need. Well, I will as soon as I figure out where I'm going to start over."

"Are you then?" he asked, looking greatly relieved.

Delia wasn't sure if the relief was that she was planning to relaunch her business, or that she'd stopped hugging him. "I am. Or I want to. I'll figure something out."

"You tell me when and where and I'll get the word out."

"Thank you, Owen. That means a lot."

"Dee?"

Delia turned to find Ford emerging from the throng behind her. "Ford," she said, happy to see him, feeling that last piece click into place, settling the part inside her that she couldn't settle herself. She wondered if it would always be like that. *If you're really lucky, it will be.* She rose up on her toes and kissed him. "Can you believe this?" she whispered.

"Frankly, no. I didn't even know there were this many people in Blueberry Cove."

He looked like he'd rather be anywhere else, and it occurred to Delia this was probably the most folks he'd seen in one place in a very long time.

"I don't think there are, but it sure looks good on camera." She smiled. "Have you met Owen Hartley?" But when she turned to make introductions, she saw that Peg had come and steered Owen over toward the row of reporters and news trucks at the edge of the park. Delia wasn't sure if that was such a great idea, considering Owen's interest in running was fledgling at best, but she trusted Peg wouldn't let him get overwhelmed. She turned back to Ford. "He said he's considering running for mayor. Isn't that great? If Brooks Winstock thinks he can just bulldoze the Cove into his own personal vision, at the very least he's not going to have the mayor in his pocket any longer. There needs to be some accountability."

"Do you think Hartley can stand up to him?"

"You'd be surprised. When Owen is passionate about something, and no one is more passionate about the Cove than he is, he can get pretty worked up. But just having Teddy not in office is a huge thing. And since he's already tossed his hat in the ring for mayor, he's off the town council as of election day. If Owen were to run and win, Teddy would be looking for new employment." Her eyes lit up. "This is very small of me to say, but it just occurred to me that would also mean that for the first time ever, Cami Weathersby won't have any political clout in this town. I mean, she'll always be a Winstock, but—"

"Being knocked down a notch or two wouldn't be the worst thing that could happen to her," Ford finished. "Might improve her."

"I wouldn't go that far," Delia said wryly. "But a girl can dream." She slipped her arm around his waist and leaned into him, surprised at how natural it felt. Then, realizing it might not feel as natural to him, and they were literally standing in the middle of the Cove's entire population, she started to pull away, but he tugged her right back next to his side.

He leaned down and said in her ear, "Don't abandon me to the horde. I'm going to need tethering at times, too."

She tipped her face up to his, kissing him hard and fast on the mouth. "Deal," she said, loving that she was finally able to give back to him even a small fraction of what he'd already been providing for her.

"I came to find you because Grace wanted to talk to you," he said.

Delia's grin grew wider. "And here we were worried about her rally idea, right?" She gestured around them. "Ha!"

"Well, she's quite happy about how things turned out. In fact, she's already delivered her sisterly I-told-you-so." At Delia's confused look, he added, "Her whole reason for wanting to have the party, or rally, was in hopes that if you saw how much you mattered to the town, it would help you figure out what you wanted to do. And . . . I hate to admit it, but she might possibly have had some small smidgen of a point there."

"Maddox insight," Delia said. "Sounds like it might be genetic." She smiled. "I'll have to keep that in mind, moving forward. I'm outnumbered."

"Funny," he said. "I was thinking about you and Grace together and feeling the same thing."

"Ah! Good point!" She slipped her arm around his waist and turned to look at the crowd. The chanting had stopped, and folks were milling and talking now that she'd made her speech to the reporters. She didn't imagine they'd see Brooks, Teddy, or Mayor Davis poke their heads out, but as the news ran the stories, there would be demands for statements, and they'd have to at least own up to their roles in the situation, facing more than just their constituents, but also their neighbors. And in the case of Winstock, if she were lucky, some of his business partners farther down the coast. "What does Grace want? Do you know?"

"Delia, there you are!" As if on cue, Grace came all but bursting through the throng of people closest to where they stood. She immediately wrapped Delia up in a tight hug. "I'm so sorry. That was a crap thing they did, on top of all the other crap things they'd already done. I'm so sorry I didn't see this coming after what they did to me and Brodie."

Delia hugged her back, and thought how good it was being on the receiving end of a hug when the need for it arose. "You couldn't have foreseen this, no one could have."

Grace let go, looked at her brother, and then at Delia. She stepped forward and pushed the two of them closer together, as if she was arranging furniture.

Delia and Ford both stared at Grace with a questioning look, sliding their arms around each other's waists as if out of long habit.

Grace clapped her hands and all but jumped up and down in glee. "My family is now perfect." Her grin turned a shade wry. "Who'd of thunk it, right?"

"I'm glad you're happy about it," Delia said, sincerely, though not surprised as Grace had only done everything but strand her and Ford together somewhere in hopes maybe something would rekindle. *Yet another thing Grace had been right about,* Delia noted with a private smile. She really was going to keep an eye out being under the watch and care of two Maddoxes now. "Ford said you wanted to talk to me?"

"I do," she said, the excitement on her face growing, if that was even possible. She looked around. "Maybe not here, but—what the hell, I can't wait."

Delia's eyes widened as realization dawned. She looked immediately at Grace's ring finger, but there was no engagement rock there, which meant—she grinned. Ford might have to adjust to that whole uncle thing a bit sooner than either of them had anticipated.

Grace had followed Delia's gaze, then laughed. "No, no, silly. The news isn't about me. It's about you."

Confused, Delia said, "Me?" She glanced up at Ford. "Do you know what this is about?"

"I'm just the tether," he told her, meaning yes, he did, but he was clearly staying noncommittal.

Grace took Delia's free hand in both of her own. "Promise me you'll hear me out first."

"Okay," Delia said, wary now. "What did you do?"

"I called Langston." She immediately put up her hand. "You promised. Listen."

"Grace, please tell me you didn't get him to step in and—"

"No, and yes. But not like you're assuming. Trust me a little, okay? I know you weren't sure what you wanted to do. And I know that having Langston step in and throw money at the problem was not what you wanted, and frankly, that wasn't going to solve the problem since Winstock would just throw more money and, well, you get my drift."

"So why call him?"

"I was worried about you. And he's my friend; he helps me sort things out. He's also your friend, which made him the perfect one to call about this."

"About what?"

"Brodie and I talked, and as part of the inn, I have always planned to serve at least a limited menu. More than a bed-and-breakfast, but not a full-scale restaurant."

Delia's heart stopped for a moment as she realized where Grace might be heading with this. "Oh, Grace, that's incredibly sweet, but I don't think I'm cut out for—"

"Still not done," she said, her tone more forceful now, a bit of the lawyer in her peeking out.

Delia nodded, but was caught between a smile and a pang that she'd have to be the one to rob Grace of the excitement high she was on.

"The kitchen we've framed out is just that, a kitchen. We planned to put in a little seating around the main pit area on the ground floor, but that was the extent of it, really. Then this happened to you, and I turned to Langston, and well, he had an idea. An idea I immediately fell in love with, and Brodie is completely on board. So you really have no choice but to say yes."

"To what?" Delia all but begged, completely thrown now.

"Brodie has more space, other boathouses, smaller ones that he has no immediate plans for. One of the smallest ones is right next to the inn. On his property—our property—complete with dockage on our piers." She couldn't stand it another minute, and she squeezed Delia's hand. "Langston wants to design a new place for you, something unique, that's all you, who you are now, to us, to the Cove. It would be separate from the inn, but would be there to provide a full-service menu not to only my guests, but all the locals as well. I mean, you know I want to keep the inn grounded in what I think of as the real Cove, and embrace the heart of harbor life. What better way to do that than to put the real heart of the harbor right into the mix?"

Delia's mouth had dropped open somewhere in the middle of Grace's rushed spiel, but actual words still weren't forming.

"Say you'll do it, please. Brodie said we can work out a sale, or a long-term lease, whatever. But you'll be protected from Winstock and the town and, even better, among the three of us, we'll be starting and growing a cluster of businesses—my inn, your café or place or whatever you want it to be, and Brodie's boat design business—smack-dab right in the center of the harbor, right in the face of Brooks's fancy-schmancy club. Meaning we'll have a fair share of control, as will Blue, over keeping the better part of the harbor faithful to its heritage. So if we grow, we'll grow in the direction that's right for all of us."

To say Delia's mind was spinning with the possibilities, with the logic of it all, the basic, well . . . perfection of it all would be the understatement of all time.

"Let Winstock open a yacht club, you know?" Grace rushed on. "With us there, and Blue on the other side, members who opt to join Winstock's place will have to also be the kind of folks who'd want to moor their yacht alongside your customers' smaller sailboats and my guests' boats. And Blue's fishing boats and the tugs—" She broke off, finally out of breath. "It's not the perfect solution, and I know you'll still lose your diner, but—"

Delia cut off the rest by wrapping Grace up in the tightest hug she'd ever given anyone. She didn't stop, she didn't analyze, she didn't deliberate. She did what Ford had been trained to do. She observed, she understood, she solved. She went with her gut. "That's maybe the best plan I've ever heard in my entire life," she said. Tears—which were apparently going to also be part of the new, improved her—spurted from the corners of her eyes. "Thank you. And Brodie."

Grace held her at arm's length. "Really? Truly? I thought I was going to have to wheedle and beg. And I would have."

"Yes," Ford said. "You did the smart thing," he told Delia. "Saved yourself a whole world of—hey!" He rubbed the spot on his bicep where his sister, who had a pretty good right hook, had socked him. But he was smiling as he did.

Delia nodded. "I've been dreading . . . pretty much everything about starting over. Just the idea of having to find the right spot was soul crushing, because I know every inch of this town and I already knew there wasn't a spot, not one that called to me. And I couldn't get my brain past that. The idea of giving up the place I loved to settle for some spot that wouldn't be right for me or my customers killed the whole endeavor for me. I even thought about going back and looking at the spot where O'Reilly's was, but that's on the far side of the Cove and the town has really developed away from there now. I just—" She wrapped her arms around

Ford's waist when he pulled her under his arm, and pressed her cheek to his chest. "This is perfect," she whispered. And she wasn't simply talking about the next incarnation of her diner. Or café. She'd rather liked the sound of that. She could feel the wheels already beginning to spin and the relief almost made her feel light-headed. "And Peg, and Pete, and Charlie—"

"It's your place," Grace said. "Your staff. Langston is still in Tokyo, but he's already sketching up some plans for you to look at and we can just move some of the guys working on my place over to start as they wrap up work on the inn. It won't take near the work that was necessary for mine. Langston and Brodie think you could have the place up and running by the time the inn is ready or close to it. I know that means you'll lose the winter months, but—"

"I was going to lose them no matter what," Delia said. "And I know I might lose Peg and Pete with the delay."

"They'd come back, don't you think?" Ford asked.

"If they knew for sure they'd have a place, and they would, then maybe they can find something temporary until then."

"It's going to take a lot of work," Grace said, shifting her gaze apprehensively between the two of them. "And you'll want to be hands-on—"

"I'll be moving my winter workload to the foundation offices," Ford said, matter-of-factly, causing Delia to jerk her gaze up to his.

"Ford, don't—"

"I'm thinking I can find somewhere to bunk in town for the winter," he went on, then glanced down at Delia. "Got any ideas?"

"Well," she said, her heart beating even harder. "I

do have a claw-foot tub that needs a history adjustment."

He grinned, and Grace just looked a little stunned watching them. Delia could relate. She felt more than a little stunned, about all of it.

"I'll have to head out to the island from time to time," he said. "Monitor some of the winter migration when the weather lets me commute. I'll talk to Blue. They work all year long, so we'll figure out a deal."

"Really?" Delia asked him.

"Really," he said, without so much as a hint of hesitation.

She knew that they still had the whole summer thing to figure out, but heck, she thought, military spouses were apart for longer than that and managed. And she could plan things differently this time, set it up so that she wasn't the one carrying most of the load. Between the inn, and Brodie's business, and yes, even the damn yacht club, she'd do well enough, soon enough. So she could probably afford to hire more local help, at least in the summer, and split time between the Cove and the island. Heck, maybe the interns would enjoy a better menu while she was there.

Unable to believe it might all be coming together in a way that not only made sense, but that she was actually excited about felt . . . well, surreal. And she knew the one person she wanted to share that surreal excitement with, the one person, the only person who would understand exactly what it was like. And he was all hers. *Why on earth did I think do-it-yourself was better? It's so much better doing it together.*

In that spirit, she hopped up on her toes and kissed Ford hard on the mouth. "You know that falling thing we talked about earlier?" she said quietly, just for his ears.

He nodded.

"Splat," she said, and then laughing at the stunned look on his face, kissed him again. "Head over heels, all the way to the ground. You?"

In response, Ford caught her up against him and took his time with a proper kiss, garnering hoots and hollers and a few "It's about time!"s from the crowd she'd completely forgotten was there. "All the way to the ground," he murmured against her ear.

When he finally put her back on her feet, a cheer went up. Pink cheeked, Delia turned and did a quick curtsy for the masses, earning another cheer, and then Grace stepped in and hugged both Delia and her own brother. "Group hug!" she cried, sniffling herself.

"Family hug," Delia said, and realized that's exactly what it was she'd been missing all along.

Epilogue

"Wait up," Delia called out to Ford, clambering over yet another rock. "How do you make it look so easy?" she huffed.

"Longer legs," he said, coming back and reaching a hand out to help her gain her balance once she'd landed on the other side.

"I wish that was all it was."

He waited until she got her equilibrium before he let go.

"I can't believe we're doing this in the dark," she said, trying to pick the same rocks to step on that he did.

"It's barely dusk."

"Like I said." She adjusted her hard hat and the light that was strapped to the front.

"We've worked this hard. I want her to have the best chance," Ford said.

"Won't it be enough that she comes back to Sandpiper in general?"

"She should fledge from the burrow she was born in. We can make that happen for her."

Delia might not love the rock scramble, but her

heart only swelled further for the man at her side. Protector and defender. How could she not love him for that? "Then we will," she said, determination in her voice. "Lead on, Dolittle."

She heard Ford chuckle, but was too busy focusing on not killing herself to watch him as he nimbly transported his little bundle farther out on the rocks.

The moon was rising by the time they made it to the large boulder that sat just in front of the crevasse leading down to the burrow.

Ford helped her up to stand next to him.

"We made it," she said, working to steady her breath. He wasn't even winded. "What do we do next?"

"We go to the front edge of the rock where it juts out over the water, unwrap her, and then we toss her up so she flies out and is on her way."

Delia looked up at him, horrified. "She's never flown before and you're just going to toss her up in the air? What if she doesn't know how? What if she—"

"How do you think it works?"

"Well . . . I don't know, exactly. Can't we just sit her in the water and give her butt a little push?"

"The waves would just toss her back. She needs to get out past the surf. Then she can land on the water and float a bit before flying again."

Delia wasn't any less dubious than before, but she nodded. "Is it dark enough? Is it too dark?"

"The sky is clear, which is good. She'll have moonlight. In fact, that's what guides her to the water, the reflection of the light on the surface. We'll have to turn our headlamps off, so she doesn't get confused and fly back toward us."

"Would that be such a bad thing?" Delia remarked in a hushed whisper.

Ford reached down and slid his hand in hers. "We can't keep her."

"I know. I just . . . this is the closest I've come to having a pet. The closest I've ever wanted to come, but still . . ." She let go of his hand and, before she lost her nerve, she opened the front of Ford's jacket. "Okay, little one. It's time for your big adventure."

Ford helped her unwrap the chick from the sling until the puffling was safely in his hands. "Do you want to launch her?"

Delia gaped. "Me?" she squeaked. "What if I do it wrong? What if I hurt her?"

"You won't. And . . . I think you'll be glad you did."

Delia eyed the chick, who eyed her right back.

"Here," he said, shifting around so he could transfer the chick from between his palms to between hers. Once she had the bird steady, he reached up and switched off both of their head lanterns.

"What do I do?" Delia asked, her voice as unsteady as her knees.

"Lift your arms up and reach out as you let her go, so she's going out over the water. I'll hold on to you." He got behind her and braced his hands on her hips, then leaned down. "Here's to new beginnings," he said, then pressed his lips to the side of her neck.

Delia's heart thumped, as it always did when he said the most amazing things, which he always did. "New beginnings," she said, and then bent down. "You ready?"

She felt the little body squirm in her hands, as if it could smell the briny tang in the air, feel the spray, the wind coming off the water, and couldn't wait to get out there.

"Good luck," she said. "Swim fast. And eat all your herrings."

"Dee," Ford said, but there was such pure affection in his voice, she didn't take the admonishment to heart.

"Okay," she said, more to herself than the baby puffin. "Here we go." She looked over her shoulder at Ford, who nodded at her. She trusted him—he wouldn't let her go, wouldn't let her do this if he thought she couldn't pull it off. So she sent that trust on to the baby bird. "Fly, little puff." She lifted her arms up and out, and the baby all but burst out of her hands before she could even toss her, her little wings flapping as hard as they could. "Oh, my God, Ford, look at her!" Delia cried.

Ford pulled Delia back against him, arms around her waist. She gripped his forearm with one hand and followed baby puff's flight with her other hand until they lost sight of her in the dark. "She did so good!" She looked over her shoulder at Ford. "Didn't she? That was amazing!" She took one last look out to sea, and then Ford was turning her around in his arms. "Thank you! Thank you for making me do that. I feel just . . . wow. You knew it was like that, didn't you?"

"Disney ending?" he said.

"Almost," she replied, feeling as if her entire body was smiling, right down to her soul.

"Almost?"

She took off her gloves and shoved them in her pockets, then reached up for his face and pulled him down closer to her. "I love you, Ford Maddox."

She was close enough to see the effect her words had on him as his eyes went all dark, teeming with emotion. And if her soul had been smiling before, it was smiling and filled with a radiant glow now.

He touched her hair, her cheek, lifted her face to his. "Delia O'Reilly, you are the love of my life. Always have been." He kissed her, and looked deeply into her moonlit eyes. "Always will be."

Delia kissed him back and, yes, she sniffled. "Now *that* is my Disney ending." He chuckled, and she kissed him again.

And they most certainly did live happily ever after.

Author's Note

I hope you've enjoyed your stay in Blueberry Cove and out on Sandpiper Island. Those places are creations of my imagination, but the work being done off the coast of Maine to help ensure the future of many seabird populations, including the Atlantic puffin, is very real. If this story has sparked your curiosity to learn more about this beautiful and entertaining seabird, or you'd like to go one step further and offer your support, check out www.projectpuffin.org and learn more. You can even adopt a puffin as a way to support the work they are doing out on Seal Island via the Audubon Society to help ensure successful nesting and migration. (I adopted two!)

If you'd like to watch the antics of the nesting puffin population on Seal Island, www.explore.org has live cams on the island every summer. Fair warning, you will fall in love with these little clowns of the sea!

Create Your Own Indoor Miniature Water Garden

In *Sandpiper Island,* Ford Maddox has created an entire world centered around the concept of sustainable living, surrounded by nature, deep in the forest, on the outer reaches of Pelican Bay.

Here's an easy way you can bring a little bit of the grandeur of the great outdoors indoors, to enjoy all year round. And you don't have to move to an island tree house to do it! (Although that would be pretty cool!)

Did you know that almost any plant cutting can be grown indoors, rooted in water? You can root coleus, spider plants, a variety of herbs, even African violets!

1. *Containers.* First comes the fun of choosing your containers. From tiny apothecary jars to old vintage teapots, the possibilities are endless. For some, the view of the root system dangling in the water is part of the beauty of the garden, and for others, the greenery that grows above water level is what their garden is all about. So when choosing your water garden vessels, you need to decide on whether you want them to be transparent (where you can see the roots) or opaque (where you'll only see what's above the surface). Or you can be like me and put together a variety of both.

2. *Location.* What kind of vessels you choose may also be determined by where you plan on locating your garden. A windowsill is perfect for a mini water garden, with vintage jam jars, drinking glasses, those apothecary jars I mentioned, or even antique teacups (yes, teacups will work!). You can also choose a larger container, maybe an old china teapot or goldfish bowl, and make it a centerpiece on a coffee table, or something unique that would sit on a mantelpiece, bookcase, or desk. Again, the possibilities are endless. Just make sure there is sunlight (natural or manmade), and that your plant is not exposed to extreme heat or cold. If an object will hold water, you can use it as a water garden container. (Hint: Flea markets make for excellent rummaging for water garden containers!)

3. *Prepping your container.* Make sure you clean your chosen container well, using a water-bleach solution made up of 10 percent bleach, just to make sure it's free of contaminants. If you are using a container made of metal, concrete, or something with an unfinished interior, you may need to use a water sealant, or leach out the lime first.

4. *Choosing your plants.* Simple! Take cuttings from your outdoor plants at the end of a season, or maybe you've been admiring your best pal's herb garden, or your neighbor's violets (ask first, of course). Snip off a 4″ to 5″ section of the plant at a clean angle, just below the leaf set, making sure there is another leaf set left above that one. The healthier the plant, the better the chances of successful water rooting. And your snippet should

not be flowering. Also, make certain your cutting tool has also been well cleaned before snipping.

5. *Setting up your garden.* Fill your container 2/3 to 3/4 full of water. You can use tap water, but it must sit uncovered for 24 hours so that the chlorine, fluoride, and other treatment chemicals have time to evaporate. There are also water purifier tablets you can use as well, or get distilled water. I just fill a clean pitcher with tap water the day before setting up a new container.

6. *Adding your plants.* Make sure there is no soil clinging to your plant anywhere. Carefully pinch off the leaves from the bottom leaf set only. This creates a long enough stem to dangle underwater. Only put the stem in the water, leaving the leaves on the next leaf grouping to rest on the lip of the container, or hang over the side. If your snipping is too delicate for this, you can also tie four bamboo skewers to create a small square, and then set it over the opening of your container, making the center square small enough so that it provides that "lip" you need. Trim the ends of the skewers so they only extend an inch or two past the edge of the actual container. Tie with decorative twine or string. Simply slip the snipping end through the square opening until it's in the water. You can also put more than one clipping into the same container.

7. *Don't have plants to clip?* You can purchase any small potted seedling, or start your seed in a small pot of soil and grow to seedling size. Gently remove the plant from the soil, shake and rinse off all soil from the root system (using distilled tap water), then immerse the root system into your

prepared water container. Instant floating root plant!

8. *Watch your garden grow.* Most plants do best in a bright sunny location. Make sure it's not subjected to extreme heat or cold. Replace the water as it evaporates and change it completely if it gets cloudy. You can go longer if your vessel is opaque. Make sure the refill water has also been distilled. I fill old milk jugs—clean them first!—with tap water, let them sit open for 24 hours, then cap. Keep your distilled water jugs at room temperature so as not to shock the root system when added. If the roots get mushy or rot, discard, clean the container thoroughly, and start again. You can pot your water root plants in soil and put outside in the spring . . . or simply move them to a bigger container and continue to enjoy all year long.

Go to www.kensingtonbooks.com and enter "Donna Kauffman" in the search box for printable directions that include photos of my own water garden! Happy rooting!

If you've enjoyed the Bachelors of Blueberry Cove, you won't want to miss the brides. Read on for a sample of *Sea Glass Sunrise,* coming in June 2015.

So, there was going to be a June wedding after all. Only it wouldn't be Hannah McRae in a gorgeous white dress, walking down the aisle.

No, she'd be in swathed in wildflower blue. Or spring leaf green. Or dandelion yellow. Or some other color found only in nature and bridesmaid dresses.

Hannah didn't slow down as she passed the colorful, hand-painted sign welcoming her to Blueberry Cove, Maine. Founded in 1715. Population 303. "Make that three hundred and four," she murmured, still undecided on when she was going to share that little tidbit with the rest of her family.

She should be happy for her big brother and his impending nuptials. And she was happy. Truly. Logan deserved all the love and fulfillment in the world and she was thrilled he'd finally found it. Alex MacFarland had gotten herself a good guy. Probably the last remaining good guy on the planet.

Not that Hannah was biased or anything. Or cynical, for that matter. Okay, so maybe she was a little cynical. All right, more than a little. Who could blame her after the year she'd had?

Hannah wove through the narrow streets of her hometown on autopilot, too distracted by her thoughts to soak up the welcoming sense of belonging, the unconditional love she always felt simply entering the Cove. She'd driven twelve straight hours fueled solely by the promise of that much-needed hometown group hug. Well, the hug and the king-sized bag of chocolate-covered pretzels presently tucked in her lap.

She dug in for another fix. They'd been an impulse buy when she'd filled her tank before heading out of Virginia. She couldn't even say why. She hated salty and sweet together. Of course, she'd also hated finding out the guy she'd been giddily anticipating a marriage proposal from at any second had already proposed to someone else. In fact, he'd not only proposed to someone else, he'd married her. Four years ago. Which meant Hannah had spent the previous eighteen months dating a married man. *Eighteen freaking months!* She was a trial attorney, for God's sake. A damn good one. She earned her living by knowing when people were lying to her.

How could she not have known? How could she not have had at least some inkling of a suspicion long before Tim's very petite, very blond, and exceedingly pregnant, sweet-faced wife stalked into Hannah's office, in front of God and everyone—and by God she meant the senior partner of the firm himself, and by everyone, she meant, well, everyone—and announced, quite loudly, using language that could only be described as salty, just what Hannah could do to herself, and stop doing to her husband?

Yeah, Hannah thought, and shoved the pretzel back in the bag. She hated salty and sweet.

As the Rusty Puffin pub came into view, she felt a tug in her chest, and a knot form in her throat. She wanted nothing more than to pull in, run inside, and be immediately folded into one of her Uncle Fergus's big bear hugs, but she couldn't trust herself not to fall apart all over him. No way would she get out of there without telling him why she was a wreck, which would be as good as telling the entire town. Instead she whispered a silent *I love you,* knowing she'd see him soon enough at the rehearsal dinner, continuing on instead toward the coast road that would take her out to Pelican Point . . . and home.

She didn't see the pickup truck until it was too late.

One second she was glancing over at the tall shoots of summer lupines, in all their purple, pink, and white stalks of glory, and—dammit—digging out another chocolate-covered pretzel, the next she was slamming her brakes and swerving to miss the tail end of the big, dark blue dually that was suddenly somehow passing right in front of her.

She missed the truck's rear bumper by a hair-breadth, but the hand-painted sign on the far side of the intersection advertising Beanie's Fat Quarters, "The best little quilt shop in Blueberry Cove!" wasn't so lucky.

It all happened so fast, and yet each second seemed to be somehow elastic, as if she could live a lifetime inside every single heartbeat of the accident as she was swerving through it. So many thoughts went through her mind as she careened toward the sign she knew Beanie's husband Carl had so proudly painted for his wife when she'd opened up her little shop, what, fifteen years ago now? Sixteen? Hannah had just graduated from high school. Carl had done the town sign, too, right in his adorable little potting shed-turned-art studio, touching the signs up like new every spring after the winter season did its number on them. And yes, okay, that made two good men, but Carl had gone to his great reward just last year, so that left Logan as the only one still breathing.

So many thoughts raced around inside Hannah's brain in those weirdly elastic, terrifying, life-threatening seconds. The things she should have said to Tim during their final confrontation, that she should have told Logan and her sisters what happened, leaned on them instead of shouldering it alone, that maybe she should have tried harder to make her newfound notoriety in the Capitol Hill legal community work for her, that she still felt terribly guilty, hating that she'd ultimately caved, quit, and come running back home to the Cove with her humiliation tucked between her legs like the tail of failure and shame that it was.

Then Carl's once-beautiful sign raced right up to the hood of her car and no amount of further wheel yanking and swerving was going to save her from smashing right into it. There was a small explosion as her air bag deployed, punching her in the face and chest, just as her shoulder harness jerked her tight against her seat back, yanking her thoughts instantly back to the present as she plowed straight into the stack of brightly colored, plaid quilting squares painted on the bottom corner of the sign. *Sorry, Beanie,* she thought inanely, along with *shit, shit, shit!* as she finally slid to a stop a mere speck of an inch before hitting the cluster of tall ash trees that stood just behind the sign.

She instinctively batted at the white, puffy bag, trying to keep it from smothering her, as she struggled to regain clarity of thought. Her head was buzzing from the adrenaline rush, her pulse was pounding in her ears, and her face hurt. A lot. So did her shoulder. Then the driver side door was being pulled open and there was a man crouching next to her. At least, given the deep voice, she assumed it was a man; she was still wrestling with the air bag.

"You okay?" he asked, his voice all deep and dark and smoky in that bass vibrato kind of way that sent shivers down a woman's spine. Though, in all fairness, her ears were ringing from the impact and she was pretty sure shock was setting in, or should be, so it could have just been an aftereffect of the accident.

He effortlessly collapsed the air bag with one broad palm. "Whoa, whoa," he added quickly, putting those broad, warm palms gently but firmly on her wrist and shoulder when she tried to wrestle off her seat belt. "Let's make sure you're okay before you move too much, all right? Just sit tight for a moment."

She wanted to be the cool, competent, in control—always in control—attorney she was. Not the exhausted, injured, bordering on hysterical idiot who stupidly and blindly dated married men, yet still got the shivers over a smoky, hot, sex voice. Sadly, the latter was the best she had to offer at the moment. "What . . . happened?" she managed, her voice sounding oddly tight, bordering on shrill. "Where did you come from?"